WATCHER IN THE WOODS

Also by Kelley Armstrong

Rockton
City of the Lost
A Darkness Absolute
This Fallen Prey

Cainsville
Omens   *Betrayals*
Visions   *Rituals*
Deceptions

Age of Legends
Sea of Shadows
Empire of Night
Forest of Ruin

The Blackwell Pages (co-written with Melissa Marr)
Loki's Wolves
Odin's Ravens
Thor's Serpents

Otherworld
Bitten   *Personal Demon*
Stolen   *Living with the Dead*
Dime Store Magic   *Frostbitten*
Industrial Magic   *Waking the Witch*
Haunted   *Spell Bound*
Broken   *Thirteen*
No Humans Involved

Darkest Powers & Darkness Rising
The Summoning   *The Gathering*
The Awakening   *The Calling*
The Reckoning   *The Rising*

Nadia Stafford
Exit Strategy
Made to be Broken
Wild Justice

Stand-alone novels
The Masked Truth
Missing
Aftermath

WATCHER IN THE WOODS

A Rockton Novel

KELLEY ARMSTRONG

MINOTAUR BOOKS ✺ NEW YORK

WATCHER IN THE WOODS. Copyright © 2019 by KLA Fricke Inc. All rights reserved. Printed in the United States of America. For information, address St. Martin's Press, 175 Fifth Avenue, New York, N.Y. 10010.

www.minotaurbooks.com

Library of Congress Cataloging-in-Publication Data

Names: Armstrong, Kelley, author.
Title: Watcher in the woods: a Rockton novel / Kelley Armstrong.
Description: First edition. | New York: Minotaur Books, 2019.
Identifiers: LCCN 2018049401| ISBN 9781250159915 (hardcover) |
    ISBN 9781250159922 (ebook)
Subjects: | GSAFD: Mystery fiction.
Classification: LCC PS3551.R4678 W38 2019 | DDC 813/.54—dc23
LC record available at https://lccn.loc.gov/2018049401

First Edition: February 2019

10 9 8 7 6 5 4 3 2 1

For Jeff

WATCHER
IN THE
WOODS

ONE

I have not seen my sister, April, in two years. Nine months ago, I called her before I fled to a hidden town in the Yukon, where people like me go to disappear. I didn't tell her where I was going. I only said that I had to leave, and she might not hear from me for a few years. Maybe I was imagining it, but I thought I heard relief in her voice.

After our parents died, I would call before April's birthday, before Thanksgiving, before Christmas, and I'd suggest getting together. For the first year, she made excuses. Then she stopped bothering, and I stopped calling. I worked through every holiday and pretended it didn't matter. Of course it mattered.

Late last night, I called from a pay phone in Dawson City and told April that I needed her help, that a man's life depended on it. She hung up on me.

Now I'm outside the Vancouver hospital where she works. She's a neuroscientist, but also has her medical degree and consults on neuro-surgery. According to her assistant, she's been here all night on an emergency call and should be leaving at any moment.

I'm standing by the parking garage. I've confirmed there's a car in her spot. Now it's just a matter of waiting.

"Looks like good weather today," says a voice beside me.

I slant my gaze to a guy about four feet away. He's six feet tall, with dark blond hair in a buzz cut. He's got a few days' worth of beard scruff, and he's wearing a ball cap, a T-shirt, and shades. He leans against the building, a paperback novel in his hand.

"Didn't your mother ever tell you not to speak to strangers?" I say.

"Nah. She told strangers not to speak to me. And I won't be a stranger after you come back to my hotel room tonight."

I laugh. "Does that line ever work?"

"Never tried it." He lifts the shades. "I can offer further incentives, if you'd like."

"Like a room-service dinner?"

"Sure . . . eventually."

I slide over and lean my head against his shoulder before putting space between us again. Eric Dalton, the sheriff in Rockton, that hidden town where I've been living. Also the guy I've been living *with*. April doesn't know Dalton, so we're keeping our distance until I introduce him. Dalton can be a tad intimidating when he wants to be. And given the runaround I'm getting from April, he *really* wants to be.

"You could just wait at her place," he says.

"That would require knowing her address," I say. "She moved here a few years ago, and I only realized it when my birthday gift for her bounced back. I called, and she said she'd gotten a job here. She didn't provide an updated address."

"Bitch."

I shrug. "Maybe I did something to piss her off."

"Yeah. It was definitely you, Casey. You're such a pain in the ass." He lifts his glasses again, so I don't miss his eye roll. "Your sister is a bitch, and if this wasn't Kenny's best chance, I'd say fuck it. If she doesn't want to know you, that's her loss."

I smile. "Thank you."

He starts to answer and then quickly lifts his book and murmurs, "I'm gonna guess that's her coming out now."

I look up. Dalton has never seen a photo of April, and if asked, I would have said there isn't much of a resemblance between us. Our mother was Filipino and Chinese, our father Scottish. April can pass for white, where I cannot, and to me that has always meant that we look very different. She's a few inches taller than my five-two. Her skin is lighter. Her eyes are blue, their shape more Caucasian.

But we have the same straight dark hair, the same heart-shaped face, the same cheekbones and nose, all inherited from our mother. When I see April through Dalton's eyes, the similarities outweigh the differences. It's just that the differences have always loomed larger in my mind, wedged in by every acquaintance who met my sister and commented on the fact that she "looked white."

It always seemed like one more way we were different. One more way that she was "better," and I feel a flare of outrage thinking that now. I am proud of my heritage. I wouldn't want to be able to "pass" for anything but what I am. Yet I cannot deny that when I was young, looking like April seemed better. Easier.

April spots me and slows. Her lips compress, and I am flung back to my childhood, seeing that same look from her every time I careened or bounced into a room. A moue of distaste for the wayward little sister who was always causing trouble, always disrupting April's orderly life. I'm only five years younger, but that gap always felt huge. Insurmountable.

"No," she says as she walks straight past me.

"I just want to talk."

"Did I say no last night?" April doesn't even glance over her shoulder. "Go back to . . ." She flutters a hand over her shoulder. "Wherever you went."

Dalton surges forward, but I stop him as I follow her into the garage. "I need your help, April."

"If you've frittered away your inheritance, I'm not lending you money."

If anyone else said this, I'd snap back a response. We both inherited seven figures from our parents, and mine has done nothing but grow since their death. Anyone who knows me—*at all*—wouldn't be surprised by this. Yet the person who should know me best is the one thinking I'd blow through a million bucks and come to her for a handout.

But I don't snap. I don't even feel the urge. With April, I am forever that little girl scrabbling up a mountain to get her attention. Forever trying to win her approval.

"I haven't touched my inheritance," I say evenly. "As I tried to explain on the phone, I need your medical assistance. For a friend who's been shot in the back."

She slowly pivots to stare at me. "What kind of trouble are you in, Casey?"

"None. Someone else—"

"A friend of yours has been shot, and you're coming to me instead of taking him to a hospital? Did you shoot him?"

I flinch. I can't help it. Thirteen years ago, I shot and killed a man. But April knows nothing of that, and it isn't connected to the current situation.

Before I can answer, she turns away again. "Get this man to a hospital. Drop him off at the door if you need to. Then go away, Casey. Just . . ." Another hand flutter over her shoulder. "Go away again. Please."

Dalton strides past and plants himself in her path. "Your sister is talking to you. Turn the hell around and listen to her."

Her gaze flicks over him. Then she looks back at me. "Tell your fuck toy to move, Casey."

"Hey!" I say, my voice high, part outrage and part shock. My sister is never vulgar. Even the mention of sex usually has her flushing bright red.

She looks up at Dalton. "Yes, that's what you are. If you haven't realized it yet, take a tip from me. My sister doesn't date men. She just screws them."

"Huh," Dalton says. "Well, then I don't know who I've been living with for the past six months, but I guess it's not your sister. Or maybe I'm just special." He looks over at me. "Tell me I'm special."

I mouth an apology, but he dismisses it with a head shake. My sister isn't far off, as he knows. Until Dalton, I hadn't had a "boyfriend" since I was eighteen, and the reason for that had nothing to do with personal preference and everything to do with the fact that the guy I shot and killed *was* my last boyfriend.

April tries to walk around Dalton. He blocks her. He has his hands in his pockets, a clear signal that he will not physically stop her, but he's not about to let her pass him easily either.

"This isn't about me," he says. "It's about your sister. Who needs your help, and believe me, she wouldn't be here if she didn't."

April opens her mouth. Then a woman in a nurse's uniform enters the garage, and April straightens so fast I swear her spine crackles.

"Yes, I understand," she says, in her most businesslike voice. "Let's discuss this outside."

She leads us through a side door to a grassy area. It's empty, but she surveys it twice to be sure.

"If you wish to speak to me, I can spare . . ." She checks her watch. "Ten minutes. Then I have a salon appointment."

Dalton snorts a laugh before catching her expression. "Fuck, you're serious." He shakes his head. "Are you sure you two are related?"

"Yes, we are," April says coldly. "We simply don't share the same sense of responsibility."

"Yeah," Dalton says. "You could learn a few things from Casey."

She looks at me. "Please tell your guard dog he's using up your ten minutes."

I explain Kenny's situation, as fast as I can. I'm a homicide detective, but I grew up in a family of doctors and had been expected to take a career in medicine, so I know enough to give April a decent assessment of the damage and the treatment so far.

"You have doctors treating him," she says.

"No, we have me, plus an army veteran who received some medic training, and a psychiatrist with an M.D. but no on-job experience."

"This man needs a doctor. A hospital."

"The situation . . ." I glance at Dalton.

He nods, telling me to continue.

"The situation is not criminal," I say. "Let me clear that up right now. I've been working in a remote community. Very remote. We're more than willing to take the patient to a hospital, but he refuses to leave. He fears that if he goes, he won't be allowed back. The community is . . . a safe haven."

"Witness protection?"

"Something like that. It's complicated. That's all I can say, April. I am not asking you to do anything illegal. I wouldn't."

She's eased back, her guard still up but flexing. "I can't go on site, Casey. I can recommend someone, but you really should get him to a hospital."

"We know that. And we aren't asking you to go on site. Just consult. The two guys working with him are excellent medics. Steady hands. Steady minds." I force a tiny smile. "Which was always what Mom and Dad said made a good surgeon."

She flinches, and I realize maybe I shouldn't bring up our parents. She was always much closer to them than I was.

"We just need a consult," I say. "Lead them through the process of removing the bullet."

"Fine. We'll go to my place and video-link them in."

"It's not a video link." I reach into my bag and hand her a satellite phone.

She stares at it. Then she looks at me. "You're kidding, right?"

"Our town *is* very remote." I pull pages from my bag. "But we have the medical equipment." I flip through the stack. "Here are photos and X-rays . . ."

She flips through them and then slows for a second pass before slapping the pages back into my hand.

"This can't be done by a satellite phone, Casey."

"It's that bad?"

"No, it's . . ." She throws up her hands. "It's actually *not* that bad. The problem is the location of the bullet. It's a tricky extraction, and I don't care how steady your psychiatrist's hands might be, you need someone on site who knows what she's doing." She consults her cell phone. "I can give you three days. Possibly four."

"What?"

"It's Thursday. I was planning to work in the lab today and tomorrow, but that's not necessary. I need to be back for Tuesday, when I'm consulting on a surgery. You can have me until then."

TWO

I have no idea how we got from "I can't spare fifteen minutes for you, Casey" to "I'm yours for the next four days."

My sister is coming to Rockton, and I can't quite wrap my head around that.

Dalton made the call to let her come, his excuse being that he doesn't want to "bother" the council with it. The council is Rockton's governing body, though they never set foot in the town.

Two weeks ago, they sent us a serial killer for safekeeping. We aren't equipped for that, and he escaped. During the ensuing chase, Kenny got shot in the back, which is why we need April. We also lost our de facto town leader, Val. A few days ago, the council sent us Phil, who used to be our radio contact for communicating with them. That means the communication system is a bit of a mess, and Dalton decides to skip it, which makes a very fine excuse.

There's an old saying about it being easier to ask for forgiveness than permission. That's what Dalton decides to do here. We don't trust the council to let us bring April in, and if we don't bring April in, Kenny will spend his life in a wheelchair. So, we'll sneak April into Rockton. She'll treat Kenny, and then we'll spirit her out of there. If we do this right, the only people who'll know are those who *have* to know—all people we trust.

We cannot tell April where she's going. In this, Dalton treats her like a new resident. She gets the usual spiel. Don't ask where you're going. Don't try to figure it out. Leave your cell phone and all electronics behind. Make one call to the person others will phone if they can't contact you. Tell him or her that you're taking the weekend off. I suggest she say she needs a stress break, an offline sabbatical. Dalton wouldn't understand the concept. April will.

She balks at leaving her tech behind. I explain that we don't have cellular or Wi-Fi access, and even recharging her batteries would mean plugging into a generator. She doesn't care. She argues that she needs her laptop, even if it's offline. I can tell Dalton's frustrated—we need to get her on a plane ASAP—but I work it out. She can take the laptop, nothing more.

We escort April to her condo to pack. She doesn't much like that either, but we're taking a huge chance here, one that could blow up with a slip of the tongue when she makes that call. I overhear it. It's brief, and I don't ask who she called. I have her put an autoreply on her email and a message on her voice mail, explaining the offline weekend.

Then we're gone.

Rockton is in the Yukon. It might seem like it'd be wise to hide that—fly commercial into northern British Columbia, and then take a small plane. That's pointless, really. No one is going to find it.

Rockton is a wilderness town of two hundred, hidden by both technological and structural camouflage. The Yukon is roughly the size of Texas with a population of thirty-five thousand people. When Dalton first told me that, I thought he was misspeaking. He had to be. In a place that size, even tacking on a zero would make it sparsely populated. Dalton never misspeaks when it comes to facts. There are indeed thirty-five thousand people, three-quarters of them living in the capital, Whitehorse. The rest is wilderness. Glorious, empty, achingly beautiful wilderness.

As the plane begins its descent, I'm like a kid, with my nose pressed against the glass. I see the mountains, the tallest still drizzled with snow. And I see trees, endless waves of green in more shades than I ever thought possible. Beside me, Dalton reaches for my hand. Across the aisle, April sees me staring out the window, and I catch her frowning reflection in it.

"What do you see?" she asks when I turn.

Home. That's what I want to say. I see the only place I've ever truly considered home. She'd grimace at that, so I only say, "We're in the Yukon."

There's no one in the seat beside her, and she leans to peer out her window for exactly two seconds before straightening with: "Trees."

"Yep," Dalton says. "That's what you get in a boreal forest."

She ignores him and returns to working on her laptop. I think back to the first time I flew in. Even then, while I'd never consider myself outdoorsy, I'd been transfixed by the view. April has granted it only a fleeting glance, and with that, I'm five years old again, showing her an anthill or a turtle, waiting for a flicker of interest, and instead getting that two-second glance before she moves on.

We have a couple of hours before our connection to Dawson City, so I suggest popping into Whitehorse. Dalton's quick to agree—sitting in the tiny airport really isn't his idea of fun. April objects. It's only a two-hour wait. Leaving the airport is unwise. We'll need to go through security again. And really, what's the point?

"The point is that your sister wants a cookie," Dalton says. "And probably a cappuccino."

April stares, as if he's obviously kidding. He waves her to the exit and then prods her along, like a shepherd with a balking sheep.

I talk too much on the cab ride. I can't help it. I want April to see the incredible views and be stunned. To see the Yukon's "wilderness city" and be charmed. We go to the Alpine Bakery, and I know she's always been pro-organic, pro-natural-foods, and I want her to be impressed at finding that here. I want her to get a cup of locally roasted coffee and a freshly baked cookie and relax.

Instead, she frets. Is it really safe to let the cab leave? Shouldn't we just grab my snack and go? My God, is that loaf of bread actually seven dollars?

"It's the north," I say. "Everything's expensive."

Dalton proceeds to buy a bagful of baked goods—bread and scones and cookies—and a few pounds of coffee. We get our snack and chat with an athletic senior couple who retired here after a chance visit. That is the story I hear, over and over, people who came to the Yukon for a work trip, for vacation, on a temporary placement, and never left.

The Yukon isn't an easy place to live—with long, dark winters that never seem to end—but it is a place that people *choose*. A place that seduces. I don't need my sister to be seduced, but I want her to see the magic. As Dalton and I talk to the couple, she picks at her scone and keeps checking her watch. We still have an hour to go—plenty of time for the five-kilometer drive to the airport and the nonexistent security line—but her anxiety is contagious, and finally, with regret, I surrender to it.

The first time I came to Rockton, we drove from Whitehorse to Dawson City. Dalton and I have made that trip a couple of times since, when he needs supplies he can't get in Dawson. If he's picking up newcomers, he'll usually fly that leg, if only to avoid being in a car with a stranger for six hours. That's what we do today. We fly into the tiny Dawson airport, and then we head into the hangar, where our bush plane awaits.

"Are you going to be okay with a small plane?" I ask.

She stares, uncomprehending, and I remember my first walk to this hangar, when Dalton handed me a couple of pills. Mild antianxiety meds for the flight. The former town doctor had known my background and sent the pills. I'd given Dalton a look not unlike April's, as I'd tried to figure out why anyone would think I needed medication.

"Your parents?" he'd said.

Because my parents died in a small-plane crash. I'd been walking to a small plane without even thinking about that. Ashamed, I'd hurried to cover it up, to not be the cold bitch unaffected by the tragic death of her parents.

When April gives me that look, I realize she's not making the connection either. I won't make it for her. I won't put her through that discomfort. So I just say, "Bush planes aren't for everyone."

"If you're referring to Mom and Dad's crash, I am well aware of the statistical unlikelihood of perishing under the same circumstances. I am many times more likely to die in a car accident, and yet I don't see people swearing off motor vehicles when a loved one passes that way."

Sorry I mentioned it.

I want to mutter that, as I would have when I was young. Instead, I stick to my adult method of dealing with April: I ignore her.

As we fly, the noise of the plane makes conversation difficult. Dalton and I still manage it, mostly in gestures, him pointing out something in the forest or me doing the same. April doesn't say a word. By the time we land and taxi into the hangar, I've forgotten she's even there, and I jump when she says, "Where are we?"

"Nowhere," I say. Then I grin at Dalton. "Everywhere."

April rolls her eyes. "I know I'm not supposed to ask for details. I simply didn't realize it was quite so . . ." A scrunch of her nose. "Remote."

"Yep," Dalton says. "That's why we warned you. No Wi-Fi. No cell service. We've got electricity, but it's strictly rationed."

"You'll be able to use whatever you need with Kenny, though," I say.

I haven't used his name before, and I expect her to comment. She only waits for the door to open.

As I help Dalton unload the plane, April wanders outside. I hear the thump of running footsteps and then a happy bark that makes me grin.

Storm must circle past April, wide enough that my sister doesn't notice a charging eight-month-old Newfoundland pup. The dog skids to a stop at my feet and dances with excitement until I give her the command. Then she jumps on me, front legs planted on my shoulders. After I hug her, she takes off to greet Dalton.

I step outside. April is about twenty feet away, at the edge of the clearing. I'm about to move away from the dark hangar when Anders jogs up behind April and pulls her into a hug.

"Didn't go well with your sister, huh?" he says.

April jumps like she's been knifed.

Anders falls back fast. "Shit. You're not . . ."

"Not the sister who allows strange men to hug her?" she snaps.

I jog out from the hangar.

"So you let strange men hug you?" Anders calls to me. "Guess that explains how you ended up with the sheriff."

I shake my head. "Will, this is my sister, April."

"Yeah, I figured that." He extends a hand. "Will Anders. Local deputy and the remaining third of the police force."

She gives his hand a perfunctory shake. Then she sees Storm and startles.

"Not a bear," Anders says. "Well, supposedly. Eric says she's some fancy purebred, but I'm still convinced someone conned our sheriff and sold him a black bear cub."

"She's a Newfoundland," I say, rubbing Storm's neck. "She's big, but she's well trained. You just need to watch out for flying fur and slobber."

"Isn't that . . ." April peers at her. "Didn't Aunt Becca's boyfriend have a dog like that?"

I light up in a grin. I can't help it. "He did. Nana—named after the Newfoundland in *Peter Pan*. I kinda fell in love with that dog, so Eric bought me this one."

She mutters something under her breath. It sounds like "Of course he did," but when I look up, she's only shaking her head.

"Her name's Storm," I say. "Because of . . ."

I rumple her white-streaked ear. April looks at me blankly.

"X-Men," Anders says. "Your sister is not afraid to let her geek flag fly. She's even got us playing D and D."

"Which was *your* idea," I say.

April stares at Anders. Admittedly, he is kind of stare-worthy. Her look, though, is pure confusion. If there's a stereotype of a guy who knows every rule in the D&D handbook, it is not Will Anders. He's six foot two, with a military buzz cut and a US Army tat on one bulging black biceps.

"Do you have an actual patient that I'm supposed to see?" April says finally.

"Casey and Will were waiting for me," Dalton says as he walks out of the hangar. "We have to sneak you into town, and I needed to put the plane to bed first. Now, let's talk about how we're going to do this."

THREE

Dalton and I have already discussed how we'll manage this situation. As we walk to town, we let Anders in on the plan.

If we play this right, we'll get April in and out of Rockton, and the only other person who'll know she was here is Mathias, our psychiatrist-turned-butcher. There's a reason Anders mistook April for me. Before we boarded the bush plane, I had her change into my spare clothing. She's wearing my T-shirt and jeans, and after we left the plane, I gave her my jacket and ball cap, too. I had her pull her hair into a ponytail and tug it through the back of the cap, the way I wear mine.

No one will walk up to April face-on and presume it's me. The thing about Rockton, though, is that there are no strangers. As long as people only spot her in passing, they'll see who they expect to be wearing that ball cap and jacket.

We don't take her through town, of course. As soon as we draw near, she's in Anders's custody. Then Dalton and I continue on with Storm. Dalton marches into Rockton and straight to the first gaggle of residents he sees.

"Where's Phil?" he says.

They all turn with blank looks.

"The council guy," I say. "Val's replacement."

"I think he's holed up in her old place," one says.

Dalton grunts a thanks and strides in that direction.

People tag along, hoping for scraps of information about Kenny. I promise an update soon. That would usually be enough to placate them, but Dalton uses the excuse to snarl and curse and make a whole lotta noise about how if the "fucking council found us a fucking new doctor, Kenny wouldn't be in this fucking mess." It's pure theater— getting people's attention while Anders spirits April around to the clinic. Fortunately, the town is accustomed to seeing their sheriff on a rant, and no one thinks twice about it. They just draw closer in hopes of some real entertainment once Dalton reaches Val's house.

"Philip!" Dalton shouts when we're within fifty feet. "Get your goddamn ass out here!"

It takes a few moments before the door creaks open. When Phil sees Dalton, he seems to contemplate the possibility of retreat. Dalton's striding toward the house, looking like he's two seconds from putting his hand on his sidearm and challenging Phil to a duel at high noon.

When I first met Dalton, I thought he looked like a Wild West sheriff. The way he carries himself. The strong jaw. The sun-weathered skin. The crow's-feet forming at the corners of gray eyes that have spent too long squinting into the sun. Put him into Rockton, with its dirt roads and simple wooden buildings, and he seems right at home. Today, he's even wearing the hat, one that's meant to keep the sun off and slow that early damage but yes, I may have picked out one that bears more than a passing resemblance to a ten-gallon hat.

Phil, on the other hand, looks like the kind of guy who, if asked to "draw," whips out his cell phone at lightning speed. Early thirties. Impeccably dressed. Chiseled face. An Armani suit model come to life. After a few days in Rockton, he's forgone the jacket and tie, but he still wears the white shirt, trousers, and loafers. The shirt, admittedly, is beginning to look a bit rumpled. We don't have ironing boards in Rockton.

Before Phil arrived, he'd been a faceless voice on our satellite receiver, and I'd always pictured a nebbishy middle-aged pencil pusher with a comb-over and paunch. I was still fighting the disconnect.

Phil steels himself and walks out, his chin lifting. "Is there a problem, Sheriff?"

"Yeah. This"—Dalton waves the satellite phone—"is a fucking piece of shit."

He whips the phone. To Phil's credit, he doesn't hit the deck. He just takes a quick step back as the phone smashes into the wall, pieces flying.

"That—that is an expensive piece of technology, Sheriff."

A few of the gathering locals titter. I hear at least one whispered request for popcorn.

"No, *that* is a fucking piece of useless shit," Dalton says, bearing down on Phil. "Or did you fall asleep?"

"What?"

I answer as I walk up beside Dalton. "We hoped to speak to April before she went in to work. You'd said the phone would be manned at all hours."

"It was. I had a nap, of course, but Sam was watching it while I slept. I was awake at daylight, which up here is four in the morning, apparently."

"We called at four thirty," I lie. "And five. And five thirty. And six . . ."

"The fucking phone didn't work," Dalton says. "Which is a problem when it's the only fucking way we have to get in touch."

"I'm sure there was some other way—"

"Like what?" Dalton says. "Smoke signals?"

"It's a direct-link satellite phone," I say. "If it fails, we can't just buy a new one. This is what happens when you refuse to give us another method of communication."

"One fucking method of communication," Dalton says. "We had a trained neurosurgeon on hand, ready to give Kenny the best goddamn care possible, and you fucked it up."

"The council—" Phil stops himself and straightens. "I apologize, Sheriff. Yes, the council has very strict communication protocols, as you know, but in this case, you are correct that we needed redundancy."

"Well, you can tell that to Kenny. The lack of fucking redundancy cost him the use of his legs."

Phil clears his throat. "Redundancy means—"

"It means a backup plan," Dalton says. "So just *say* you didn't have a backup plan. You decided Kenny's future mobility wasn't worth making an exception to your goddamn rules."

"The rules are there for security, Sheriff. Providing an unsecured satellite phone introduces the possibility of an intercepted call. Even letting you take that phone was dangerous. We allowed it to show that we do care about Kenny's situation. Now we'll need to get him some-place else, which means he cannot return to Rockton."

"Not yet," I say. "My sister gave me detailed notes based on the X-rays and photographs. Mathias and Will will attempt to remove the bullet. My sister believes that will be enough. Then, on Monday, we'll fly to Dawson and provide a phone update."

"I don't think the council will want you leaving again so soon—"

"We are," Dalton says. "For Kenny."

A chorus of approval from the crowd. This isn't just about Kenny. It's us versus them. Rockton versus the council.

Not everyone here is a fan of our sheriff. He's tough as hell, and even those who obey our laws don't appreciate his endless rules. But they know each of those rules is designed to ensure they are safe here and return home alive.

Dalton is the one living with them, enduring the same conditions, and he'll be here long after they return to twenty-first-century life down south. In contrast, the council represents nameless, faceless bu-reaucracy. They enjoy hot showers and fine dining and modern tech-nology from their high-rise towers, while dictating our conditions here. Even when they do show up, they're like Val and now Phil, se-questered in their house, putting in time until they can flee back to civilization.

The truth is that Phil could be the nicest guy imaginable, and the residents would still side with Dalton. The fact that Phil seems like a real dick doesn't help matters at all. He isn't an idiot, though. He hears those rumblings, and he looks out over the crowd, and he's very aware that he's no longer hiding behind the safety of a satellite receiver a thousand kilometers away.

"All right," he says. "I will convince the council that, in light of this mishap, you should be allowed to return to Dawson City to consult with Detective Butler's sister. I will also authorize funds to purchase additional supplies, so long as you are making the trip."

Phil raises his voice. "If anyone has items you need purchased, please compile a list. I will ensure the council authorizes extra funds, in light of everything you've been through in the past week."

"Bread and circuses for all," Dalton mutters.

Phil frowns over at us. "Hmm?"

"Nothing," I say. Then I turn to the crowd. "I want to get working on Kenny, and I'm going to ask for minimal distractions. I know everyone is worried about him, but this is a delicate operation, without a trained surgeon. If you can give us time and space, we would appreciate it."

"Sam?" Dalton calls into the crowd. "Jen? Nicki? Round up the militia. Those who aren't on patrol, I want them keeping a wide berth around the clinic. No one comes in or out until I say so. That includes you guys. Last thing Kenny needs is someone slamming a door when Will's got a scalpel next to his spinal cord."

Nicole is closest to the front. "Understood. We'll maintain a twenty-foot barrier and clear the houses on either side."

"Thank you," I say, and then we head to the clinic.

April is already in the clinic when we arrive. She's assessed Kenny. Now, as he talks to her, she looks like she's wondering how soon she can anesthetize him. Of everything she's done, that pisses me off the most. While I'll be the first to admit that Kenny can be a bit puppy-dog eager, what she's doing feels like kicking that puppy, especially given his situation.

"Ignore my sister," I say as I walk in. "She's a scientist these days, and I think she's forgotten her bedside manner."

She shoots me a look of mingled annoyance and bafflement.

"Or," Anders murmurs beside me, "that's *why* she's a scientist."

Kenny gives a strained chuckle. "So it's been a while since you put someone under the knife, huh?"

"No," April says, with a glare for me now. "I have a medical license with a specialization in neurosurgery. I practiced full time for five years before deciding my talents were better utilized in research, so I earned my Ph.D. on weekends."

"Oh, wow. That's . . ." Kenny shakes his head. "You and Casey are living proof that pretty girls can be smart, too."

I cringe, but this is typical Kenny.

"Of course they can," April says as she assesses our equipment. "The genetics required for both intelligence and attractiveness are independent. Which doesn't mean that one can achieve a medical license and Ph.D. effortlessly, regardless of IQ. I worked hard. My sister could have done the same, despite her lower intellectual starting point."

"Wow," Anders whispers. "Just . . . wow."

"I'm a slacker," I say.

That makes Anders chuckle, but he still shoots me a concerned look, as if I might not be taking this so lightly. I am. Mostly. I grew up with this. My parents had my IQ tested as soon as possible. It's 135. My sister's—as theirs was—is above 140. To them, my "inferior" intellectual ability only meant I'd need to work harder. When I became a homicide detective, it proved I didn't have the fortitude to do that extra work, to their everlasting disappointment. The fact that I'd dreamed of being a detective since I was a kid, running around with my fingerprint kit? Irrelevant.

Before anyone can speak, the door opens. In walks a slender man in his forties, carrying a wolf-dog cub.

"Uh, Mathias?" I say, pointing at the cub. "No spectators allowed."

"He will be quiet. He is very sleepy."

April blinks at the cub. "You can't bring—"

"You must be the sister. It is a pleasure to meet you. *Parlez-vous français?*"

She stares at him.

"*Non?*" He looks at me and sighs. "Why did you not teach your sister French? This is most inconvenient."

"Your English is fine, Mathias, but if you're having trouble comprehending: *Dépose le foutu chien.*"

"*Loup chien.* And his name is Raoul."

"Did he say . . . wolf-dog?" April says.

"Ah, she does speak French. Excellent."

"She understands it," I say. "She won't speak it. Now take that damn—"

He covers the cub's ears and lays him on a blanket. "I have not yet decided upon a suitable sitter."

"I can hold him for you," Kenny says with a smile. "I'm not going anywhere."

"Sadly, that would, I fear, be unhygienic. He will stay in his corner and sleep. But when we are finished here, I would like the doctor to take a look at his leg." Mathias moves to the operating table. "It was caught in a snare. Casey did an excellent nursing job, but I would appreciate your opinion, Casey's sister. When surgery is over, of course."

"I'm not a veterinarian," April says.

"The cub will not mind."

"Mathias?" I point to the operating table.

The cub pitches to his feet and toddles after Mathias.

Dalton scoops up the canine. "I'll take him on my rounds."

"Excellent idea," Mathias says. "He requires socialization to enhance his dog nature. Not too much, though. It would not befit my carefully crafted personae to have a *friendly* wolf-dog."

Dalton shakes his head and leaves.

"Can we start now?" I ask.

"I will scrub up," Mathias says.

April nods at Mathias as he crosses the room. "I take it he's your psychiatrist."

"*Non,*" Mathias says. "Casey does not require a psychiatrist. An occasional therapist perhaps, but we all do at times. My specialty is psychopathy and sociopathy, with the occasional borderline personality thrown in for good measure, but only if he has committed the requisite number of atrocities. I have very exacting standards."

"Mathias?" I say. "Scrub."

"Have you ever conducted surgery?" April asks him.

"Not medically. However, I am the town butcher."

"Yeah," Kenny says. "No offense, Doc, but I think we'll let Casey's sister do the cutting."

"I cut very well," Mathias says. "And the human anatomy is not so different from—"

"Mathias?" I say. "Stop freaking out the patient. April is the surgeon. Will is assisting. You're the gofer."

"Gofer? That is rather degrading. What are *you* doing?"

"I'll be playing anesthetist today. Unless you plan to *talk* him to sleep. Now go scrub up while I put Kenny down."

I catch Kenny's look.

"*Under,*" I say as Anders chuckles. "I mean put you under. Sorry."

April sighs, and we begin.

FOUR

The bullet is out. And right now, that's all we can say.

"The bullet had shifted," April says as we're cleaning up. "There is still a possibility of permanent damage, and if that is the case, it is due to the movement of the bullet before I arrived."

"No one's going to blame you if Kenny isn't up and running to-morrow," Anders says. "We know how delicate an operation that was, and it went perfectly. Anything after this is because of unavoidable shifts in the bullet's location."

"They were not unavoidable," she says, and I wince behind Anders.

She continues. "The patient should have been kept immobile after the bullet struck. I realize that he had to be transported, but proper precautions were not taken."

When Anders tenses, I jump in with, "We did what we could, April. And the patient's name is Kenny."

"The fault might also be his own," she says. "He did not ensure his own immobility."

"You're blaming—?" I begin.

"April." Mathias extends his hand. "On behalf of Rockton, we would like to thank you for your fine work. Will you be leaving soon? We can take matters from here, and I am certain you have work— very important work—to continue back home."

April blinks, taken aback.

"Eric will fly her out Monday," I say. "That gives Kenny time to wake up and, with any luck, the swelling will go down enough for April to evaluate his condition before she leaves." I turn to my sister. "You'll be staying in my old house. Will is going to escort you through the woods. I'll see you in the morning."

"So your sister's a bitch," Dalton says as soon as we get home.

I laugh at that. A full-blown whoosh of a laugh, as if I've been holding myself tight all day and can finally relax. Which is true. Our door closes, and I am home with my guy and my dog. There's no one I need to pretend for anymore.

"Now you see where I get it from," I say as he follows me into the kitchen.

"Fuck, no. You're tough, and you can be . . ." His lips purse as he searches for the word. "Reserved. That's not a bitch." He jabs a finger in the direction of the clinic. "That's a bitch. You might look like sisters, but the resemblance ends there."

"She's smarter than me."

He rolls his eyes. "For someone like that, IQ is just a number they hold up to make themselves feel superior. You know how many times residents announce their fucking IQ when I try to give safety instructions on chopping wood?" He shakes his head. "Like intelligence will keep them from cutting off their damned hand."

I reach for the fridge, but Dalton stops me. He takes a bag from the counter, one that wasn't there when we left yesterday. From it, he pulls out the loaf of bread we bought in Whitehorse. Then he produces something even more magical.

"Is that butter?" I say. "Real butter?"

"It is."

We get fresh bread from our bakery, but butter is a perishable we can't afford.

Dalton waves for me to sit as he saws off four thick slices and slathers them in butter. I may start to drool. He takes out our peanut butter and adds a layer. Then he steps back and eyes the open-faced sandwich.

"Missing anything?" he says.

"Gimme."

He pulls chocolate chips from the grocery bag. "Are you sure it's not missing anything?"

I laugh then and say, "I think I love you."

His brows rise. "Think?"

I stand and put my arms around his neck. Then I kiss him, a deep, long kiss that ends with me on the kitchen table, my legs around him. I'm pushing up his T-shirt when his stomach rumbles.

"Dinner first," I say as I pull down his shirt. "Also, this confuses the dog."

Sure enough, Storm sits by the table, her head tilted. We've trained her to retreat to the kitchen when things heat up elsewhere in the house. So when they heat up *in* the kitchen, she has no idea where to go. The last time, she hid under the table . . . and then went zooming out when it started rocking.

Dalton puts chocolate chips on my sandwich and on one corner of his. Then he pours glasses of water, and we sit and eat.

"I knew your family was fucked up," he says. "But I thought it was just your parents."

"Messed-up parents; messed-up kids."

His lips tighten at that. He chews and then says, "She's your older sister. If there were problems with your parents, she should have looked out for you. That's what older siblings do."

"It's what *you* do with Jacob. But I don't get the impression there were any serious issues with your birth parents."

He takes another bite, avoiding the topic of his birth parents altogether, as usual.

"I'm not sure April ever saw issues with our parents," I say. "I was the underachiever. The disappointment."

"So April piles on and treats you like shit, too?" He shakes his head.

"I knew you weren't close. I didn't know it was this bad. Otherwise, I'd have found another solution for Kenny."

"I'll be fine."

Another two bites. Then, "I still wish you'd talk about it more. Your family."

"I will when you will."

He stops in midbite and nods, acknowledging the point. That's all he does, though. Acknowledges it and keeps eating.

"I don't talk about it because I don't want to go back there," I say. "I've moved on. I know I sometimes push myself too hard because I still hear their voices, but you make sure I don't overdo it. My life isn't all about my job anymore, and that wasn't entirely their fault."

"I know."

"I'm not the messed-up kid I used to be. April will see it and . . ." I shrug. "Even thinking that puts me right back there. When I was little, I wanted her attention so badly. More than I ever wanted my parents'. I'd do goofy things to make her smile. I'd find interesting science tidbits to make her listen. It never worked, and instead of backing off, I'd just try harder, make a fool of myself."

"You were a kid who wanted her big sister to notice her. That's normal. Remember what Jacob said, about how he'd follow me to my hideaway, go in after and play with my stuff? I feel bad about that. He wanted my attention, and sometimes I just had to be alone."

"*Sometimes.* That's the difference. You needed a break from being a big brother, and April . . ." I lean back in my seat. "There was nothing to take a break *from.* There was no relationship there. I thought I'd accepted that, and then I find myself right back in that old dynamic. I want her to see what I see here. In the Yukon. In Rockton. I'm like that little kid, hoping for a reaction, and ultimately, making a fool of myself."

"Pointing out a moose is 'making a fool of yourself'?"

I give him a look.

"I do know what you mean," he says. "Reminds me of when you first came here. You'd show sparks of interest—in the animals, the

landscape, the life—and I'd jump on it . . . and then you'd back off. I'm the one who felt like the overeager kid, tripping over myself to impress you."

"Uh, I don't remember anything vaguely like *tripping* over yourself. I do remember that I was worried about seeming *too* interested in Rockton and maybe . . ." I slant a glance his way. "Too interested in you."

"I definitely don't remember that."

"You were fascinating and infuriating and . . . unique. I couldn't tell what to make of you. I just knew that I wanted to get to know you better."

"I felt the same about you. I also felt like I tripped over myself chasing those sparks of interest."

"While I was trying to play it cool. We learn that, don't we? Hit high school and you need to chill, tone it down, which usually means showing no interest in anything."

"Good thing I never went to high school."

"Yeah, it's crazy, huh? But I didn't come from an exuberant, expressive family to begin with, so I know I can be . . . what's the word you used? Reserved."

"You can."

I look up at him. "You do know I'm happy here, right? Even if I'm not screaming it at the top of my lungs?"

"I do."

"And you know how I feel about you."

He hesitates, and my heart slams against my ribs.

"I'm crazy about you," I say. "I hope you know that. I say I love you, but that always seems weak. This is . . ." I take a deep breath. "It's miles beyond anything I've felt before."

"Yeah, I know." He eases back in his chair and smirks. "I just like to hear you say it."

"Jerk."

"Not 'asshole'? Pretty sure that deserved an 'asshole.'"

"I'm being nice to you, because I'm done." I walk over and straddle his lap. "And I was promised dessert."

"Pretty sure I never actually . . ." He watches as I shed my shirt and bra. "My mistake. I definitely promised dessert."

"Just not in the kitchen."

He laughs and then scoops me up and carries me past Storm, out of the kitchen.

We're out for a walk. Just the two of us, which feels like parents sneaking away on their kid. As much as Storm loves her jaunts, sometimes we need to take one without her, relax and enjoy the night as a couple.

It's past midnight, the sun finally dipping below the horizon. It's warm, too. I haven't spent a summer here, but I'm told to expect temperatures in the low- to mid-twenties—Celsius, that is—which is damn near perfect for me, since I've never been fond of hot and humid.

Despite the romantic stroll, we aren't completely slacking off. We're also patrolling the town's borders. Warmer temperatures mean residents throw off the shackles of the long, cold, dark winter, and they go a little crazy, also throwing off the rules that keep them inside our boundaries. There isn't a fence around Rockton. The council tried that, but it just made people feel like they were in an armed camp. Better to treat them like adults. Which works better when they act like it. We've already had incidents this spring, with people sneaking off for a moonlight walk—or moonlight sex—in the woods.

When we spot a figure in the woods, Dalton opens his mouth, ready to launch a profanity-laden tirade that'll send the offender tearing back to town like a dog caught off its property. But before he can say a word, I grab his arm, my fingers tightening.

He looks down at me.

"Can you tell who that is?" I whisper.

He squints and then shakes his head. It's a figure in a dark jacket, hood pulled up. The size looks male, but even that is an educated guess.

"If you shout, you'll lose him," I say.

Most times, Dalton would be willing to just do that. It's not worth his time to punish someone for being ten feet outside town. Yet when the town's under a strict lockdown, a scare isn't enough.

Dalton slips off. I count to ten, and then I circle the other way, approaching the figure from the rear.

The man is just standing there, looking toward Rockton. Which is odd. The point of sneaking out is to put town life behind you for a while. The only reason to be on the edge looking toward it is . . .

If you're watching someone inside.

Did someone spot April? See enough in the shadowy twilight to realize she wasn't me?

Yet we aren't near my old house. Nor are we near the clinic.

My next guess is, unfortunately, a male resident paying unwelcome attention to a female one. Guys make up three-quarters of our population. At least a third of the women are here to escape a partner—a stalker or abusive ex—which means they aren't exactly looking to strike up a new relationship. That leaves a serious shortage of available partners for heterosexual men, which can lead to guys having trouble hearing the word "no."

I mentally map the town. Two of the border buildings nearby are storage units, and the only house belongs to Anders. That doesn't mean this *isn't* a stalker. Our deputy gets his share of unwanted attention from both sexes.

I ease to the side for a better look and realize this guy isn't behind Anders's house. He's looking between the two storage buildings. He has one hand raised. I didn't notice that at first—it's on the other side of his body—but when I move, I see he's holding something to his face.

Binoculars. I'm trying to remember whether we have a compact pair like that when a shadow moves through the trees. A dark figure heading right for the man.

Dalton.

I swear under my breath. Of course Dalton is coming. While I've been trying to solve this puzzle, he's been waiting for me to approach the guy. If I don't, he will.

"Did you miss the goddamn announcement?" Dalton says, his voice ringing out. "We're under a fucking cur—"

He stops. Goes completely still and then says "Casey!" as his hand flies to his holstered gun. The guy wheels, and I see his face.

A face I do not recognize.

FIVE

I go for my gun. The guy lunges to the side and hits the ground.

Dalton yells for the guy to stop, stay where he is or we'll fire. The man scrambles into the underbrush, and even a warning shot from Dalton doesn't slow him. The guy disappears in the bush, and I'm racing after him, gun in hand, but by the time I get there, he's on his feet, a distant shadow in the twilight. I don't aim my gun. From here, there's no chance of anything except a potentially fatal shot. Instead I run. I get about twenty feet before a hand grabs the back of my jacket, Dalton saying, "No."

Adrenaline pumping, I spin to knock his hand off, but I stop myself before I do. I take a deep breath and holster my gun. Dalton's right. It's nighttime in the forest. Tearing after a fleeing man is a very stupid idea.

Dalton holsters his weapon and gives his arm a shake. It's still weak from last week's injury, and he's been too busy to bother with the sling. When I point at his arm, he waves me off and scowls into the forest. Then he looks toward town. Wondering whether we should track the guy ourselves or call out the militia.

He doesn't glance over for my opinion, which means there's no real question in his mind. He gives an abrupt nod and starts circling around the border.

I don't ask what he's doing. "Equal partners" can't apply to our professional lives. He's the sheriff. He's in charge.

Dalton actually has a harder time with that than I do. I've always frowned on supervisor-and-underling relationships. If a guy is your boss at work, isn't that going to carry over at home? For Dalton, the discomfort goes in the opposite direction—he'd rather be partners across the board. But Rockton requires a leader. *One* leader.

Dalton still only gets about twenty steps before he glances over his shoulder and then lowers his voice, saying, "We'll get Storm and track him. Leave the militia out of this for now."

I nod. By not chasing the guy, we let him think he got away. Let him slow down. Let him get careless.

"He's definitely not a hostile," I say.

"Yeah."

"A settler?" I ask. "Not from the First Settlement—his clothing's too new for that—but has anyone left recently?"

Dalton shakes his head.

Rockton has been around since the fifties. That means thousands of people have passed through, and almost all complete their stint and go home. Some, though, choose the forest instead.

Rockton was born as an exercise in idealism—a place for people who needed refuge, and in those earliest years, it was often their ideals that brought them there, when they fled McCarthyism and other political witch hunts. But as with so many lofty humanitarian ideas, eventually the coffers ran dry and someone saw the opportunity for profit. When capitalism moved into Rockton, a group of residents moved out and formed the First Settlement, which is now in its third generation.

There are also smaller settlements, plus people who chose not to join one, like Dalton's birth parents. They were twenty-first-century pioneers, living off the land, hunting and gathering, building shelters, and sewing clothing from skins.

Then there are the hostiles. People who have left Rockton and reverted to a more . . . I want to say primitive form. They *are* tribal. They are also ritualistic—painting and scarring themselves and setting out totems to mark territory. But in no way should they be confused with tribal societies. The hostiles are a grotesque stereotype of that, as if someone read too many *National Geographic*s as a child. I used to think they'd lost what makes us human, but that implies they're animalistic, and the hostiles' sheer capacity for violence is far more human.

"His clothes were clean," I say. "Dark jacket. Jeans. Boots. He didn't have any more beard stubble than you do. So he likely hasn't been out here longer than a week."

"Yeah."

Dalton opens the back door to our house. Storm races into the kitchen and skids to a stop, knowing better than to barrel through an open door. Dalton goes inside and returns with two flashlights and a Newfoundland on a leash.

"His clothes seem to rule out a miner or trapper," I say, picking up where I left off. "I don't think he's a hiker either. Those weren't hiking boots, and that jacket was too heavy. Dark hair. I couldn't make out eye color. I think brown skin, but he didn't seem indigenous."

I'm running through all the possibilities because I don't want to jump to the paranoid conclusion. I'm hoping Dalton will find an angle I've missed. Instead, as we head into the forest, he says, "You think it's connected to Brady."

I don't answer. I'm hoping not. We both are. Oliver Brady was the serial killer foisted on us two weeks ago. He's gone now, but I suppose someone could have come looking for him.

"That's possible, but it doesn't feel right."

"You think it's a new problem."

"I hope not."

God, I hope not.

Getting Storm is a good idea—she's a tracking dog. However, she's still in training, and so far we've always given her an article of clothing to sniff. We don't have that for our mystery man.

We take her to the spot where we saw him, and I have her sniff the ground, but I can tell she's confused. I know the direction he went, so I head that way as she sniffs. Dalton has grabbed treats, which helps her think this is a new phase of training.

Storm seems to understand what we want, but after about a hundred feet, she loses the trail as it crosses a path. There are other scents there, familiar ones, and she keeps trailing those and then stopping, as if realizing that's not correct. She backtracks, as she's been taught, and tries again.

After a few rounds, she gets bored and requests her treats in that halfhearted way that says she knows she doesn't deserve them. At some point the work outweighs the reward, particularly for a well-fed and well-loved dog. She tracks for the fun of it, and when that wears off, so does her interest.

She can't pick up the man's trail on the other side of the path, which may mean he followed the path itself. So we walk her along that. It's a major trail, though, and well traveled, and I'm not sure she'd be able to find his scent on it. Someday, yes, but at eight months, she's a little young for tracking at all.

We stop and peer into the darkness. Storm nudges my hand. She knows she's failed, and while she may not care about the treats, she hates to disappoint us. I pat her as Dalton motions that we'll return to where we last detected our intruder, and he'll use his tracking skills from there.

We've walked about ten paces when Storm lets out a happy yip and lunges into the undergrowth. Her nose is up, not sniffing the ground, which means she's catching a scent in the wind.

"Could be him," Dalton says.

"Or could be a bunny rabbit."

He shrugs. "Let her have her fun."

Even if this scent *is* our mystery man, we won't catch him. We have an eighty-pound puppy hot on a trail through dense forest. A charging bull moose would be quieter.

I motion that Dalton could give me the dog and circle around, in hopes of seeing our target, but he shakes his head. He won't leave me. A stranger in the forest is always trouble.

We keep going, Storm straining at the lead, snuffling and slobbering. Finally, she gives a giant-puppy pounce and lands in the middle of a clearing. Then she looks up at me, her dark eyes glittering.

"Uh, great," I say. "You've found . . ." I look around. Then I grin, lower myself, and hug her. "Good girl. Very good girl."

"Shit, yeah," Dalton says.

Storm hasn't found her target, but she's discovered something that could prove equally valuable: his camp. It's only a couple of hundred feet from Rockton, and it doesn't look as if he's actually slept there. He's just left his pack. Abandoned it in the middle of the clearing, like he's on a beach, dropping his stuff to go exploring. Not a guy accustomed to the forest. Otherwise he'd know that, presuming there's food in that pack, it won't last long.

Dalton reaches to open the backpack.

"Whoa, hold on," I say, grabbing him back. "It could be a trap."

He frowns. "In the bag?"

To Dalton, a trap is a literal one, like a bear trap.

"An IED," I say.

When his frown deepens, I start to say, "A bomb," but he nods and says, "Improvised explosive device." While he might never have encountered such a thing, he's read more than anyone I know.

"It's unlikely," I say. "But I want to be sure. This screams setup. Can you hold Storm back, please?"

He hesitates.

"I'm not going to attempt to disarm a bomb," I say. "I'm just looking, and I don't want to have to worry about either of you."

He backs off with Storm. I examine the ground for signs of a trigger. Out here, it'd need to be a literal trigger—trip wire or such. I get close to the bag and crouch. It's an oversize backpack, the sort campers use. This one is so new that it smells of polyurethane. I can even see a plastic fastener around the handle, where he's ripped off the tags. That sets my alarms flashing—he could have bought this to house an IED. Then I notice open pockets, and when I aim my flashlight beam inside, I see energy bars and a bottle of water.

I examine the main zipper. It isn't quite closed, and I poke at the hole with a twig and shine my light through on rolled-up clothing.

Next I pick up a tree, which sounds more impressive than saying I haul over a downed sapling. I use it to prod the backpack. Nothing happens.

None of this proves the pack isn't rigged to explode, but without any way to test it, at some point I need to make a judgment call. My call is that it's exactly what it looks like. The guy doesn't know his way around the Yukon forest, and he's bought a bag, stuffed it with supplies, and dumped it to go check out the town unencumbered.

Of course, this would all make far more sense if we weren't a week's hike from the nearest town. There's no way an amateur can buy a few supplies, set off into our forest, and reach Rockton. Not unless he's seriously lost, wandering for days, about ready to give up all hope when he finally sees signs of civilization and . . . Takes off at the first sign of a rescuer? Not a chance.

I wave to Dalton that the backpack is fine. Then, before he's close enough to get hurt, I yank down the zipper and there's a tremendous boom—

No. That isn't what happens. Even my paranoia cannot imagine the point of putting a triggered explosive device here. It's not exactly like dropping it off in the middle of Union Station.

I open the zipper all the way and start unpacking while Dalton moves closer to stand guard. As I go, I tell him what I find, so he can keep his attention on the forest, in case our mystery man returns.

"Water and energy bars, like what you'd take on a daylong hike. There's a change of clothes. Sweatshirt. Tee. Track pants. All brand-new. And . . ." I pull out a smaller case. "A toiletry bag. With toothbrush, paste, comb, razor . . ."

"Did he think he was going to a hotel?"

"Actually, it looks like that. Half-emptied paste. Used razor. Old bag. It's what I kept in my bathroom to grab for work trips. Judging by the new clothing, though, his 'work trips' aren't usually into the backwoods."

My hand touches something familiar. I pull it out.

"Ammo?" Dalton says. "Fuck."

"Nine-mil. Odd choice for up here."

His brows rise.

"Yes, that's what I carry," I say, "because that's what I'm accustomed to. But it's a city gun."

"For shooting people, not wildlife. Yeah, I'd be a whole lot happier if you found shotgun pellets in there."

"Let's switch spots," I say. "Now that we know he's armed, the person on guard shouldn't be the one who'll have trouble firing straight."

He doesn't say he'll be fine. Until his arm heals, he's hampered. I'm not.

Dalton isn't nearly as good at announcing what he finds in that backpack. For years, it's been just him and Anders, and our deputy is an army boy. When he trusts his commanding officer, he doesn't expect details until that officer is ready to give them.

"Anything?" I say finally.

"Stuff."

"Helpful."

A jangle. "Car keys. Got a parking-garage ticket, too. From the Calgary airport. Dated . . . Fuck. Dated this morning?"

"You can fly Calgary to Whitehorse, right?"

"In the summer, yeah."

"So he flew in from Calgary, and somehow got out here. He sure as hell didn't walk." I squint up at the sky. "Where else could a plane touch down, if not our airstrip?"

"Plenty of clearings. With the right plane, if you know the area, you can do it."

"Which means he hired someone to bring him in. Packed a quick bag, bought supplies for the woods, dropped off his car in Calgary, flew to Whitehorse, and got a charter from there. Seems very . . ." I follow a noise in the forest, but it's only an owl swooping past. "Seems very last-minute."

"It does." Dalton rises. "You want this repacked the way it was?"

I consider. "No, let's take it. I can go over it better in town. And, if we take his food and water . . . He's seen Rockton. He knows where to get more."

One of the endless dilemmas we face as law enforcement in Rockton is also one I faced as a homicide detective down south. Only here, it's multiplied a thousand times. How much information on potential threats do we release to the public? From a layman's point of view, the answer is a no-brainer: tell them everything. Yet as cops, we know how wrong this can go. Tell people there may be a thief targeting their neighborhood, and you damned well better hope no teen tries sneaking through a window after breaking curfew.

Up here, it is so much worse. For the average resident, Rockton is an extended summer camp. To some it's a grand adventure, the chance to experience another kind of life and go home enriched by the experience. To others, it's like being sentenced to camp by working parents, forced to endure a cell-phone-free and Starbucks-free hell before being released back to civilization. Either way, as the "camper" you are a guest. You don't need to worry about paying bills or putting food on the table. Sure, you have chores. And rules. Plenty of rules. But you trust the grown-ups to lock the doors and arm the security system and replace the batteries in the smoke detectors.

We have had death in Rockton. Murder and kidnapping and assault, and yet no one looks around and says, "Holy shit, is this the murder capital of North America? Let me outta here!" They understand the issues with this life, the volatile elements we are dealing with. They see that we catch and deal with those responsible, as quickly as we can.

This does not mean, however, that it's impossible for us to break their trust. I can use the analogy of children, but these are adults, and the more complicated the situation, the more armchair law enforcement we see, residents taking a critical look at our methods and saying, "That's not how I'd do it."

We *have* made mistakes. It's unavoidable. It's like installing a security system on your home. You think you've covered every possibility, and then someone breaks in through the chimney, and you kick yourself for leaving a point of entry unguarded. Sure, you weren't expecting cat-burglar Santa. Yet others will judge the omission, and you feel the full weight of that.

Now we have an armed stranger in the forest. Which, in itself, is like saying we have grizzly bears in the forest. Yep, we do. Lots of grizzly bears *and* armed strangers, with the settlers and the hostiles. The difference here is that this guy seems to have come here for us. For Rockton. That is alarming on many levels.

So do we *raise* the alarm?

Yes, we must.

It's *how* we raise it that's in question.

"When we get back to town, I'm waking Will," Dalton says. "Fucking shitty thing to do, after leaving him in charge, alone, for two days."

"He'd want to be the first to know."

"Yeah. I'll also recall the patrols for the night so they don't bump into this guy. First light, though, we're tracking his ass down. I want you to stay in town. Pick two militia to stay with you. You're gonna need to make a statement."

I don't argue. I'm the one who insists we make public statements. Before that, it really was a parental situation, where the grown-ups handle everything and explain nothing. That isn't my way, and Dalton has come to see the value in these public statements, if only because they keep residents from pestering us to update them each personally.

Dalton and I part ways at the edge of town. I'm heading home. He's keeping Storm—she knows what our mystery man smells like, and if he comes near, she'll warn Dalton.

Our back door is unlocked, as usual. I make a mental note to add this to my morning statement—tell people to lock their doors. Most don't. For them, there's nostalgia in that, hearkening back to a time before most of us were born, when you could pop out for a few hours and leave your door open. For Dalton, an open door is also a statement. If someone wants to break in and steal his belongings, they can go right ahead—he'll have fun tracking down their asses. Needless to say, Dalton has never had a break-in.

As I walk in, I'm thinking about that, and so when I hear a creak, I freeze, hand dropping to my gun. Any other time, I wouldn't have even noticed. It's a wooden house. It creaks. But I've just been reflecting on our unlocked door, so a creak puts me on full alert.

I scan the moonlit kitchen. Our dinner dishes are still out. Even the chocolate chip package is there, morsels spilled onto the table where I grabbed a handful as we left.

I shrug off my light jacket, so I can better access my gun. Then I take a step and . . .

Another creak sounds, this one from the bottom of the stairs. I ease forward, but even if I could see through the doorway, I wouldn't have a direct sight line to the stairwell. So I withdraw, close the back door quietly, and turn the lock. My intention is to lock the intruder inside, but I'm aware that I'm potentially trapping myself, too.

I pull my gun from its holster. Then I take one careful—

Footsteps sound on the front deck. Damn it. Dalton has circled back.

When a rap sounds, I go still. Dalton would *not* knock on our door. I check my watch. Who the hell would be—?

"Casey? It's Di. I know you're up."

Diana? Seriously? It's *three A.M.*

"I saw you head in the back way, and I saw Eric take off across town. I know something's up. Also? I know who you've got in town, and I'm offering my help."

Shit . . .

There is one resident who could catch a glimpse of April and not be fooled into thinking it's me. Diana. The person I came to Rockton with. The person who *knows* my sister.

Go away, Diana. I appreciate the offer. I really do. But can we talk about this in the morning—

The front doorknob rattles. The door starts to open, and I'm lunging forward as I hear her step inside, the door shutting behind her.

"I know April's here, Case," she says. "And if you guys are up at three A.M., you're dealing with a problem, and you'll need help taking care of Kenny."

I wheel around the corner.

"There you are." Her gaze drops to my gun. "What the—?"

A figure steps out behind her. My heart thuds.

"Stop!" I lift my gun. "Stop right there—"

Diana lets out a squeak . . . as a pistol barrel presses against her neck.

SIX

"Lower your gun," a man's voice says.

"You first," I say.

"I'm the one with a target."

I aim my gun over Diana's head. "Mine's just fine."

He laughs softly. "Then we're at an impasse. But I'm still going to suggest that you won't want to take that chance."

"Let her go—"

"No, sorry. She's obviously a friend, which means I know the value of *my* target." His voice is calm, casual even. *Just stating facts.*

He continues, "You and I need to have a conversation. I propose we lower our weapons together, but I'll keep your friend close while we chat."

I could bluster. Say I won't talk while he has Diana. But he can't surrender his hostage and trust in a civil conversation. That'd be stupid.

"Count of three," I say. "Guns holstered."

"Lowered."

"*Holstered.*"

He doesn't argue. So he *has* a holster, which means he's accustomed to carrying a gun. In Canada that suggests he stands on one side of the law or the other. I'm not sure which side would be more troubling.

"Yours goes in the holster first," he says. "I'll follow."

"Not a problem."

Diana snorts at that. It's a little ragged, but she meets my gaze with a smirk. She knows how fast I can draw my weapon. She also believes I won't hesitate to pull the trigger. She's been my friend since I did exactly that, once upon a time. Pulled the trigger and changed my life. Ruined my life, but I don't think Diana ever fully understood that.

I do the countdown from three, and we lower our guns together. Mine goes into my holster, but my fingers linger on it until the man lifts his empty right hand. Then that hand grabs Diana's upper arm. She jumps and starts to twist.

"It's okay," I say. "He's going to bring you over here. You two will sit on the couch. I'll take the chair. We'll talk."

"First, lock the front door," he says.

"That's a bad—" Diana begins.

"It's fine," I say.

I walk to the door and turn the lock. He makes me pull on it, proving I've done as he asked. Then we head into the living room. He waits until I sit before he prods Diana to the sofa. As he lowers himself to it, I take a closer look at him in the moonlight.

In size, he's somewhere between Dalton and Anders. Formidable enough. He's older than us, maybe early forties. Dark hair salted with gray. Brown skin. I won't guess at the racial makeup—I get tired of people doing that with me.

"You have someone here that I need," he says.

I don't reply. To say a single word risks betraying Rockton.

"I know what you have in this town," he says. "You're hiding criminals."

"You have been misinformed."

He meets my gaze. "I don't think so."

"Look at the woman beside you," I say. "Please tell me, what's her crime?"

His gaze flicks to Diana. "I have no idea."

"Mass murder possibly? She *does* look dangerous. I'd sit further away if I were you."

The corners of his mouth twitch, and his chin dips, acknowledging my point. Pink tips still linger on Diana's blond hair. She's cute in a pixie-girl way. Even her body language says she's no violent criminal, as she struggles not to flinch.

"Pretend she *is* 'hiding' as you say," I continue. "Is it not more likely she's hiding from someone?"

"That's none of his business," she says, and she pulls her hands into her sleeves, looking smaller as her gaze drops to her lap.

Ah, Diana. We might have a hellishly complicated relationship, but there are times when I remember why we used to be best friends. She understands what I'm doing, and she comes to my aid, playing the role of abused wife. It helps that she *was* abused, though, again, that was complicated, as everything is with Diana.

She really *is* here hiding from a crime: conspiring with her abusive ex to steal a million bucks from her employer. But this guy's never going to look at her and see a double-crossing schemer.

"Theoretically," I say, "what if people here *were* hiding . . . under our protection."

"Some might be," he says. "Maybe even most. I'd suggest, though, that you may have residents who've come under false pretenses."

Buddy, you don't know the half of it.

"That would make it your word against theirs," I say. "Maybe you can start by telling me who you are."

"I'm going to reach into my back pocket and take out my ID."

I tense. I know what that means. Even the way he says it—warning me that he's about to reach for something—tells me what he is.

"Left hand," I say. "If it goes near your holster, I'll draw."

"Fair enough."

He takes out a wallet and passes me a badge. US Marshals Service. The branch of federal police who, among other things, chase down fugitives.

He meets my gaze. "I saw you in the forest. I see the way you've handled yourself. The way you handle your gun. The way you're handling this situation. I believe we're on the same side."

"Whatever you've heard about our town—"

"I've been told my target is here. That's what matters." He locks gazes with me. "Nothing else."

Just give me my fugitive, and let me leave. That's what he's saying. He's also making it clear that he's not walking away empty-handed, which is a helluva lot bigger problem when he's holding a badge.

"And your target is?" I say.

"At this point, I'm not prepared to say. We will call my target Pat. I use the male pronoun for simplicity, but do not presume that to mean my target is male."

I open my mouth to say I obviously need to know who he's here for, but he continues.

"Pat told someone that he was going away. He apparently wasn't supposed to say more, but this person is close to him, and he wanted her to know he'd be safe. He said he was going someplace where he was guaranteed safety. Hints from what he said reminded me of something I'd heard. Long story short, I found you. Your settlement."

"How—"

"That's all I'm saying. Don't ask for more."

I *need* more. I'm sure that over the years more than one of our residents has broken the rules and reassured a loved one that they were going someplace safe, someplace off the grid, some secret town. But getting from that to Rockton itself involves much more, and we have to know where our vulnerabilities lie. That conversation can come later. It will come, though. It must.

"So you found us and—" I start to say.

Footsteps sound on the step. Heavy bootfalls, accompanied by the scratch of dog nails.

The man's head snaps up.

"Yeah," Diana says. "That'd be her boyfriend. The local sheriff, with their very big dog." She points toward the rear of the house. "The back exit is that way."

Dalton tries the door.

"I need to let him in," I say. "Otherwise—"

"Otherwise he's ten seconds from knocking down that door," Diana says.

I stand. Dalton's twisting the knob a second time, certain that he's mistaken about it being locked. Then—

His fist booms against the door. "Casey!"

The guy on the couch rises, and his mouth opens, like he's ready to tell me not to answer, but he can already see that's not an option, and as I reach for the lock, he hesitates only a second before grabbing Diana's arm.

She lets out a yelp.

"Case—!" Dalton begins . . . and I pull the door open.

Storm lunges. I grab her before she makes this situation a whole lot worse. Then I stand in Dalton's way, so he can't see inside.

"We have a visitor," I say.

"What the—?" He tries to shoulder past.

"Eric, hold on a sec. I'm going to let you in."

"No," the intruder says. "Please ask your sheriff to stay—"

"Not happening," I cut in, Dalton echoing my reply in far less polite language.

"Eric?" I say again. "Hold on, please. He has Diana."

"Really?" Diana says. "Could you tell him it's Nicki? Petra? Isabel? Someone he wouldn't actually like to see dead?"

Dalton aims a glower her way. I roll my eyes for him. He doesn't want Diana dead. He just doesn't like her very much . . . and the feeling is mutual.

"The situation is under control," I say. "I'd like you to put Storm in the kitchen, and then come back, sit down, and join the conversation. Okay?"

He nods. There isn't a moment of hesitation. My speech is more for the guy on the couch. Diana has painted our sheriff as a hothead. A man our intruder might not want to mess with. True, but Dalton's also never going to shove me aside and roar in, guns blazing. He isn't an idiot. Diana just prefers to think he is. Again, the feeling is mutual. Which is going to make this fun. Really.

As Dalton passes the living room, he doesn't fail to stop and give the guy a slow once-over. Taking his measure. Nodding, as if to say, *Yeah, I can handle this.* Then he continues on and locks Storm in the kitchen. She sighs, and the door thumps as she settles against it.

"Who the fuck are you?" Dalton says as he strides into the living room.

I pass him the man's badge.

"Mark Garcia," Dalton says.

"That's not the important part," the guy says.

Dalton tosses the badge back at him. "It's the important part for me. You're a US marshal. Your jurisdiction?" He jerks his thumb west, toward Alaska. "It's a long walk. I'd start now."

"I'd like to get through this without the posturing, Sheriff."

"I'm not posturing. Get the fuck out of my town."

Garcia opens his mouth.

"Yeah, you're going to remind me that I won't want you going to the authorities. And I'll say, 'Go ahead.' The Mounties have a station in Dawson. It's only a two-week walk. Watch out for the grizzlies. And the moose."

Garcia tries again and gets a single syllable out before Dalton says, "Next, you're going to remind me that you come from this big American agency and can call down giant fucking helicopters on our heads. And I say, yeah, you've got a point. So hand over your satellite phone."

The guy laughs. "You've got balls, man. I'll give you that much."

"I do. What I don't have? A fucking gun to my head."

Garcia starts to smile. Then he follows Dalton's gaze to me, standing beside the sofa, pointing my weapon.

"Yeah," Dalton says. "I'd suggest spending a little more time in our forest. Develop a proper sense of awareness for your surroundings." He puts his hand out. "Phone."

Garcia's gaze slides my way. "If she shoots me, she'll also shoot her friend."

"Don't think that'll stop her," Diana says. "I might have kinda earned it."

"The trajectory is wrong," I say, "as you can see. Just give the sheriff your phone and your gun."

"Right," Dalton says. "Forgot about his gun."

"That's why I'm here."

"You two are cute," Garcia says. "And I really do admire your balls—both of you—but there is no way I'm handing over—"

Diana attacks. I don't see it coming. Even when it happens, I'm not quite sure what *is* happening at first. Garcia's sitting there, holding her arm, his head turned to address us, and then she's on him, scratching and kicking like an enraged kitten.

Dalton and I recover from our surprise at the same time. I go to grab Garcia, but Dalton beats me to it, catching the front of the marshal's shirt and hauling him from the sofa while Garcia is still fending off Diana.

Garcia reaches for his gun—finally—but Dalton snatches it from the holster and tosses it aside. Then he has Garcia on the floor. The marshal tries to throw a punch . . . and I press my gun to his shoulder. That stops him faster than if I put it to his head.

"Good idea," Dalton says. "I wouldn't call her bluff on that shot."

He pats the man down. He lets Garcia keep his wallet but takes a satellite phone from his jacket and a knife from his jeans.

When Dalton straightens, I say, "He's here for someone. He wants us to turn them over."

"Figured that. Wasn't going to ask because I don't actually give a fuck. Whatever he wants, he's not getting it." He pauses. "No, that isn't right. He's a fellow lawman. I gotta show some respect for the badge."

He marches into the kitchen and comes out with the backpack. He opens it, takes out the ammo and a knife, then tosses the bag at Garcia.

"You want those directions again?" Dalton says. "Sun sets in the west."

"You're—"

"Making a mistake? Please don't tell me those were the next words out of your mouth. I hear them all the time, and they don't seem to mean what folks figure they do, because they're never right. Same with 'You're going to regret this.' A man reaches a point where he actually hopes he *will* regret it, just for a change of pace."

Garcia looks up at Dalton and shakes his head, a smile playing on his lips. "I like you, Sheriff. I get the feeling you and I could sit down with a beer and have a really good talk."

Dalton vanishes into the kitchen and comes back with a bottle. He sets it on the floor as Garcia sits up.

"There's your beer. Now give me your next line, about how this guy you're hunting is a dangerous bastard, and I need to let you take him for my own good." He looks at me. "Is it a guy?"

"He won't establish gender. Apparently, it's Pat."

Dalton's lips tighten. It's a split-second reaction, and anyone looking at him would see only calm resolution. But he's furious. While he's keeping the upper hand, to him it feels like treading water, one second away from going under.

This *is* deep water. Piranha-infested. We both know it.

"Fine," Dalton says. "So Pat is dangerous. That's the next thing you'll tell me, whether it's true or not."

"True or not?" Garcia uncaps his beer and rises to the chair I vacated earlier.

"Are you gonna tell me Pat ran a Ponzi scheme, cheated little old ladies out of their retirement savings? No. You could try that, hope I want to kick the fucker all the way over the border myself, but you don't know me. I might hate little old ladies. If you say Pat's a dangerous bastard, though, I'll pay attention. So consider it said and skip that part."

"I don't think you want me to."

"You gonna tell me what Pat's done?"

"I will tell you that Pat is likely someone you trust, someone who seems like a very average resident, maybe even involved in the running of your town. A committed citizen . . . who should be committed to a psych hospital for the criminally insane."

I glance at Dalton. Dalton gives a nearly imperceptible nod, telling me to pursue this.

"We had someone who might fit the description," I say. "He was brought here a couple of weeks ago for safekeeping, but you'll notice I'm speaking in the past tense."

There's no hint of dismay in Garcia's eyes as he shakes his head. "This would have been more than a few weeks ago."

"How long?"

He gives me a hard look. "I'm not telling you that."

"Yeah?" Dalton leans over Garcia. "Fuck. You."

"Is that really how you want to play——?"

"No. I want details. I want a name. I want to be treated the same way you seem to think *you* should be——like a fucking fellow officer of the law. I want some sense that you are what you seem to be——a righteous man on a righteous mission. But I'm not going to get any of that, am I?"

"You have my word——"

"Fuck your word. I don't know you. Give me a name. Give me details. Treat me with a whole lot less of your patronizing bullshit."

"Patronizing?"

Garcia's brows shoot up, and even that gesture carries a whiff of exactly what Dalton is talking about. As a homicide detective, I met too many guys who remind me of Garcia. They'd pat me on the back. Tell me I was awesome. *So* talented. *Such* a hard worker. We were going to get along great, because I was a real cop's cop, just like them.

Which warned me I'd be fighting them every step of the way. All those pretty words were pats on my adorable baby-cop head. Tell the girl what she wants to hear. Make her feel important. Make her feel like part of the team. Then, as part of the team, she'll toe the party line, do what we want, not get in our way.

I can't say that *is* Garcia. But it's what Dalton's picking up with the marshal's smiles and "You've got balls" and "I like you" and "I feel like you're a guy I could talk to over a cold beer." A whiff of the snake-oil salesman.

"Name," Dalton says. "Details."

"See, now here's the problem." Garcia lowers his bottle. "First, you might not know Pat by the name I have."

"A description will do."

"That can change."

"Gender? Oh, right—that can change, too. So what you're asking is for me to gather my people and you'll pick out Pat. Expose all my citizens. Trust you to take the right one . . . after you've just admitted Pat might not look like your mug shot. I don't know what you're actually here for—"

"I will give you details, Sheriff. Descriptive details that will allow you to bring me a subset of people, and one of those will confess to being Pat. Trust me on that."

"I don't trust—"

"Neither do I." He looks at Dalton. "I don't trust you, Sheriff. Like you said, we don't know each other. You might very well realize what kind of lowlifes you have here, the wolves among the sheep, but someone is paying you to keep the entire flock safe. If that's the case and I give you a description, you'll tell me to just wait here while you go round up the people who match it . . . and you'll make damned sure I don't see the one I'm looking for. *Sorry, Marshal, but Pat doesn't seem to be here.*"

Dalton's cheek tics, his jaw flexing. This hits a little too close to the mark.

We do indeed know about the wolves among the sheep, and I think, in some ways, it would be easier if we were mercenary shepherds, happy to protect the entire flock for the right price. But there is no price. And we are not happy. We're just trapped.

"Nice speech," I say. "You know what ruins it? Not even being willing to tell us the *gender* of the person you're looking for. There is no way in hell you can argue your point that far."

"I'm not trying to. I don't want you to parade your town before me. I will provide you with details after we agree to a process. You three are the only ones who know I'm looking for someone. Therefore, if you want me to trust you, you will not leave my sight until I have Pat."

"We agree to stay where you can see us, so we can't sneak off and hide Pat, and then you'll give us a complete and full description, along with proof."

Garcia looks over. "Proof?"

"Of Pat's crimes," I say. "You don't honestly expect us to hand over a resident on your say-so. You provide a description and proof—"

"Proof is for a court of law. You know that. I'm arresting someone, not sentencing them."

"By removing them from our protection you *are* sentencing them. I'm not asking for irrefutable proof of guilt. I'm asking for a warrant."

He starts to laugh. Then he sees I'm serious.

"You say we're fellow law enforcement?" I continue. "Then as the sheriff said, treat us like it. Give us the warrant. The proof that Pat is a fugitive, whom you have been sent to retrieve."

"Yeah, that didn't make it into my luggage."

"Would you expect a sheriff in the States to hand you over a federal fugitive on your say-so?"

"Actually, yes. The badge is usually enough."

"Not here. Not with people who've never seen a USMS badge. For all we know, you bought that online."

"So it appears we're at an impasse."

"Seems that way."

He gets to his feet. Crosses the room and picks up his backpack. Then he turns to Dalton. "Gun or phone. Give me one."

"What I'll give you is a chance to explain yourself," Dalton says. "In detail. And then we will fly you to Dawson. You'll provide a warrant. You'll provide proof."

"How the hell would I get that in Dawson City?"

"It's called the internet."

Garcia shakes his head. "You're being unreasonable, Sheriff."

"Sounds reasonable to me," I say.

Garcia's jaw clenches. It lasts only a second, but it's enough to shatter the good-ol'-boy persona.

"You're making a very big . . ." He trails off before finishing that cliché, and his jaw tightens again. Then he hefts his backpack. "I'll give you time to think about it, Sheriff. It's late. You're tired. You're not thinking this through. So take your time. I'll call again in the morning."

He heads for the back door.

"Eric," I say, leaping to catch Dalton's arm. "Let him go."

Dalton hadn't made a move to go after him, but he grumbles, "Fine," as if I had indeed yanked him back. Then I hurry to grab Storm. As Garcia strides past, she growls. He ignores her and keeps going.

As the door shuts behind Garcia, Diana spins on us. "You're really just going to let him walk away?"

Dalton ignores her and watches out the window as Garcia disappears into the woods. Then he turns to me.

"See if Will's radio is working," he says. "By now, he's out there with the boys. Nicki's patrolling in town. Have her wake everyone Will didn't roust earlier."

SEVEN

Dalton has gone after Garcia. He gave him enough of a head start, before he left the house and loped silently into the forest to pursue.

I leash Storm and go out the front.

"You don't think he's really a marshal, do you?" Diana says as she jogs to keep up.

"I have no idea. That's the problem."

"But if you had to speculate . . ."

"If I had to speculate, I'd say he's trouble either way."

Which is not entirely true. If Garcia is a US marshal, he is a far more dangerous threat. That would mean his superiors know where he's gone and what he's doing. A federal officer can't just jump in a plane. Even on vacation, he needs to file his plans and check in daily. A marshal is not a bounty hunter. Not a lone wolf. That's what makes Garcia's story suspicious. I wasn't lying when I said I wouldn't know a USMS badge if I saw one. I've met FBI. I've met CIA. I've even met a US Postal Service agent. I have never met a marshal. Which means I don't know what their badge looks like or how they operate. Yet I cannot believe they operate like this—one lone agent flying into the wilderness.

So what is he? A bail bondsman is one possibility. A bounty hunter is another, and sometimes they're the same thing, but that isn't always the case. A bail bondsman is looking for a fugitive who skipped bail. A bounty hunter may be looking for anyone he's paid to find.

If this is not an actual marshal, I'll bet my inheritance he's a professional, and not just some guy out to settle a score. Garcia knows what he's doing. He knows how to act like an officer of the law. He has the badge and the confidence, as if he's played this role many times. Which he might very well have done, if he's a bounty hunter. Swagger into town, pick up his target, and if the local cops interfere, wave that badge—which probably *would* be enough, as he said.

When I reach the station, I hand Storm to Diana, go inside, and call Anders. Tonight I get lucky and the radios actually work, probably because . . .

"I'm five minutes away," Anders says when he answers. "Three if I run."

"You don't run very fast then, do you?"

"Yeah, yeah. What's up?"

I tell him, starting with "Don't come back to town." Otherwise, by the time I finished he'd have been here. It's not a short story, as much as I condense it.

When I finish, he says, "Shit. You think he's really a—" He stops himself. "Doesn't matter right now. Point is to get him and bring him in, right?"

"No. We could have stopped him if we wanted to. Garcia thinks he's giving us time to reconsider, but he's got things a little backward, considering where he is."

"In the middle of the Yukon wilderness, armed with a few protein bars and a bottle of water."

"Yep. No gun. No phone. He's screwed and—"

The station door opens and Diana leans in as I have the talk button pressed. "Casey? Tell Will to come back to town. Now."

"Uh, no," Anders says when I release the button. "I'm sure you have this under control. I'll pull the militia back, but I'll look for this Garcia guy—"

"You don't need to." Diana pushes the door wider, and I hear a distant commotion. I turn to follow it, and I wince as I realize what it means.

"Will?" I say.

"On my way."

We're outside. Diana still has Storm, and we're running across town. Doors swing open. People poke their heads through. Someone asks what's wrong. Someone else asks if we need help.

It might be not yet five in the morning, but the sun is rising, and up here, it is as if we adopt the old ways of adjusting to the seasonal light pattern. In winter, people routinely get ten hours of sleep. Now, the bakery opens at seven to a lineup.

This is one time when I wish—I really wish—people slept in. I can hear raised voices at the edge of town, anger and confusion and fear, and I know what it is. I hope I'm wrong, but I know, and I wish it were 2 A.M., everyone too deeply asleep to know what is happening.

I'm telling people it's okay, go back inside, but more doors open. That's when I channel Dalton, snapping, "Inside! Now! Stay in your fucking houses!"

As doors slap shut, Diana snickers and says, "Nice."

I hear running footsteps behind me and snarl over my shoulder, "Get back—!"

"That doesn't apply to me, Detective," Jen says. "Or it better not."

"Keep people inside," I say. "If that fails, just keep them away. Please. Diana? Take Storm and go with Jen."

"I don't need Blondie—" Jen begins.

"Diana, go with her. Jen, put Diana to work. Keep people *back*."

I can see the situation ahead, and it is exactly what I feared. Garcia stands on a front porch near the town border. It's a duplex, with both residents outside, demanding to know who the hell he is and what the hell he's doing in Rockton. A few others are gathered around, which tells me this isn't the first house Garcia has tried.

As I jog, a young man leans over a second-floor balcony. "Everything okay, Detective Butler?"

It's our newest resident. At twenty-one, Sebastian is also our youngest, and he looks even younger tonight, watching the scene ahead with obvious dismay, as if thinking this place isn't nearly as safe as he's been told. Great. . . .

"It's fine," I say. "Go back inside."

He does. I keep jogging and shout, "Marshal! Get the hell out of our town."

Garcia ignores me and strides off the porch. "I have my job, ma'am, and if you won't help me do it, I'll do it myself."

My heart pounds so hard I can barely breathe. I'm panicking. Honestly panicking. Every face he sees is a face we have sworn to keep hidden. I'm also keenly aware of the dilemma I've been trying not to think about.

A stranger knows about Rockton. A stranger can tell the world about us if he does not get what he wants. He can tell them even if he *does* get his quarry. He's seeing face after face, and he knows they could all be fugitives, could all have a price on their heads. If he's a bounty hunter, this is *his* Klondike gold.

What the hell are we going to do about that?

What am I going to do about *this*?

Handle it.

I run to the next porch he's climbing. I shoulder him aside, and I slam my back against the door, and I take out my gun.

"You don't want to do this," he says.

"Whoever is inside?" I say, raising my voice. "Do not come out. We have a situation."

I continue raising my voice until it echoes through the still morning. "There is a stranger in town. He tells us he's looking for a fugitive, and that he will take that person when he finds them."

"Hey!" Garcia says.

"We do not trust this man," I shout. "Remain in your homes. The sheriff and the militia are on their way."

"You're—" Garcia begins.

"Making a mistake?" I say. "Yes, this time, I think you're right. Letting you walk away was a mistake." I aim my gun. "One I should probably rectify right now. How about you give me the excuse?"

"You've got balls—"

"No, actually I don't. And you're a broken record, Mr. Garcia. Like one of those dolls. Pull the cord, and it gives you another prerecorded line. I do not have balls. I am not making a mistake. I do want to stop you." I lift the gun. "And I really want to use *this* and solve our problem for good. So go ahead. Move me aside. Try that house over there. Walk farther into town. See what happens."

Someone claps. I don't take my eyes off Garcia, but I know who it is, and I say, "Looks like the cavalry is here, Mr. Garcia."

"Looks like you don't actually need it," Anders says as he walks over, two of the militia following. "Whoever you are, sir? I'm going to suggest you move along."

Garcia glowers. As he strides off the porch, he bumps Anders with a look that says he really hopes Anders will bump back, give him a reason to brawl. Our deputy just stands there, his arms crossed, lips curved in a smirk that sets Garcia seething as he heads from town.

"If you want to talk," I call after him, "you know where to find us."

Garcia keeps going. When he nears the edge of town, I turn to Anders and lower my voice. "I'm going after him. We need to see where he sets up his new camp so we can keep an eye on him." I raise the radio. "Tell Eric I have this, and he can join me as soon—"

The thump of boots on wood cuts me off. It's the sound of someone climbing onto a porch, coming from Garcia's direction.

There's only one house past this one, and it's empty. It's been empty since I moved in with Dalton—

"April," Anders whispers.

Oh, shit. That house is *not* empty.

We both take off at a run. Garcia is on my old porch, raising his fist.

"Hey!" I shout. "Get away from that house."

Garcia pounds on the wooden door. The sound echoes in the quiet morning.

"She won't answer," Anders murmurs beside me. "I was very clear on that. She's not supposed to answer unless one of us announces ourselves."

Garcia bangs again. We're almost there when a figure emerges from the forest, running full tilt toward my old house. It's Dalton, and I swear he's breathing fire.

"Eric—!" I begin, to tell him it's okay, we have this under control.

Anders's hand lands on my shoulder, cutting me off. "At this point, it's probably best we just let him do his thing."

Garcia is lifting his fist to knock again when Dalton hits him. Garcia staggers. Dalton grabs him by the shirtfront and throws him clear through the railing, the wood cracking and splintering.

Garcia thuds onto the ground below. Before the marshal can even start to rise, Dalton is off the porch and on him. Behind me, footsteps pound, and I turn to see that the onlookers from earlier have caught up with us, ignoring the militia's orders to get back. This spectacle is too entertaining to miss, even if it earns them a few days of chopping duty.

Dalton lets Garcia stagger to his feet, and our sheriff stands there, fists clenched, waiting for it. If Garcia had an ounce of brains, he'd see that look in Dalton's eyes and surrender. *You win, Sheriff. Now let's talk.*

Garcia swings. Dalton blocks and hits him with a right hook to the jaw. Garcia slams into a tree. The marshal recovers, massaging his jaw, looking like he's ready to give up. Dalton straightens, as if he's falling for it, but when Garcia swings, he grabs him by the arm and throws him into the side of my house.

Dalton's bearing down on Garcia when my front door opens. April rushes onto the porch. She sees the two men and her mouth forms an "Oh!" Then she's quick-stepping backward when she spots the others: Anders and the militia and the half dozen local onlookers.

April wears my oversize sweatshirt and a pair of my track pants, but even if I weren't standing ten feet away, there's no chance anyone would mistake her for me. Her eyes round, and she darts back inside.

I jog toward the house. I glance at Anders, who motions for me to go on, they can handle this. The fight hasn't stopped for April's intermission. Neither man seemed to realize the door had opened. Blows have been traded. Garcia's nose streams blood, and his shirt is torn. There's a smear of dirt on Dalton's face, where one of Garcia's swings made contact. I'm about to go inside when Dalton shakes his left arm.

His left arm. Shit. His injured *dominant* arm.

I glance at Anders, but he's already seen it, and he's jogging toward the men.

"Hey, boss," Anders says. "You want this guy in lockup? Or you trying to put him in the infirmary?"

Dalton snorts and moves back. "Yeah, lock him up."

I open the front door. As I'm stepping through, Anders goes after Garcia while Dalton bears down on the assembled gawkers, now dispersing quickly.

I close the door behind me. April's on my sofa.

"I'm sorry," she says, and that stops me dead. Even makes me check over my shoulder, certain my sister is apologizing to someone behind me.

"I heard a commotion, and I thought the patient was in distress." She pauses, and then adds, "Kenny," as if she had to recall his name. "I thought that's why someone was banging on my door. It didn't occur to me that anyone would be up this early."

I say nothing. I can't tell her it'll be all right. I have no idea how to handle this, and considering what's happening with Garcia, this wrinkle is the last thing on my mind. It's more than a wrinkle, though. We've smuggled my sister into Rockton. I don't even want to consider the implications of that.

"Kenny's fine," I say. "This is a whole other situation, and I need you to stay inside. Lock the doors. Don't open them unless it's me or Will."

She nods, and then gives herself a shake, throwing off the confusion of sleep. She stands, straightening, and when she speaks, there's a snap in her voice I know well.

"They are being ridiculous," she says. "The council or whatever you called them. You had a man in serious need of medical attention, for a spinal injury, and your sister is a neurosurgeon. They should be grateful that the"—she flutters her hands—"stars aligned. What is the chance of that? And the fact that they don't have a full-time medical doctor is breathtakingly irresponsible. I cannot believe you allow such a situation, Casey."

"Breathtakingly irresponsible is my middle name."

She gives me such a frown that I half expect her to say, *I thought it was Analyn.* Instead, she waves it off and says, "Your town needs a doctor."

"Are you volunteering?"

The horror on her face makes me sputter a laugh, and she frowns again in confusion.

"Yes, April, I am well aware of our need for a physician. We lost ours last year, and we've been pestering for a new one ever since. Right now, though, I need you to stay put."

I make it halfway to the door before there's a shout. An angry shout. Then a gunshot.

"Was that—?" April begins.

"Yes, it was. Now *stay put.*"

EIGHT

I race out the door. There's a distant commotion, and I have a flash of déjà vu, of running out of the station what seems like only minutes ago.

No, it *was* only minutes ago.

This time, this disturbance is Anders and a couple of others. Dalton's voice booms from another direction. "What the hell is going on?"

I run toward Anders, which is also the direction of that shot. I see someone on the ground, and I catch a flash of dark skin, and my heart jams in my throat. It's not Anders, though, I see that in a second, as I notice dreadlocks.

"Sam?" I say as I race over.

He's getting to his feet.

"Are you okay?" I say.

"No." He gives an angry shake of his head. "I'm not. I'm a goddamn idiot. That's what I am. He got away."

"Garcia?"

"He—" Sam tries to take a step. His leg buckles, and he swears.

"Where's Will?" I ask.

Sam gestures toward the forest, and I pick up the sound of people running through it.

"I heard a shot," I say.

"That was Will," Sam says. "Trying to spook the guy into stopping. It didn't work and—"

I cut him short. The point is that Garcia hasn't gotten hold of a gun. He's just escaped, and he's running. Which means I don't need to know how this happened—I just need to bring him back.

I'm taking off when I spot Dalton running toward us.

"Garcia's gone," I say. "He bolted. Will's giving chase."

"Along with a few of the guys," Sam says.

"Is your leg hurt?" Dalton cuts in.

"It's fine. I—"

"It's hurt, and you can't run. So get your ass to the station. We'll talk later." He turns to me, Sam already dismissed. "I'm going after Garcia. You stay here. Town meeting. Now."

"Do I get to use my bell?"

He gives a strained smile. "You do." He leans down for a peck on the cheek and then looks around. "You!"

The only person in his sight line is Mathias, casually walking his wolf-dog cub toward the forest, as if nothing is happening. When Mathias doesn't turn, Dalton booms, "Atelier! I'm talking to you!"

Mathias looks at us. "Me?"

"Get your ass over here."

"Raoul needs to relieve him—"

"Do you want to keep that mutt?"

Mathias scoops up the cub and comes over.

"Town meeting," Dalton says to Mathias. "Go door-to-door. Tell people to get their asses into the square now."

I brace for Mathias to make some crack about not being the town crier. He only nods. Before he can leave, another figure comes around the corner, moving fast.

"Sheriff," Phil calls. "Whatever is going on here, I should have been notified—"

"Yeah, that's not how your job works. Go with Mathias. He'll tell you what to do."

Dalton starts leaving. Phil grabs his arm—the bad one—and Dalton wheels. Mathias pulls Phil away.

"Do you see that look?" Mathias says. "It is not the sheriff's this-is-negotiable look. Or his I-wish-to-chat-about-it look." Mathias purses his lips. "To be honest, he does not have either, so it is safest to . . . I believe the English would be: shut up and do as he says."

Dalton strides off.

"Detective—" Phil begins.

"Here," Mathias cuts in. "You may hold Raoul as you follow me." He extends the cub.

Phil falls back. "That's the rabid—"

"Not rabid. Not dangerous." Mathias smiles, showing his teeth. "Not yet."

Mathias hefts the cub under his arm as he leads Phil away. "Do you know what we wish for most in this town? A council representative with an iota of competence. A mere iota. Is there any possibility we might find that with you, Philip? The early signs are not promising."

I shake my head and jog off to ring the bell.

I hold the press conference. I explain that we found a stranger in the forest and tracked him to his camp, and we'd just initiated a militia search party when the man began approaching people in their homes. I say that he's claiming to be a US marshal seeking a fugitive. I leave out the part where he broke into our home and we questioned him and let him go again. That opens our actions to far too much second-guessing.

The only other option would have been to throw him in jail. Take a supposed officer of the law, treat him as a criminal, and hope for a peaceful negotiation.

Yeah, the "throw him in jail" part would have annihilated our chance for a quiet resolution. We *had* hoped for quiet resolution. *Tell us who you came for. Tell us why. Let us figure out what to do about it.* If it turned out we were harboring a dangerous criminal, then the answer *might* have been to let Garcia arrest his target for the safety and protection of others.

That isn't an option now.

I tell the residents that we're actively hunting the intruder. When he is found, the council will deal with the situation. That's our only option now. Turn him over to them. Let them make the call. Let them handle it, and if handling it means a shallow grave for Mark Garcia, well, my only real concern is that the council doesn't insist Dalton carry out that sentence. I trust they won't. That isn't their way. They'll send someone for Garcia, and he'll get on a plane. The problem will go away, and for once, maybe I'll actually be thanking them. It's not the resolution I would have wanted, but I'd be lying if I didn't say it might be the best.

"For now," I say, "all excursions are canceled. Militia will receive double credits for overtime. Other militia-trained citizens may assist patrols for full pay. We will lock down the border of this town. You may continue to wander freely during the day. However, we will be imposing an after-dark curfew, meaning . . . well, this time of year, that's midnight to four A.M., when you should all be sleeping any-way."

I get some laughs for that, people relaxing.

I continue, "At night, lock up and draw your blackout blinds. Do not answer your door to anyone. If we need you . . ."

"If they need you, the sheriff has the master key," says a voice be-side me, "and he isn't afraid to use it."

I look to see Isabel on her upper balcony, wearing a silk wrapper and sipping a coffee.

"That's right," I say. "So doors stay closed and locked. Any ques-tions?"

"Who's the woman?" someone calls from the crowd.

"Isabel," I say. "I know, you don't recognize her in that robe. She's come out to announce free morning coffee with a whiskey chaser for everyone. Just pop by the Roc. Tell her I sent you."

That gets a laugh, drowning out Isabel's reply. It does not, however, distract from the question, and as soon as the laughter dies down, that voice in the crowd says, "No, the woman staying in your house."

There's a momentary urge to pass this off, pretend he's mistaken.

Woman? What woman? But a couple of others join in, one saying, "She looks like you. She's a relative, right?"

I take a deep breath. "Yes. There is a woman staying in my house. She has nothing to do with the man we're hunting. She's . . ." *Oh, hell, just get this over with.* "She's my sister. She's a neurosurgeon, and we brought her in to treat Kenny."

There's a movement in the crowd, and I look to see Phil striding to the front, his expression warning that he'd better be mishearing me.

I continue. "As you know, Kenny was shot in the back, and we were unable to airlift him out for the emergency medical attention he required. We decided to bring my sister in. Our hope was to make it a very quick visit and to segregate her from the population, for your privacy."

Phil looks positively apoplectic by this point, his eyes blazing behind his hipster glasses.

I keep going. "I am pleased to report that my sister conducted surgery on Kenny yesterday, working with Will and Mathias. They were able to dislodge the bullet. We don't know the prognosis yet, but the surgery was successful."

A round of applause. Phil plants himself at the foot of my platform, blocking my exit once I'm done.

"If I may." Isabel's dulcet tones cut through the chatter as well as Dalton's shout would have. "I believe I speak for us all when I say we are very grateful to your sister, Casey, for her time and expertise. I hope she will give us the opportunity to say as much. I understand your concern for our safety, in keeping her sequestered, but she is your sister. That is enough for me."

A chorus of agreement follows.

"We appreciate the council's thoughtfulness in this," she continues. "We would hope that if any of us were in the same situation as Kenny, we would receive the same treatment."

Phil aims a glare Isabel's way. She heads inside, as if this ends the matter. I take my cue from her, thanking everyone and imparting a few final warnings while assuring them this matter will be resolved as soon as possible.

As I turn to climb down, Phil ascends. "You—"

"Can't talk," I say. "With Eric and Will gone, I need to organize the volunteers."

"Your sister—"

"—is a highly trained professional," Mathias says, climbing the steps behind him. "We are grateful for her expertise, as Isabel said. Grateful too, to the council, for displaying such understanding in this matter."

If looks could kill, Phil was preparing to launch a nuclear warhead. I hop from the platform and start for the station. Isabel is outside now, and she joins me, still in her wrapper, legs and feet bare.

"So you snuck your sister in," she says as we walk. "Well played."

I make a noise under my breath. "I'd rather not need to play games at all."

"I know. But you're so good, it would be a shame to deprive us of the entertainment. Eric's performance yesterday was breathtaking. Even I never suspected he was distracting us while he snuck your sister into town." She pulls her wrapper tighter. "Phil will be fine. He just needs to learn his place. Which is *not* with the big girls and boys. A shame really. He's terribly pretty."

"Enjoy."

"I still might. I sense a great deal of repressed anger in that one. If properly channeled, it could make for excellent sex."

I shake my head and turn toward the station, but she catches my arm.

"Let's detour to your old house, Casey," she says. "Introduce me to your sister. I'll take over her care from here."

"So you can pry out blackmail information on me?"

She gives me a look. "No. Admittedly, I am curious to meet your sister, but I will contain that curiosity better than others. They will pry—only to satisfy their curiosity, but in doing so, they'll invade your privacy."

"All right. I'll introduce you to April."

———

I take Isabel to meet April, and my sister stares. Just stares, as if a mirage has emerged from the wilderness. Or, possibly, the saloon mistress has emerged from her fine establishment.

Isabel looks like she belongs on the set of a Wild West movie. She's mid-forties. Dark hair with a few strands of gray—we don't import dye into Rockton. No makeup—also not a priority. But the lack of more modern feminine grooming only adds to Isabel's aura of old-time glamour. Her silk wrap and bare feet cement the image, and when she swans into my old house, her hand extended, I half expect her to say "Charmed, I'm sure." Which wouldn't be Isabel's style at all. Instead, it's a firm handshake as her gaze assesses my sister.

"Isabel Radcliffe," she says. "I will be your hostess for the next couple of days, freeing Casey to go about her duties."

April's gaze flicks to me. "All right . . ."

"The town knows you exist," Isabel says, "but we will refrain from parading you about. That would be . . . unwise."

April's brow furrows.

A knock sounds at the door, and Isabel murmurs, "Our boys are fast on the draw. One must give them that."

I open the door to find a trio of locals. All men. All trying to peek around us at April. I block their view.

"Yes?" I say.

"We just, uh, thought your sister might, uh, want breakfast. We could escort her—"

"Unnecessary, boys," Isabel says, stepping around me. "I have this under control. Please, pass the word on to the others. While I'm here, Miss April will want for nothing, particularly companionship."

Isabel shuts the door. "Reason number two why I offered to care for April. The local wildlife have caught wind of prey."

April looks alarmed. "Wildlife?"

"The men," Isabel says. "We have a lot of them. It's a problem."

April frowns.

"Three men for every woman," I say.

My sister continues to look confused.

"Sex," Isabel says. "They want sex. As men often do. Well, no, that's unfair. Women want it, too. In this town, though, that is much easier to come by for us." She looks out the front window to see the trio of men talking to another group, warning them off with a shake of their heads.

Isabel sighs. "Did you have to tell them she was your sister, Casey? Wouldn't great-great-aunt have sufficed? You realize the stream will be nonstop."

"You can handle it," I say as I turn to leave. "Drum up some business for the brothel."

April blinks. "Did you say—?"

"Your sister has a very special sense of humor, April," Isabel says. "Come along inside, and let's discuss how we can get your breakfast without attracting a conga line."

NINE

I spend the day running on a treadmill while madly juggling a half dozen grenades. It's a solid day of absolutely zero progress, and the best I can say, at the end of it, is that nothing exploded.

Kenny runs into postsurgery complications. None of them are April's fault, but my damn sister can't just trust that I have the medical IQ to realize that. Nor can she seem to see those five other grenades I'm juggling. She has to summon me and make it very clear that she did not cause any of Kenny's complications. *We* did, through our unacceptable presurgery treatment of the situation. The fact that the "unacceptable" part arose from the situation itself—Kenny being shot five miles into the forest, and us having to convey him to Rockton—doesn't matter. It's our fault. All ours. Specifically mine, because I knew better.

Phil is furious about April being here. More furious than he is about Garcia, which spikes *my* temper even higher. The April situation is a well-controlled bonfire; the Garcia one is a full-blown wildfire. We need the council's help with the latter. We do not need their bullshit threats over the former.

Currently, the council's stance on Garcia is "get him." Find him, bring him in, and then they'll decide what's to be done. Which would be awesome if we could manage the "finding" part. He's disappeared into the woods, and the council is baffled as to how that happens—how that *keeps* happening. People continue to escape, and we continue to have a helluva time finding them.

It's like dealing with my sister harping at me over Kenny's care. I want to grab the whole damn council and throw them into the wilderness for a few days. Give them a sense of the circumstances we are dealing with. People down south have died of exposure while lost in a few miles of forest. Imagine if that person is in a forest a thousand times that size . . . and doesn't want to be found. Garcia can literally plunk his ass down in some bushes, and unless someone stumbles over him, he'll be safe.

I haven't seen Dalton since he left this morning, but I know he's fine. Give him a waterskin and an energy bar, and he doesn't need to come back before nightfall. Hell, in this weather, he'd be fine indefinitely, sourcing water, hunting and gathering. He also has a gun, and Garcia does not. This doesn't, however, keep me from wishing our sheriff would swing by once or twice. He doesn't.

I'm juggling as fast as I can, powered by caffeine and cookies. When I zip into the station to refuel on both, footsteps follow me.

"If you're volunteering for patrol duty, go speak to . . ."

I turn to see Petra closing the door behind her, and there's a moment where I think *Thank God*. In this town, I have more female relationships than I've ever had in my life, and I am grateful for that. They are complicated, at times fractious, but they are real, with none of that sugarcoated crap I grew up reading and seeing on television, girls linking arms and vowing to be BFFs forever, them against the world. Of all these relationships, there is only one that is truly steady. One friend who is always there for me and never complicates my life. Who never needs more than I can give, never demands anything.

That is Petra.

No, that *was* Petra.

Three days ago, Dalton and I were bringing Oliver Brady back to face whatever fate the council decided for him. He never made it. Someone in the forest shot him. Dalton and I both saw who did it: the woman standing before me, the woman I thought I knew, the woman I apparently did not know at all. Petra shot Brady, and when we called her on it, she told us we were mistaken.

Nope, sorry, you've got the wrong person. Wasn't me. Uh-uh.

At the time, Kenny was the bigger concern, so I tabled this discussion. With Garcia on the run, I'd like to keep tabling it.

"Yes?" I say, my voice chilling.

"I saw you gave Storm to Brian and Devon."

"Yes." I take a couple of cookies from the box that Brian dropped off. "Someone needs to watch her."

"That someone has always been me."

"It isn't now."

"I'd like to talk about that."

I spin on her. "Really? No, Petra, you will not be dog-sitting for us again, and that is the least of your worries. If it seems like we've dropped what happened with Brady, we have not. It's on the back burner while we extinguish other fires."

I take a step toward her. "I saw you. Eric saw you. There is absolutely no doubt in either of our minds who killed Oliver Brady, and I would strongly suggest that, instead of worrying about losing your dog-sitting gig, you take this time to worry about that. Because it has not been forgotten."

"I know."

"So you came here to admit to it?"

She moves back. "I came to suggest that you *do* drop the matter."

I stare at her. Then I burst out laughing.

She has the grace to flinch at that laugh. "What I'm trying to say, Casey, is that it's a moot point. Whoever shot Oliver Brady did not kill an innocent man. In fact, I'd say they did—"

I surge forward, and she backpedals so fast she smacks into the wall.

I advance on her. "If you are about to say they did me a favor, I'd remind you that I've had zero sleep in forty-eight hours."

Petra straightens, her features setting in a look that, a week ago, would have surprised me. It is hard, and it is unflinching, and it warns me to step the hell back—now.

I stay in her face, waiting.

"I was going to say that whoever did this made the right move," she says. "The move that you, understandably, could not. I would also remind you that Oliver Brady wasn't the only person to die in that clearing. And I didn't pull *that* trigger."

"No, you did not. The difference is that I killed a direct threat to Eric. Oliver Brady was in custody, and no threat to anyone."

"No threat?"

"If you're saying he could have escaped again—"

"No, I'm saying he didn't need to escape to be a threat. What would have happened if you brought him back alive?"

"Phil would have taken him into custody, on behalf of the council."

"Exactly. The council would have whisked Oliver Brady away. And Rockton doesn't trust the council. I'm sorry, Casey, but you and Eric—and others—have made sure of that."

"Excuse me?"

She sidesteps past me and walks farther into the room. "You have reason to mistrust them. The situation here has been mismanaged. No one is arguing that. But the upshot is that the town trusts you, and they do not trust the council. People wouldn't trust them to properly handle Brady."

"Whatever issues we have with the council, we don't broadcast those to the town."

"You don't need to." She sits on the edge of the desk. "Your contempt is clear."

"That's—"

"Fine. Forget contempt for the council. Forget mistrust of the council. Forget paranoia of the council. Let's pretend people trust the council to take Brady back to face justice. The fact remains that Oliver Brady hated us. He had every reason to want to destroy Rockton and all it stood for. What was to stop him from doing exactly that once he left here? He could not be *allowed* to leave."

"If you believe that, then say so. Just don't tell me that you acted alone, spurred by your conscience to kill a man for the greater good."

"Would that be so wrong?"

"Not wrong, just very unlikely, especially given your impassioned defense of the council."

The door opens, cutting off Petra's reply. Sam slips inside and stops.

"Is this, uh, a bad time?"

"No," I say. "It's perfect timing." I glance at Petra. "You want to see the difference between what you did and what I did?" I turn to Sam. "I shot Val."

"Okay . . ." he says.

"She had a gun on Eric," I continue. "She would have killed him. I couldn't see another solution. So I shot her."

He nods. "Okay."

I appreciate that Sam will never see me in a worse light for what I've done. But that nod tells me Sam has never had to kill anyone. And I hope he never needs to.

"So what's the problem?" he says, with genuine confusion.

"I want people to know what I did. I don't want them whispering and guessing. I take responsibility."

"Okay."

"The council already knows. I'd rather you didn't tell anyone right now—there's too much going on—but as soon as the rest is settled, I will tell them that I'm the one who shot Val and why."

He nods. "Sure."

I turn to Petra. And I wait.

She shakes her head. "It's not that easy, Casey."

"Of course it is. Just try."

She says nothing as Sam watches in confusion. After a moment, he says, "Is this about that Garcia guy?"

I look over at him.

"If you're hinting that I need to take responsibility for him escaping, I do. I totally do."

"I know," I say. "This is something else, between Petra and me. You already accepted responsibility for Garcia, and I don't blame you for his escape. He's a professional, and it was bound to happen."

Which is the truth. That's the problem with our militia. Very few people with law enforcement experience pass through here, so it's comprised of amateurs.

Sure, there are plenty of residents who harbor a secret power fantasy of being a cop. Dalton doesn't want *them* near a gun. That means our militia didn't grow up developing skill sets that qualify them for this work. That's the price we pay for not having a town of redneck militia, ready to shoot the first person who won't let them cut in the dinner line.

I reassure Sam that it's fine. We'll review the situation, and we'll use it as a training example.

"If you came here to talk about that," I say, "that isn't necessary. If your leg is fine, we really need you out there, making sure Garcia doesn't sneak back."

"I know. It's just . . . Well, if—*when*—Eric catches him, you might need long-term lodgings. Something other than this." He nods toward the cell in the next room.

"We might. Fortunately, we have the place we built for Brady."

"So you want Roy back in here?"

"Roy?" It takes a moment to even place the name. "Shit. I forgot about Roy."

Sam manages a smile. "Yeah, I think we all did. Or we tried to. Someone's been feeding him and whatnot. But Eric wanted him in the new place."

Add another grenade to my juggling pile. Roy's a new resident who has been troublesome since the start. Then Brady came along, and Roy tried to lead a damn lynch mob. He'd been in custody ever since, mostly because we haven't had time to decide what to do with him.

I'm about to say I'll let Dalton handle this when I see Petra still standing there.

"Leave Roy where he is," I say. "Put Petra in this cell."

Sam laughs.

"I'm not joking." I turn to Petra. "You're under arrest for the murder of Oliver Brady."

"Casey . . ." she says. "Don't do this."

"I gave you the chance to talk to me, as a friend. You refused. This is the next step. Do you want to get in the cell yourself? Or does Sam need to escort you?"

She walks into the cell room.

"Lock her in please, Sam, and I'm going to ask you to be in charge of her care. Hourly checks. If anyone asks why she's there, refer them to me. I'm hoping to handle this situation without a public announcement."

He still looks confused but nods. "Sure."

"There's one other thing I need you to do. Find Phil. Take him aside and tell him I've arrested Petra for shooting Oliver Brady. Tell him that I want the council to know that immediately. If he makes excuses, come see me. The council *must* be notified. Okay?"

He nods again. I grab my cookies and head out to keep juggling.

TEN

It doesn't take long for me to hear that Phil "needs to talk to me about Petra." I ignore the summons. I have cast my die, and I will wait to see how it plays out.

It's nearly 10 P.M. when I'm back in the station to grab my flashlight. I'm opening the drawer when the rear door creaks open. I riffle through the drawer, listening to the slow footfalls, and then I spin, gun raised . . . to find it trained on Dalton.

"Shit," he says. "That was stupid of me. Sorry."

I set the gun down, pat Storm, and then put my arms up for a hug from Dalton. He practically collapses against me and I say, "Long day?"

He chuckles and straightens, his hands looped around my waist. "Yeah. Fucking long day."

Then, in answer to my unspoken question, he says, "Not a damned trace."

I arch my brows.

He shrugs. "Okay, a few traces. But they didn't lead anywhere. Even if he's not a US marshal, he knows how to throw someone off his trail. He headed straight for rock. Waded through a couple of streams on the way. I kept thinking having Storm would help . . ."

"Not for sneaking up on him. And you're going to need to sneak up."

"Yeah."

"We'll have to teach her stealth, too. Which won't be easy with her size."

He sighs. "I didn't really think it through. Getting a Newfoundland."

I put my arms around his neck again. "You got me my dream dog, Eric. I'm not trading her in for a bloodhound, so don't even ask."

He chuckles. "A bloodhound would be fucking useless in the winter anyway. As for Garcia, I give him three days before he comes knocking on our door again, wanting to cut a deal."

"I give him one *night* out there." I move back to perch on the desk. "Speaking of nights, I hope you're calling it one."

"Yep, just picking up my bed buddy first."

I glance down at Storm.

Dalton laughs. "No. She snores and drools and sheds. So do you, but not as much."

"Thanks. I'll be there in a few minutes. I just have a couple more things—"

"Nope."

"I just need—"

"Nope. If you don't stop working, I won't either."

"Damn."

"Yep, that works better than ordering you to quit." He's about to say more when a noise from the cell room stops him. Before I can explain, he says, "Petra?"

"Uh . . . yes. How'd you know?"

"Educated guess. She pissed you off, huh?"

"She wasn't taking me seriously. Putting her in there, though, is about testing a theory. One that I would prefer to discuss *after* you've gotten a good night's sleep. But I really do have a few more things I need to do."

He sighs. "All right. I'll rest my eyes while you finish up. Just sit with me for a minute first."

He leads me to the fireplace bearskin rug. Rockton is full of hide rugs and blankets. It adds a nice "wilderness lodge" touch, but it really is about conservation—using as much as possible of any animal we need to kill.

We sit on the rug, Storm taking a spot beside it. Then Dalton stretches out and tugs me to lie beside him. I prop up on my elbow. He kisses me—a long, slow kiss that washes over me like a warm bath, and I relax into it, feeling the pull of my exhaustion. When he lowers his head to the rug, his eyelids are flagging. He keeps me there, though, his hand on my hip.

"So," he says. "How was your day?"

I laugh at that and shake my head. "Long. It felt like running in place while juggling hand grenades, so the best I can say is that I didn't drop any."

"That's the main thing."

"Progress would be nice."

He shrugs. "Move too fast, and you'll drop a grenade. Then you won't need to worry about making progress."

"True. Slow and steady just isn't my style."

"I know. But I gotta say, it made a difference, knowing I didn't need to worry about what shit was happening back here. Knowing you'd be on top of it."

I hesitate and then say, "So I shouldn't ask to go with you tomorrow."

One nearly shut eyelid opens. "Is that what you want?"

"For a while, if I could. Will can handle the grenades. None are in imminent danger of exploding. I know you're fine out there but . . ."

"You worry about me."

"Sorry."

"Hey, if you get a little concerned for my safety, then I won't feel so bad when I completely overreact about yours."

I smile. "True. So may I join you?"

"You may. You can bring the coffee. Got a feeling we're going to need . . ."

He trails off, eyes closed, and I think he's joking, proving the point about needing coffee tomorrow. But his next breath comes deep as his face goes slack.

"Not tired at all, were you?" I say with a smile.

I lean down and press my lips against his and then cuddle in beside him, closing my eyes, just for a second . . . and the world darkens.

I wake once in the night, rousing just enough to feel soft blankets, where someone has draped them over us. The station smells of wood fire, someone setting it to ward off the night chill. Storm is pressed up against my legs, a furry hot-water bottle. Dalton sleeps so soundly he's snoring, and I can't summon the energy or the will to wake him and go home. I'm back asleep in moments.

I wake again to the smell of coffee, a mug wafted under my nose, Dalton crouching beside me. I reach out, and he starts to hand it to me, and then kisses me instead. When we part, I smile and say, "Good morning."

"Now just give you your damn coffee?"

My smile grows. "I'd never say that." I take the steaming mug, and he passes over the box of cookies from yesterday. "Saved them for you."

"I'm spoiled."

"It's my detective-retention program. In return for sticking with a shitty, shitty job, you get fresh coffee and chocolate chip cookies delivered to your bedside. Also, sex. The last one's a sacrifice, but I really need a good detective."

I laugh and grab his shirtfront, pulling him into a kiss. The door opens. I don't let go of Dalton. I just look over, hoping whoever it is sees that they're intruding, backs out, and lets me have a few quiet minutes with my coffee and my guy before the day implodes.

It's Phil. He stands there, looking at us, bewildered, as if he's walked into the wrong movie theater.

"I need to speak to you both," he says.

"Of course you do," I say. "Because it's four A.M., the sun is peeking over the horizon, and God forbid we get to enjoy our morning coffee in peace."

"I'll . . . come back in a few minutes."

"Don't bother," I say. "Sit down. Have coffee. Behave, and I'll share my cookies. Not sharing my rug, though. Or my sheriff."

Phil blinks at me.

Dalton snorts a laugh as he goes to pour another coffee. "She's in a good mood, Phil. We both are. Roll with it. Under the circumstances, it's not going to last."

He holds out the coffee. Phil looks down as if checking for cyanide.

"Oh for fuck's sake," Dalton mutters. "Do you prefer us in a pissy mood?"

I stand up, take the coffee, and hold it out to Phil. "Eric's right. We're in a good mood. Neither of us cares to start our day off with a confrontation, so I'm going to be more bluntly honest than usual. This is your turning point, Phil. Your moment of reckoning. You are stuck in Rockton. Hopefully, it's temporary. We both know it might not be. So you have the same choice Val did when she arrived. You may become part of this town, however much you hate it."

"Or you can say 'fuck that,'" Dalton says. "Fuck making the best of it. Hole up in your house. Come out when necessary. Fight us every step of the way. And hope that works out for you."

"Hope I don't shoot you," I say.

Dalton winces and glances my way. "I didn't mean *that*."

"I know. But it's true."

Dalton turns to Phil. "I fucked up with Val. I didn't understand her. I couldn't relate to her. The first time we met, I could feel her contempt and I don't have the patience for that. I gave as good as I got. That was my mistake."

"Mine was the opposite," I say. "I thought I did understand her. Or I tried to. I reached out. I wanted to help bridge the rift, mostly for Eric and Rockton, but partly for her, too. She saw that, and she had just as much contempt for me. In my case, she hid it. Right up until the end."

"When she left you with one choice," Dalton says.

I shrug, gaze shifting to Phil's mug.

"One choice," Dalton repeats. "Val made *her* choice, and she pushed us to ours, and the upshot of that is that Val Zapata was a bitch. A fucked-up, narcissistic, homicidal bitch. That's who the council gave us as their representative." He meets Phil's gaze. "You'd have to work hard to be worse. Wouldn't have to do much to be better. Bar's set pretty low. But ultimately, it's your choice."

Phil takes the mug from me. Then he looks around and very gingerly lowers himself to the floor as we join him on the rug.

I pass him the cookies.

And so, in the wee hours of breaking dawn, Dalton and I share cookies and coffee with Phil, and we all come to a better understanding of one another's position, and we leave committed to working together for a better Rockton.

Yeah . . .

That is my fantasy version every damn time I sit down with someone who's locking horns with us, whether it's debating the gender politics of brothels with Isabel or dealing with Jen's Greek-chorus critique of my every move. Yet none of my attempts to broker peace approached my efforts with Val. None approached the degree of success I enjoyed with Val. In light of how that turned out, I should really stop trying.

I don't think I'll extend myself that way again. At least, not for a very long time. I'd say "once burned," but it's not the first time.

I reach out, I get slapped back, and I keep reaching out. Sometimes I do make inroads, but right now I'm about ready to do exactly what Dalton did with Val. To look at Phil and say, "You don't want to help us? Fuck you, too." Except Dalton's approach didn't resolve the Val issue either.

One problem with having Dalton and me in leadership roles is that we're both stubborn as hell. And we stubbornly hold on to the notion that the average person is good—or can be, at least, like Mathias, an ally in our cause, whether he believes in it or not.

Another thing we both have in spades? Pride. Which means there is no way we'll beg Phil for help. We can't even pretend that we need his assistance. We will meet him halfway and nothing more.

We don't reach that midpoint during this meeting. To be honest, if we did, I'd suspect Phil's motivation. What we do manage is a civil conversation.

Phil agrees that getting Garcia is our priority. He agrees that any fallout over bringing in April can wait until we have Garcia. Regarding Petra's shooting of Brady, he's utterly confused. Or so he pretends to be, as does the council. Both are convinced we've made a mistake. When I tell Phil that Dalton and I both saw Petra do it, he tries coming up with alternative explanations. I cut him off—we have a search to conduct. We can resume this conversation once we have Garcia. Until then, Petra remains in custody.

We haven't dallied long with Phil. We're the first search team on the ground, out as soon as the sun fully crests the horizon. Others are still mingling in the town center, where volunteers pass out coffee and egg sandwiches. Dalton and I drop off Storm and then grab food. I say a few words to the assembled searchers, like "Thank you for your time—we really appreciate you getting up at this hour," and then I run to catch up with Dalton, who's already in the forest.

"Water," Dalton says as soon I fall in beside him.

I pass over ours.

He shakes his head. "I mean he'll go to water. That'll be his first step once the sun's up. Find water. Wash. Refill his bottle. My guess last night was that he'd head for the mountain. I can't track him over rock, and he probably hoped for shelter there. With the late sunset, there's a good chance he found it. If he's smart, he'll have picked a cave near water."

"Perfect."

"Nah. *Perfect* would be a mountain spring near a cave. In the direction he headed, the water sources are all at ground level, meaning I can't just match up a cave and a stream. Fuck, he might not even have found a cave—or know enough to pick a spot near water. Face it, I'm flying blind and pretending I can see."

"No, you're flying in fog, knowing you can't see very well. You have a search area in mind. I know you do, or you wouldn't mention it. Unless you've come up with a better idea in the last thirty seconds . . ."

"No."

"Then you're explaining your reasoning while telling me not to get my hopes up. You can skip the last part, Eric. It's just me here."

"Yeah, I know. Thanks."

What Dalton has is a theory that provides a better sense of purpose than wandering aimlessly in the woods, hoping to stumble over the marshal's sleeping body. Yet for the rest of the searchers, stumbling over his body is really their only hope. Their orders are to stay close to town and sweep in groups, which is more about guard duty than searching. Their presence will convey a message to Garcia: that he has no hope of sneaking into town again. We can guard our border longer than he can survive in the wilderness. Best to just come out and negotiate. Hot meal and lukewarm shower included.

We check a few shallow caves close to ground level, within easy reach of streams. There's no sign of Garcia. Then Dalton cuts through thicker trees, off the main path, following a wildlife trail—a thin line of trampled undergrowth and broken twigs. We're quiet, me moving behind him, mimicking his rolling walk, putting each foot down with care.

When a brace of ptarmigan fly up, I fall back. Something whistles through the still air overhead. A ptarmigan thumps onto my head and then bounces to my feet with an arrow through its breast. I yank out my gun, my gaze sweeping the forest for the archer.

Dalton grabs the arrow and curses under his breath. Then he shouts, "Jacob!"

A figure appears through a stand of trees. He's a little shorter than Dalton. A little thinner. His light hair is much longer and neatly tied back, and he has a short beard. Squint past the differences, though, and Jacob is the spitting image of our sheriff. Not surprising, considering this is his little brother. Like Dalton, Jacob grew up out here, with their settler parents. Unlike Dalton, he has stayed in the forest.

"That is not funny," Dalton grumbles.

"No, *that* is breakfast." Jacob takes the ptarmigan. "Hey, Casey."

"Don't *hey* her. Ask if she's okay, after having a dead bird fall on her head."

Jacob's eyes round. "Are you all right? I didn't mean—"

"I'm fine. Your brother's just being cranky."

Jacob's smile returns. "Nothing new, huh?" He turns to Dalton. "Got your message. Something's up?"

The "message" would have been Dalton setting out an indicator that he wants to talk to Jacob. Jacob is illiterate, with no interest in changing that, which drives his book-loving brother crazy.

Dalton starts to explain when I see another figure in the forest. A huge one, rearing up on two legs, its shaggy brown hair having me reaching for my gun before I see that the bear wears clothing.

"Could you cut your hair, Ty?" I call. "Or shave? Otherwise, one of these days, I'm going to see an actual grizzly and start chatting with him."

"Probably a better plan than shooting him," Cypher says as he lumbers over to us. "That little gun won't do more than piss him off, kitten."

"You got my message?" Dalton says.

"Yeah. Got it. Then found Jakey here, crashing through the forest."

Jacob arches a brow. "I'm not the one who makes enough noise to scare game for miles."

Tyrone Cypher. Six foot four. Well over two hundred pounds. With his grizzled brown hair, he does indeed resemble an aging bear. Cypher is a former sheriff of Rockton. Before that, he was a hit man, which in Rockton apparently qualifies as law enforcement experience.

"That Brady kid get away on you again?" Cypher says when Dalton tells them we're looking for a fugitive.

"Not unless he's a zombie," I say. "And Eric has promised that whatever else we have in these woods, there are no zombies."

"Yet," Dalton says.

"No, you said there were no killer *rabbits* yet. You said there were no zombies at all. You were very, very clear on that."

"Which only means I've never seen one." He turns to the other two. "Brady's dead. This fugitive is a different problem."

While the three of them talk, I wander off. As always, Dalton keeps one eye on me. I joke that he'd like to have us all on leashes . . . with shock collars that will zap us if we stray too far.

I check out what looks like a berry bush. I'm hunkered down examining it when something moves in the undergrowth. It's the size of a rabbit. Too dark to be an Arctic hare, though, or any of the other small critters we get out here. When I squint, I realize it's twice the size I thought—it just looked small because it's lying on the ground.

When the thing gives an odd bleat, I go still.

Another bleat and then it snuffles, raising a black furry head with a black nose. It reminds me of what Anders said the other day, joking about Storm being a bear cub. That's exactly what I'm looking at: a black bear cub.

It lifts its head and bleats, and it is so adorable that I stifle an "Awww" of appreciation. I know to leave it alone, so I just smile and step backward.

Then a snort sounds behind me.

I turn slowly to see Mama Bear twenty feet away.

ELEVEN

I take a deep breath to calm my stuttering heart. I'm not bothering her cub. I'll just step sideways, get farther from it, and hope she hasn't noticed me. . . .

Mama Bear rises up on her rear legs, and her nearsighted eyes lock on me.

I open my mouth to shout. That's how we deal with black bears: stand our ground, make ourselves as big as possible, and shout in hopes of scaring them off.

Thankfully, before I shout, I realize the logic flaw in that. If I'm standing between a sow and her cub, I really *don't* want to put on a threat display.

The sow is in front of me, the cub to my left. The bear keeps snuf-fling the air, her head bobbing as she assesses. When I step backward, away from the cub, the sow snarls, baring her teeth.

"Casey?" Dalton's voice, sharp with anxiety.

I slide my gaze his way. He's on the other side, just out of the sow's sight line.

"I thought you said black bears aren't like grizzlies," I say. "They don't attack if you get between a sow and her cubs."

"I said that'd always been my experience." He's right, of course. He'd never say such a thing couldn't happen, only that he'd never known it to. Apparently, this sow has not read the black bear behavior guide.

"Advice?" I say.

His gaze is on the bear, assessing just as hard as she is. He has his gun in hand. When he shifts, the sow glances his way and waves one paw, brandishing inch-long claws. I'm closer, though, and I'm the threat to her baby, so her attention swings back to me.

"She doesn't want me to move," I say. "But I need to get away from her cub."

"Yep."

"Which requires moving. . . ."

"Hold on a sec." He squints over, still assessing. Also lining up the shot.

I have my gun in hand, but I haven't lifted it. A voice in my head says we haven't reached that level of threat. Which is ridiculous. This isn't a human, who might be provoked by me raising my weapon. So I do, but I feel guilty about it. I know, better than anyone, never to raise my weapon unless I am prepared to fire, and I really don't want to fire. I am between an animal and her young, with no way of telling her I don't pose a threat.

I do not want to kill her for protecting her baby. But I still raise my gun. I must.

"Take one step directly to your right," Dalton says. "Away from the baby *and* the mother."

The sow growls as soon as I lift my right foot, and Dalton quickly tells me to stop.

"You're gonna have to shoot her, kitten," Cypher says. "No way around this."

"Casey?" Dalton says. "I have my gun trained on her, but you know it's my bad hand. Jacob has an arrow nocked. Neither one of us has a sight line to the best shot."

"But I do."

"Yeah." A pause. "Sorry. We'll try something else, but I need you to be absolutely ready to fire if she charges. She'll drop to all fours. Aim downward at her head. Empty your weapon. Do not hesitate."

"I know."

The sow growls and bares her teeth. She's getting impatient.

"Walk backward," Dalton says. "It's clear ground behind you. Don't hurry, or you'll trip. Keep your gun ready. If she drops—"

The sow drops to all fours.

"Casey?"

"Got it."

She's going to charge. Her muscles bunch. Her eyes fix on me. She will charge, and I can empty my gun, but I'm still not certain it will save me.

The cold thud of that hits me square in the gut. This is a black bear. Up until now, I've paid them only healthy respect. It's the grizzlies I worry about.

This bear can kill me, though. She has fangs and she has claws and she's twice my weight, and I'm between her and her baby.

She can kill me.

And I'm not sure anyone can stop her.

I wheel and run. Dalton shouts. The bear snorts in rage. A gun fires and an arrow *thwangs* . . . and I race straight for the cub. I scoop it up in my arms. As it bleats in alarm, I throw it, a low and easy pitch that sends the cub smacking into its charging mother. The sow skids to a halt, and then I do run—toward Jacob's shouts of "Over here!"

Nine months ago, I'd never have led an enraged bear toward anyone I cared about. If I made a mistake, I'd pay the price alone. But Jacob is correct. I need to run to where three people stand ready to help me.

When I reach the others, I wheel to see the bear prodding her cub, making sure it's all right. She glowers and snarls our way, but there are four of us, a tight-knit mass of large predators. She has her baby. That's all she wanted. She picks him up by the scruff of the neck and marches into the forest.

"That was . . ." Cypher begins. "I am torn between 'awesome' and 'the fucking craziest thing I've ever seen.'"

"I'll go with the latter," Dalton mutters.

"Nope," Cypher says. "I think we gotta admit to both. Awesome *and* crazy. She *threw* a cub. At a charging bear."

Jacob snickers. "It was kind of—"

"No, no it was not," Dalton says. "You know what you're supposed to fire at a charging bear, Casey? *Bullets.*"

"I know."

"What if you just pissed her off more?"

"I know."

"Actually," Jacob says, "the first thing any mama's going to do is make sure her baby is okay, so—"

Dalton wheels on him, and Jacob steps back, his hands raised.

"I wouldn't have done it with a grizzly," I say.

Dalton glowers at me. "Well, *that's* good to know."

"I didn't drop my gun. If the baby toss failed, at least it would have startled her enough for me to get a good shot. As long as I kept hold of my weapon, I was okay."

"She has a point, Eric," Jacob says.

Dalton turns his glower on Jacob.

"In any other circumstances, I'd have shot," I say. "But if I killed her, we'd have had an orphaned cub, and we've already given Mathias the wolf-dog. I don't know who'd take the bear. It just seemed unwise."

Dalton turns to me again. "You know what's *unwise?*"

A hug throws him off guard. "I know. I'm sorry. I won't say I'll never do that again, but I promise I won't try it with a grizzly."

"You couldn't lift a grizzly cub," he grumbles.

"Nah," Cypher says. "Casey's got some guns on her. She could *lift* a bigger cub—just couldn't *throw* it." He slaps me on the back. "Creative thinking there, kitten. And it proves my point: you don't always need to use a gun. Now let's split up and get out of here before Mama comes back."

———

Cypher and Jacob each goes his own way. They're both experienced trackers—with very different methods—so it's best if they separate. Also, too much of Cypher could drive even Jacob to justifiable homicide.

Dalton and I stick together. I'm just lucky he doesn't tie a rope around his waist and make me hold on to it. As it is, he settles for checking over his shoulder every dozen steps to be sure I'm still there.

When we reach a wider path, he brings me up beside him, his hand locked in mine. I know that bear standoff spooked him even more than it did me. Dalton's world is one of both endless wonder and endless danger, and he fears that one day he'll lose me to it. Either I will fall prey to those threats or I'll simply declare "enough" and leave. So I let him grumble about the bear, and I let him clutch my hand, and I push branches aside to walk beside him along a path that's really too narrow for both of us.

We do keep an ear and eye out for the black bear. I don't know what the chances are that she'll come back. Bears aren't as territorial as wolves and cougars. That might change if it's a sow with a cub. Still, there's no sign of her. I didn't hurt her baby, and she seems to have decided retreat is the best option.

When we catch a noise, at first it does sound like a bear. The hair-raising yowl of an ursine in distress. Then the yowl becomes a word.

"Helloooo!"

As we listen, it comes again, a very clear human cry echoing through the forest. Dalton breaks into a jog.

The shouts are sporadic, as if the person knows he has little chance of getting a response. We run more than a kilometer into mountain foothills. Then, as we draw near, I grab Dalton's arm and say, "Trap."

I hate being the one who hears a person in need and immediately expects the worst. It makes me feel like a horrible human being. But that won't stop me from slowing to be sure, even when those extra moments could mean the difference between life and death for another person.

We continue slower now, tracking the sound, pausing when it stops. Finally, we're close enough to hear ragged breathing. We still can't see anyone, which worries Dalton. He slows and squints at the open rocky landscape.

"Hello?" the voice calls. "Is someone there?"

The sound seems to come from less than twenty feet in front of us. The only thing there, though, is a low boulder. Dalton's eyes narrow as they fix on it.

"I thought I heard footsteps," the voice continues. "If someone's there, I need help. Please."

It's undeniably Mark Garcia. Calling to us from behind a boulder.

"I've fallen," he says.

"And I can't get up," I mutter under my breath.

Dalton only glances my way. A lifetime of incomprehensible pop-culture jokes has taught him not to ask.

I motion a plan. It's virtually the same one we had when we first encountered Garcia in the forest. Dalton will slip around the far side of that boulder, and I will be the bait.

While Dalton lopes off to get in place, I scuff my boot against the rock.

"Hello?" Garcia calls.

I scuff again, distracting him from Dalton's muffled footfalls.

"Look," Garcia says. "If you're human, just say something." A rasp-ing cough. "I really don't have the energy to be talking to wildlife."

I take two thumping steps toward that boulder.

"Please be human," Garcia says. "Please be a *friendly* human. I have . . . Oh, hell. I don't have shit. That's the truth. But I can get it. The couple hundred bucks in my wallet is useless to you, but I'll bring you supplies. Whatever you need. Just help me. Please."

Another two steps. Then I lift my gun and check the ammo. It's full, of course. I don't leave without a full cartridge. But the sound will be unmistakable to a lawman.

"Sheriff?" he says. "Is that you? No, you had a revolver. The deputy had a big-ass forty-five. That's a nine-mil, which makes it the detec-tive. Or so I hope. Is that you, Detective? I don't know your name. Seems we never progressed that far. But I heard someone call you a detective."

"It's me," I say.

A loud, ragged exhale. "Oh, thank God. Please tell me you have the sheriff or deputy with you. No offense, but you're going to need help. I can't make it back to town on my own."

Why, no, I'm afraid it's just little ol' me, Marshal. All alone in the forest with my basket for Grandmama.

"They're out searching," I say. "I can go get—"

"No. Get me out of here first, please. Then you can bring help."

Of course.

I continue forward, my gun out. I'm dividing my attention between the boulder and the forest behind it as I watch for Dalton. He appears and signals something, but the sun is blasting down, and I can only tell that he's pointing to the boulder. *Yes, Garcia's there, Eric. There's no place else he could be.*

I continue forward. The boulder is five feet away. Any second now, Garcia will lunge—

"Casey!"

Dalton's shout startles me, and I pitch forward. My foot keeps going, and I stumble. Thankfully, my instinct is to pull back and right myself. I look down . . . *way* down.

There's a crevice right in front of me. Another step, and I'd have walked into it.

"So the sheriff *is* here." Garcia gives a hoarse chuckle. "Okay. I should have seen that coming."

I follow his voice. He's to my left, wedged into the crevice. He's fallen at least a dozen feet. Splotches of blood paint the rocks.

Dalton walks to the edge, looming over Garcia's head. He looks down at the marshal and grunts.

"Yes, Sheriff," Garcia says. "I got myself in some trouble, as you predicted. And, no, I can't get out."

"Figured that or you would have."

Dalton hunkers down on his side of the divide. I do the same on mine.

"Are you going to help me? Or just stare at me?" Garcia says.

"We're admiring your predicament," Dalton says.

"Yeah, yeah. Fuck you." There's no venom in Garcia's curse, only exhaustion laced with the recognition that he has indeed ended up in exactly the kind of straits we warned him about. "Can you get me out, please?"

"You want to tell us who you're hunting?" I say.

He turns a glower on me, and his dark eyes snap. "Really, Detective? I'm not lying here enjoying your fine Yukon air. I'm hurt, okay? I'm trying to hide it. Bit of machismo in that. More than a bit, maybe."

I take a closer look. There's blood on his clothes, and they're torn far worse than I'd expect from a ten-foot tumble down a crevice.

"So," Garcia says, trying for nonchalance. "Apparently, you have wolves up here."

"We do," Dalton says. "You met them?"

"You might say that. I went to a stream this morning, and I'm trying to wash dust out of my hair, when I look up to see a goddamned pack surrounding me. They attacked. I wasn't expecting that. Sure, they're wolves and all, but I'm the idiot city boy who's thinking how cool this is. Real wolves, close enough to touch." His voice is shaking now, bravado fading. "Close enough to rip my damned throat out."

He twists, and I see that the front of his shirt is torn. There's blood, too.

"I'd set my knife down. That's the only thing that saved me. I'd put the knife right beside me while I washed my hair. When the wolf lunged, I grabbed it and . . ." He holds up his hands, fingers and forearms stained red. "I fought like something out of a damned lost-in-the-wilderness movie."

"You killed the wolf?" I say.

His laugh dissolves into a pained cough. "I wish. The version in my *head* was like the lost-in-the-wilderness movie—the intrepid hero vanquishes an entire pack of wolves armed only with a knife. I just wounded the one attacking me. As soon as it let go, I tore up the mountain. I don't think they followed me far, but I never checked. I just kept going. Blind panic fueled by pure adrenaline. Which is how I ended up down here. For a moment, I was like a cartoon character, running on air. Then I dropped. I've been trying to climb out but . . ."

He grimaces as he straightens one leg to show a bloody gash. "I hit the side when I fell. Between that and this"—he waves at his clothing, slashed with bloody holes—"I'm *still* running on adrenaline. And fear. Probably shock, too. That wolf did a number on me. I'd like to say I did worse to it, but that'd be a lie. I'm in rough shape."

"Hold on," I say. "We'll get you out."

TWELVE

We set about extracting Garcia. I joked earlier about a rope. I actually have one. I put it into my pack last week after Storm took off chasing a young cougar.

I clamber down into the crevice and check Garcia's wounds before we move him. After Kenny, I'll err on the side of extreme caution in any situation that might result in spinal injury. There doesn't seem to be one here. Garcia's ankle hurts to the touch, as does his knee, but the bones are fine.

Garcia has a half dozen puncture wounds and tears from the wolf attack. I can't see how deep any of them go. They're bloody and ragged, and they're causing him a lot of pain. Same goes for the leg gash. The upshot is that none of his injuries requires leaving him in this crevice while we run for help.

With my support, Garcia rises to his feet. Lots of wincing and heavy breathing and a couple of pained gasps, but he manages it. Dalton lowers the rope, and I support Garcia as he climbs it. Dalton helps him out.

I don't need the rope for more than a handhold. A week ago, I survived clinging to the side of a cliff. This is nothing.

As dire as Garcia's predicament had seemed, I suspect that once the shock and fear passed, and he assessed his situation with a clear head, he'd have gotten out of that crevice. Not that I'll tell *him* that. If he thinks his injuries are worse than they are, that'll ensure he doesn't try making a run for it. Just in case, as I clean his wounds up top, I tell him he's lucky we came along. Injured and bleeding, he was sure to attract predators. Then I list them, from cougars to black bears to grizzlies to wolves to wolverines.

"That's not even counting the wild dogs," I say. "And the wild pigs."

Dalton's glittering eyes suggest I might be overselling it.

As for Garcia, he manages a snorting laugh at the mention of dogs and pigs.

"I'm serious," I say, as I plaster one of his chest wounds. "Our town kept pets and livestock years ago. The animals either escaped or were turned loose, and they've thrived. That's the biggest danger out here, really. Domestic animals aren't afraid of humans. You're lucky we came along when we did."

"Believe me, after those wolves, I'd be glad you came along even if I hadn't fallen into that crack. You guys win. I'm ready to negotiate. Just take me back to your town, and let me see a doctor, please. I'm pretty sure I broke a rib or two falling down that hole."

Getting Garcia to Rockton isn't easy, not when Dalton is still trying to hide the fact that he's injured his dominant arm. We don't need to carry the guy, but he's limping badly, and his breathing suggests he's not wrong about those ribs. Dalton supports him on his right side, and I drape his other arm over my shoulders. It's slow going, and when Jacob whistles, warning us he's approaching, I'm about to breathe a sigh of relief. Then I see Dalton tense, and instead, I tell the guys I need a "restroom" break and hurry off to warn Jacob away. We've learned our lesson about introducing newcomers—however unwittingly—to Dalton's younger brother.

I tell Jacob we have our man and ask him to please let Cypher know. Then Dalton and I continue our trek back to town with Garcia.

When we're close to town, I try the radio. It's not working great, but I manage to get a message through to Paul, telling him we're bringing Garcia in, wounded. He takes off to tell Anders and gather a party to meet us.

It's at least fifteen minutes later before I catch the distant sound of voices, and we're almost at town. So much for getting help carrying Garcia. I'll need a good shoulder massage after this. A hot bath would be even better, but that's not a—

A crack sounds behind us, like someone stepping on a dried branch. I'm turning with "Will?" when Garcia falls against my arm.

"Casey!" Dalton says.

My first thought is that Garcia has collapsed, and thank God we're only a hundred feet from Rockton. Then there's another crack, and I realize it's not a branch.

Someone is shooting at us.

Dalton pulls me down just as I start to drop on my own. He looks over at Garcia, but I drag Dalton off the path, as I flash back to a week ago, Dalton trying to protect Brady, lucky to end up with only that bullet wound in his shoulder.

This time, I'm ready to haul Dalton into the undergrowth and hold him there if I have to. I don't have to . . . because he looks at Garcia and sees the blood pumping from his chest and knows it is already too late.

THIRTEEN

I lift my head. Dalton goes to push it down, but I duck and peer out at the path. There's a dark shape about fifteen feet away, in the bushes alongside the path. It's too hidden by that bush for me to see more than a shape.

"Cover me," I whisper to Dalton.

"My arm—"

"—is fine for cover fire."

I inch behind a tree and rise to a crouch. The dark shape has vanished, and I'm aiming my gun at the bush instead. I lean out.

A bullet whizzes past. I drop. Dalton fires. There's a crash of undergrowth as the shooter takes off.

I lunge again, but the shooter fires, and I can't see anything to fire back at. Dalton shoots twice in quick succession, but I know he's also firing blind. Firing high, as his bullets *thwack* into trees, his shots intended only to make our assailant dive for cover. The shooter just keeps running, and with the thick growth here, I see only a dark blur dart between two massive evergreens, already fifty feet away.

I'm about to fire—a wide shot, still hoping to spook the shooter—but a shout from deep in the forest stops me. Running footfalls say someone else has heard the shots and is coming our way. I can't risk firing off another round.

"Casey?" Dalton says.

He jogs up beside me.

"Take Garcia," he says. "I'll go after the shooter."

I race back to Garcia. As I do, I shout, "Man down!" and "We need help!" I can already hear shouts and footfalls.

I drop beside Garcia. He's been hit twice. Both to the back. The first shot is low and off to the side. The second is to the upper left of his chest, and even if it missed his heart . . .

I won't think about that. He's still breathing. That's the main thing. Breathing and conscious, but in shock, his eyes wide, mouth working.

"We've got you," I say. "We have two doctors in town. You'll be fine."

He will not be fine. I know that. But as long as he's breathing, there's a chance to find out who did this. To find out who the marshal came for.

God, I'm a cold bitch, aren't I? A man is dying in my arms, and all I can think about is keeping him calm enough to find out who he came for. But that's my job. Garcia is here for a fugitive, and the town knows that, and his target has lain in wait for us to return. Lain in wait to make sure Garcia fails in his mission.

My job is to make sure *that* person fails in his—or her—mission to dodge justice.

Right now, Garcia wouldn't be able to answer my questions. He's going into shock. I assess and field-treat Garcia's wounds, mostly trying to stop the bleeding. By the time help arrives, Garcia is unconscious. April appears right behind the first group. That surprises me. I don't know what I expected—that she'd hear shots and hide? That's unfair, but honestly, it's what most people do. It's the sane thing to do.

April arrives and only needs a ten-second assessment to look up at me.

"We're going to move him to the clinic," I say.

Her brow furrows, and her voice takes on a tone I know well, the big sister to the younger one who, time and time again, proves she's not quite as bright as one might hope.

"This man—" she begins.

"—is going to the clinic." I meet and hold her gaze. "We are taking him to the clinic."

"He's—"

"Will moving him to the clinic hurt his chances of survival, April?"

She starts to answer. I'm ready to cut her off again when a light-bulb flashes behind those blue eyes. Well, maybe not so much a flash as a flicker, with the faint hope that her sister is *not* so medically incompetent—that I realize even firing a bullet into Garcia's head wouldn't "hurt" his chances of survival. He has none.

"I would like him in the clinic," I say, and she finally seems to get the message.

"All right," she says, but cannot resist adding, "I don't think it'll make any difference, treating him here or there," for the benefit of the three gathered townspeople. But she doesn't clarify that he has no chance either way. For that I'm grateful.

When more locals arrive, I shoo them off. Anders has come running from the forest, and between him and the three others, they're able to lift Garcia. Anders does frown over at me when he sees Garcia's condition, but when I say, "I'd like him in the clinic," he nods, needing no further explanation.

As we walk, I clear the way with my best Dalton impersonation, warning the residents that we have a gravely injured man, one who has been shot, and anyone who takes too great an interest will zoom to the top of my suspect list. That clears them fast.

When I catch sight of Diana, I call, "Gather up any militia in town. Have them wait outside the clinic," and she takes off.

The clinic isn't meant for long-term patients. There's one examination room, where Kenny is currently enjoying morphine dreams. We wheel Kenny into the other area, used for supplies and equipment, which feels like sticking him in the closet. I'll apologize later.

As soon as Garcia's on the table, I shoo off our three helpers with thanks. By that point, Garcia is barely breathing. Anders has already figured out my plan, and he's jumped in to work on Garcia. April thankfully follows his lead, and the last thing the trio of residents see is the two of them heroically trying to save a man who cannot be saved.

They don't stop as soon as their audience is gone. We *do* make every effort to save the marshal. When he breathes his last, we all step back from the table.

"He's comatose," I say.

April gives me that are-you-an-idiot look again. "This man is—"

"Comatose," I say. "We have about forty-eight hours before the smell will prove otherwise."

Anders chuckles.

April stares at him. "I realize you are a police officer, Deputy Anders, but let me assure you, I do not share my sister's sense of gallows humor."

"Yeah, pretty sure you don't have a sense of humor, period," he says under his breath.

"Excuse me?"

"We aren't making jokes here, Doc," Anders says. "But you're right that we're law enforcement. Your sister is a detective first, medical assistant second, same as me. She has a killer to catch. A killer who shouldn't know that he succeeded."

"Or that *she* succeeded," I say. "I realize you're using the masculine for simplicity, but I didn't even see enough to establish gender." I turn to April. "Marshal Garcia came to town to catch an alleged fugitive. Unfortunately, he made his intentions clear."

Anders looks at the body. "Fatal mistake, I'd say."

"Everyone in town knew what he was here for," I continue. "I had to tell them. After Garcia went door-to-door, enough people knew for the news to travel like wildfire. Better for me to clarify. Someone in Rockton knew there was a supposed US marshal here to arrest them. That person tried to make arrest impossible."

"We don't want them to know they succeeded," Anders says.

I nod. "I'll put out the word that Garcia survived but has gone into a coma, from which we hope he'll recover. I'll make it clear that Marshal Garcia did not reveal his suspect's identity, but that he certainly will when he awakes. With any luck, our shooter will move to ensure Garcia never wakes up."

April thinks this over and then nods slowly. "All right."

"I'll set up guards right away," Anders says.

"Hold off for a bit," I say. "First, I'm going to need to figure out which militia members we can eliminate. For now, that'll just be everyone who was in sight at the time of the shots."

Anders lifts his hand. "I was with Jen and two volunteers." He looks at April. "You have no idea what a relief that is. Around here, that's step one in any crime: eliminate the law officers from the suspect list."

She stares at him.

"You think I'm kidding," Anders says.

I shake my head. "No, she just hopes you are. Okay, let's go talk to the militia."

I'm heading outside with Anders when Dalton comes striding through town. From his expression, I know he didn't catch the shooter. I retreat into the clinic, leaving Anders in charge of getting militia alibis.

"How is he?" Dalton asks as he throws open the clinic door.

"Comatose," I say.

I'm tucked back, out of sight of the militia, waving for Dalton to come in and shut the door, but he says "Fuck. What are his chances?" as the door still's shutting.

"Pretty good," I say. Then I lead Dalton into the back room. "Garcia's dead."

"What?"

"Lower your voice please," I say. "It was a fatal wound. He survived long enough to get here, so I'm saying he's in a coma, in hopes of flushing out the killer. If you disagree, let me know, and he'll suffer a sudden fatal relapse."

"No, you're right. It's a good idea. Given our track record, the shooter will figure he can break in here no problem."

"I know you're being sarcastic, Eric, but yes, the shooter has to think they have a chance of success."

He slumps into a chair. April is rattling about, cleaning, but he ignores her.

"I didn't see anything except a shape," I say. "Adult human. That's all I have."

"That's all I've got, too. I picked up the trail, but whoever it was, they made a beeline for town. Reentered by the lumber shed. By the time I got there, people were all over the place. They heard the shots and came out to see what it was."

"Maybe one of them saw someone enter town from that direction."

"Yeah. Hope so." He waves at Garcia. "He's not gonna be any help." He exhales. "Fucking shitty thing to say."

"Earlier I wanted to make him name his suspect before I rescued him. But I felt like a ghoul. Poor guy was attacked by wolves and thought he might die in that hole, and I wanted to barter for his release. I should have. I really should have."

"Wouldn't have helped. He would have just made shit up."

"Now he didn't even survive our rescue. He might have been better off staying in that hole."

Dalton grunts. Then he rises, walks over to the table, and pulls back the sheet tugged up to Garcia's neck. He grabs a probe from the surgical tray and starts poking at the puncture wounds.

"Excuse me, Sheriff?" April says, turning on him.

"It's Eric. 'Sheriff' is what folks call me when they're showing respect or being patronizing." He meets her gaze. "You demonstrating respect for my position?"

She doesn't answer.

"Yeah, didn't think so. It's Eric." He examines another hole. Then he starts poking at Garcia's shredded shirt, lifting it with forceps and examining the damage.

"Can I help you, *Eric*?" April says.

"Actually, you can." He rocks back on his heels. "You got any experience treating dog bites?"

"Dogs?"

"Garcia was attacked by a wolf. Those are the puncture wounds you see here and here."

She takes a cursory look and glowers at him. "If you are testing my expertise, Sher—Eric, I do not appreciate it. While I am hardly an expert in wounds inflicted by animals, I did see dog bites as an intern in the emergency ward."

"And these are different?"

"Those holes are near perfect punctures. If a dog bit him once, then yes, these could be correct. But an attack involves ripping."

Dalton nods. "Ragged punctures. Tears." He lifts Garcia's arm to examine the gash on the underside.

"That is not a wound caused by an animal either," April says.

"He didn't say it was. He got this one sliding into a rock crevice."

She takes a closer look. "That's possible."

"It's shallow, though. Like the punctures. Lots of blood, but shallow wounds."

"Yes."

"Shit," I say. "He wasn't attacked by wolves, was he? I wondered when he said that—I know it's not normal behavior for them. But you didn't question, so I figured . . ." I shrug. "First rule of dealing with wildlife: the wildlife doesn't know the rules."

"Yep. Basic animal behavior supposes no external mitigating factors."

"Like human behavior. Mental illness, physical impairment, drugs, alcohol, extenuating circumstances . . . they all play a role."

He nods. "For humans, wolves are probably the least dangerous predator out here, all other things being equal. The 'big, bad wolf' lore is bullshit. Livestock is more likely to attack you than a healthy wolf in the wild. A pack of wolves setting on Garcia at a stream makes no fucking sense. There's plenty of water to go around. Plenty of prey—wolves sure as hell aren't starving this time of year. Plenty of land, too—we aren't encroaching on their territory. That doesn't mean a wolf couldn't have attacked him. Maybe he did something he failed to mention. Maybe there were cubs nearby. Hell, maybe a wolf ate something it shouldn't have and wasn't thinking straight."

"You suspected Garcia's story was bullshit, but you wanted April to check the wounds first."

"Nah, I wanted to get him back here first. Which didn't turn out so well."

I walk over to the body. "He *wanted* to come back, didn't he? That's why he faked the attack. He heard us in the woods. He hopped down into the crevice. Cut himself up a bit, nothing so serious he couldn't get out again."

"That makes no sense," April says.

I wince. She's been following our conversation, as if genuinely interested in the exchange. But now she must treat me like an idiot drawing a ridiculous conclusion.

"Is that a statement or a question?" Dalton asks.

"What?"

"Well"—he leans back against the counter—"if you're curious about our reasoning, you should presume we have a motivation in mind and ask. Which might be what you meant. But the way you word it sounds like you're just rendering judgment."

"Of course I want an explanation," she snaps. "I pointed out that your reasoning does not—to me—make sense, which is your opportunity to explain it."

"Yeah, that's not actually how people phrase a question. Unless they want to be a dick about it."

"I do not appreciate—"

"I'm sure you don't. Get used to it. I'm not putting up with your bullshit. If you have a question, phrase it as one."

I cut in. "Here's our reasoning, April. Yes, it seems to make little sense to fake being injured in order to return to a town you escaped. But if we tracked Garcia down, we'd toss him in the cell. At best, we'd put him under house arrest. That means there'd be no way he could grab his fugitive and run."

"If he's injured, though, presumably he'd come to the clinic instead of a cell," she says.

"Right. He'd be a patient, not a prisoner. He told us he twisted his leg and hurt his ribs. That's hard to prove. The guy just escaped a pack of ravenous wolves—we aren't going to be questioning his injuries."

"He would be allowed to stay in the clinic," she says. "Then he could sneak out, find his fugitive, and leave."

I nod. "That seems to have been his plan. He faked being injured . . . and ended up dead."

"Would have been better taking his chances out there," Dalton says, jerking his thumb toward the forest. "The wolves in here are a lot more dangerous."

FOURTEEN

Our theory makes sense. Even Dalton rarely sees wolves around here. Garcia likely heard them howling at night and presumed they were close. Even if he encountered a pack of the more vicious wolf-dog hybrids, they wouldn't leave such neat and shallow bite marks. Nor would they have let him escape so easily.

There's also the issue of coincidence. In all this wilderness, Garcia just happens to fall into a crevice where we're searching? And just happens to be calling for help while we're within earshot? Sure, it's possible. It's a whole lot more possible, though, that he heard us talking to Cypher and Jacob, our voices echoing through the quiet forest. Then Garcia formulated a plan, which ultimately got him killed. There's a lesson about the dangers of crying wolf in there. Maybe a joke, too, a little of that gallows humor my sister sniffed about.

We leave April in the clinic, cleaning Garcia's body, hooking up a dummy IV, and making it appear as if the patient is sleeping. When Kenny wakes, we'll have to break the news that he's stuck in that supply room. He won't want a dead roommate . . . and we also don't want him near Garcia when we expect someone will try to break in. As for letting Kenny in on the secret, well, it's not as if he's a suspect.

For everyone else . . .

April thought Anders was joking about eliminating ourselves from the list. Down south, I'd never turn to my detective partner and say, "Where were *you* the night our victim was killed?" Up here, with such a restricted population, everyone *must* be a suspect.

I know Dalton didn't do it, and he's my alibi. So that's sorted. Anders is cleared, too, which really does make this easier.

Dalton takes off to speak to Phil and update the council. I head to Anders, who has found the militia members with solid alibis. We station them outside the clinic, with orders not to disturb the patients.

Next comes the public announcement. I spin our story—Garcia is comatose, and he has not told us who he came to collect, and we hope he'll make a full recovery. In the meantime, someone shot the guy, and it's my job to figure out who.

After that, everyone wants to tell us where they were at the time of the shooting, with cries of "I'm sure someone saw me" and "Hey, Jim, didn't you see me?"

Dalton would tell them not to be too eager to claim an alibi, because if it turns out they can't produce a good one, that's suspicious. I try his tactic. The roar of the crowd drowns me out. Anders gets up on the porch with his trained-military bark, and people hear that, but well, there's an ingredient missing from our bluster: Dalton. With him, it's never mere bluster, and they know it.

Someone shouting for my attention stops midword and goes crowd-surfing. Or, more accurately, he does an impressive imitation of a bowling ball, the people around him serving as pins. Dalton strides through and grabs the guy—Artie—by the back of his shirt. Then he drags Artie over and dangles him in front of me.

"You have something to say to my detective?" Dalton says.

"Uh, y-yes. I wanted to tell her that I was over at the Roc—"

Dalton cuts him off with a firm shake. "I'm not holding you up so you can convey your alias, Artie. What you just did is the proper way to speak to her. What I heard before? It's not the proper way."

"I'm sorry, Casey. I just wanted—"

"You just wanted what everyone else wants. You think you're special?" Dalton raises his voice. "Sam? I find Artie's enthusiasm suspicious. Go search his quarters. Bring me anything that looks like a weapon . . . or contraband."

Dalton tosses Artie aside and nods for me to address the now-silent crowd.

"I need to handle this one person at a time," I say. "Which is going to take a while. I'll start with those who were on search parties or had volunteered for town patrol. If you were helping us with the current situation, you move to the front of the line. If you do not have an alibi, give your name to Will. If your alibi is 'maybe someone saw me around town,' give your name to Will. We'll follow up with you later. For now, I only want to speak to those who were in the presence of at least *two* other people. Patrol volunteers to my left. Everyone else with a two-person alibi, queue up on my right."

The council will see us now.

We're almost done gathering preliminary alibis when Phil comes to say there's someone on the line. That's how he phrases it. *Someone.* At first, I think he's being pissy, refusing to grant his replacement a name. But then I see his expression.

"Who is it?" I ask as we walk.

"I . . . I don't know."

"Someone you aren't familiar with."

There's a pause. A long one. That look intensifies, until he seems as adrift as he did when he first discovered he had to stay in Rockton.

When Phil arrived in town, he'd marched in like he owned the place. Undaunted by a new situation, or by meeting people who had every reason to hate his guts. There'd been a touch of the junior executive in that. The thirty-year-old AVP striding among the cubicles, unable to hide his disdain for the grunts who lacked the education and connections to rise higher.

Then Phil was told he had to work alongside those grunts, and his orderly world tilted, his career path jolting out of sight. Now he has that look on his face again, as if he's just discovered that not only is he condemned to purgatory with the office drones, but the entire upper-management structure has changed, his connections disappearing . . . and with them, his chance for escape.

"Phil?" I say. "Is there a problem with the council?"

He gives his head a sharp shake, coming back to himself. "Of course not. They need to find a temporary replacement for me, which is understandably not easy."

Dalton snorts at that.

Phil gives him a hard look. "I mean given the security clearance required, Sheriff. In the meantime, someone from the board will be speaking to you."

"The board of directors?" I say.

"Yes. I don't deal with them, so I'm not familiar with this person."

"Did you get a name?"

"No." A long pause. "She didn't give me one. I have also been told it's a private audience. I cannot stay."

"Huh," Dalton says. "Well, that's a problem."

"I'm sure you can manage without me." Phil's tone is cool, but I hear the hurt—and the worry—in it.

Dalton continues, "I mean it's a problem if you don't know this woman . . . who won't give her name and doesn't want you listening to the call."

"Any chance the communication system has been hacked?" I ask.

"She provided all the necessary credentials. The call is legitimate. It is just . . . not our standard operating procedure."

That's one way of putting it.

FIFTEEN

We're at Val's old house. We've told Phil he can move in—he was originally in the fortified box we constructed for Brady. His suitcase sits by the front door. One latch is undone, suggesting he's been using it but keeps it there, like that AVP sentenced to a cubicle, his briefcase ready to grab as soon as his superiors realize they've made a terrible mistake.

The house seems ready for a new occupant, with not so much as a piece of art on the walls. That's because Val never truly moved in herself. Three years in Rockton, and the only personal touch she added was small shelf of journals. I take one down, and with no small trepidation I crack it open. I know now what Val thought of us, and I'm not sure I care to see the extent of her contempt. Within these journals, though, I might find insight into a mind I can't quite fathom.

And I do. Because they aren't journals at all. They're filled with algebraic equations. I remember seeing her doing that once. She'd said something about trying to solve a problem. Later, I learned she'd been a mathematician. Still, I expected that at least some of these notebooks would contain her thoughts, her musings, her words. They do not. I flip through all four to find only numbers and symbols.

Trying to solve a problem of her own.

You never found it, did you, Val?

And neither will I. There is no solution to the problem of Val Zapata. Certainly not in these books.

Or maybe there is, indirectly. These books speak of an obsession. One that is meaningless up here. Solving a math problem wouldn't have set her free. Nor would it have improved her life. It was a distraction. Expending energy better directed toward getting outside these walls and engaging the world. But that wasn't her way. Never had been. And so she worked through a math problem, filling books with her computations, all that effort about to be consigned to flames, recycled as fire starter.

"Casey?" Dalton says, his voice soft.

I nod and walk to the satellite receiver. Phil has it set to the proper station. I press the call button to let our mystery board member know we've arrived.

A woman's voice comes on with "Hello?" as if she's answering the phone.

"Detective Butler and Sheriff Dalton," I say.

"You're alone?"

"We are."

"Before we start," Dalton cuts in. "I don't like this. I don't know you. Phil doesn't know you. You're a faceless voice on a radio, telling us you're a member of the board of directors. So tell me, who am I?"

A dry chuckle. "That sounds like an existential question, Eric. I have the feeling, though, that you know exactly who you are. On a purely biographical level, you are Eric Dalton. Formerly Eric O'Keefe. Or Eric Mulligan, if your parents gave you your father's name. I'll go with the matrilineal O'Keefe."

Dalton goes still. Very still. Panic touches his eyes, and I realize he's never known his parents' surnames. Now a stranger is telling him, and that is humiliating. This woman joked that Dalton knows exactly who he is. Yes, he does, in the sense that he knows his place in the world and has a better grasp of his strengths and weaknesses than most people twice his age. But knowing who he is on a familial level, the one that we take for granted? That is entirely different.

The woman continues, her voice calm, as if not realizing she's telling him anything he doesn't already know. "Your parents were Amy O'Keefe and Steven Mulligan. Your dad came to Rockton as a newly minted police officer who'd tried to expose corruption in his force and ended up on the wrong side of some very dangerous people. Your mother had arrived two years previously, a master's student fleeing the unwanted and dangerous attentions of her thesis advisor."

Dalton's eyes are shut, tightly shut, and he looks queasy, as if he wants to tell her to stop, just stop. This is all new to him and it's too much, hearing it calmly recited. He wants to tell her to stop, yet he doesn't dare . . . because he *doesn't* want her to stop. These are tidbits he's secretly longed for. I opened Val's notebook hoping for insight into her, but that's mere curiosity. This is vital information. It is the truth of where Dalton comes from, of who he is on another level.

"Your mother was due to leave six months after your father arrived. By then, the young couple were deeply in love, and they applied for an extension on her stay. When it was denied, they gathered supplies and headed into the forest. You were born two years later. When you were nine, the Daltons found you in the forest and took you in."

Dalton's cheek twitches. He's holding back words. The ones that say the Daltons did not take him *in*. They just took him.

The woman continues. "Gene Dalton said you were filthy, un-kempt. According to the town doctor, you were severely malnour-ished."

Dalton's mouth opens now, his eyes flashing. He pulls back then, his jaw snapping shut, gaze still simmering.

"I don't know if that's true," she says. "At the time, I questioned it. I wanted to speak to you personally. I was overruled, as I was when I questioned the council's decision not to extend your mother's stay. As the sole woman remaining on the board, I was often accused of sentimentality."

"I was fine," Dalton says, and he speaks through his teeth, as if he's struggling against saying words that cannot be kept in. "When they found me, I was fine."

"I feared that," she says. "But Gene Dalton was insistent that he'd rescued you from terrible conditions. His wife begged to be allowed

to keep you. It was . . . I will say only that Gene Dalton was an excellent sheriff, and even I agreed that Rockton desperately needed
him. The Daltons had lost a child shortly before they arrived and . . .
We let them keep you, Eric, and we stifled our doubts in return for
Gene's pledge to stay in Rockton until you were grown. That was
necessary—you couldn't be allowed to leave until you were old
enough to understand that you had to keep Rockton's secrets. As it
turns out, you wanting to leave wasn't an issue."

There's a pause. Then, "I'm sorry. I'm making light, and this isn't
a light situation. It's an awkward one, and any apology I can offer isn't
enough. The point is that I know you, Eric. I have known you since
you arrived in Rockton. I knew your parents since *they* arrived. If you
want further proof, test me. Ask me what Rockton looks like. Where
to find the nearest stream or lake in any direction. Ask me what it
smells like in the spring, after the ice melts. Ask me what it sounds
like at night, when the wolves sing. It may have been fifty years since
I lived there, but I still wake up smelling that, hearing that, and when
I don't look out my window to see evergreens, I feel as if I have lost
something. Something I gave up when it seemed convenient to do
so. There were so many other important things to be done . . . and
now I can barely remember what those were, and why they were so
important."

"You lived in Rockton?" I say.

"I was one of the pioneers."

"The founders?"

A light laugh. "No, I'm not that old. Close, though. Rockton had
been operating for about ten years when I arrived with my husband.
We were newlyweds. Young and idealistic. We'd made some rather
foolish political choices, and his parents sent us to Rockton before
we landed in jail. We lived in what is now the main kitchen. There
wasn't a need for such a thing in our time, with barely thirty residents. We stayed for eight years. Gave birth to our son and daughter,
and then returned home."

"And now you're on the board of directors?"

"We *were* the board, at one time. My husband, myself, and another couple—friends we made in Rockton. When we came home, my husband returned to his family business. A very prosperous business. His friend also came from money, as they say. When Rockton over-expanded and needed investors, we offered. My in-laws saved our lives by sending us to Rockton, and the town itself saved us too, giving us a fresh outlook that we were able to bring home. The board has grown, obviously." She goes quiet for a moment. "It has retracted, too. My husband is gone, as is one of the dear friends who founded it with us. The other is . . . unable to perform his duties. Dementia. Which means, of the original four, only I remain. There are several newer members, too, who joined as former Rockton refugees. Fellow idealists. And then there are the rest."

"The investors."

"Yes, and if you're hoping for tales told out of school, you have the wrong woman. I know neither of you is particularly fond of anyone on this end of the receiver. I will not defend them. Nor will I con-demn. I am here to mediate the current situation. After the upheaval with Val and Phil—and the situation with Oliver Brady—I have used what little power I retain to grab the microphone, so to speak. I will be clear. My job here is to resolve the current situation, not to inter-fere with the town's management. That would be beyond the limits of what I'm permitted to do in this capacity."

She's warning us that she doesn't dare overstep her bounds. That might be true. Or it might be a convenient way to fend off complaints. It doesn't matter. We aren't looking for someone to complain to. We wouldn't trust anyone who offered to listen.

"What can we call you?" I ask.

"Émilie," she says, giving it a French pronunciation, though I don't detect an accent in her voice. "That is my name, and that is what you may use. Now, the situation at hand . . ."

"Mark Garcia is dead," I say. "We just aren't letting residents know that yet."

"I see . . ."

"I don't know how much Phil told you. Eric and I found Garcia. He'd apparently fallen into a crevice after being attacked by wolves."

"Wolves? That's never happened before, has it?"

"No, and it still hasn't. Garcia lied. The alleged bite marks don't correspond to a wolf attack. They were shallow puncture wounds, which he made out to be much more serious, as he did with his supposed injuries from falling into that crevice. We believe he heard us talking—we were with Tyrone Cypher, whose voice carries."

She chuckles. "That is putting it mildly. I remember Tyrone. I heard you'd made contact with him recently."

"We have, and we're using him for tracking. Anyway, we believe Garcia heard us, lowered himself into the crevice, and made the wounds himself, so he could be brought back to Rockton as a patient, giving him the chance to escape the infirmary and grab his fugitive."

"Clever . . ."

"He'd've even been more clever if it didn't get him killed," Dalton mutters.

Émilie chuckles. "True. So from what Phil told me, as you were returning Garcia to town, he was shot by a sniper."

"Not a sniper," I say. "Just a person with a gun, hiding in the bushes. Garcia was shot twice. The first wouldn't likely have been fatal—it was poorly aimed. The second was the lucky shot—lucky for the shooter, that is. Garcia survived until we got him to the clinic. I could tell he wouldn't survive much longer, so I shut down access to the clinic. He died shortly after. Only Eric, Deputy Anders, and my sister know that. Oh, and Kenny will—we needed to move him. Otherwise, we're telling people that Garcia slipped into a coma without revealing his target. We're hoping whoever shot him will come back to finish the job before he wakes up."

"Excellent. You have the situation under control."

"Yeah," Dalton drawls. "A federal marshal died retrieving a fugitive from Rockton. That is *not* a situation under control."

"Our immediate concern is finding Garcia's killer," I say. "But the larger issue—the one that we'll need the council for—is figuring out how serious this leak is. First, we must determine whether or not

Garcia was actually a US marshal. I doubt it, given that he came here alone. My hope is that we have a bail bondsman or private bounty hunter who didn't file a trip plan with anyone down south."

There's a pause. Too long of a pause.

"He's a marshal, isn't he?" I say finally.

"We've found a Marshal Mark Garcia who works out of Spokane. I have his photo here. Getting it to you is obviously a problem. I can't determine height from the photograph, but he seems physically fit. He's forty-five. Dark eyes. Dark hair with some graying at the temples. His mother is Caucasian, father Hispanic. Does that match your intruder?"

"Yes, but I'd like more."

"So would we. You are correct that his behavior is inconsistent with what we'd expect from American federal law enforcement. The marshals do not operate like this, a lone wolf chasing down a fugitive. However, as I'm sure you're aware from your own law enforcement experience, Casey, how officers are *supposed* to behave is not always consistent with how they *do* behave. Even within a department, there can be variation in how 'standard' standard operating procedure really is. There can also be exceptions."

She's right, of course. It only takes one superior officer to sign off on something like this, for whatever reason. Maybe Garcia's partner was unavailable. Or his partner was supposed to join him later. Or, simply, Mark Garcia was a pain in the ass to work with, and his superiors gave up on him. It's not supposed to happen. But it does. I'd gone out on cases without my usual partner for various reasons. I wouldn't fly into the Yukon wilderness alone, but I can't look at Garcia's situation and say it could never, ever happen.

"Then he's filed a flight plan," I say. "They're going to come looking for him."

"We hope not. Our hope is that he got a lead and chased it without pausing to follow proper procedure. That may be unlikely."

"It is."

"We know that, and so we're already pursuing other avenues. We have contacts within the USMS, as we do in most federal agencies. That has proved advantageous over the years, allowing us to ensure that we do not permit dangerous criminals into Rockton."

Dalton and I exchange a look at that.

Émilie continues. "We are, of course, very circumspect with those contacts. Which means we can't simply phone and ask if they're missing a marshal. But if this man is Marshal Mark Garcia, and he was working a case with a registered travel plan, then we have every hope of resolving the matter before it becomes a security threat."

"Resolve it how?" Dalton says. "Their marshal is dead."

"Which means, I fear, that our best hope of resolution punts the ball back into your court."

"Find his killer," I say. "Offer them that."

"Yes." She pauses. "And while your focus is, of course, on who killed Marshal Garcia, have you given any thought to how he found Rockton?"

"He said his target had talked to someone before coming to Rockton," I say. "Reassuring a loved one that they'd be safe. Garcia says he got enough to remind him of something he'd heard, about a town out here. Obviously, it's more complicated than that, given that he managed to find us."

"He followed the plane," Dalton says.

I glance over.

"He tracked the plane somehow," Dalton says. "That's the best I can come up with. He arrived the same day we flew back from Dawson. It doesn't seem likely to be coincidence."

"No, it doesn't," Émilie says. "Which leads me to make a very uncomfortable suggestion about a potential suspect."

"Who?" I ask.

"Your sister, April."

"What?" I laugh. "Uh, no. Trust me. There is no way in hell that my sister has attracted the notice of a Washington State marshal. Not as a fugitive, at least."

"Your sister attends regular conferences in the US. Including one last year in Seattle."

"Right. Because she's a very successful neuroscientist. She speaks at conferences and presents her papers."

"I'm not going to argue about this with you, Casey. I'm simply putting forward a theory. You went to get your sister's help, via a conference call. Instead, she offered to come with you. Shortly after she arrives, we have a marshal who apparently followed your plane here."

"But Garcia said he spoke to someone. A person connected to his fugitive. That can't be April. It doesn't fit."

"Because it was a lie. A deflection to keep you from guessing his target. Marshal Garcia's story contained no details, correct? Just a vague account of speaking to someone whose words reminded him of something he heard about a town out here."

My gut screams that she's wrong—she must be. But if we weren't discussing my sister, I'd have already jumped to this conclusion. Earlier, Anders said we need to consider everyone, and I agreed. I must always consider every possible suspect, whether it's a friend or my sister.

"But they saw each other," Dalton says. "Garcia knocked on April's door, and she answered. There wasn't any sign that he recognized her, right?"

I open my mouth to say, yes, he's correct. Then I mentally play back that moment and shake my head. "I'm not sure Garcia saw April. She came to the door while you two were brawling."

"But *she* would have seen *him*," Émilie says. "She might have recognized *him*."

Yes, she might have.

SIXTEEN

I find April tending to Kenny. He's awake but groggy. I speak to him for a moment and then take April into the next room. When the door shuts, I cross the floor, getting far from it, which unfortunately puts me next to Garcia's corpse.

"You know why Marshal Garcia was here, right?" I say.

"I know why that man was here." She nods at the body. "And I know he may be a marshal."

"It seems he is."

"Then I hope there are procedures for handling such a security breach, Casey. I came here to help you. I did not intend to get caught up in an international crisis."

"I—"

"If there's even a hint of that, I expect to be flown out immediately."

I study her expression. She looks pissed off. Worried, too? Frightened?

"Why?" I ask.

"Why would I not want to be here when a branch of the United States government descends on you for the murder of one of its officers?"

"You know why he was here, right?"

She flutters her hands and starts reorganizing implements. "Is this a test, Casey? Do you want me to pretend I don't know he was here chasing a fugitive? Pretend I don't realize not everyone in this town is here for an innocent reason?"

"No, I just want to know why *you* were in such a hurry to get here."

She looks up. "What?"

"You haven't seen or heard from me since last fall. I show up and ask to speak to you, and you treat me the way you did when I called last time—like I'm your kid sister who just keeps popping up, annoying you with petty demands. You wanted nothing to do with me . . . until you got a better sense of the situation. A sense that I was offering to take you someplace far away, someplace hidden. Then you jumped. Forget a conference call. Let's pack a bag and go."

She tries to answer, but I continue. "I should have questioned that. Years ago, you gave me shit for trying to surprise Mom and Dad with an anniversary family trip. You said six months' notice wasn't enough. You accused me of springing it on you at the last minute. That was your idea of spontaneity. So I should have known something was up when you dropped everything to come with me."

"Are you . . . ? Are you asking if this man came for *me*? Followed *me*?"

"Yes."

"If this is one of your very poor attempts at humor, Casey—"

"It's not. It's an honest question. You went from 'get away from me, Casey' to 'how soon can we leave' in ten seconds flat. The only way this guy could have shown up is if he followed us." I meet her gaze. "Did he follow us here, April?"

"You're serious. You honestly believe that I'm a fugitive wanted by the American government."

"I honestly believe that I don't know shit about you, big sister."

Her eyes narrow. We exchange a look that scorches between us, and when she speaks, she barely unhinges her jaw. "That is not *my* choice."

"Hell, yes, it is. You're the one—" I stop short. "The point is that

I do not know you nearly as well as I should. I do know that you make regular and frequent trips to the States."

"For medical conferences. For seminars. Dear God, I know you aren't a genius, but this is a new low, even for you."

"No."

"No, it's not?"

I advance on her. "No, you will not play this bullshit card with me, April. I'm not a child anymore. I'm not going to be humiliated into silence anymore, terrified that if I open my mouth, I'll only prove you and Mom and Dad were right, and it's a miracle I have the brain cells to spell my own name. I'm smart. I know I am. But more than that, I'm capable. I earned my job, and I'm good at it. That is the one thing even you can't make me doubt. I might only have one skill, one real talent, but this is it, and you're treading on my turf here, big sister, so tread carefully. Tread very carefully."

"I—"

"Let's rewind. Right now, I'm not Casey, your little sister making stupid accusations. I'm a detective questioning you in regards to a murder investigation."

She fixes a cold stare on me. "All right, *Detective*. Ask."

"What made you change your mind so quickly?"

It takes her at least sixty seconds to answer. When she does, her voice is as cold as her stare. "My little sister asked for my help."

"Oh, don't you—"

"You want to play this out, Casey? Then close your mouth and listen." She crosses her arms. "My sister took off last fall. Called with some rushed message about needing to go away, and said I might not hear from her for a couple of years. I thought she was just being her usual dramatic self."

"Dram—?" I stop and nod. "Sorry. Continue."

"The next thing I know, she's actually gone. Quit her job and left with her friend. Diana, who has never been anything but an albatross around Casey's neck. But no, Diana needs her, so Casey quits a very good job to move away with her. And what do I get? A twenty-second phone call. But that's my sister. She's careless, thoughtless, selfish, and reckless. Zero sense of responsibility. I should be used to it by now. But I'm not, and when her leaving hurt, it proved that I needed to sever that link, and if she ever came back, I was not giving her the power to hurt me again."

I can only stare at her. It's as if I really am hearing her talk about a third party, our nonexistent other sister.

She continues, "But when she asked me for something—the first time in her life she's ever asked me for anything—I saw the look on her face, and I saw how much she needed me. She needed help saving another person, and I was the one she came to. So I said yes. God help me, I said yes. And now I wish I hadn't."

"That is bullshit," I say. "Complete and total bullshit."

"Excuse me?"

I move toward her again. "Do you really think that'll work, April? Spin some bullshit story to make me feel terrible. Convince me that you came here for *me*? You really do think I'm an idiot."

Her voice rises. "Excuse me?"

"So I'm careless, thoughtless, selfish, reckless, and irresponsible? Is that the full list? Are you sure you don't want to add anything?"

Her mouth opens.

"You call me thoughtless and selfish . . . for giving up my job, my home, my life to help a friend escape her abusive ex. Careless? Irresponsible? I defy you to find someone else who would apply either of those words to me. Yes, I can be reckless. But never by endangering others. My brand of recklessness is doing stupid things like throwing a bear cub to avoid shooting its mother."

"You threw—?"

"Not important. The point, April, is that I call bullshit on your story, and I'd really think you'd have the *IQ* to come up with a better one."

"So you're not careless? Not thoughtless and selfish? What about the hell you put our parents through, always racing off, riding dirt bikes and skateboards? Even that dog of yours. You know how our parents felt about dogs, especially big ones. They've been gone five years, and you're still defying them."

I laugh. I have to. Her expression, though, is perfectly serious.

"I did normal kid stuff, April. Yes, Mom and Dad didn't want me to do those things, but I wasn't running wild, hot-wiring cars or selling drugs on the street corner."

"No, you just *dated* a drug dealer. Who left you to be beaten nearly to death."

"Are you saying *that* was my fault, April?"

She stiffens. "Of course not."

"No? Dad did. Mom did. Does that seem normal to you? Parents who stand beside the bedside of their comatose daughter and decide 'She deserved that'? Tell her so when she wakes up?"

"They didn't mean it. They were angry. Do you have any idea how scared they were? Mom never left your bedside. Did you know that?"

No, I didn't. All I remember is waking up and hearing her railing at me for being stupid, for dating a boy like Blaine, for fighting back against those thugs, for walking down a dark alley, for every little thing I'd done that landed me in that bed.

"I couldn't live the life they wanted for me," I say slowly. "That wasn't rebellion. It was just . . . living. I was never going to be the daughter they wanted. I didn't need to be. They had you."

"Exactly. You didn't need to be that daughter. I did. I followed every rule. I never caused them a moment's worry. I achieved everything they wanted. I was *perfect*. And they didn't care. All that mattered was you. All they cared about was you."

Tears well up in her eyes, and I stare. I am transported back to that hospital bed, to hearing my mother berate me for every mistake I made, while tears rolled down her cheeks. She railed at me, and she cried, and she told me never to do anything like that again, never to scare them like that again.

I had reached out and hugged her and told her not to worry. I'd be fine. I'd recover. I'd bounce back, like I always did. It was the first time I'd seen her cry. The first time I reached for a hug and got one. Mom had fallen against me as she sobbed. And over her shoulder, I saw April. Just standing there. Watching. And then turning and walking past Dad out the door. She left, and no one noticed.

I'm looking at my sister, and I don't know what to say. No, I do know. I could sympathize and commiserate . . . or I can be honest.

"That wasn't my experience, April," I say softly. "To me, there were three people in our family and one interloper. One cuckoo among the warblers. You were the one they were proud of. Their success story. I was the screwup. But, yes, I understand what you're saying. You gave them what they wanted, and that freed me to do my own thing. If they were disappointed in me, I knew they had you. They could take comfort in you. That placed a burden on you, and I'm sorry. I honestly never saw that. I was a kid. I was so much younger than you, and I don't think you ever realized that. To you, I was stupid and selfish and irresponsible. To me, I was the screwup little sister you wanted nothing to do with. I could never make you laugh. Never catch your interest. Never even make you smile. No matter how hard I tried."

Her cheeks go bright red, and I'm not sure why. Before she can speak, Kenny calls, "Uh, Dr. Butler?"

April ignores him and fidgets with the hem of her shirt.

"April?" I say. "That's you. It's Butler here, remember?"

"Dr. Butler?" Kenny calls again. "I, uh, spilled water on my legs and I . . . I can't feel it."

We look at each other and then jump up and hurry for the supply room.

SEVENTEEN

This is the first time Kenny has been awake enough to assess his condition. He's surfaced before this, dopey from the morphine, and April wanted to assess him, but I'd said no, hold off. I wanted him to be awake enough to understand the questions . . . and awake enough to be reassured if the answers were not what we all hoped for.

They are not.

Kenny has no feeling in his legs. No movement either. When he starts to panic, I begin the reassurances. Surgery went well. There's still swelling. It's too soon to tell.

April glowers at me. She wants me to prepare him for the worst. I will not. Anyone who has been shot in the back knows the worst scenario. Kenny might be the town carpenter, but down south, he'd been a high school math teacher. He is perfectly capable of reasoning through a problem on his own.

When April conducts her prick tests, I am vindicated. He has sensation. Not a normal degree, but when she pokes his legs enough, he feels it.

"So, that's good," he says.

When April opens her mouth, he says, "Yeah, Doc, I understand what I'm facing. Damage to the lumbar region. Not paralysis but nerve damage. Loss of sensation." He manages a strained chuckle. "Thankfully, I don't seem to have fully lost my sense of . . ." His cheeks flush. "Bladder and bowel control, I mean. That's a start. So what's the next step?"

"Letting the swelling subside and seeing where we stand," I say.

"Seeing if I *can* stand, you mean."

I pass him a smile. "You should be able to. You just might need help."

"Braces," he says. "Lots of rehabilitation. Possible permanent loss of some motor function."

I nod. "As soon as we see what's what, we can transfer you down south. The council would ensure you have access to full medical care and physiotherapy."

"And if I don't want that?"

"Don't want physio?"

"Don't want to leave."

"If Oliver Brady hadn't shown up, you'd be gone by now, Kenny," I say. "Your term ended. You were packed and ready to go."

"And if I've changed my mind? If I want to apply for an extension?"

"I don't believe this town is equipped to provide either medical care or rehabilitation," April says. "I could not, in good conscience, advise that you stay. Nor could I support such a course of action."

He looks at me. "Eric said I could get an extension. My carpentry skills plus my militia training meant I qualified to stay the full five years."

Yes, they had discussed it . . . before that bullet meant Kenny might not be such an asset to Rockton. That's what it came down to, as horrible as that sounded. We had no capacity to accommodate anyone with serious medical, psychological, or intellectual issues.

"Let's see how it goes," I say.

I leave April with Kenny. As soon as the initial stress of testing him— and talking to him—passes, it's obvious she wants me gone. I could hope, like with Phil, that airing our differences would lead to a break-through. But life doesn't always work like that.

We see others through a window fogged with condensation, catching only a warped and shadowed image and presenting the same. We squint to see through that condensation, but we use our fog, too. We hide behind it. Wiping it away lets us see clearly . . . and lets us be seen clearly.

For better or worse. I see my sister better now than I ever have, and I understand, too, that the damage goes both ways. The damage our parents did. The damage we did—however inadvertently—to one another. I can also see that it might not be the kind of damage we can ever repair. We are two people who wouldn't have had anything to do with each other if not for kinship. That isn't hatred or even dislike. It is a simple lack of common ground. I see my sister clearly now, and I still don't understand her, and I know she looks back at me and says the same.

I have not ruled April out as a suspect. That is painful to admit. I realize, too, that in saying that, I wipe away the condensation between myself and the world, and I expose myself for what I am. A detective first. And maybe, yes, a person second.

Nothing my sister has said clears her of the charges. She's given me no excuses, no explanations that I can rely on. I would love—*love*—to think she came to Rockton for me, but that is not the April I know, not the one I have ever known, and so I cannot trust even this new image I see. I cannot pretend to miss the blur of condensation lingering at the edges.

I spend the rest of the evening alibiing those I can. I've worked through the militia, dividing them into those with clear alibis and those without. The former will be given shifts guarding the clinic, and the latter will not. That's the only distinction we make for now.

Once the militia and patrol volunteers are covered, I move on to friends. That feels biased. Everyone is waiting for their chance to tell me where they were. Many have excellent alibis, having been at work with others when the shots rang out.

To begin with my friends smacks of favoritism. It's not. These are the people I rely on, the ones I ask for help and advice on a case. As Dalton says when we pause to share updates, "Gotta know who you can trust."

"In Rockton? That'd be you and . . ." I look around. "You."

He chuckles and kisses the top of my head. Then I continue on.

Nicole has an alibi—she was on patrol as part of the militia. So was Jen. Mathias was in the butcher shop serving two people when the shots fired. Diana and April had been in the clinic. The list goes on, those with—and without—alibis.

It's after eleven. Dalton is off putting out a fire. A figurative one, fortunately. But the fact that we're hunting a killer doesn't mean the town stops to let us investigate. While he's busy, I'm walking Storm and joining Nicole on patrol. Or that was the plan. I'm heading into the woods with her and one of the militia guys when Isabel strides from nowhere.

"Walking the pup?" she says.

"While patrolling."

"Excellent. I will join you." She falls in step, and I know that means she wants to talk, so I send Nicole and her militia partner the other way.

"So this is patrol?" Isabel says as we walk through the quiet woods, twilight just beginning to fall. "I'm disappointed. I should at least get to carry a gun."

"You should have brought yours."

Her brows lift. "I don't have a gun, Casey."

"Just checking."

She chuckles at that. "I know I'm on your suspect list. You unreasonably failed to accept my alibi."

"You were brewing beer. Alone."

"I always do it alone. And the beer should provide my alibi. If I left it at that stage to go shoot Garcia, I'd have had to throw out the brew and start over. I may be capable of shooting a man, but I'd never cut into my profits like that."

I shake my head.

"The question of who had a gun is the main one, isn't it, though?" she says. "You keep those tightly regulated."

"We'll know more when we get that bullet."

"So your sister hasn't dug it out of the corpse yet?"

I know better than to react. "For that, we'll require a corpse, and we aren't ready to write Marshal Garcia off prematurely."

She smiles. "Ah. Yes. Of course." She walks a few more steps and says, "It's actually your sister—not the case—that I wished to speak to you about. I believe she'd have an easier time in Rockton if others were aware of her condition."

"Condition?"

She studies me. "May I presume your sister has never been assessed for ASD?"

"ASD?"

"Autism spectrum disorder."

"April?" I laugh. "She has her quirks, but no. She's a freaking genius. Yes, people with autism can be gifted in some areas, but April was an A-plus student in *all* areas."

"Autism is a spectrum. There are so-called savants, gifted in one subject, such as math or art, but others can be like your sister, intellectually unimpaired. It's the social and affective areas where I see the signs. Has anyone ever described your sister as socially awkward?"

I tug Storm away from a deer dung pile. "Sure. She lives for her studies, her work. She's not a people person, so she lacks some . . . okay, *most* social skills."

"Has her demeanor been described as chilly? Unemotional? Detached?"

"Yes, but so has mine."

"You're reserved. There is an abundance of emotion there. You prefer not to show it, a stance I can understand. As women, over-expressiveness can be seen as a weakness. It seems proof we are not rational beings."

"But when we're *not* emotional, we're seen as cold bitches."

"The eternal struggle of a professional woman. You and I both deal with it by accepting 'cold bitch' as a sobriquet far more acceptable than 'hysterical bitch.' In your sister's case, though, I believe it isn't so much restraint as a restricted emotional range. Would I be wrong in that?"

I walk for a few paces before saying, "No."

"And her sense of humor? How would you describe that?"

"Uh, nonexistent."

"She doesn't make jokes."

I smile at the thought. "Definitely not."

"Does she get them? Understand them? She didn't seem to when I met her."

I remember all those times I tried so hard to amuse her. Other people would laugh. She just scrunched her brow and told me to stop being silly.

As a child, she might not have realized why I was being "silly," but at the age of thirty-seven, she could not fail to realize that she lacked a sense of humor. What would it be like, constantly knowing others found something funny and not understanding why? A good sense of humor is one of the traits we look for in others. Someone who doesn't understand jokes is dull, stuffy, boring . . .

"Did your parents ever have her assessed?" Isabel asks when I don't respond. "Did she ever see a psychologist?"

I shake my head. "I did. Well, a psychiatrist. My parents were concerned about my rebellious tendencies."

Isabel laughs. Then she sees my expression. "You're serious? Well, apparently the therapy worked."

"My parents' idea of rebellion was me refusing to follow some of a very, very long list of rules, like 'don't eat cookies before dinner.' After a few meetings the psychiatrist called in my parents for a family session."

"And they refused."

"No." I steer around a corner. "We did a couple. Dad didn't want to. He considered psychiatry junk science." I glance at her. "Sorry."

"Oh, I am well aware of the attitude. At one time, it led to a lovely little solution called lobotomies. Because carving out part of the brain is much simpler than talking about a patient's problems. So your parents did the family therapy, and I'm going to guess that the doctor suggested the problem might originate beyond you."

"She hinted at that, but she also thought I did have a real problem. I overheard her with my parents while I was in the waiting room with April. I didn't catch much of what the therapist said, but my father was furious. He'd brought me there for help, and now she was suggesting his child should be assessed for . . ." I break off. "Oh."

"Autism?" she says.

In a blink, I'm back there. April and me in that room, her deep in a book, as I paced the room, bored and restless.

I brought Casey here for help, and now you want my daughter assessed for autism? There is nothing wrong with her. She's brilliant, accomplished . . .

I remember how my heart swelled at those words. I wanted to run to the door and press my ear against it. My father called me brilliant. Accomplished. My therapist thought I had some kind of problem, and Dad was actually defending me.

That's the problem with you people, he continued. *If you can't find a problem, you make one up. I ask you to look for horses, and you go hunting unicorns. My daughter is fine. And we are done here.*

I remember April sighing and saying, "What have you done now, Casey?"

Even she'd presumed they were talking about me.

I look at Isabel. "It wasn't me. The doctor was talking about April."

"I suspect so. I also suspect she wasn't the only one to raise a flag. That does not mean your sister has ASD. Even if she does, she's as high functioning as they come. Intellectually, that is. Do you have any idea how she does socially? I know she isn't married. She said she wasn't living with anyone or seeing anyone. Is that an unusual situation?"

I shake my head. "She's busy."

"With work. Very, very busy. It makes an excellent excuse, and I suspect it's one you've given in the past yourself. I know Eric is the first man you've lived with. He might even be your first committed relationship since you were a teenager. But that, I believe, is learned experience rather than natural inclination. As for being too busy to have a relationship, that is complete nonsense. I doubt you've ever been busier in your life. A good partner is an asset—moral support, help at home, easy access to sex."

I snort at the last.

"Oh, that's as important as the rest," Isabel says. "We just don't like to admit it. Good girls don't care about such things."

"Then I was never a good girl."

"Nor was I. Thank God." She pauses to skirt a spiderweb. "On that topic, I shouldn't presume your sister would be interested in *men.* Or that she has any interest in sex at all. Is there a chance she's asexual?"

"I-I don't know."

I assumed April was straight because she dated guys in high school, but I realize now it's just a presumption, my mind settling on the default. Since high school, I haven't heard her talk about dating, and I've learned not to ask about my sister's life.

"It's not important," Isabel says. "What matters is opening your mind to the possibility. If you or I are rude or abrasive, it's because we wish to be. With April, it might not be a choice, and it could help *you* to remember that. At the very least, that might help you survive the weekend."

"We talked earlier. Had a bit of a blowout actually. She—"

My arm flies up to stop Isabel as I spot a figure in the woods. It's Artie, the guy who'd been so eager to give his alibi at the town meeting. I never did get one from him—he vanished when we insisted on two-person alibis. Now he's hovering behind the clinic, watching the guards.

EIGHTEEN

I mentally race through what I know about Artie. He's in his fourth year here, and Dalton is pissy about that. Residents get a minimum of two years, maximum five. Other than Dalton, the only person who's been here longer is Isabel. In her case I'm certain she's blackmailing the council with tidbits from her bag of secrets, gathered from years as the local bar-and-brothel owner. Mathias is coming up on five years and has expressed an interest in staying. Again, the council may agree out of self-preservation—I'm sure Mathias has filled his own treasure chest of secrets.

Getting past five years is damned near impossible. Getting beyond the minimum currently only requires you pull your weight and don't give us trouble.

Artie did not qualify for an extension. He's gone through seven positions since he got here. I'm not even sure what he does now. While he isn't a troublemaker, he's constantly whining and complaining, and honestly, I think Dalton *prefers* the troublemakers.

So why is Artie now in his fourth year at Rockton? When other residents complain about Artie's extensions, Dalton says, "I have no fucking idea." In private, he suspects that Artie is one of our white-collar criminals and he's buying his longer stay.

I'm surprised to see Artie staking out the clinic. I can't imagine him shooting Garcia. But I've learned that in Rockton those assessments are bullshit. Maybe they're bullshit everywhere. As a homicide cop, I never actually knew the people I arrested. Yet even down south, how many times were a killer's friends and coworkers stunned? How many offered to be character witnesses, convinced that the police had made a horrible mistake?

As Artie watches the clinic, I motion for Isabel to take Storm and retreat the way we'd come. I slip through the trees until I emerge two houses down from the clinic. Then I loop along the street and through the clinic front door, after briefly speaking to Sam, who's stationed there.

Diana is inside, watching over Kenny. I talk to her. Then I grab the radio we left in the clinic and head out back, where one of the militia stands guard. As I walk out, I'm talking into the radio.

"He's out here. You want me to send him over?"

Pause.

"Sam's on the front door. That's covered. Diana's looking after Kenny and Garcia, but Kenny's fast asleep. I'll send both and cover nursing and back-door duty myself."

Pause.

"Got it. They're on the way."

I send the back-door militia guard inside, murmuring, "Talk to Diana." He doesn't question. A minute later, they're on the front porch, telling Sam that they need to go handle something for Dalton. Then their footsteps retreat along the hard-packed dirt road. Five minutes later, my radio beeps with an incoming call. I answer, keeping it close to my ear so Artie won't hear.

"I can't find Eric or Will," Diana says. "I'm using the radio at the station."

Shit. That's not ideal.

"Okay," I say, and when I speak, I do it loud enough so Artie *does* hear my side of the conversation, "it's quiet here. I really can't imagine the shooter would dare try again. Between you and me, Will, I think Eric's overreacting."

"Eric's *always* overreacting," Diana says. "Sadly, he usually has good reason. And I can't believe I admitted that."

"Sure," I say. "Give me five minutes, and I'll be there. Sam's got the front door. Good enough. Just don't tell Eric."

"I wish I *could* tell Eric this plan of yours," Diana mutters. "You're going to handle it on your own, aren't you?"

I laugh. "Okay, sure. I'll be right there."

"And I'm going to find Eric or Will," Diana says. "Hold on, okay. Don't try this without— Oh, hell, why do I bother? Just be careful, Case, okay?"

I sign off and head inside. I walk through and out the front door, where I speak to Sam. He takes off across the road, giving the sound effects I need—those running footfalls.

I slip back into the clinic. Then I hide in the room with Garcia's body, crouched behind a chest of instruments. Yes, that feels ridiculous, but it's a small room, and I don't have a lot of options. A moment later, Artie tries the door. I locked it, but I didn't pull it shut all the way, and there's a sharp intake of breath as he discovers it isn't actually closed.

Artie slips inside and shuts the door behind him. He looks around and sees the partly open door into Kenny's room. He creeps to it and peers through the gap. Then he pulls the door shut. A moment's pause as his gaze sweeps the tiny exam room. There's moonlight coming through the window, and thankfully he decides that's enough and doesn't light the lantern I just extinguished on the counter.

Artie looks down at Garcia's still form. The marshal's eyes are shut, the sheet pulled to his chin. An IV drip is attached to his hand. He looks like he's sleeping, and from here I see nothing to destroy the illusion. April even left an open bottle of disinfectant to cover any odor of decomp. Artie certainly seems fooled. He's not paying close attention to Garcia, just gazing at his body, as if trying to drum up the courage to act.

He watches Garcia for at least thirty seconds. Then he glances at the back door. Garcia. Door. Artie marches toward the door and grasps the handle. Damn it. He's changed his mind, and he's about to leave. I'm ready to step out and confront him before he goes. But then he releases the knob and moves into the room again.

His shoulders straighten, and his gaze sweeps the room. It stops on a pillow left on a chair. That is not accidental. This room has been staged. A pillow on the chair. A scalpel left on the tray. Even a bottle marked MORPHINE with a needle beside it. So many ways to kill a man, should you have forgotten to bring a tool. I'm helpful that way.

Artie picks up the pillow. He steps beside Garcia. His Adam's apple bobs. Then he lowers the pillow . . . and sees me, crouched in my imperfect hiding spot.

I straighten. "Okay, Artie, put down the pillow."

He lunges for the scalpel. I'm already coming at him, and when he sees he's not going to make it, he knocks the tray instead. The scalpel skates across the floor. He dives, grabs it, and rolls onto his back, brandishing the tiny blade . . . to see me calmly holding my gun on him.

"Go ahead," I say. "It's better than the pillow. Take your shot. I'll take mine."

He whips the scalpel. It bounces off my jeans as he scrambles for the door. He grabs the knob, twists, and—

"You need to unlock it first," I say.

He goes to do that, but I'm already on him. I've holstered my gun, and when he reaches for the lock, I grab his arm and throw him to the floor. Behind me, I hear a snicker, and I glance over to see Sam watching the show.

"I'd have helped," Sam says. "But I figured I'd just get in the way."

"Good call."

I wrench Artie's arm, pulling him to his feet just as footsteps sound on the front porch. Dalton runs in.

"It's under control," I say.

"So I see."

"He threw a scalpel at me," I say.

"I'll add that to the charges." He walks over and takes Artie. "Arthur Grant, you're under arrest for the murder of Mark Garcia."

"What? No. I never—" Artie twists to face me. "Casey, tell him. I never used the pillow."

"Only because you saw me."

"I *wouldn't* have used it, and you can't prove otherwise. Even if you try, that's *attempted* murder."

"Nope," I say. "He's dead."

"He can't be. That pillow never touched him."

"Your bullets did. That's the murder you're being charged with, Artie. The man you just tried to kill? He's already dead."

"I didn't do it," Artie whines as Dalton strong-arms him into the station.

"Here's a thought," I say. "Surprise us. Upend our expectations. Stand tall and proud and say, 'Yes, I did it and by God, I'd do it again if I could.' If you really, really must proclaim your innocence, just don't whine about it, okay? The whining really gets on our nerves."

Artie gapes at me. Then he says, "You—you aren't supposed to talk to me like that. I have rights."

"No and no," I say. "You signed off on those rights when you came up here. Literally signed them away, in return for safety. And while down south I wasn't supposed to talk to suspects like this, I sure as hell wanted to. Up here . . ." I glance at Dalton. "May I speak to him like this, sir?"

"Fuck, yeah. I'm sick of his complaining too. Four years, Artie, and I don't think I've heard you say a sentence without whining it. I'm beginning to suspect it's a speech impediment."

Artie straightens. "Fuck you, asshole."

"Nope, apparently not a speech impediment. Good thing, 'cause I'd have had to apologize if it was, and I might even have felt bad. Truth is, you're just a whiny little shit. Now you're a whiny little shit murderer. Not sure if that's a step up or down."

Dalton pushes Artie into a chair, and I secure his hands. Artie's cursing the whole time. We ignore him until I'm done.

Then he says, "I have an alibi."

"Yeah, heard that one," Dalton says. "Also noticed you didn't stick around when we started *asking* for the alibis."

"Because you needed two witnesses, and I only had one. I was waiting my turn. I was doing what you told me to, asshole." Artie looks at me. "At the time of the shooting, I was with Mindy. I had . . . arranged for her company."

Mindy is one of Isabel's "girls." She's relatively new to Rockton, and she came after being a sex worker down south, where she saw a crime that put her in witness protection . . . which did not protect her as well as it should. When she came up here, she happily resumed her former occupation for extra credits. She was the idealized version of prostitution—a healthy and capable woman who said "my body, my choice."

"At the moment the shots were fired . . ." I prompt.

He meets my gaze with a smirk. "I was firing my own. Just ask Mindy. She made a joke about it. Fireworks and all that."

I will check with Mindy, obviously. There's a tendency to think that a woman who'd sell her body might be equally willing to sell her integrity, but that's bullshit. I'm sure many people in town would sell an alibi—or trade one—which is why I'd asked for doubles.

"So you're claiming you didn't shoot Marshal Garcia," I say.

"Uh, yeah." He rolls his eyes, confidence soaring.

"Then why did you just try to murder him?"

"I wasn't—"

"Yeah," Dalton says. "You were just giving him a pillow. Making him comfortable. The problem with that? Most of us prefer the pillow *under* our heads."

"You tried to murder Marshal Garcia," I say. "I saw it. The question is what we tell the council. What we recommend to them. Do we say you're a cold-blooded murderer? Or do we plead extenuating circumstances and ask for leniency? Ask them to let you stay. Because that's the fate you face. Being forced out of Rockton. Given all your extensions, I get the impression you don't want that."

"I wouldn't have gone through with it."

"Don't care," Dalton says. "What matters is what Casey saw."

"You wanted to stop Marshal Garcia from waking up," I say. "You were afraid of what he'd say when he did. Which means you thought you were his target. There's a US federal warrant out on you—"

"Hell, no. I'm Canadian."

"Yeah," Dalton says. "That doesn't actually matter. If you committed your crimes in the United States—"

"I didn't commit any crimes. I'm the victim here. I heard people saying he's not a real marshal. I mean, come on. I've only ever seen them on TV, and I know one guy isn't going to come into the Yukon wilderness chasing a fugitive. He was with one of those drug cartels."

"You stole money from a drug cartel?" I say.

"I didn't steal anything. Are you listening to me? I'm the victim here."

"The victim who bought his way into Rockton," Dalton says. "Who is buying his extensions. You don't get that kind of cash working as . . . a social worker, wasn't it?"

"I didn't steal that money."

"So a drug cartel gifted it to you?" I say.

"Yes, actually. In payment for services rendered."

"You worked for a drug cartel."

His nose screws up. "Of course not. Like I said, I'm not a criminal."

"So they paid you to keep quiet about something. A client came to you with information, and you extor—convinced a cartel to pay you not to reveal that information to the police."

"Believe me, my 'clients' would never have information worth that sort of payoff. Bunch of deadbeat addicts, never worked a day in their lives. You haven't heard whining until you've sat in my chair. I put myself through school, all the way to a *master's* degree, and where did it get me? A shit-paying job listening to losers."

"If you wanted a lucrative career, social work may not have been the way to go."

He scowls. "I planned to be a psychologist, like Miss Holier-than-Thou Whoremistress Isabel. But I got fucked over. Couldn't get into grad school, because I'm a white male."

"Uh-huh."

"So I went into social work, thinking I'd get my psych doctorate once I had some work experience, but that never happened. So I was stuck listening to druggie losers all day. That's when I hit on a plan to make some extra cash. I started getting details from my clients and going after their suppliers. Cutting my own deals. Five grand here, ten there . . . It adds up. I made a better detective than you, Casey. I climbed higher and higher up the food chain until I was trading serious info for serious cash."

"Until you climbed *too* high and attracted the attention of the wrong people. A cartel."

"Apparently. So I ran, and now they've found me. Obviously."

"Why 'obviously'? What made you think Garcia was after you?"

He looks at me like I'm a moron. When I don't react, he taps his cheek.

"You recognized him?" I say.

"Exactly how many Mexican marshals do you think are out there? Obviously he's with a cartel."

I stare at him. Then I turn to Dalton. "Better let Phil know we're shipping Artie home."

"What?" Artie says. "You said if I had an excuse—"

"You don't," Dalton says. "We'll verify your alibi, and then you're gone."

NINETEEN

I let Petra out of the cell. I have to. Last week we doubled our secured space by constructing long-term lodgings for Brady. Now we've
got Roy in there and Petra in here, and we need someplace to stash
Artie.

Petra's incarceration has served its purpose. The council has been
advised that we've charged her with the murder of Oliver Brady. And
they've said nothing. Phil desperately wanted to talk to us about that,
so I'm presuming he notified them, but Émilie didn't comment on the
situation. I'm not sure what to make of that. At this point, I no longer care. I'm back-burnering this murder to solve one where I don't
know whodunit.

"So this is like . . . bail?" Petra says when I tell her she's free to go.

"We've been told to release you," I say.

"By who?" She gives a soft laugh. "Nice try, Case, but no one said
to let me go. You need the cell space, and you know I'm no danger
to you or anyone here."

I wave for her to leave.

"I mean that," she says. "I'm here to help. I'm on your side."

"Good night, Petra."

"Well, I suppose I should thank you for locking me up. Otherwise, you'd be accusing me of shooting this marshal guy. Someone did you a favor there, too, from what I hear."

"Yeah, murdering an on-duty US marshal? I can't see how that could ever turn out badly for us."

"The council will take care of it."

"Like they took care of Oliver Brady?"

She says nothing.

"You know what I wish?" I say. "I wish people would stop doing us favors."

I escort her out the door before she can answer.

No one has "done us a favor" here, and I spend far too much time seething over Petra's words. A dead marshal is serious trouble. Even if it wasn't, it's wrong. This wasn't Oliver Brady. It wasn't Val Zapata. It wasn't even my ex, Blaine, who, whatever his mistakes, did not deserve that bullet. On a scale of deservedness, though, the murder of Mark Garcia ranks far below even Blaine. This was a US marshal. An officer of the law doing his damn job, and if the execution of that job proved inconvenient to us, too bad. We could have dealt with it once we'd stopped butting heads and come to a place where we could negotiate.

Yes, Garcia was a pain in the ass. Yes, he threatened our security here. Yes, he tried to trick us with his "attacked by wolves" crap. But Dalton saw through that. We'd have brought Garcia back, gotten him secured in Rockton, and then thwarted his plan to sneak out and find his suspect.

We'd have bested him, and he'd have thrown up his hands and said, "You win. Let's talk." That's not wishful thinking. I've known too many men like Garcia. His issue with us was a territorial pissing match. A battle of law enforcement wits. When we won, we'd have gotten our reasonable conversation and solved this. Now we can't. Now we are screwed, and for Petra to suggest—

That's my hurt feelings talking. I'm still smarting from her betrayal. More than smarting. Which means she has far too much power over me right now. When she leaves the station, I'm tempted to slip after her. See where she goes. But Petra's secrets are a matter for another time. Like she said, I know she didn't kill Garcia, being locked in the cell the entire time. So I can put her out of . . .

Am I *sure* she was in there the entire time?

The moment I think that, I want to dismiss it. Chalk it up to more hurt feelings. I'm angry with her, so I don't want her getting a pass on this. I want to go after her, for something, anything.

She was locked in a damn cell, Casey. No one has a better alibi than that.

Here's the problem, though. I am almost certain Petra works for the council. It's the only solution that makes sense. Someone sent her after Brady, and that someone also supplied her with a gun and a silencer. We don't have silencers here. There's no point. But when I think about the gun, I remember another one that went missing.

When someone shot Dalton in the arm, the gun came from our locker, which had stymied us. Only Dalton and Anders have keys. I'd asked whether the council might have a spare, and Dalton had allowed that it was possible. Considering that Val was the one firing that gun, we presumed I was right. But if Val had that key, might she also have one to the cell? If so, it'd be easy enough for Phil to slip it to Petra. No one would have been guarding her cell. It's locked. We don't need to watch over prisoners—we just make sure someone pops by regularly to see if they need anything.

The station door opens. Sam walks in.

"Sam," I say. "Do you know who was assigned to Petra earlier today? Around the time of the shooting?"

"Jen, I think. She went home an hour ago. She might still be up but . . ." He looks at the dark window, and I check my watch. 2:10 A.M.

"Okay," I say. "I'll talk to her tomorrow. Shouldn't you be done, too?"

"That's what I came to talk to you about. Paul was supposed to take over for me at one thirty. I figured he was just running late, but when I went by his apartment, no one answered. Do you know if he's been reassigned? I can't find Will to ask."

Anders is in charge of the militia scheduling. With so much going on, that schedule exists only in his head, subject to constant juggling as he makes sure everyone gets enough time off.

"I saw Paul heading home earlier this evening," I say. "I was busy gathering alibis, but I think he was grabbing a few hours of shut-eye before his next shift. Given how much you guys have been working, he's probably just overslept. Go on in and check."

"I would, but his door's locked."

I curse under my breath. "Right. Because I told everyone to keep them locked. Let me find Eric and grab the master key. You can call it a night. I'll get Paul up and on duty."

I get the skeleton key from Dalton. Paul lives on the second floor of a four-unit building. I climb the external staircase and head along the balcony to his apartment. His windows are dark. Everyone's are— blackout blinds must be pulled at sundown to minimize our glow to passing aircraft. Some light still seeps out at the edges when the oc-cupant has a light on. At this time of night, they're all dark, including Paul's.

I knock twice. Then I unlock the door and crack it open.

"Paul?"

No answer. As I slip inside, I do see a faint glow from the bed-room at the back. The door's shut, and I walk in, calling Paul as I go. I rap on the bedroom door. Still no answer.

"Paul?"

Knock. Call. Knock again. A light definitely shines from beneath the door. A wavering one. Has he fallen asleep with a candle going? I'd hate to report one of our key militia for what seems like a minor infraction. But it's not minor. Fire is our greatest threat, and while we allow candles, they're meant for winter, when it's dark by four in the afternoon. They aren't even supposed to be taken into a bedroom.

I'm tempted to leave. I know that's wrong. But it's two thirty in the morning, and I'm tired, and I do not want to chew out an overworked militia guy.

I try one last knock and call, in hopes he'll wake up and put out the candle himself.

He's not responding, though, so I take a deep breath and decide that if it is a candle I'll let him off with a warning. I'll also tell Dalton. I have to be careful with that. As the detective sharing the sheriff's bed, I need to tell him when I issue warnings for serious infractions. Otherwise, it'll look like I consider my authority equal to Dalton's.

I ease open the door. The first thing I see is that damn candle, flickering beside the bed. And then Paul himself, sound asleep in bed.

All the simmering frustration of the day ignites. I slam open the door and march in with, "Get your ass out of bed. Sam's been waiting for you to take his shift, and you're sleeping with a goddamn candle on."

Paul doesn't move. I pull up short, heart pounding. But then I see his chest rise and fall. I catch the faint wheeze of his breathing. I set my lantern on his nightstand and pinch out the candle. As I do, I spot the bottle. It's a glass pill bottle with a mailing label neatly affixed. On that label is Beth Lowry's careful script.

I lift the bottle. It's a prescription for a midlevel sleep aid. The date is two years ago, around the time Paul arrived. He must have had trouble sleeping then—not surprising given that he came at this time of year, when the sun only naps. He must have saved the pills to use as needed. That explains his deep slumber. I sigh. There's no point waking him. If he's this deeply asleep, he'll be in no shape to work.

I'm taking my lantern as I set down the pill bottle. As I do, I realize nothing jangles inside. The bottle is empty. The hairs on my neck rise, but I tell myself I'm overreacting. He used up his last ones. That's all. Still, I glance at Paul's sleeping form, and when I do, I spot two pills on the sheets . . . and a bubble of foam in one corner of his mouth.

TWENTY

I'm in the clinic. We've brought Paul there, which means we had to put Garcia's body on the floor so we'd have a bed for Paul. Dalton can't even fit in the damn examination room with us—there's no space with a corpse on the floor. In the supply room, Kenny's awake and asking what's going on, and I want to throw up my hands and walk out and clear my head. I haven't had more than a few hours' sleep in three days, and my brain is about to shut down from overload.

It doesn't, of course. We have a man who just attempted suicide. That's a problem that cannot wait until I get my shit together.

We pump Paul's stomach, and even that makes me feel like I've slid into some twilight zone nightmare. A few months ago, we had to pump Diana's stomach when she'd been drugged. We also did it with Brady, who poisoned himself. And before that, Anders had never even *assisted* in a stomach pumping in Rockton. It seems impossible that we'd be doing it for the third time in six months. The truth is that situations like this are contagious. Someone drugs Diana with sleeping pills . . . and then Val remembers that when she needs to get Brady out of the jail cell. And then, I suspect, Paul recalls both those cases when he decides to take his own life.

I remember standing at his bedside, ready to walk away. If I hadn't realized the bottle was empty? If I hadn't spotted the foam on his lips? I don't want to think about that. I'm just glad that I did.

I'm by Paul's bedside when he wakes. Dalton tried to get me to go home and sleep. I refused. That's not just guilt. It's the very real possibility—likelihood even—that guilt is what drove Paul to take those pills. Guilt over what he'd done. There's no other reason for him to decide this is the time to commit suicide. He tried to kill Garcia, and when he failed, instead of making a second attempt, he tried to take his own life before Garcia woke and named him.

I'm dozing there, in a chair. Dalton's asleep in the one beside me. We've moved Garcia's body into the front room. I know how callous that sounds, stashing his corpse here and there, but we've had no time to do anything else.

"C-Casey?"

Paul's groggy voice wakes me. I get to my feet and move to his bed. He's trying to prop himself up. He accidentally tugs against the IV line and follows it, blinking at the drip bag in confusion.

"Wh—where—what—?"

"Paul, I need to ask you a question."

I don't ask whether he feels up to answering. Down south, I'd have to do that. I'd need to read him his rights. I'd need to give him the option of not speaking without a lawyer present. None of that counts here. He's still dopey from the drugs, and he could very well say something that incriminates himself, and I am okay with that.

"Do you remember what happened?" I ask. "Do you remember taking the sleeping pills?"

His eyes half shut, shame darkening his face, telling me there's no chance someone force-fed those pills to him.

"You were attempting to take your own life, yes?" I say.

He nods.

"Because of something you'd done."

Another nod.

"Do you want to tell me about that?"

"He—the marshal. He's here for me. For what I did. It was a federal offense, and he's a federal agent."

"So you shot him."

Paul's eyes round. "What?"

"You're the one who answered the radio. You knew we were bringing him in, and he'd tell us it was you, so you shot him."

"N-no. *No.*" He pushes up onto his elbows. "At that time, I figured he'd already told you it was me. There was no point doing anything. Not that I would have anyway. When you called, I ran and got Will. Then I heard the marshal got shot and . . ." Paul swallows. "I'd be lying if I said I wasn't glad. But when you said he'd pull through, that gave me time to think about it. *Really* think about it. I realized I couldn't go back. I committed a federal offense, and then I fled the country. I was going to jail for a very long time. I . . . I couldn't do that. So I took the pills."

He goes quiet. I'm ready to ask something else when he blurts, "Can I speak to him?"

"Hmm?" I say, my mind elsewhere.

"The marshal. May I speak to him? Maybe if I do that—if I talk to him, if I explain—we can work something out. I know, I should have thought of that before I swallowed a bottle of pills, but I panicked. I didn't see any other option."

"What's he want you for?" Dalton's voice comes from behind me, and I turn to see him awake, straightening in his chair.

"Tell us about this federal offense you committed," Dalton says.

Dalton knows Paul's official story. He doesn't say that, though—he wants to hear it from Paul.

"It was a really stupid mistake," Paul says. "And it's a long story."

"From the beginning," Dalton says.

Paul nods. "It began on my lunch hour. I worked in Manhattan. Sales. Boring as hell, but it paid the bills. I was thirty-four. Divorced for a year. No kids. I was just kind of plodding along in life. Waiting for things to get better but not doing anything to make them better. I was coming back from lunch, alone, with my headphones on, when this girl falls right in front of me. I look up and see a guy coming at her. A scrawny kid, looked like he just crawled from an alley. I used to play quarterback in high school, kept it up with a few hours in the gym each week. So I fend him off. Turns out I was so lost in my music that I walked straight into the middle of a protest. It was Manhattan. Honestly, you learn to ignore them. Anyway, she was a protester, and that's why this neo-Nazi creep went after her. I stayed to make sure she got help. The next day, she called to thank me and asked me out for coffee. I said yes. Hell, yes."

He pauses and looks up at me. "Did I mention it's a long story?"

"Keep going," Dalton says.

"So, fast-forward a year. We've been dating, and I'm crazy about her. Sure, Cindy's too young for me—twenty-four—but I'm still smarting from my divorce, and this is the ego boost I need. She's cute and smart and sweet, and I'm smitten. She's also into social activism. *Really* into it. So I'm right in there with her. It's like when I met my wife, and she was a dog trainer, and all of a sudden, I was the biggest dog lover ever. And it wasn't as if Cindy and I had different political views in general. So I was right in there with her, protesting so much shit I had to set reminders for myself. Tuesday is animal rights, Saturday is pro-choice, and make sure I grab the right sign for each, 'cause screwing that up is really embarrassing."

He offers a weak smile. "I was an activist poseur. Stupid as hell, but it made her happy, and when Cindy was happy, I was happy."

"So what happened?" I ask.

"Déjà vu all over again, to quote . . ." He squeezes his eyes shut. "I don't even remember who said that. Sorry, I'm trying to play this cool, so maybe we can all forget I tried to kill myself tonight. That's just not . . ." He looks at me. "Does anyone else know about the overdose?"

"Will and my sister assisted us. Anyone else only knows it was a medical emergency."

"Could we not tell people? It's just . . . It's not the image . . ." He shakes his head. "Sorry, I'm supposed to be defending myself against attempted murder, not worrying what people will think of me."

"Paul?" Dalton says.

"Sorry, boss. So, déjà vu. A year later. Another protest. Another attack on Cindy. We're in there, shouting and whatever, and it's chaos.

I look over to see her go flying, just like that first day. I go off on the guy who did it, even more than I did the first time, because now this is my girlfriend he's attacking. I beat him until Cindy's friends pull me off. That's when I discover she wasn't attacked by another neo-Nazi asshole. It was a federal cop, who pushed her by accident. He got hit, and he stumbled into her. That's it. He had the jacket on, the one that said he was a cop, and I never noticed it. I just saw Cindy go flying. I beat the shit out of a federal officer. The moment I realized what I did, I made the next-biggest possible mistake. I bolted."

"You fled the scene," I say.

"Oh, yeah. Ran like the devil himself was on my heels. I walked five miles to our hotel room—we were in DC for the protest—and when I arrived, there were cops waiting. They grabbed Cindy and her friends, and someone gave me up. I saw the cops, and I got out of there. The group helped me. I don't know if that was the right move. I'm pretty sure it wasn't. But it's not like they were experts. I should have gotten a lawyer. Instead I panicked and ran. Someone connected to Cindy's group knew about Rockton, as a place for political asylum, and they figured I qualified. That's how I ended up here."

"And the officer?" I ask.

His brow furrows.

"Did you kill the guy?" Dalton says.

Paul's eyes widen. "No. I broke a couple of ribs and fractured his orbital socket or something like that. He made a full recovery and was back to work in a month." He hurries on. "Which doesn't diminish what I did. Jostling Cindy was unintentional. He was a federal officer doing his job keeping the peace, and I put him in the hospital. I know now I should have stayed and muddled through. Running made it worse. I became a federal fugitive."

He pushes up straighter in bed. "I didn't face the music three years ago, so I'm doing it now. Just let me talk to this marshal. I probably can't convince him to let me stay—not after all this—but I want him to know exactly what happened before he takes me. I want him to know I'm not some maniac who attacked a federal agent."

I glance at Dalton. He shakes his head.

"He's dead," I say. "The marshal . . . has succumbed to his injuries."

"What?"

I repeat it. It takes at least a minute for the news to penetrate. When it does, Paul hovers there, like he's waiting for more.

Then, slowly, he slumps onto the bed. When he speaks again, his voice is barely above a whisper. "I should be glad, shouldn't I? Not that he's dead, of course. He was just like that agent I beat up. A guy doing his job. But as shitty as that is, and as guilty as I'll feel, it means I'm safe. Except . . ."

He swallows, and he looks up at me. "I was kind of glad. Happy I'd been caught. Part of me always wanted to be. Right from the start. When I went back to the hotel and saw those cops, I wanted to turn myself in. I kept hoping someone would talk me into it, hoping Cindy would tell me she loved me and she'd see me through this and once it was over, we'd be together."

He gives a short laugh. "That was my fantasy. I'd made a mistake, but I'd redeem myself and win the girl. Instead, she told me I had to run, for the sake of the cause. She wished me all the best. A kiss-off. That's what it was. Thanks for saving me, Paul. Thanks for protecting me. Now get the hell away from me."

He shifts in the bed. "Today I had the chance to fix it. I panicked, like after I beat up that officer. That's why I took the pills. But when I woke up, I was relieved. Relieved that I was alive and relieved that I could turn myself in. I know that sounds crazy. But I just wanted to be caught. And now this poor guy is dead—because of me. And I get to go free. That's not fair. Not fair at all."

TWENTY-ONE

I'm behind the station with Dalton. Isabel and April came to take care of the patients, and we ended up here, on the back deck. Dalton takes my hand and sits, and he pulls me down with him. I'm sitting there, his arms around me as I lean back against his chest.

"That's what *you* felt like, isn't it?" he says.

I don't ask what he means. I know. He's asking if I wanted to be caught for the murder of Blaine Saratori. If, while I'd been unable to turn myself in, there'd been some part of me hoping I'd be found out. Hoping I'd face justice.

"Yes," I say.

Silence. I feel his heart thudding against my back.

Then he asks, "Do you still feel like that?"

"No."

He nods. I twist to face him and say it again, to be clear. He needs that. A part of Dalton will always be that boy taken from his parents. The boy who lost his family and came to Rockton, to a world where he loses everyone. Every person who comes into his life leaves again. While he's accepted that, he's not sure how to deal with actually wanting someone to stay.

We all learn that lesson, in our way. People enter our life, and whether or not they stay isn't really up to us. The uncertainty is so much easier to cope with if we just inoculate ourselves against it, as Dalton has. People come, and people go, and he's learned to enjoy what time he has with them, but he allows no one to be so important that he'll grieve their loss for long.

Now he has me, and he had to acknowledge this fear. The fear that I might go or that I might be taken from him. If I still feel like Paul—if I'm secretly hoping to be caught—might I decide to turn myself in someday? Is this just another of the endless ways he could lose me?

So I reassure him, and then I lean against him as his arms tighten around me.

"I remember when I met you," he says. "You thought you were in danger of being arrested, and how you still tried to cut a deal with me. If we took Diana, you'd stay behind."

"Because you didn't want me here."

"I didn't want you because you didn't want to come. I needed a detective who gave a damn."

"I did."

"You cared about your job, yeah. But up here your job is your life. You can't care about one and not the other. You do now. But if someone like Garcia came for you . . ."

I twist to look at him again. "I can't imagine that ever happening. It's been thirteen years, and no one's looking anymore. I was attacked because my boyfriend was a rich-brat student dealing drugs on someone else's turf. A few months later, Blaine was shot. The police figured it was the same guys, and my biggest worry, at the time, was that they'd catch them and they'd have alibis for Blaine. That never happened. It's a cold case that no one cares about."

He nods, but I can tell he's still worrying.

I continue. "When I thought Blaine's grandfather had tracked me down, yes, I was ready to accept my fate. I was also willing to come up here with Diana until you made it clear you didn't want me. If the council had let you take her and not me, I wouldn't have turned myself in, Eric. I still wasn't ready for that."

"The council didn't refuse your deal with Diana. I never asked them."

My brows lift. "What?"

He shrugs. "I didn't like your offer. Fucking martyrdom. I wanted you to fight. To tell me you'd be a damn fine detective if I let you come. When you tried to cut that deal, I wanted to take you up on it. But . . ."

"You decided to give me a chance?"

"No. I really needed a detective, and there wasn't much chance of me getting another one."

I thump back against his chest, laughing. "Fair enough. I can't imagine anyone will reopen my case, Eric. Even if they did, I'm here. But on the very, very slim chance that someone comes for me, I'm not going to put my hands behind my back for the cuffs. Nor am I going to swallow a bottle of sleeping pills."

"You think Garcia did come for Paul? It happened in Washington, and that's where Garcia's from."

"He's from Washington State, not the city."

Dalton pauses. "So what state is Washington *city* in?"

"None. I'll explain later. Garcia said his fugitive was dangerous. Someone who attacked a federal officer is dangerous . . . especially in the eyes of another federal officer. But Garcia made it sound like we were dealing with a homicidal maniac. That's not a guy who beats up an officer at a protest march. On the other hand, Garcia may have played up the crime to spook us into handing him his guy."

"So, no strong feeling either way?"

"Unfortunately, no." I ease off his lap and turn to face him. "Is Paul's story the one you know?"

"Yeah. It's true, too. When he wanted to join the militia, I looked it up. If he assaulted a federal agent, I had to be sure it went the way he said it did. I found the story online. No red flags there."

"Then whether or not Garcia came for Paul is a moot point. The problem is that Paul thought he did. He won't be the only one, either. Finding out who Garcia *did* come for doesn't necessarily solve his murder."

Which made our job a whole lot harder.

––––––––

I tell the town that Garcia is dead. I have to. If Paul's suicide had succeeded, his death would have been on me. My attempt to trap a killer
would have taken an innocent life.

Now I'm back at square one. I can't even narrow it down by looking at residents accused of US federal crimes. Yes, Dalton knows resident backstories, and he shares them with me on a need-to-know
basis only. In this case, I need to know. The problem is twofold. One,
the entry stories aren't necessarily true. Two, Artie tried to kill Garcia
thinking he was a cartel goon posing as a federal agent. The killer
could very well have mistaken Garcia for a hired killer or a bounty
hunter. Hell, at this point, we aren't even absolutely certain he's not.

I get some sleep. I have to. I'm running on fumes.

Dalton brings Storm home. We pull the blackout blinds and keep
the alarm off and crash into dreamless sleep.

Six hours later, Dalton comes downstairs to find me in my bra and
panties, stretched out on the bearskin rug, as I jot notes in my book,
Storm by my side. He walks past me without a word and bends in
front of the fire, which is down to smoldering ashes.

"Sorry," I say. "I forgot to stoke it."

"Kettle won't boil without fire," he says, nodding at the kettle I set
over the wood. He pulls the handle to bring the kettle in. As he hefts
it, he frowns. Then he tilts it. Nothing runs out.

"There *was* water," I say. "It must have boiled dry."

"Do I even want to ask how long you've been up?"

He shakes his head as he takes the kettle into the kitchen, and then
brings it back, hangs it, and relights the fire.

Dalton sits cross-legged beside me. He doesn't say a word. Just sits
and watches as I write. When I finish jotting a few notes, I glance up.
He's wearing only his boxers, and I tilt my head to admire the view
as my fingertips tickle his bare thigh.

"Don't start something you can't finish," he says.

I sigh and roll onto my back. "Sorry. Just . . ." I make a face. "Busy."

"Nah." He tucks a strand of hair behind my ear and taps my temple.
"Busy."

"Same thing."

"No." He shifts closer and leans over me. "Garcia is dead. His killer isn't going anywhere. Nor is that killer likely to be a danger to anyone else. You could sleep more. You just . . ." He taps my temple again. "Can't sleep more. Your brain's spinning like a clothes dryer."

I smile. "Clothes dryers don't actually spin very fast."

"Tornado then. I've never seen one of those either, but I *know* it's fast." He pauses. "I've used dryers in hotels. Just never paid any attention to how they work."

I laugh.

"What?" he says.

"The way you say that. As if you have inexcusably missed an opportunity by not observing the normal operating habits of clothes-drying machines. But yes, your point is taken. My brain's spinning. I did manage to sleep for a few hours. After that, I couldn't, and it made more sense to spew my thoughts on the page."

He looks at the open book. "Doesn't look spewed."

"That's because you arrived at the right time, as I'm organizing the mess into helpful categories and tables. You want to see spew?"

I leaf back and lift the book. It's an entire page of questions, almost all crossed out.

He leans closer. "Trying to narrow down the subpopulations of suspects."

"Yep, same damn thing I do every time. And the same damn thing that fails every time."

"It doesn't fail. It just doesn't work as neatly as it does down south. We're a unique situation up here."

I snort a laugh. "That's one way of putting it." I flip onto my stomach, and he stretches out beside me as I point to the list. "I initially tried to figure out who Garcia came for. That's when I was still half asleep and forgot it doesn't matter. So anything he may have told us about his target—which is precious little—is meaningless."

"Not meaningless. Just because his target may not be the killer doesn't mean I don't want to know who his target *was*."

"He didn't specify gender. Didn't specify how long the person had been here. He said the crime was violent, but as you pointed out, that might be bullshit. The point, however, is that the killer thought they were his target, which gives us a bit to go on. At first, I thought, 'Ah-ha, that means they're American!' But no, Artie isn't, and he thought *he* was the target. So, ultimately, we are left with knowing only that our killer has committed a crime that would warrant someone—US marshal or bounty hunter or hired killer—coming after them. I'll just say that I'm really glad Will and I are off the list, because otherwise, we both fit. So do about a dozen people in that little black book of yours, plus God knows how many whose real stories we don't know."

"Huh. So it's like one of those murders in the city where you find a body and don't have a line of suspects queued up behind it."

I knock my shoulder against his. "Yes, smart-ass." I move forward in the book. "Which is why I gave up trying to narrow my suspect pool and started compiling a list of physical evidence. First and fore-most is the bullet. We have a limited number of guns here and a limited number of people who have access to them. As soon as my sister digs out that bullet . . ." I catch his expression. "She already has, hasn't she?"

"Yeah. Last night. You were busy, so I handled it, and then after Paul, there wasn't a chance to talk. It's a nine-mil."

"Wait. What? The only person who carries that caliber is me. You were there. There's no way in hell I shot Garcia."

"There's another nine-mil in town. Just not one of ours."

"Who . . . ? Garcia. Right. He brought a nine-mil. It was in lockup." I see his expression again. "No, not in lockup. In our house."

"Yeah. When we let him go, I stashed it in the drawer, along with his sat phone. I meant to get it to the locker that night. Then he came back to town, banging on doors, and I got busy hunting him. Yester-day, I took the gun and the phone and put them into the locker. Which means, not only did I leave a gun out to be used in a crime, but I fucked up your scene by moving it."

"I forgot all about the gun myself," I say. "As for messing up the scene, your prints were already on the gun. You just added more, and you aren't a suspect anyway. Did you notice anything when you opened the drawer? Was the position changed?"

"The other day, I was just concerned with getting it out of sight. I didn't pay attention to how I put it into the drawer."

"So who knows it was in our house? Me, you . . . Oh, and Diana. Did you tell anyone else?"

He shakes his head. "I mentioned it to Will, when I took it to the locker, but that was after the shooting."

"So only Diana knew. She has a solid alibi. She was with Kenny and April in the clinic. She must have told someone the gun was there." I snap my book shut. "There. I have a lead."

When I get up, Dalton says, "You might want to dress first. Not that anyone would object to you walking around like that, but it's a little nippy out."

"Ha ha. I'm not *that* distracted."

As I head for the stairs, he says, "You want this coffee I'm making? I'd insist on breakfast too, but I know that'd be pushing it."

I pause. "Actually, now that I have a lead—and it's not going anywhere—yes, I'll take the coffee and the breakfast." I walk back over, eyeing him, still stretched out by the fire. "Anything else on offer?"

"You're heading this investigation. I play support staff. So just tell me what you need."

I grin. And then I do.

TWENTY-TWO

I'm on the case forty minutes later. I may have a lead, but it's not like I'm going to fritter my afternoon away, however much fun the frittering might be. I leave the house, rested, caffeinated, fed, and back on my game.

Diana works as a seamstress. Down south, she held a string of accounting jobs, the sort that come with interchangeable titles. There isn't much use for that here, so like many people, she's fallen back on hobby interests. She's always had an eye for fashion and used to make some of her own clothes. Up here, being able to repair or resize clothing is a valuable skill.

I find Diana working at home, sitting on her apartment balcony, sewing in the sunshine.

"I need to speak to you," I say as I climb the stairs.

"Nice to see you, too, Casey. Keeping busy, I see."

"You know what the great thing is about knowing a person for fifteen years, Di? Getting to skip the small talk when I *am* keeping busy. Like investigating a *murder*."

She nods and folds the jeans she'd been hemming. "You're right. Sorry. I just keep hoping we'll reach the point where you come over for something other than work."

"The way I see it, you're lucky I don't send Eric to interview you instead."

"That would require delegating. Not happening. Pull up a chair."

"Better if we take this inside."

She nods, gathers her sewing, and we go in. Diana's apartment is even smaller than Paul's. It's basic accommodation, where people have a choice between sharing a larger space or taking a bachelor apartment, which is the size of a hotel room with a kitchenette.

"Park yourself on the bed or the sofa," she says. "They're in the same room anyway."

"Hey, you always wanted to move to Vancouver. Think of this as practice for microapartments."

She snorts. "No kidding, huh."

I could also say it's far more comfortable lodgings than the jail cell she'd have gotten if she hadn't ended up in Rockton. But that'd take us places I don't want to go to with this conversation.

Contrary to her snark, there's more than a sofa and a bed. I lower myself into an armchair, and she perches on the sofa . . . which, to be fair, is really more of a love seat.

"Mark Garcia was shot with his own gun," I say.

"He . . . shot himself?"

"Eric took his weapon, remember?"

"Please tell me this story ends with our sheriff being the one who shot the marshal, and sadly, Eric will now be forced into exile, and you'll take over."

I just look at her.

She sighs and leans back. "Okay, I'm being bitchy. You're fond of the guy, and you don't need the extra work of being sheriff. It wasn't Eric who shot him, was it?"

"No, I was with Eric—and Garcia—at the time."

"Wait. So you're the sheriff's only alibi? This seems highly suspicious. I think we should investigate."

"I'm glad you find the situation amusing, Diana, but since I know you're not actually accusing Eric, I'd suggest you might want to take this a whole lot more seriously. Someone used Garcia's gun to shoot him. Three people knew we had that gun in our house. You, me, and Eric. Since Eric and I alibi ourselves out . . ."

She straightens. "What? Are you suggesting I shot him?"

"I'm just pointing out—"

"I have a double alibi. Your sister and Kenny. I was in the clinic when we heard the shots."

"There's actually been some question about that," I lie. "You might want to reconsider."

She sputters. "Question? What question? I was there. April, Kenny, and I discussed the sound. And why the hell would I kill this guy? You know what I did, Casey. I embezzled funds from my employer, and then Graham convinced me the cops were getting close and I had to run. He double-crossed me."

"Shocking."

She glowers. "Yes, you saw that coming. Maybe someday you and I will have a conversation about how your best friend could be such a flaming idiot. Or maybe now that you've actually fallen for a guy, you have some idea how that works."

I don't point out that Dalton has never lifted a hand against me, and if he ever did, I'd be gone forever. That's victim blaming. The truth is that I don't think I can ever understand how Diana could still love Graham after what he put her through. I simply have to accept that she did. Which doesn't ever excuse the rest. I don't care how much you love a man, you don't betray your best friend for him.

"Graham has the money," she continues. "I'm stuck up here for at least another year. A US marshal wouldn't be involved because it's not a US case, and Graham isn't going to send someone after me, because I'm no threat to him. Never was. I'm not you, as he reminded me, over and over again."

"Well, if you didn't shoot Garcia, then we have a problem, because only the three of us knew where that gun was."

"Someone else must have."

"Eric and I forgot about it. Otherwise, we'd have secured it in the gun locker."

"I presumed it *was* in the gun locker."

"Did you mention to anyone that we took a gun from him?"

I've been hoping she'd volunteer this information. That's why I lied about her alibi being in question. The obvious defense would be to say that she mentioned the gun to someone. I even prompted her by saying *we* hadn't told anyone.

Diana might insist she's not "like me." That's she isn't a threat. She might not know how to take revenge on Graham or how to make him pay for what he did, but she has a finely honed survival streak. I've tossed her a life raft here, and it didn't matter if saving herself meant tossing someone else to the sharks. She'd have done it in a blink. The fact that she hasn't tells me she doesn't have the answer I want. I still ask, outright, but I'm not surprised when she says, "I didn't tell anyone, Case."

"If you did, it's in your best interests to tell me."

"You think I don't know that?" She pulls her legs up, crossing them. "I didn't tell anyone *anything* about what happened at Eric's house, because I knew that wouldn't help you guys. Also, admittedly, I wanted to prove you could trust me. So, because I kept my mouth shut, I'm now your prime suspect. I think they call that irony."

"What about after Garcia ran? Maybe you mentioned something about him being unarmed? Maybe people worried that he was running around with a gun, and you said no, he wasn't."

She shakes her head. "No one realized that I'd met Garcia, so I didn't volunteer that information. To anyone."

I rise from the chair. "All right then."

"Can you talk to April and Kenny again? I don't know how there can be any confusion about my alibi."

"It's fine. Your alibi stands."

She gets to her feet. "You lied?" Before I can answer, she says, "Wait. You lied about my alibi, expecting me to toss you other suspects to save myself. Wow."

I meet her gaze. "And you wouldn't have?"

Her mouth opens. Then it shuts. She sits down. I let myself out, and she's still sitting there, staring into space.

———

I head to the station. Dalton's there, doing paperwork. One huge advantage to working in Rockton is the lack of paperwork. It's a running joke with law enforcement that our job looks so much cooler in TV and movies, where we're constantly on the move, out in the field solving crimes. The TV audience doesn't want to see us stuck behind a desk, two-finger-typing endless reports. Down south, besides reports for our supervisors, everything must be detailed, as meticulously as possible, in hopes of an arrest and trial. Or, if we fail to find a suspect, we want those notes for future investigators.

In Rockton, my only supervisor is the guy sitting at the desk. There isn't an aspect of my cases that I don't verbally share with him. The council doesn't require reports or documentation. They don't give a damn. There are no prosecutors to worry about either. Dalton, Anders, and I are the entire judicial system. The only people we need to document anything for is ourselves. That's what Dalton is doing. He's handwriting a report on Garcia's death for our files. I'll add to that as the investigation proceeds.

Dalton writes while Storm snoozes at his feet. He doesn't look up when I come in. I put a coffee and a few cookies in front of him. The coffee is in a travel mug. The cookies are in a Tupperware box. That's another oddity to Rockton living. You won't find the ubiquitous cardboard cups, cookies in a paper bag, or even cookies wrapped in a disposable napkin. We are the most eco-friendly town in the world, I suspect. For us, it's pure practicality. We can afford the water and the manpower to wash dishes far more than the cargo space to fly in disposable items. By the door, there's a blue recycling box with an assortment of mugs and plates and plastic containers. Every other day, someone from the dishwashing unit will stop by to grab it. The contents will be cleaned and put back into circulation.

Dalton sips his coffee and absently takes a cookie. He still says nothing. Anyone else might raise a finger or murmur "Just a sec." For Dalton, that is implied by the fact that he's not acknowledging my presence. Sheer efficiency.

I sit on the edge of the desk and wait. When he finishes, he pushes the pages aside and tugs me into a kiss. After that, I hop from the desk and pick up my coffee and the box of cookies. I want to talk to him about Diana, and that means going out back. Not for privacy but because that's where he's more comfortable. He'll write his notes indoors. Otherwise, though, he's out on that deck, if the weather's halfway decent. And his version of "halfway decent" only means "temperature above freezing."

He grabs his mug and a hide blanket, and we go out. There are two Muskoka chairs, where there used to be one. He tosses the blanket onto mine, for cushioning. Storm lies between us as Dalton settles in. There's an oversize tin can below his chair, almost filled with beer caps. I remember the first time I saw that, how my hackles rose, fearing it meant I'd walked into the kind of police station where officers drank on the job. It's true. Dalton has no problem cracking open a beer midday. If we weren't both in need of caffeine, that's exactly what he'd be having now. But if Dalton didn't drink while on duty, then he'd never crack open a beer. He's always working, and he never drinks more than one. If I pick up that can of caps, I'll see that beyond a layer or two, they're old and rusted.

We sit and sip our coffee for a few minutes. He's in no rush to get my report, and I'm in no rush to give it. He knows what that means—I didn't come away from Diana with any hot leads.

"She didn't tell anyone," I say. "She didn't mention that she'd even met Garcia."

Dalton just nods. He doesn't ask whether I believe her—he won't—but I still add, "She isn't lying. I pretended her alibi was in question, and she was our main suspect. She'd have given up names if she could. She didn't."

Dalton nods and takes a bite of his cookie.

"I don't know what to make of that," I say. "We didn't tell anyone. Diana didn't tell anyone. Yet someone knew there was a gun in that house."

"People knew," he says.

I look over. "Diana might be a lying bitch, but I really do believe her here, Eric. Yes, that probably means I still don't want to think the worst of her—"

"Nah. If anything, you're the first to think the worst of her."

"I—"

"I don't mean that how it sounds," he says, shifting in his seat. "You have every reason for not trusting Diana. She earned that. What she did to you is unforgivable. The problem is that you don't want to cut *yourself* slack. If you *don't* suspect the worst of her, then you feel like you're making excuses for yourself. Making excuses for why you were friends with her. You don't need excuses, Casey. You were good to her. You were a friend. She repaid you by being a backstabbing bitch. That doesn't mean she doesn't care about you. I might have no fucking clue how you can care about a person and do that to them, but I can see that she cares. She's proven it. Over and over. She is on your side. She wants you back, as a friend. So she's sure as hell not going to protect a potential suspect. I suspect the only person she gives a damn about is you."

"But you just said—"

"I don't mean Diana's lying. I mean people figured it out. They knew Garcia claimed to be a marshal. A federal agent. If the guy's a cop, he's got a gun. So where was it? Why didn't he pull it on me? Why'd no one see it? They'll presume we took it from him earlier."

"But I never announced that we had an *encounter* with him earlier."

"Doesn't matter. He's missing his gun, and he sure as hell didn't drop it in the forest. Hell, whoever took it might not have even gone looking for the gun. They only needed to suspect we'd spoken to him and search our house for clues. Trying to figure out if we knew who he came for. The gun was right there in a drawer."

"Next step, see if our neighbors noticed anyone coming around our house."

He pushes to his feet. "I'll handle that. Got something else for you."

He heads into the station and returns with an evidence bag. "Murder weapon. Straight from the locker."

"Murder weapon?" a voice says. We turn as Mathias appears, with

Raoul on a makeshift lead. Mathias looks at the bag. "Please tell me it is not a gun in that bag."

"That'd be the murder weapon," I say.

He sighs. "How terribly pedestrian."

"The guy was shot, Mathias. What else do you think killed him?"

"I simply hoped that was not the cause of death. Perhaps you discovered that the bullet was coated in a rare poison."

"Gun would still be the murder weapon," Dalton says.

"Yes, it's a boring homicide," I say. "So unless you're here to confess, I'm sure you have more exciting ways to spend your afternoon."

"I have brought Raoul for a playdate."

I look back at Storm. She's on her feet, Dalton's hand hooked in her collar as she strains for the wolf cub . . . who hides around the corner of the building.

"I hope you're joking," I say.

"Yes, 'play' may be an exaggeration. But I do hope to begin the process of convincing Raoul to accept Storm as a pack mate. Canine socialization is extremely important."

"I meant that I hope you're joking about being here for that. We're kinda in the middle of a murder investigation."

"I realize that, and so I am multitasking. Our canines shall become acquainted while we discuss your case. I may have something of interest."

Dalton passes me Storm. "As much fun as this sounds, I'm going to go interview our neighbors."

He heads inside before I can stop him. The door opens again, but only enough for him to toss Storm's leash outside for me.

"Thanks!" I call, and then grumble under my breath. I turn to Mathias. "You'd better have an actual lead, and not be using the excuse to socialize your damn mutt."

His brows shoot up. "Damn mutt? I take it the investigation is not going well."

I clip the leash onto Storm and head into the yard.

TWENTY-THREE

I walk into the middle of the backyard and plunk myself down. Mathias scoops up Raoul and approaches. When the cub sees Storm, he convulses in a fit of panic.

"Watch out," I say. "He's going to—"

Raoul chomps Mathias's arm. Mathias stops walking, calmly dislodges the cub's fangs, holds his jaws shut with one hand, and taps him on the snout with the other as he says a firm "*Non.*"

Mathias sits where he is, about ten feet from us. Storm whines and belly-crawls forward, but when I put my hand on her back, she lays her muzzle on the ground and sighs, her jowls wobbling.

Mathias turns the cub around to face Storm. When Raoul tries to twist away, Mathias holds him there.

"You are safe," he says in French. "I will protect you from the giant bouncing puppy."

"So, Raoul, huh?" I say. "Your wolf-dog's name means 'wolf.' Got creative, huh?"

"Wolf?" His brows arch. "I named him after a boyhood friend who had freckles, just like this." He rubs the spots over Raoul's nose, the one sign of his Australian shepherd heritage.

I shake my head. "Okay, so the pups are a safe distance apart, becoming accustomed to one another. What's your lead?"

"I would not necessarily call it a lead."

"Mathias . . ."

"Tell me about Petra."

"What about her?"

"She is your friend. A good friend. You did not toss her into the cell because she beat you at poker. She has done something. A criminal act."

"I don't divulge—"

"I know it is criminal, because you would not incarcerate her for anything personal. Nor, given the chaos of the current situation, would you confine her to the cell for a misdemeanor. She has committed a felony. A serious one. Yet you released her two days later. So whatever she has done, you are in no fear of her re-offending."

"I needed the cell."

He waves off my excuse. "She committed a serious breach of town law, yet you do not deem her a dangerous offender. It is connected to Brady, yes?"

"Do you have a lead, Mathias? I don't have time to satisfy your idle curiosity."

"My curiosity is never idle."

I look at him.

He shrugs. "*Rarely* idle."

I keep looking.

"All right," he says. "I have a curious mind, and to keep that mind from *being* idle—which is dangerous—I must pursue intriguing information."

"Yeah . . ." I start to rise. "When this case is over, I'll be happy to socialize our canines."

"Yes," he says. "I ask about Petra because I am curious. Very curious. I have, until now, dismissed her. She does not annoy me. She does not interest me. Therefore I have paid her little mind. But her arrest tells me there is more to Petra than meets the eye. She is not what she seems."

"No one here is, Mathias."

"Mmm, no one here is who they say they are. But most are who they seem. There is a difference. I prefer those, like you or William or Eric or Isabel, who do not claim to be anything at all. Isabel says, 'I was a therapist' and no more. Her entire past is summed up—like yours—in an occupation. You both allow yourselves to be judged instead on what you do here. Others make up an elaborate backstory and then attempt to fulfill it. Petra does neither. She was an artist, yes?"

"Comic-book artist."

"Do you think she really was?"

"Back to idle curiosity. . . ."

"No, I'm posing questions that you're already asking yourself. I am proposing, Casey, that you indulge my curiosity by using me to solve the problem that is Petra. I will investigate her for you."

I glower at him. "Don't pretend you'd do that for me. You're bored, and I don't want you taking on Petra for a project. Not yet. As for socializing Raoul . . ."

I tell Storm to stay. Then I march over and take the cub from him. I cuddle Raoul for a moment. He knows me—I was his nurse and keeper when he first arrived. He wriggles and licks at my hands. As I pet him, I ease closer to Storm. Raoul notices and tenses, but he's too busy accepting my attention to pay much mind. When I'm a few feet away, I kneel, saying, "Stay, Storm."

She whines but does as she's told. I take a strip of dried meat from my pocket. I break it in half, and then give Raoul one piece and Storm the other. While he's chewing, I creep closer to Storm. I extend my hand, and she snuffles it. Then I pet her and let the cub smell my hand afterward. As he does, he peeks out at her while I hold him tight, reassuring him he's safe.

Then I rise, hefting him, walk to Mathias and hand him back.

"He was curious," he says. "He would have gotten closer."

"I know. Always leave them wanting more. Step one accomplished. Now Storm and I have rounds to make."

"Do you still want my lead?"

I look up at him. "You actually have one?"

"I may misdirect, but I do not lie. Not to you. I would suggest you take a closer look at Sebastian."

Sebastian is that newest and youngest resident who popped out when Garcia began knocking on doors. He hasn't had any contact with us—either by committing crimes or by being quick to volunteer his help solving them. He works as general labor, so I don't encounter him in the shops. Nor do our social sets overlap. He belongs in the fifty percent of Rockton's population who come and go, and never leave a mark, and considering they're here to hide, I can't blame them for lying low.

"What about him?" I ask.

"I do not like him."

I roll my eyes as I walk back to Storm. "Really, Mathias? You don't like ninety-five percent of the people here."

"Not true. I have no interest in ninety-five percent. They are leaves passing on the breeze, making no sound as they go, not attracting my attention in any way. There are actually only . . . five people I dislike. No, make that four. Valerie is deceased."

"So what does it take to incur your dislike?"

"Attracting my attention in an actively negative manner. For example, my neighbor Ronald. He has sex. It is loud, and it is bad. One of those things would be acceptable. Both is very annoying in a neighbor. It is like listening to an amateur sex tape every weekend. I have considered ways to rid myself of Ronald."

"Note to self: if Ron goes missing, arrest Mathias."

"I would not kill him. That is wrong and unjustified. I simply mean getting rid of him as my neighbor."

I rock my weight onto one hip. "Mathias, is there a point—?"

"There are others that I dislike because, in them, I see traits that remind me of my former patients."

"The sociopaths and psychopath patients? Here's a thought—if you notice that, maybe you should tell me."

"I am. Sebastian Usher is a sociopath."

When I start to sputter, he says, "Possessing some degree of sociopathy does not mean one is a dangerous killer. I myself score uncomfortably high on the scale."

"Whew. Okay, that's so much better, because I know *you* aren't a killer." I pause. "No, wait . . ."

"Your sarcasm is charming, Casey. Has anyone told you that? You have quite a gift for it. In this case, I deserved it. I misspoke. Sociopathy does not mean a person will kill without cause, or poor Ronald would have been dead months ago. A self-aware sociopath is able to form relationships and understand that murdering people without just cause is wrong. Also inconvenient." He purses his lips. "Mostly inconvenient."

"So Sebastian shows signs of sociopathy, and you didn't think to notify me?"

"I would have, once I'd concluded my field study."

"And told the council."

"Yes, that is my role here, as you know. I am a mental-health spy for the council. I report on persons of concern. However, I would have told you first. At one time, I naively presumed they passed my concerns on to Eric."

"They don't."

"I realize that now, and I feel foolish for my naiveté. While I have been here nearly five years, and I have the utmost respect for our sheriff, we have never been what one would call friends. I am, to him, a very foreign creature. One he cannot quite understand. He is the same to me. I find him fascinating, but his ethical rudder is as unfathomable to me as mine is to him. Which is the long way of saying that I never expected him to discuss residents with me—and I presumed that he did not know who made those reports—so I never questioned whether they were being passed on. In fact, while I hate to defend my naiveté, there were several cases where he kept a particularly careful eye on residents that I had identified as potential problems. Likely, I realize now, because he has his own sixth sense for that."

"And Sebastian . . . ?"

"I'm ninety percent convinced he's a sociopath. I can give examples of his behavior that led me to this conclusion, but I would prefer you to interview him without that. Draw your own conclusions." He tightens his grasp on Raoul. "Come see me afterward. Oh, would you possibly do me a favor?"

"Maybe."

"Take Dalton to that interview. I would be interested in his conclusions as well. A test of his sixth sense."

"I'll see what I can do."

TWENTY-FOUR

I *will* get Dalton to help me interview Sebastian. That isn't to satisfy Mathias's curiosity. I'm not even completely sure what I'm looking for here. I know what sociopathy is, but it's not an area I've studied in depth. Dalton knows more.

Finding someone in Rockton isn't a matter of dialing a cell phone number. I know Dalton's not "at work" in the station. I know he won't be at home in midafternoon. Last I heard, he was going to talk to our neighbors. I'm heading to the bakery, where a couple of our neighbors work, when Sam catches up with me.

"Paul would like to talk to you," he says.

I check my watch. "Where is he?"

"At the clinic. Your sister's releasing him soon. She'd also like to speak to you."

I sigh under my breath. I glance down the road, but there's no sign of Dalton.

I swing into the clinic and collide with my sister, coming out backward. She jumps, her hands fluttering, and I realize she was backing out while pulling Kenny's bed. With Kenny on it.

Before I can comment, she says, "Can't you just walk, Casey?"

"Pretty sure that's what I was doing," I say.

"No, you were bouncing. As usual. Bounce, skip, sail . . . crashing into everything as you go."

Kenny snickers. "Sorry, I'm trying to picture Casey bouncing."

I look at him. "I was a very energetic kid. My sister has failed to realize I'm well past my bouncing and skipping stage in life."

She gives me that frown, the one that says the words coming from my mouth don't make sense. Not to her, anyway.

"Yes, I did kind of swing through the doorway," I say. "And I did crash into you, April. Sorry. Do I dare ask what you're doing with poor Kenny?"

"I said I'd love some fresh air," Kenny says. "I didn't mean I expected her to single-handedly wheel me out. I've objected. She told me to shut up."

April blinks. "I most certainly did not—"

"She said, 'Please stop.' Talking, that is. Which is progress. Usually, she just makes this face, like the sound of my voice hurts her head."

April's face reddens. It takes me a moment to realize she's blushing. "I do not—"

"Totally do," Kenny says. "Anyway, I mentioned fresh air, and now she's wheeling me onto the front porch, and since I can't physically stop her, all I can do is protest, and she doesn't like that. So I'm keeping quiet and letting myself be wheeled out."

"He's been stuck in a supply room for two days," she says. "That is not conducive to recuperation."

I grab the end of the rolling bed and motion for her to take the head. We navigate through the doorway as I say, "It's warm out, so you might as well stay here, Kenny, until Paul's gone. Apparently, he needs to speak to me first."

April opens her mouth. I cut her off with, "Yes, and so do you. I got the message. Everyone needs to speak to me."

"I don't think *everyone* does, Casey," she says. "I realize you're a very important person here, but an overinflated sense of self-importance—"

"—is not a problem Casey has," Kenny says. His voice is low, gentle, but April still stiffens. He continues with, "Casey meant that it *feels* as if everyone needs to talk to her."

I expect my sister to snap something back, but she only nods. She might even look a bit chagrined. I wave her inside and make sure Kenny's comfortable before I follow. I close the door behind me. We're in the tiny waiting room, with the door to the exam room shut.

"Will I still be home by Tuesday?" she asks.

I swear under my breath. That makes her wince, but she says nothing.

"I know you need to get back," I say. "Your job here is done. It's just a little complicated with the marshal's murder. But we did promise you. I'll talk to Eric. He should at least be able to fly you to Dawson Monday morning, and you can catch a flight from there and be home for Tuesday. That gives us two more days."

"It's Sunday, Casey. Late Sunday afternoon."

"What?" I think fast and then start cursing again. When she opens her mouth, I lift my hands. "I can do this. I'm really, *really* sorry. I will talk to Eric right now. . . ." I glance at the closed exam-room door. "Right *after* I talk to Paul. We'll make the arrangements. There are more flights out of Whitehorse at this time of year. We'll have you to Vancouver tomorrow night. I promise."

I take a step toward the exam room.

Behind me, she says softly, "Are they going to let me leave?"

I turn. "What?"

"I realize you snuck me in." Her hands fly up to ward off my protests. "I knew that when I came, so I am not accusing you of anything. I . . . understand that I sometimes speak too bluntly, and what I do not intend as an accusation may sound like that. I have been told as much in the past, but with you, I fear I slip into old habits. Isabel has spoken to me about this, and I have enlisted Kenny's assistance in reminding me of it."

"Kenny?" I must look confused. Kenny is not the person I would ever expect my sister to reach out to for help. She points to the front porch, as if to remind me who Kenny is.

April continues, "As I was saying, I realized that I was being brought in secretly, so I am not complaining. But these people know about me now." She pauses. "I acknowledge that is my fault . . . although, I might point out that I was not fully aware of the extent of the situation and the need for secrecy."

That's not true. We told her more about the situation than Dalton was comfortable revealing. She just thought we were exaggerating. Typical Casey, being dramatic. I don't say anything, though. Even admitting that she came of her own accord is progress, and I'll take it.

"Are they going to let me leave?" she asks again.

I want to say of course they will. She came here in good faith. She came to help us. She's my sister, and she knows nothing about Rockton that she cannot know. I would never—ever—have let her come if I thought there was any chance she couldn't leave.

But now, as she says the words, ice nestles in my gut. It's like when our parents would tell me not to take a shortcut to school because ten years earlier a girl had been assaulted there. I wanted to laugh and say they were being ridiculous. That girl had been attacked by a family friend who stalked her, and since then, the city had added lights and removed shrubs, making it safer than the streets. Yet once they put that idea in my mind, my heart pounded every time I took that shortcut. Every shadow made me jump.

"The council can't keep you here," I say firmly.

"They're keeping Diana. I heard that. She wanted to leave, and they won't let her."

"That is a very long and complicated conversation, April. One I'm happy to have someday, but I have a feeling it won't interest you."

"Why not?"

Because it's about me. Because nothing in my life has ever interested you, and you've made that abundantly clear.

"Diana made a commitment to stay here for two years. She wanted to renege on that, and under most situations, they'd allow her to do so. This is different, and honestly, as patronizing as it sounds, she's better off here. If she *had* to leave, though, I'd get her out. We made you a promise. We will honor that. The council couldn't keep us from bringing you in. They can't stop us from taking you out."

They can just make it very, very difficult. There may be repercussions. But that's on us. It's on me. Not you. I made the choice, and I'll deal with the fallout.

I don't say that either. She'd hear it as virtue signaling. *See what a good person I am, April?* It's not that at all, so I stay silent.

"I'll talk to Eric. Just let me see what Paul needs first."

She nods and heads back outside to Kenny. I take a moment to compose myself. After that talk, I want to grab Dalton and run to Phil and make sure there won't be any problem taking April home. No, I want to grab Dalton and leave with April before anyone can stop us. My sister did me a favor here. The biggest she's ever granted me, and if any trouble comes to her because of it . . .

Dalton would not have let me bring April if he thought she could be trapped here. We're fine. Talk to Paul. Talk to Dalton. Get reassurances about April, and then take Dalton to interview Sebastian.

I push open the door. Paul is sitting on the edge of his bed, as if just about to get up.

"Hey, Casey," he says.

I ask how he's doing before finding out what he summoned me for. It takes conscious effort for me to do things like this—my natural proclivity is to just jump to the point of the visit. It's not that I don't care how he's doing. But I can see he's okay, up and around, and I'm here on business. I wonder if that's how April processes things, too. It's not that she doesn't think about others, but just that social niceties seem like a waste of time and energy when there is important work to be done. The problem is that if you skip the niceties—especially as a woman—it comes off as cold, abrupt, even bitchy. I've been called all three. I can only imagine what April gets.

When I do get to the point, Paul fusses for a bit before answering. Then he blurts, "I screwed up."

I lean back against the counter. "I should say no, you didn't. But if you want that, you've come to the wrong person. Attempting suicide was a mistake. An overreaction. I understand the impulse. Everything seems so bleak that you don't, in that moment, see any other solution. Just . . . ask for help, okay?"

"I know. And I'm embarrassed about the whole thing. But that wasn't what I meant. I made another mistake, one that added to my guilt and made everything worse. Then, when you saved me, I didn't want to make the situation worse by admitting . . ." He takes a deep breath and meets my gaze. "I didn't kill that marshal, but his death may have been my fault."

"How?"

"I was guarding Roy when you called."

"Right . . ."

"I was inside the secured house talking to him. I'd just brought his lunch, and I've been trying to talk sense into him. He's an asshole. There's no two ways about it. Back in my protest days, he'd have been the guy on the other side of the line. Cindy used to say if we could just talk to people like that, we could open their eyes, wake them up. I grew up with guys like Roy, and I know it isn't that easy, but with Roy, I figured since he's stuck here with us, maybe he'll listen to reason. I was wrong."

I nod and say nothing.

He continues, "And that's no surprise to you, huh? Yeah, it's pointless, but I still tried. I told him about this marshal guy. I was trying to impress on him how tough a job you guys have with law enforcement. How hard you work to keep us safe, and the last thing you need is garden-variety assholes like him making it worse. I talked to him about that when I brought his breakfast. Then I brought his lunch, and he wanted an update. I gave it, and we were chatting—sports stuff—when you called. I took off to get Will and . . ." He takes a deep breath. "When I came back later, Roy's door wasn't locked."

"Someone opened it?"

He shifts on the bed, his hands clenching the edge. "I think I left it unlocked. No, I *must* have. There's only one key, and I had it. When I found it open, I tried to remember locking it, and I couldn't. I was busy thinking about where I'd last seen Will, so I could pass on your message, and I must have walked out and forgotten the door."

"Was Roy there when you got back?"

He nods.

"Did you say anything to him?"

Paul shakes his head. "I was hoping . . ." He swallows. "I hoped he hadn't noticed the door. It was closed, of course, and I figured since he was still in there, with no sign that he'd left, I'd gotten off easy. It never occurred to me that he could be the killer. This Garcia guy was a US marshal, and Roy is Canadian. Then last night, I was talking to Jen, and she said she thought this guy was lying about being a marshal. That he would know there was no way for you guys to check. I remembered Roy had asked me that over breakfast, when I first told him about Garcia."

"He asked if Garcia was really a marshal?"

"He said something like 'You think this guy's really American?' and I said that's what he says, and he has a badge, but Roy looked worried. I didn't think anything of it until Jen, and then I wondered, *What if Roy thought the same thing?* I know the marshal came for me—for my federal warrant—but no one else realized that. Roy sure didn't. And he was worried. Really worried."

"About Garcia."

Paul nods.

TWENTY-FIVE

I like Roy as a suspect. Paul's right. He's an asshole. It's always so much easier when the bad guys are jerks. Even if Roy isn't responsible for this, I'd love an excuse to get rid of him. He's a powder keg waiting for his match.

The problem with Roy as a viable suspect is timing.

Garcia's killer used Garcia's gun. From our house. That gun could have been taken at any point after Dalton put it into the drawer and returned anytime before Dalton put it into the locker.

I would presume that the killer got the gun when Dalton and I went searching for Garcia. The house was empty, no people, no dog. Then the killer waited for us to bring Garcia back. Now, it's possible they waited in the forest, but that's hours of hanging out in hopes that we returned with our quarry. With the militia and volunteers scouring the forest for Garcia, it's unlikely anyone could stay out there half the day and not bump into someone who'd escort them back to town.

The more likely answer is that someone heard we had Garcia. After I called, Paul had been running about, searching for Anders, telling everyone what happened so they could help find our deputy. This means there were dozens of residents who knew we were slowly making our way to town with a wounded marshal.

This timing only works if the killer already had the gun. Roy didn't. He's been in custody since before Garcia arrived. Roy would have needed to take off after Paul left, run to our house, ransack it in hopes of finding a weapon, and still make it in time to intercept us. That's twenty minutes maximum. Not impossible, but highly improbable.

I've barely started my hunt for Dalton when I spot Anders. I jog to catch up.

"Seen the boss?" I ask.

He chuckles. "He just asked me the same thing."

"So he finally admits I'm the boss?"

A louder laugh. "No, sorry. But he is looking for you. I told him I was too, and whichever found you first got dibs. He's swinging by the station, so we might be able to catch up to him."

As we head in that direction, I say, "You wanted to speak to me?"

"Actually, you wanted to speak to me. You just didn't realize it. Sam says you're looking for the person who'd been in charge of Petra yesterday. That would be me. Given the circumstances, I figured you didn't want anyone else in contact with her. Too many questions. So I handled it myself. I'm going to guess you wanted to be sure she was safely incarcerated at the time of the shooting. She was. I opened the door with her lunch about ninety minutes before you called. I returned thirty minutes later to let her use the facilities. I locked her in and double-checked it."

"You need to teach that skill to your militia."

His brows arch. Then he winces. "Paul and Roy."

"Good guess. You must be psychic."

"No, unfortunately. Just an educated guess. Paul's been on my shit list. First, that fiasco with guard duty last winter, when he let Jen distract him. Then failing to back you up with Roy's lynch mob last week. I was already planning to speak to Eric about relieving Paul of his militia duties. Two strikes is enough for me. Now, since I know he was guarding Roy when the call came in, I'm guessing he made it three."

"He did. He forgot to lock the door when he took off to find you."

"Now I have to fire a guy who just attempted suicide. Awesome."

"Can you put him on light duty for a while?"

"Yeah, I will. Paul's a good guy, but he's a screwup, and while I appreciate how hard he's worked for the militia, we can't have that. At least you know Petra was safely in her cell, though, which is a start."

"So you saw her an hour before the shots. When did you see her *after* that?"

"Speaking of screwing up . . . With everything happening, I totally forgot about Petra until dinnertime. Let's just say she was very happy to see me."

"As far as you know, then, was anyone inside the station between those visits?"

"If they were, she'd have been shouting for her bathroom break. But the cell door was locked, Casey. I'm absolutely sure of it. I don't walk away without checking. I had the key on me the whole time." He pats his pocket.

"I'm sure it was locked. I'm sure you had the key. I'm just not sure there isn't a second key."

"There is. Eric has . . . Oh, you mean a *third* key. You suspect the council?"

"They had one to the gun locker. That's how Val got the rifle. She—and now Phil—may have keys to everything."

"So Phil slips Petra the key earlier. Or he lets her out when Paul starts running around telling everyone that you're bringing in the prisoner. Phil knew you guys had Garcia's gun, right?"

I pause. Then I curse. "Yes, of course. We told him we'd taken the gun and satellite phone. I totally forgot about it."

"So if Petra works for the council, Phil shows up, hands her the gun, unlocks the door, and she slips out the back. Straight into the forest."

"Where we're bringing in Garcia."

TWENTY-SIX

Anders is certain Dalton's in the station, but when I walk in, there's no sign of him. I'm looking around when hands close around my waist. I jump as Dalton pulls me into an embrace.

"Have I warned you about sneaking up on me?" I say.

He hops onto the desktop and kicks his heels against the desk, legs swinging like a kid's. "Missed you."

"Uh-huh. Someone's in a very good mood. Had a productive afternoon, I take it?"

"Nope. Had such a fucking shitty and utterly pointless afternoon that the mere sight of you—even when you're annoyed with me— puts me into an exceptionally good mood."

I lift my brows. Then I spot the tequila bottle on the desk.

"Ouch," I say. "That bad, huh?"

He gives a half shrug. The tequila is mine. Dalton isn't accustomed to hard liquor. He'll drink it only with me, when he's free to be like this, a little carefree, a little boyish.

"It was drink a shot of tequila or collapse on the floor sobbing," he says. "I don't think anyone needs to see me cry."

I press between his knees and put my hands around his neck. "Wanna talk about it?"

Another half shrug. "I'm being silly. Tired and frustrated and slightly punch-drunk. I got nothing from the neighbors. No one saw a damned thing. I was hoping to bring you a lead, and I hit a brick wall so yeah, I'm tired, frustrated, punch-drunk, maybe even a little actual drunk."

"Well, I have leads. First, though, we need to talk about April."

He squeezes his eyes shut and shakes his head. "Fuck. What's she done now?"

"Nothing. She's actually on her best behavior. But it's Sunday, Eric, and we have to get her to Dawson tomorrow."

He nods. "I know, and we will. We should go to Dawson anyway. You wanted to research Garcia, and there are a few background stories I'd like to verify."

"April wonders whether she'll be allowed to go."

"What? Fuck, yeah, she can leave. We don't need a doctor badly enough to kidnap her. And not badly enough to want *her*."

"She means the council. Since we snuck her in—and now she's a suspect—will they let her leave?"

He groans, and his gaze slides to the bottle. He doesn't reach for it, though. Even his glance over is a joke. Law enforcement and isolated northern communities are both known for alcohol abuse. Being law enforcement *in* a northern community? That's a trap we don't even want to skirt. Anders already drinks more than we'd like him to. It's not alcoholism—Dalton wouldn't put up with that—but here, it doesn't take much to worry us.

"Does April have a reason to be concerned?" I ask.

He exhales, air hissing between his teeth as he leans back and studies the timbered ceiling for answers.

"Fuck," he says. In other words, yes. Like me, he hasn't considered this, but now that he does, he sees treacherous ground ahead.

"I promised her, Eric," I say.

"We both did. Don't go making this about you. I want my share of the blame."

He leans back far enough to almost collapse on the desktop before he rights himself.

I chuckle. "How many shots did you have?"

"One. I'm a cheap drunk."

I lean against his shoulder. "You are. And I'm sorry for putting you—"

"No." He gives me a stern look. "Having met your sister, I now understand why you're so quick to take all the blame. Because she takes none. If she's putting the screws to you on this, Casey, please remind her that she knew we were sneaking her in. She chose to ignore our warnings."

"She realizes that. She's trying to take her share of the blame, which, yes, isn't easy for her. Isabel thinks she might be on the spectrum."

His brows lift.

"Autism," I say. "It's a spectrum disorder, which is—"

"A mental condition that can manifest in different ways, to different degrees. We had a guy with Asperger's a few years back. High functioning. I did my research." He considers, his head tilted. "Yeah, now that you mention it, I can see hints. It's not nearly as marked as the guy we had, but like you said, it's a spectrum disorder."

"And, as usual, I'm prepared to explain something to you, and you've read more about it than I have."

"That's what happens when you don't have a television. And you have six fucking months of darkness."

"Well, April's actually doing better. Isabel has spoken to her, and April asked Kenny to call her on it, when she sounds harsher than she intends."

"Kenny?"

"That's what I said. No idea how that happened, but it does mean April's making an effort. She isn't blaming me if we run into trouble getting her out of here, but I really don't want there to be trouble. It's tough enough between us without adding one more reason for her to treat me like a screwup."

He mutters under his breath at that, but says, "We'll take her with us to Dawson tomorrow. Fuck the council. I'm not even telling them."

When I tense, he says, "Val's dead. Phil's been exiled here. Protocol's blown to hell. When we ask to talk to someone, we get that

Émilie lady. As far as I'm concerned, until they get their shit together, we're on our own here."

"That's your story, and you're sticking to it?"

"Yep. No one told us April can't leave. They never even said much about it after Phil's hissy fit. No one from the council has reprimanded us for bringing her in, so now that her job is done, off she goes. Now, did you say something about leads?"

I tell him about Sebastian and Roy.

"Roy seems like a long shot," I say. "If it was anyone else, I'd dismiss it outright. The timeline is too tight. But he otherwise makes a good suspect. He hasn't been here long, and Paul's right that he's a troublemaker. I don't know if that's enough to warrant you giving me his backstory, though."

"Good enough excuse," he says. "That's all I need."

The only person here who is supposed to know a resident's "real" story is Dalton. The problem is that I've been brought in as a detective. Sometimes I need those stories to solve a case.

As soon as Garcia showed up, Dalton and I had discussed residents who might be the subject of a federal warrant. It was a very short conversation, one that went something like this.

Me: Has anyone in town committed a US federal crime?
Dalton: Not that I know.

Even with Paul, Dalton had only been told that Paul accidentally struck a law enforcement officer during a protest. Without more detail, it's a huge jump from that to "has a federal warrant out for his arrest."

Neither of us is even completely clear on what justifies a federal warrant. I gave Dalton the short rundown of what qualifies in Canada. He still had nothing.

If Garcia is actually a bounty hunter or a hit man, that throws the playing field wide open, encompassing, well, everyone really. Our hidden criminals. Our white-collar criminals. Those legitimately here seeking refuge. . . .

So when we have suspects, I'm going to need to know the back-story they gave. That's the only way I can even begin to determine how likely it is that they've caught the attention of a bounty hunter or hit man.

"Roy's a white-collar guy," Dalton says. "A capital-A asshole hustler who ran a pyramid scheme, cheating folks out of their retirement money. I grumbled. I always grumble with guys like that. If they cheat a big company, I realize it trickles down to the little guy one way or another, but actually cheating regular people feels worse, you know?"

I do. Unfortunately, I know, too, that Dalton's grumbles had been only a token show of protest. The council doesn't care. When it comes to white-collar criminals, all that matters is whether their checks clear. If we complain, we get a lecture from Phil on the costs of running Rockton and the fact that even if guys like Roy are indeed capital-A assholes, they aren't a threat in a society that runs on a strictly regu-lated economy of credits.

"We will investigate his story," Dalton says, "but it wasn't throwing up red flags for me. He's here for being an asshole, and he's continued being an asshole. That isn't a sinner pretending to be a saint. Attack-ing you over that lynch mob bullshit, though, took it to a whole other level."

"He came at me hard, and I have no doubt he'd have seriously hurt me if he could. But he lacked the skill. It was rage and bravado."

"Yeah, as you said, he's not a great suspect. Too bad. I'd love the excuse to kick his ass out."

"Agreed."

Dalton stretches his legs and looks toward the back door. Looks at it longingly. Given what we're discussing, we can't move this con-versation outside. Even in here, we have Artie in the cell, and while that room is soundproofed, Dalton and I still speak quietly.

"Sebastian's interesting," Dalton says. "Mathias is right. Some-thing's off with him. I don't know how to explain it, which is why I haven't brought it up. I figured, if he caused trouble, I would, but he's been a model nonentity, if you know what I mean."

I do. For us, a model citizen is someone like Nicole or Sam or

Kenny. They're the first to pitch in during a literal fire, and the last to cause a figurative one. Others just want to do their work, pull exactly their share of the load, and otherwise keep their head down. They're model residents rather than model citizens. Nonentities who pass through Rockton without leaving any impression, for better or worse. That accounts for probably two-thirds of our population.

Dalton continues. "When I read Sebastian's story, it reminded me of Abbygail's. I wanted to talk to you about it. Just . . ." He rubs a hand over his mouth. "Talk. In the back of my mind, yeah, I hoped maybe Sebastian might be my chance to set things right. That sounds crazy. I just figured, if another kid like Abbygail came here and everything went smoothly, I might feel like the scales are balanced." He runs his fingers through his hair. "Fuck."

I take his hand and entwine it with mine. I don't say anything. What happened with Abbygail wasn't his fault, but he knows that. Everyone who knew her still feels the sting of her death, of misplaced guilt. She died before I arrived—her murder is what brought me here. Abbygail came to Rockton at nineteen, younger than residents were supposed to be, and far more messed up than they were supposed to be. For her, a hellish childhood led to a life on the streets and teen prostitution and drug abuse. When she tried to escape that life, it followed her, old associates setting fire to her parents' house. Her mother and father died in the blaze. After that, someone got her to Rockton.

Like me, Abbygail hadn't wanted to come here. And like me, this town saved her. Isabel and Dalton and others got her on the right track, destined for nursing school once she returned down south. Only she never got that chance. She was brutally murdered, and it doesn't matter if no one could have foreseen or prevented that, they still feel as if they failed her. To them, it's as if she'd been drowning, and they grabbed her hand, and when they relaxed too soon, a shark pulled her back under.

"Sebastian reminded you of Abbygail," I say.

"His *story* did. I read it, and I wanted to talk to you, but I couldn't, of course. I figured maybe I would anyway. Fuck the rules. They didn't apply in a case like that. Like with Abbygail—we didn't go around telling everyone her background, but some people had to know. Sebastian seemed like that. But then . . ." Dalton shrugs. "He wasn't."

"Wasn't like Abbygail."

"Wasn't what I expected. His background's similar. Shitty fucking childhood. Tossed around by his relatives, like a puppy no one wanted. Had some arrests. Petty theft, selling pills. Ended up in group homes. Things got worse after that. He joined . . . I don't know what you call it. I'd say a gang, but it wasn't like that. Wasn't like the mob either. Somewhere in the middle. He wanted out, and they weren't letting him go, so a guardian angel sent him here."

I pause. "That's . . . not what I expected. We haven't talked much but that wouldn't have been the background I picked for him."

"No, shit, huh? I expected him to be like Abbygail, a tough kid fighting me every step of the way. Or maybe a scared kid, happy to get out of there. He's a little older than her, but still a kid. What I got was . . ."

He throws up his hands. "I don't even know what I got. He's there, but he's not there. I meet him, and he does whatever I tell him to. He answers whatever I ask. It's like dealing with a fucking robot. He never acts. He just responds. Usually, when someone's like that, I can get a sense of what's behind it. Maybe they're uncertain, feeling out the situation, careful not to cause trouble. Maybe they're pissy, doing as they're told and nothing more. With Sebastian?" He shakes his head. "Nothing. I was going to talk to you about it, but what would I say? The kid creeps me out? What kind of bullshit is that?"

"A valid personal reaction. A gut feeling."

Dalton makes a face. "Based on what? He's polite. He does as he's told. There's no sarcasm there, no snark, no sense of repressed anger. Guy's a fucking perfect resident, and I'm complaining?"

"Well, Mathias thinks there's something wrong with him."

"Like what?"

"For now, he'd like us to just speak to him. Get our responses." I hop from the desk. "We can do that right after we tell April about tomorrow."

TWENTY-SEVEN

I find April at the clinic and promise she's leaving tomorrow, and there's no reason to tell anyone other than Kenny and Isabel. The council hasn't refused to let her go. We just aren't asking permission.

April doesn't like that. She doesn't actually complain, but she fusses and frets, and I can tell she's uncomfortable with the subterfuge. Still, the important thing is that she's leaving. Definitely leaving. If that causes trouble, we'll deal with it after she's gone.

Before we leave, she picks up a pill bottle from the counter. "I presume you need this. It should be put somewhere for safekeeping."

I lift the bottle. It contains the bullet she took from Garcia.

"We've identified the caliber," I say. "That's really all we need. We already know the gun used so . . ."

I'm holding the bottle at eye level. Just casually looking at the bullet while I talk. I stop.

"April?" I say. "Can Eric and I have a moment?"

Her brow furrows.

"She needs to speak to me in private," Dalton says.

April nods and heads into the exam room, where Kenny rests.

"What's up?" Dalton asks.

I uncap the bottle. Then I lay out a cloth on the waiting-area counter and tip the bullet onto it.

"This isn't a nine-mil," I say.

"What?"

He takes a closer look. "That's a nine-millimeter-caliber bullet."

"Right. The cartridge is nine millimeters in diameter, but it would be longer than an actual nine-mil. Rimless, too. I'll return to the scene, find the casing, and confirm that, but I'm ninety-nine percent sure this is a three-eighty. It's definitely not from my gun. We'll have to fire Garcia's to check the bullets. I think this explains why the gun was full. No one took it out of that drawer. They used an entirely different weapon."

A look crosses Dalton's face, the horror of a kid who's bet his year's allowance on a quiz answer, so certain he's right.

"I . . ." He can't even finish that.

It's hard for me to remember that I'm older than Dalton. Even if it's only by two months, it's significant because I *feel* younger. He doesn't act like a thirty-one-year-old. He can't, as sheriff in a town where ninety percent of the residents are older than he is.

I got my badge younger than most. I spent years hearing how that was because I was a woman and a visible minority, and I won't say with absolute certainty those things didn't play a role, but I also earned it, through my education, my experience, and the fact that I worked my ass off. Even when I left the force, I was the youngest detective in major crimes. So I was accustomed to older coworkers watching my work carefully, double-checking and, yes, second-guessing. As much as that rankled, I appreciated it, too, because they had the experience I lacked.

Dalton doesn't have that older partner. He hasn't since his father left. I've wondered at that sometimes. Five years ago, Gene Dalton retired and put his twenty-six-year-old son in charge of Rockton law enforcement. I made detective around the same age, and I hated anyone suggesting that was too young. It felt old enough. For a junior detective, maybe. For sheriff of a town as volatile as Rockton, without even an experienced older officer as mentor? Hell, no. When I asked Dalton once how he'd handled that, he'd shrugged and said,

"What's the expression? Fake it 'til you make it." It wasn't entirely a joke.

Dalton's formal training in ballistics is nonexistent. As in everything else, he's self-taught. It's just easy to forget that when I'm working with him.

"This is my fault," I say. "I should have confirmed ballistics first. Especially when Garcia's gun wouldn't have been easy for the shooter to get. I just . . ."

"Trusted me when I said it was a nine-mil." He slumps into a waiting-room chair. "Fuck. I'm sorry. I was completely sure, based on nothing more than overweening confidence. I have no fucking idea what a three-eighty is, so I sure as hell shouldn't be playing gun expert."

I pull up a chair in front of him. "We'll share blame on this one. I'm accustomed to not questioning my partner's findings. The problem is that you *aren't* my detective partner. Like you've said before, you're a junior partner. I'm uncomfortable with that, so I don't focus on it. But junior doesn't mean less competent. It means less experienced. I do you no favors treating you like a full detective and not questioning your work. For your part, yes, less confidence in your detective skills helps. You're not alone in this anymore, Eric." I point at the door. "I understand why you can't waffle and second-guess out there. But when it's just me, you can say 'It *looked* like a nine-mil,' and let me follow up. If you don't, I should follow up anyway. Likewise, you are free to check and question my work at any time."

"I was trying to save you a few minutes, and I added endless fucking hours chasing the wrong damn gun." He shakes his head. "How much does this screw up your investigation?"

"Not much, really. Let's walk."

I pocket the bottle and lead Dalton outside into the forest. His face stays tight, gaze distant, and I wait until he shakes it off and glances over.

"A three-eighty, huh?" he says.

"It's very similar to a nine-mil," I say. "In law enforcement and the military it's mostly used as a backup weapon. It's smaller than a nine-mil, cheaper, and has less kickback. Not as much force behind it, though. For a cop, there's no reason to use one instead of a nine-mil. It's mostly a personal weapon. Well, if you're American. Not a lot of self-defense pistols in Canada. I'd say that could be significant, but either way someone smuggled a weapon in, which is damn near impossible."

I take a few steps. "Is there a chance the gun predates you? We're allowed to pick our own sidearms. Could someone from a previous force have brought one in? What happens when one of Rockton's officers leaves? What do you do with their sidearm?"

"Get it the hell out of Rockton. We don't want more than we absolutely need. Sidearms for you, me, and Will. Rifles for militia and hunting."

"How careful were they about that before you? Could one have been left behind? Stuck under a floorboard?"

Dalton shakes his head. "Ty and Gene were just as careful as I am. The sheriff before Ty fucked up once. He let a deputy leave, saying his sidearm was under the bed. No big deal. Except a half dozen people heard him say that, and by the time the sheriff went to get it, the gun was gone."

"It was used to shoot someone, wasn't it?"

"Yeah, the moron who took it."

"He killed himself with it?"

"Not intentionally." Dalton's grip relaxes on mine, as his mind moves away from the misidentified bullet and he finds his rhythm. "The guy who took it was militia. They'd never let him carry a rifle. Didn't trust him with it. For good reason, it seems. He swiped the deputy's old sidearm, and two weeks later, he's dead in the forest. He was out doing target practice, gun jammed and he blew his face off trying to clear it."

"Ouch."

"It gets worse. The only reason the guy was on the militia was because the council insisted. He was the son of some rich asshole paying a shitload of money to keep him here. Rich asshole wanted his money back after his kid shot himself. The council repaid it to shut him up. When a random resident dies in an accident, the council doesn't give a fuck. But if it costs them money? That changes their perspective. Since then, sidearms are tightly regulated, and our asses are on the line if we screw up. When you came in, they found out in advance what kind of gun you wanted. It arrived in Dawson City, and I picked it up when I brought you in. Same went for Will. When my previous deputy went home, I had to take his sidearm with us to Dawson and drop it off at the usual spot. We can't even keep them on site. So right now, we have four handguns in Rockton. Yours, Will's, mine, and Garcia's."

"Five."

He looks over. Before I can say anything, he curses. "Petra."

"Yep. That was a handgun. And I have no idea what caliber it is, because we haven't gotten that far. The bodies are still lying in the forest, waiting until we have a moment to breathe and bury them. After we dig out the bullet."

"Fuck."

"The to-do list gets longer. Question is where do we start?"

"Interviews," he says. "We've got the advantage of daylight. Talk to Roy and Sebastian. Then get our asses out to fetch that bullet."

TWENTY-EIGHT

We tackle Roy first. Dalton comes along for moral support. And, I suspect, protection, though he knows better than to actually say that. I've already kicked Roy's ass. Dalton's still fuming over Roy attacking me, and so I suspect he tags along in hopes Roy will try something, and he'll get a chance for some retributory ass-kicking. Of course, the fact that the sheriff is with me means Roy won't so much as posture. He's a stereotypical bully. He's tough when he's got hangers-on backing him up. He's tough when his only adversary is a woman literally half his size. Strip him of his posse and put him up against a younger, fitter male opponent, and he shuts up fast. Well, no, "shutting up" is too much to ask for when it comes to guys like Roy. With Dalton around, though, he'll only run his mouth off, as if he totally *could* kick our sheriff's ass . . . he just doesn't feel like it today.

"The moron left the fucking door open?" Roy says after we explain. "Figures. That's your entire militia right there, Sheriff. Bunch of pussies. The toughest ones you've got actually *have* pussies." He shakes his head. "You want a decent force? Try hiring real men."

"The men I have are just fine," Dalton says. "I'd rather have them backing me up than the assholes who *think* they're tough guys. Loud-mouths who can barely throw a punch, swagger in here and try to sign up for militia duty. All they want is a gun in their hands, and they probably aren't even sure which end to hold."

Roy's face reddens. From day one, he'd been negotiating for a militia spot. Not offering to join. Not asking if he could. Trying to sell his services—*I might be persuaded to join, Sheriff, but you gotta make me a sweet offer.* Dalton told him he wasn't interested. He's been telling him the same thing everytime Roy comes into the station, seeing if Dalton's changed his mind.

"My militia is my business," Dalton says. "You know what Detective Butler's business is? Solving this murder."

"What the hell does that have to do with me? I've been locked in this damned cell the whole . . ." He trails off. "Oh hell, no. You're telling me that moron left the door open while someone shot this FBI guy?"

"US marshal."

"Whatever." He turns to me. "You're framing me, Detective. I took a few shots at you, and now your feelings are hurt, and you want me gone. Typical chick."

"Happened before, has it?" I say.

His face darkens, which tells me I'm guessing right—that he's smacked around a woman or two in his life, and then rolled his eyes when she had the audacity to complain.

"I'm not out to get you, Roy," I say. "I kicked your ass. I kinda like having you walk around with that story trailing after you."

His face goes even darker. "You caught me off guard."

I don't even answer that. There's no point. However he may be spinning this in his head, I know—as does every witness—what really happened.

"Paul—" I begin.

"—is a loser. A wuss. A cowardly, sniveling cubicle monkey."

"Brian," Dalton says.

Roy spits out a stream of homophobic slurs.

"Huh," Dalton says. "Interesting. Isabel?"

A couple of racist slurs, plus "stuck-up bitch," though he uses a word other than "bitch."

"Huh," Dalton says. "You don't even need to feed him quarters."

Roy's broad face scrunches up. "What? If you're telling me those three claim they saw me do anything—"

"Nope. I was just listing random names. Seeing if it works. It does."

"If what works?"

"You'll spit back insults like a goddamn vending machine. Life really sucks for you, doesn't it, Roy?"

"What the hell are you talking about?"

"Just an observation." Dalton leans forward. "We're going to play a game. Call it reverse vending machine. Instead of me feeding you quarters, you're going to donate them to the town picnic."

"What the hell are you—?"

"Every time you insult someone in my hearing or Casey's or Will's, you will donate one credit to the town fund. We'll include profanity, too, just for fun."

"Does that last one apply to you?" I ask Dalton.

"Fuck, no. I'd go broke."

"I'm glad you two find this so damn amusing," Roy says.

"One credit," Dalton says. "And, yeah, knocking assholes down a peg is always fun. Penalty still stands, though. You know why? 'Cause it's *our* fucking town. We own your ass while you're here. You signed away whatever rights and privileges you had down south. Willingly signed them over. I can make up whatever stupid fucking laws I want. No one will stop me. So, you're down one credit. Considering you're incarcerated and only earning the base amount, I'd suggest you consider each fucking word that leaves your mouth. Understood?"

Roy glowers at him.

"Casey?" Dalton says.

"Marshal Garcia is dead—" I begin.

"And it wasn't me. I'm Canadian. No US cop gives a rat's ass about what I did."

"Robbing people of their retirement savings?"

He crosses his arms. "That's what I was accused of. I never said I did it. I was a legitimate investment professional specializing in high-risk, high-reward ventures. Some of my clients ignored the 'high-risk' part. When they lost money, they went crying to the securities commission. I was under investigation, and I knew where that would lead. Prison. People hear stories like mine, and they never give us the benefit of the doubt. It's the rich asshole robbing little old ladies. The one percenters strike again. It's a bad time to be a rich white guy." He looks at Dalton. "Bad time to be a white guy altogether. You wouldn't know anything about that, but if this town was down south, I guarantee you wouldn't be sheriff. It'd be her." He points at me. "Or the black guy. Or is it African-American? African-Canadian? Who the fuck knows."

"Two credits," Dalton says. "And the answer is Will."

"What?"

"You were wondering what to call him. 'Will' works. Or 'Deputy Anders.' I don't think he answers to 'Hey, black guy.'"

"Roy," I say. "Not being American—or guilty of a federal offense in the US—only gets you off the hook if our dead man was actually a marshal. Paul said you were speculating on that. Maybe suspecting he wasn't . . . and if he's not, he could be here for you. One of your clients could be looking for revenge and sent a bounty hunter to bring you back."

"Yeah? Logical flaw there, Detective. In order to hire a bounty hunter, my former clients would need to have money. That's the problem. They don't."

"Because you cleaned them out."

"Right." He pauses. "Wait. No. I didn't—" He cuts himself short. "Don't put words in my mouth. They made the investments. If they got greedy and risked all their savings, that's not my fault. I'm an investment manager, not a financial advisor."

"That doesn't mean someone didn't find the money to send a bounty hunter."

"Well, if they did, I'd expect you guys to protect me. That's what I paid for. Safety. I'm paying a damned fortune to be here. And yeah, I swore. Another credit. Fuck it, make that two more. If you're trying to frame me, you're going to need to do a better job than saying Paul left the door open. Try finding someone who saw me out of my cage. You won't. You know why? I never left. I don't check the door when your militia morons leave. What's the point? Where would I go? Run into the forest to be eaten by bears? I'm not an idiot."

And that is where we must—with deep, deep regret—leave this conversation. Dalton walks to the door, throws it open, and says, "Go."

Roy looks at me.

"No," Dalton says. "I don't speak to my detective like that. I mean you, Roy. You're done here. Go home."

Roy's eyes narrow. "Yeah, I'm not falling for that. The minute I walk out, you're going to say I escaped and throw a punch at me."

I shake my head. "Here's a tip for life in Rockton, Roy. Don't presume others are like you."

"What's that supposed to mean?"

Dalton rolls his eyes at me. Then he leans outside and says, "You! Come here."

It's two random residents, just passing by. They carefully approach.

"I want witnesses," Dalton says. "I'm letting Roy leave. I will not penalize him in any way for leaving."

"So I can go?" Roy says.

"From the holding cell, yeah. I'm passing sentence. You attacked my detective, and I needed a cooling-off period or my judgment might have been overly harsh. Now I'm ready. Roy, in front of these witnesses, you are sentenced to six months of sanitation duty."

"What? Six months emptying toilets?"

"That's the penalty for assaulting an officer. It always has been. Feel free to ask around." Dalton steps out the door. Then he stops. "Hold on. I might be jumping the gun here. There is one defense to the charges. You mentioned that Detective Butler attacked you first. If she did, then you have the right to defend yourself." He turns to Roy. "Was that right?"

Roy drops his gaze and mutters under his breath.

"What's that?" Dalton says. "This is your chance to escape six months of shit duty, Roy. Tell me that Casey attacked you first, and I'll check with the witnesses, and if it's true, you're a free man. If you're lying, though, that doubles the sentence. So, who threw the first punch?"

Roy's answer is inaudible.

Dalton motions for him to speak up as the witnesses snicker.

"Me," Roy says.

"Then I think you owe our detective an apology."

"I was mistaken," Roy says.

Dalton opens his mouth. I silence him with a look. I know he's making a point, but a forced apology is worse than none at all.

As we walk away, Dalton says, "Can you believe that asshole?"

"Are you asking whether I believe his defense against shooting Garcia? Actually, yes. As much as I'd like the excuse to ship his ass out of Rockton, he makes a lousy suspect. I can't see anyone coming to Rockton after him, and I can't see him realizing the door is open and formulating a murder plan on the fly."

I look over at Dalton. "If by 'can you believe him,' you meant colloquially—can I believe he's such an asshole, again, actually yes. When I first came to Rockton, I remember thinking of Jen as a real-life troll. You get people like her online all the time. No matter what you say, they're going to argue with you and mock you in a way they wouldn't do to your face. The internet is anonymous. You can be whoever you want to be. You can also be whoever you really are. That's what Roy is. He probably used to hide his true colors in public and let it spew online or among friends. Here, he doesn't feel the need to filter. If you asked him, he'd say he's just being real, speaking his mind, saying what others think but are afraid to say."

"Is he right?"

"I would love to say no—that hardly anyone thinks the way he does. The truth . . . The truth is more complicated than that. Scarier, too, for someone like me. We deal with chauvinism and racism in real life, but we tell ourselves that's a minority opinion and then we go online and . . ." I shrug. "I still don't think it's a *majority* opinion. I have enough faith in people to believe that. It's just becoming a louder and louder minority, which lets people like Roy *feel* as if they're voicing a common opinion."

We walk a few steps in silence, and then Dalton says, "Should I be worried? He had his posse for that fucking lynch mob."

"I think that's mostly about violence. An excuse to vent another unsavory impulse. I'd like to believe even Roy wouldn't have gone through with it. But mob mentality is a dangerous thing. We know who was in his posse. We'll keep an eye on them, and we'll let them know we're keeping an eye."

"Already doing it."

We want to interview Sebastian next. We can't. He's off on chopping duty.

"Chopping duty?" I say when we find out. "I thought he hadn't caused any trouble."

There are two jobs Dalton uses for punishment. One is sanitation— emptying the portable toilets. When we don't have anyone serving that as a sentence, we offer triple wages to whoever will do it in the interim, and even then, we only get those desperate for credits. The next step down is chopping duty. It's not nearly as unsavory as emptying toilets, but it's backbreaking work. At this time of year, between the mosquitoes and the blackflies, few people do it even for double wages.

"He offered," Dalton says.

"He needs credits already?"

"No, he didn't realize you get extra for chopping. He just volunteered. We don't have a regular job for him yet, so he said he'd like to try everything. Will joked about chopping duty, and Sebastian said sure. He's been on it for two weeks. I'm sure the extra credits don't hurt, but we've told him he can quit. He said he's fine with it for a while longer. The only job he won't do is hunting."

My brows shoot up.

He shrugs. "Some people get here and can't wait to try hunting. Some say hell no. That was Sebastian."

"He'd rather do chopping duty?"

"Apparently."

"Interesting."

TWENTY-NINE

We're on body retrieval. It's me and Anders for this. Dalton got called off on a problem, and it's probably best if he sticks around town, considering we'll both be gone tomorrow. That was Anders's reasoning. I tried to talk him out of it—after his army experience he doesn't need to see more death—but he insists.

We take the big ATV, the wide one that will let us transport Valerie and Brady, one at a time. We leave Storm behind. Dead bodies make her anxious. Hell, they don't make anyone *happy,* but Storm doesn't need to come along, so she stays with Dalton.

Eventually, we need to leave the main trail, and the ATV won't go on the narrow path. That means walking. It will also mean carrying the bodies back on a stretcher.

As we walk, I tell Anders about the bullet mix-up.

"Ouch," he says. "How's Eric handling that?"

"Not well."

"He won't. But . . . I hate to say this, but it's not entirely a bad thing. Eric's still learning that he's not the pro anymore, at least not when it comes to investigating. Better that he screws up on small things, easily fixed, and learns his lesson. Does that sound patronizing?"

"No, you're right. My first partner would let me make mistakes, just to show that the hotshot young college grad hadn't known as much as she thought she did. At first, I thought he was undermining me. Then I realized he never let me mess up when it made a difference, and he never told our superiors about my mistakes. It taught me that experience trumps education."

"Yep, and that's a lesson Eric's still learning. It's not his fault. He's had to step up, which may be partly *my* fault. He does know what he's doing, most of the time, so I didn't question. I'm a good army boy, as he likes to remind me."

"He doesn't mean it as an insult."

"No, but he does mean it as a kick in the ass. A reminder that I'm a little too quick to follow orders, too quick to trust that my superior officers know what they're doing." He peers ahead. "How much farther?"

"Just up ahead."

I start marching toward it, but Anders catches my arm. He doesn't say anything, just rubs his finger against my forearm. I pause and take a deep breath.

"I could say that you didn't have a choice shooting Val," he says. "But that's bullshit."

I stiffen.

"You chose this job," he says, "like I chose to be a soldier. And neither of us got into it because we wanted to kill people. We got into it despite that. Despite knowing it might come to that."

I glance over at him.

He releases my arm and eases back, hands going into his pockets. "When I signed up for the army, I was supposed to be a medic, and that suited me just fine. Saving lives, not taking them. Then there was a skirmish, in the barracks, and I handled it, and someone decided I made a better cop than a medic. Still, I figured, that's cool, at least I won't see actual combat." He shakes his head. "Didn't quite turn out that way."

I squeeze his hand, but he keeps talking, lost in his thoughts. "I spent a lot of time thinking 'This is *not* what I signed up for. It's not fair. I got tricked.' That's bullshit. I joined the army. This was what I signed up for. Yes, I didn't want to see combat. I wanted to support the troops in other ways. But if I had to fight, and I whined about it, did that mean I thought I was better than them? That I deserved to have better? Safer? Easier?"

He shakes his head. "People talk about soldiers, about cops. They disagree with war. They disagree with how we handle crime. That's fine. You know what? I agree. But someone still has to do the job. It's better if it's someone like us, someone who gives a damn. Someone who's going to *feel* it."

He looks over at me. "Feeling it's not a bad thing, Casey. It just sucks that we have to. It really, really sucks."

I lean against his shoulder. "It does. Thanks. I did sign up for this. And I hope it always hurts. That I always second-guess and wonder whether I had another option. With Val, it feels like I didn't stop to process. I think that's the worst. It feels like it did with Blaine. No thought; just reaction."

"And if you could go back?" he asks softly.

"Honestly?" I exhale. "I'm glad I didn't hesitate. It wasn't pure re-action. I understood the situation and realized I had a split second to respond. If I'd stopped to think it through more, she'd have taken Eric, and when she was done with him, she'd have killed him. I have *no* doubt of that."

"Then you made the right choice."

"Unless he could have gotten away. He probably could—"

Anders puts his hand over my mouth. "Nope. Don't go there. There are always questions. We see every possibility. What if Eric could have escaped? What if Val had a sudden change of heart? What if a grizzly got her? Mountain lion? Or maybe the heavens would open and God would strike her down with lightning because she deserved to die, and Eric's a good guy who doesn't."

I laugh softly. "I've never actually seen that last one, unfortunately."

"Me neither. That's why I'm an atheist. There are always 'what-if' scenarios, Casey. You know that. You also know that you had to shoot Val. Doesn't mean it won't hurt."

"I know." I give his hand another squeeze before dropping it. "So how are *you* doing? We haven't had much time to talk."

"Doing okay. Too busy to do much thinking. Or much drinking, if that's what you're asking."

"You know it's not."

"It's not really what you're asking, but it kinda always is, a little. You worry. I appreciate that. I'm doing fine. Could use some down-time to sit and process, you know? When this is over, I propose a day of spelunking. Leave Eric behind and just get out, take some time to clear our heads."

Before I came to Rockton, Anders used to sneak off to do exactly that. Go caving by himself. Spend time in the absolute darkness and the absolute silence. Spend time being himself, dealing with what he's seen, what he's done. These days, I've convinced him to take me—at least for safety—and he does.

I nod. "We'll do that."

"Onward then?" He waves ahead. "Are we ready for this?"

"Ready to see two bodies that have been left to the elements and scavengers for four days? Who *isn't* ready for that?"

He smiles and shakes his head.

"You don't have to be," I say. "Ready, that is. You can skip this."

"I volunteered. Had to argue to get the job too, with you and Eric so eager to protect my delicate sensibilities."

"We just—"

"I know. Now let's get these bodies home."

He waves for me to lead the way. I do steel myself as I walk through into the clearing. It's not the condition of the bodies that will bother me. I've seen worse. Saw it on my very first day in Rockton, with a mangled corpse.

But Anders is right. This isn't about seeing a body. It's about seeing Val. Seeing a woman I knew, a woman I tried to help, a woman I shot, slumped on the earth, brains splattering the trees, blood soaking the earth, body ravaged by the elements and every hungry beast that has passed this way.

Oh, yeah. I knew exactly what I was about to see. I could picture it in vivid Technicolor detail.

I still had to see it, though. Had to face it. Anders is right in that, too. I signed up for this, and that's not saying I wanted this—it's saying that I accepted the very real possibility that Blaine Saratori wouldn't be the only ghost hovering in my mind's darkest corners. That he might not even loom the largest.

He still does, though. For now. I can take comfort in that. That seems an odd word to use, but it is comforting in its way. Val's death weighs lighter than Blaine's. The hostiles I had to shoot in combat weigh lighter still. Things like this should not be compared on a scale, but they are, for people like me. For people like Anders. Those who've had to kill. And those who've killed when they didn't have to.

Val falls on the middle of that scale, yet she does slide just enough to the "had to" side that there's no danger of me slipping back into that dark hole where I had been after Blaine. This is a temporary hollow, where I'll lie for a while, bruised but still able to function.

I take a deep breath, pull back a pine bough, and . . .

The clearing is empty.

I pause. Then I step through and look around. Anders walks in behind me.

"Wrong place?" he says.

"I . . . No, I'm sure it's not. Brady and I came down this path. Eric held that bough back for me as we left. It's broken, see?" I point to where the branch hangs, base cracked, needles already brittle.

I turn around. "I had Brady. I stood right here." I walk over, the memories rushing back. "I heard a voice behind me, and I turned. Eric was standing there. Val had led him in at gunpoint. She mocked him. She'd lain on the path, and he'd rushed to help, never thinking to draw his gun, never thinking it was a trap."

"He saw her hurt, and he ran to help."

I nod. "She mocked him for it. For being a decent person."

"Bitch."

I nod. *I'm sorry, Val. I'm sorry that you had a shitty life. I'm sorry it broke something in you. I'm sorry you grew up cold and empty. But I'm not sorry I shot you. I had to. There was nothing good in you, and I could not trust you to let him go.*

I walk around the small clearing, checking each spot before I put my foot down. Anders stays where he is, awaiting orders. Yes, Dalton sometimes not-too-subtly pokes him for being a "good soldier," but that also means Anders is a good cop. Dalton and I have no problem taking charge. We don't need our deputy fighting for the reins. Right now, I don't want Anders poking about, trying to find clues and prove he's a detective. He's not. So he'll stay out of the way, and the moment I need him, all I have to do is ask.

"The only predator that'll drag off prey whole is a cougar," I say. "And our forest isn't exactly teeming with those."

We're north of their traditional territory. There's been one female, and she's a man-eater. She's also had cubs up here. I had to kill one a few weeks ago. Another death to weigh on my conscience, one I'd rather have avoided.

"I can see a cougar dragging off Val," I say, "but Brady wasn't a small guy. He'd outweigh the cat. Even if she managed to take one body and cache it, why come back for the second?"

Anders says nothing. He knows I don't expect a response. I'm just thinking aloud. If he disagrees, he'll speak up. He doesn't.

"Any other predator would only take pieces," I say. "Maybe they could eventually cart off the scavenged remains but . . ."

I don't see signs of that. I find blood. I find trampled undergrowth. I find exactly what I'd expect to remain after we took the bodies.

"Someone cleared the scene," I say.

"Petra?" he asks.

"Maybe. At this point, we have no shortage of council spies who could have gotten the order to move the bodies. Petra, Phil, Mathias . . ."

"Me."

"I wasn't—"

"Yeah, I know. But I need to address it, right?"

This is why Anders got into Rockton despite his violent past. He's here to spy on Dalton and report back to the council. They'd told him that Dalton was violent himself—and corrupt—so Anders had been fine with the task . . . until he realized the council was full of shit. He still plays spy. He just gives them small indiscretions that can never be used against Dalton. We know that's the best way to play it, even if I'm pretty sure by now the council realizes where Will Anders's loyalties lie.

"I didn't clear the scene," he says. "They never ask me to do anything like that."

"Someone has, and I doubt they did it as a favor. I came here to see if the bullet that killed Brady matched the one that killed Garcia. Now I can't."

"Petra's your most likely suspect for cleanup, too," he says. "I can't see Phil or Mathias dragging around dead bodies."

"Hmm."

"How many shots did Petra fire?" he asks.

"Just one. He was standing over here."

I position myself in Brady's place and then turn to see the trajectory of the bullet. It's possible that it passed through Brady. I wasn't paying enough attention to that—I only know that he died. Anders and I both search for the bullet. Then we go to where I saw Petra, and we hunt for the cartridge. We search for at least an hour. As the sun drops, we shine our flashlights on the ground, in hopes the beams will bounce off the metal cartridge.

"It's not here," Anders says. "Which really suggests it's Petra."

"Or that she grabbed it before she went." I sigh and ease back on my haunches. I'm tired, though, and when I shift my weight, I topple onto my ass.

"A fine idea," Anders says, plunking down beside me. He lies down, arms braced behind him, and says, "Does it even matter?"

"Does what matter?"

"Any of this. Petra shot a serial killer. Someone shot a guy threatening to expose Rockton. Do we actually care?"

I look over at him. "Do we care whether our resident comic-book artist is a highly trained assassin? Do we care whether someone may have murdered a law enforcement official who came to enforce a federal warrant?"

Anders sighs. "Yeah, I know. I'm tired and cranky. Sometimes it just feels like we're killing ourselves trying to solve crimes no one cares about. No one except us. Fighting the council. Fighting the people we're trying to protect. Everyone watching, everyone judging, no one giving a shit how much we put into this, how much we risk for it."

"Like being back in the army."

He barks a laugh. "Actually, yes."

"It's like policing down south, too. The difference is that there, we hear only the criticisms. We have to trust that the silent majority appreciates what we do—the risks we take, the constraints we work under. Up here, I actually see that. I hear that. I *feel* appreciated. It just gets hard to remember that when I'm running on two hours' sleep while watching other residents toddle off to bed at ten P.M."

"No shit, huh." He stretches out on his back. "We could stay here. Pretend we're searching *all* night. Super, super busy, doing super, super important police work."

"Do you think Eric won't notice?"

"He's probably already on his way, making sure we haven't been devoured by cave bears."

"Those damned cave bears. They're everywhere."

He flashes a smile my way at the old joke. "Fortunately Eric will always protect us. He'll be here any moment, and then you'll have to sweet-talk him into staying with us. Sleeping under the stars." He squints up at the thick tree cover. "There are stars, right?"

"There will be, once it's dark."

"Perfect." He rolls his head to the side to look at me. "And do not tell me that we can't have the entire police force spend the night in the forest, how it's irresponsible and shit like that."

"I wasn't going to say a thing."

He sighs and pushes himself up, sitting again. "I suppose we should go."

"Never said it."

"Yeah, but I still hear it." He starts to rise and then pauses. "Speak of the devil."

"Hmm?"

He nods, and I catch a glimpse of a dark shape. He opens his mouth with, "Hey, we—"

I cut him off by gripping his arm. He looks over at me. I shake my head. He frowns. I shake it again, and he peers at the figure long enough to realize it is not Dalton.

I release his arm, and his hand goes for his gun. I'm already gripping mine.

Again, Anders and I communicate through seamless gestures and expressions. A frown. A jerked chin. A gaze cutting left. A nod. It's not even so much an attempt to be silent as it is almost second nature, an effortless telepathy, our minds working so in sync that we don't need to whisper a plan. It's my plan, but he does consider a moment before nodding, assessing and agreeing rather than simply following the chain of command.

Anders stays where he is, still crouched, moving to one knee as he watches that still figure.

It's nowhere near dark yet, but the sun has begun its descent, long shadows stretching through the forest. The figure is nestled in one of those, making it little more than a featureless blob. I can tell it's human. I can also tell it isn't tall enough to be Dalton.

THIRTY

The figure moves. It's hunched down, creeping forward, gaze on the clearing where we were sitting. It stops, and its head tilts, and something in that tilt suggests it's a woman.

She starts forward again. Soon she'll be close enough to spot Anders poised on one knee, looking straight at her. Through the undergrowth, he catches my eye, and I make a split-second decision. I tell him to turn around. Put his back to the approaching figure. He does, without hesitation, and my breath catches, heart thumping harder. He trusts me implicitly. Now I need to prove I deserve that. I lift my gun, finger still off the trigger.

I take another step. The woman creeps forward and then ducks her head, as if to see through an opening. She must spot Anders, because she goes still. Then she sees that he has his back to her. She reaches up, and my gut chills. There's something long and dark in her hand.

My mouth opens to shout a warning to Anders. Then she pulls back a branch for a better view, and she uses the hand holding the object. It's not a gun. I squint. The object is black, maybe a foot long, thin enough that she can move that branch while gripping it. Thinner than a knife. Lighter, too, from the way she moves it. A stick?

My gaze moves to her other hand. She's holding something in it, too. Something round. A rock? A stick and a rock?

Anders keeps his back to her, and she takes another step. I can't see her face, but I see her clothing. It's hide, which isn't unusual out here. Some settlers wear well-mended jeans and shirts. Others wear clothing homemade from hides. The homespun clothes are works of art, craftsmanship well beyond what we buy down south. What this woman wears is another thing altogether. The hides have been roughly cut out and roughly sewn, the sort of thing you might expect to find on someone lost in the forest for years, forced to create her own clothing lest she freeze.

Yet this woman isn't lost. Not in the literal sense of the word. She's chosen to be here, like the settlers. She hasn't chosen their lifestyle, though. She's chosen one beyond my comprehension.

She is a hostile. That's our name for those who go into the forest and revert to something baser. When I met hostiles, though, I didn't see people who'd *willfully* reverted. No more than I'd see someone ranting on a street corner, lost in the throes of mental illness, and decide they'd chosen that. Yes, people do choose to not treat their mental illness, deciding the cure is worse than the disease. Yes, people do choose to live on the streets. But I don't believe they choose *that*— wandering the cities, lost in the mazes of their own disturbed minds. They make a choice, and it turns into something they wouldn't have imagined. I've talked about my past as falling down a dark pit. That's an exaggeration. The true pit is the woman I see before me.

She takes one more step, and a lone strip of sunlight illuminates her face. With no start of surprise, I realize I know her. The moment I saw that it was a woman, I'd thought immediately of Maryanne, whom we'd met in the forest a week ago. Shot by Val, she'd taken off into the forest before we could stop her. Now she's here, and I proceed as carefully as I can, knowing one false move will send her fleeing like a spooked deer.

I move forward, and so does she, slipping toward Anders, who still stands with his back to her. She's focused on him, and even when a leaf crunches under my foot, she doesn't notice. She takes two more steps. Then she crouches, dropping from view. A moment later, she rises, her hands now empty, and she steps backward, retreating.

Another step. Then another. I match each, my feet coming down in time with hers. Soon I'm so close I can smell the sweaty musk of her. One more step, and I'll be able to touch her. To grab her.

I force myself to stop. Then I holster my gun and say, "Maryanne?"

She wheels, leaves crackling. Her hands fly up. Mine do, too, rising to show her they're empty.

"It's me," I say. "Eric's girl."

A curse sounds to my left. Maryanne spins that way. It's Anders. He's turned, and when he saw her, he'd let out a curse of shock. Horror fills his face, as if he's stumbled onto something far worse than a scavenged body.

The rough hide clothing is the least of it. Her hair is matted and wild. One ear blackened and ragged, lost to frostbite. The ends of two fingers the same. She's filthy, and a week ago, the dirt had seemed rubbed on like war paint, patterns clear. Now it's smeared and smudged, revealing ritualized scars below. Her mouth is open, showing her teeth, the edges of the front ones filed into rough points. Thousands of years ago, she could have stepped onto a battlefield, a Neolithic warrior woman. Today, she seems to have stepped straight out of a nightmare.

She sees Anders. She sees his expression. And deep in her eyes, there is a flash of realization. A long-buried hint of the woman she'd been. She sees what she looks like to Anders, and she lets out a gasp. Then she spots his gun. Her gasp turns to an animal shriek. She wheels and charges into the forest.

"Maryanne!" I shout.

I take off after her. Anders is at my heels. He's already apologizing.

I ignore him and run, calling after her, telling her it's okay, we won't hurt her. She only runs faster, easily cutting across paths I don't see, leaving me dodging and darting around obstacles as she disappears into the shadowy forest.

"I'm sorry," Anders says once she's gone. "Shit, Casey. I am *so* sorry. I've just never seen . . ."

"I know."

"She startled me. That's all. I'm sorry."

I nod and start walking back.

Anders jogs to catch up. "I know I don't do as well with this stuff as you and Eric. The hostiles. The settlers. Even Brent. I just . . . I'm not used to that. I'm sorry I scared her off."

"It's okay," I say. "I know that was a shock."

"She's the woman from the forest, isn't she? The one you mentioned."

I nod.

"Everything Eric's said about the hostiles . . . it still didn't prepare me for that."

"She used to be a professor."

"What?"

He's fallen a step behind and catches up now.

"She's a university professor," I say. "She has a Ph.D. in biology."

"That—that—"

"Yes," I say, simply, and the word hangs there.

"How . . . ?"

"That's the question, isn't it?" I pause to get my bearings and then steer left. "That woman came to Rockton like anyone else. She has a doctorate. She taught at a university. She's a naturalist, and when a group of residents decided to go into the forest, to become settlers, she went with them. Eric knew her. She'd taught him." I catch his look and say, "Not *that*. Just friendship and a shared interest in the natural world. Gene Dalton didn't let people just go off into the forest, so Eric had to search for her. They found a ruined and abandoned camp, with what looked like signs of attack. They were presumed dead. A year later, Eric ran into Maryanne, and she attacked him. She was out of her mind. She didn't recognize him. They'd been friends, and he remembered her as a kind, gentle woman who loved the wilderness, and then she attacks and he thought he'd have to kill her to escape."

"Holy shit."

"He hadn't seen her since. Then, last week, she was with the party we ran into."

"The ones who attacked you."

"*She* didn't. She stayed out of it. Afterwards, Eric recognized her. He talked to her, and she was different, more like what you saw. She remembered him, but vaguely. Have you ever talked to a person with Alzheimer's? If you feed them enough information, you get flickers of recognition? That's what it was like. Eric was making progress. She remembered who he was. She remembered that she liked him, trusted him. We had a chance there, to get her to Rockton. Then Val started shooting. She winged Maryanne, and she took off."

"She seems okay."

I give him a look.

"You know what I mean," he says. "She's recovering well from the gunshot."

Yes, if it doesn't get infected. I can't imagine how it *won't,* given her state. I don't say that, of course. I don't blame Anders for spooking her. I came to Rockton better prepared for people like Maryanne, or the settlers or the hostiles. As a city cop, I cultivated contacts everywhere I could find them—the homeless, the addicts, the mentally ill. For me, policing meant getting comfortable with people that I hadn't often encountered in my upper-middle-class life. Anders grew up in the suburbs, too. He's not cold or cruel or close-minded. He just lacks experience, like the average person who crosses the road to avoid someone talking to themselves.

I find the clearing again and then the spot where Maryanne had stood. It takes only a moment to see what she set down. The "stick" is a raven feather. The "rock" is the skull of a small animal.

I lift the skull. "Predator," I say when I see the canines. "Weasel maybe?"

"She put those there?" he says.

I nod. "Set them down and backed away. Leaving them for us. She must have heard me talking and recognized my voice. Maybe she expected Eric to be with me."

"And those are what? Gifts?"

I turn the feather over in my hands. As I do, I remember Maryanne talking to Dalton.

"The boy with the raven," I murmur.

"Hmm?"

"That's how she remembered Eric. The boy with the raven. She'd told him that studies suggest corvids can use tools, and he tested it, trying to train one."

"Wait. Isn't this the guy who rolls his eyes at you for training that raven behind the station?"

"Yep. Believe me, I am not going to let him forget that. But this"—I lift the feather—"means the message is for him."

"Message?" Anders looks at the skull. "Didn't Eric say the hostiles use skulls as territorial markers?"

"Human ones. *Old* human ones. I don't know if this would mean the same thing or—"

At a movement, I turn, hand going to my gun. A figure approaches at a jog, and before I can pull my weapon, I recognize the newcomer.

"We're over here!" I call.

"Yeah," Dalton says as he slows to a walk. "I can hear you two a kilometer away."

"Just scaring off the cave bears," Anders says. "As you can see, we did an awesome job, so you didn't need to worry about a thing."

The cave bear joke comes from early in my stay, when Anders took me deeper into a cave, away from the others. Dalton hadn't let us be gone long before he came to check on us, and Anders had joked about cave bears.

At the time, I figured Dalton was just being his usual overcautious self. I realize now what Anders must have realized at the time—that Dalton hadn't loved the idea of his deputy sneaking me off for a private tour.

"We saw Maryanne," I say, and I explain, handing him the feather and skull.

When I finish, he's examining the skull. "I have no idea what it means. If she thought I would, then . . ." He shrugs. "I'm glad to hear she's okay." He squints into the forest. "I'd like to get her back to Rockton."

"I know," I say. "If she's coming out when she hears us, maybe we'll get a chance when you're around."

"And when I'm not," Anders says. "I spooked her."

"Everything spooks her," Dalton says. He puts the feather and skull into his pack. "What happened to getting the bodies?"

I tell him. He searches the clearing for clues but finds nothing, and we head back, talking the whole way, partly in hopes Maryanne will hear Dalton and come out. She doesn't.

THIRTY-ONE

It's midnight by the time we get to Rockton, and the sun has dropped low enough to leave only a glow in the night sky. We head for Sebastian's apartment.

"He was supposed to share a place," Dalton says as we walk. "That's the one time he was a pain in the ass. He got downright snappy about it. The whole flight up from Vancouver felt like sitting beside a fucking mannequin. Most people have questions about Rockton. Even you did. Sebastian didn't say a word. It was sp—" He rubs the back of his neck and doesn't finish.

"It was what?" I ask.

He shakes his head.

"Eric? It's me." I wave around the empty street. "Just me."

He wrinkles his nose and hesitates before blurting, "Spooky."

I have to laugh at that. "What's wrong with saying it was spooky?"

"It sounds . . ." He waves his hand. "Nebulous. People give off vibes, especially when I first meet them, ready to bring them here. Anxious. Nervous. Scared, even. Or defensive. Angry. Belligerent. Sometimes relieved. Happy. Excited."

"What vibes did I give off?"

"Not a damn thing."

"Like sitting beside a mannequin?"

"Nah, with you, I could tell there was more, and I just couldn't get a read on it."

"But Sebastian's vibes were spooky."

"No. See, that just sounds weird. I just . . . I don't know. Last time I felt anything like that was when I brought Mathias in. I met him at the airport, and he was charming and polite as fuck, and all I could think was 'I should leave him here.' I did not want the guy in my town. Which proves that my sixth sense for people is bullshit."

"Uh, not sure I'd go that far. Mathias . . ."

"Yeah, yeah, I know. He's manageable, though." He pauses. "Where was I going with this?"

"Sebastian's apartment."

Dalton shakes his head. "I'm tired and rambling. All right, so, two hours into the trip, I'm the one feeling anxious. I want to get him talking, reassure myself he's fine. So I start explaining the living arrangements, telling him he'll be bunking down with someone, and he turns and gives me this look. He's a kid, right? But that look, it was . . ."

"Spooky?"

I'm smiling when I say it, but Dalton still glowers. "No. See? Now you're not going to let me live that down. The look was *not* spooky. It just wasn't what I expect from a kid. It reminded me of when I bring fifty-year-olds in and tell them the rules, and they give me this look, like 'Who the hell are you, boy?' Sebastian gives me that look, and then he says, in this ice-cold voice, 'That is not what I was told.' I said whatever he was told was wrong, because he's a new resident, and the place we have ready for him is shared accommodations."

"And then?"

"He opens his mouth, like he's ready to snap at me. He stops. Regroups. And that look vanishes. He asks if there are any options. His voice changes when he asks it. His whole demeanor does. Have you had any encounters with him?"

"Just a quick hello as we pass. He seems nice. Quiet, but very polite. Kind of sweet, actually. A nice, respectful kid."

"Exactly. That's what he changed into. He politely asked for options, and my back went down. I explained that the only alternative is . . ." He waves to the building ahead. "A really shitty bottom-floor apartment that we've been using for storage. He says he'd take that, if possible. He'll clear it and clean it, whatever we need, and he's very sorry for the inconvenience, but he has anxiety issues and would prefer to not have a roommate."

"So you gave him this place."

"We've had people who'll sleep in a damned closet if it means they don't have a roommate. Personally, I understand that. I used to tell women that my place was a mess, so they'd never expect to come in, let alone stay. Then I'd give some story about how I need—by law— to sleep in my own house, so people can find me. That gave me an excuse to get the hell back to my place as soon as I could after . . ."

I snort a laugh.

He glances over. "Too much information?"

"Never. So I'm special, huh?"

"I thought you'd figured that out by now. But, yeah, I understand when someone says they'll do anything to avoid having a roommate, so I let Sebastian take this place."

"Interesting."

His brows rise as we climb onto the porch. "Interesting how?"

"Just interesting."

"You'll explain later?"

"I will."

Sebastian answers the door groggy, his hair mussed, as if he was asleep. Dalton doesn't ask if we woke him. He acts as if he doesn't care, and Sebastian lets us in without a word.

Dalton said that the look Sebastian gave him on the plane made him seem older. Normally, Sebastian looks like a high school senior, though, admittedly, I've reached that age where teenagers seem like they should still be in grade school. There's a smattering of acne on his baby-faced cheeks. Dark blond hair hangs to his shoulders. His hair flops over one eye, and he makes no motion to push it back. He never does. He just lets it hang there and hides behind it.

He's wearing sweatpants and no shirt, showing an average physique for a guy his age, thin but not skinny, muscle tone from youth and casual sports rather than gym time. As he leads us in, he grabs a T-shirt and tugs it on. There's a university logo on the front, and I recognize it, saying, "Alma mater?"

"Uh . . ."

"Sorry," I say with a smile. "You don't have to tell me. That's the rule. Say nothing you don't want to say."

"Nah, it's not that. I'd love to say yes, it's where I went. I wanted to. It just never worked out. A girl I knew went and gave it to me. Like one of those stupid vacation shirts. *Someone I know went to Western, and all I got was this crappy T-shirt.*"

He smiles when he says it, a little self-conscious, hands shoved into his pockets. As I study his face, I curse Mathias. He's told me he sees signs of sociopathy in Sebastian, so now I'm looking for them. Sociopathy, like psychopathy, is a manifestation of borderline personality disorder. As for the difference between the two, well, I've heard so many theories that I'll have to ask Mathias for his personal distinction. I know that either type is dangerous.

Of the mental disorders, schizophrenia gets the worst PR. People hear about that in conjunction with horribly violent crimes, and they think every person with it is a frothing madman. I know people with schizophrenia who manage it just fine, and even at their worst they've never committed a violent act. It's sociopathy that scares me, because a sociopath isn't that ranting killer, lost in delusion and madness. It's the person who commits crimes because they see no reason *not* to.

Mathias says he has traits of sociopathy. I won't argue that self-diagnosis. He is charming. He is manipulative. And while I believe—perhaps naively—that he's capable of caring about people, it seems an active choice, which he applies to very, *very* few people. He is definitely dangerous. He has definitely killed people. And I doubt he loses a moment's sleep over it.

Mathias told me that this young man shows sociopathic traits, so

I'm analyzing his every move. I don't want to. I prefer to form my opinions without bias. But that's why I have Dalton with me. I've told him nothing, and yet he's already admitted that Sebastian reminded him of Mathias.

Sebastian leads us inside. The apartment has the same setup as Diana's, and he motions to the sofa. We sit, and he starts to lower himself to the armchair and then stops, hovering over it.

"Drinks," he says. "Would you like . . . ?" He looks at the cold fire. "Uh, I've got water."

"We're fine, thanks," I say. "We're sorry for coming by so late. I'm sure you were sleeping."

He doesn't say no, that's fine. He doesn't argue either. Just nods.

I continue, "We're burning the midnight oil on this case. Making the rounds to those who don't have alibis."

His hands tighten on the arms of his chair, almost reflexively. "Right. That'd include me."

"Can you tell us where you were at the time of the shooting?"

"Here. Alone. Sleeping." He pauses. "Lousiest alibi ever."

"Sleeping?" My brows lift. "In the middle of the afternoon?"

"I worked a split shift. Chopping duty in the morning, and then dishwashing after dinner. I was off from noon until four. We'd headed out at five A.M. for lumber, so I was beat. I came back and crashed."

"Can anyone confirm that?"

He shakes his head. "They can confirm I had a split shift. Marlo might remember me saying I was wiped out and planned to nap." He pauses. "Which, if I intended to commit a crime, would sound like I was setting up an alibi."

"Uh-huh," I say.

He manages a weak smile. "Yep, I have some experience with that. Needing alibis. Setting them up, too." He looks at me. "I'm not sure how much you know about my background, Detective Butler, but I understand Sheriff Dalton has been briefed. While I'd rather it wasn't broadcast around town, I'm okay with you knowing my past. I'd rather you did, actually. Get it all out in the open. My personal twelve-step program for criminal rehabilitation."

"So you've committed crimes."

"What's that joke? I don't have a rap sheet—I have a rap book?" He shakes his head. "I got an early start. Shoplifting by eight. Jacking cars by fourteen. B and E. Petty larceny. Possession with intent to distribute." He folds his hands in his lap, an odd gesture that I notice. "I could blame a shitty home life and shittier friends, but we all make choices, and I wasn't a dumb, naive kid. I made bad choices. Lots of them. When I wanted out, I learned it wasn't that easy. So now you're stuck with me. If you need a car jacked, I'm your guy. Considering you have no cars here, though, I'm pretty much useless."

"You prefer bump keys or jumping the engine?"

He smiles. "Been a while since I actually jacked anything, but at the time, it was bump keys."

I hope my expression doesn't change. You don't jack a car with a bump key. Or by "jumping the engine"—whatever that means.

Sebastian leans back, getting comfortable. "One thing you won't find on my records is violence. I'm sure Sheriff Dalton can confirm that. I hurt people. I don't deny that. When you steal their stuff or sell them drugs, you're hurting them. But I've never physically assaulted anyone."

"Do you know why the victim was in Rockton?"

"I heard he was a marshal. That rules me out too—I don't even own a passport." He looks at Dalton, who nods.

Sebastian continues. "It caused me some trouble getting in. No passport. No driver's license. But I didn't lead the kind of life where I'd be going on vacation to Disney World anytime soon. Didn't have the kind of family who'd take me, either. As for driving, well, they weren't my cars, so I didn't see the point in getting a license."

"What about your drug crimes?"

"Possession with intent. That's it. I never hit the big leagues. I guess that's a good thing. I can honestly say that whatever trouble I got myself into, no one is coming up here after me. My rap sheet might be long, but it's penny-ante charges."

"Which brought you up here?"

He hesitates. It's only a split second before he shrugs, but I notice that pause. "Like I said, it was a long sheet. I pissed off some people. No one who'd have the brains to find this place, though."

I glance at his shirt again. "What did you want to take at Western?"

His eyes light up. As we've been talking, he's been calm, relaxed. Distant, though. Like a guy interviewing for a job he'd like, but if he doesn't get it, well, there are others.

When I ask about the university, it's as if I've finally hit the internal switch that engages him.

"Law," he says. "I wanted to get an undergrad degree at Western, double major, criminology and economics, and then go to Queen's for law."

"Good plan," I say.

He shrugs. "It was. It still is. I just need to get through some things first. Clean up my life and get it on track."

We chat more about his plans, and Dalton keeps shooting me looks. He knows I'm going somewhere with this, but he can't see it. Finally I end the interview and thank Sebastian for his time.

Once we're away from the house, Dalton says, "He's never stolen a car, has he?"

"He might have," I say. "But only if the keys were in the ignition."

"What about the rest? The questions about where he wanted to go to university, what he wanted to take?"

"I was following a hunch," I say. "He seemed very well spoken. Polite. Intelligent. At ease. Confident."

"Yeah . . ."

"Like Abbygail when she arrived, right?"

Dalton snorts.

"Would you have called her well spoken?" I ask.

"Fuck, no."

"Extensive vocabulary? Good diction?"

Another snort. "If we're talking profanity, yeah, she had an even better vocabulary than me. But that wasn't her fault. School wasn't exactly a priority in her life. She was barely literate when . . ."

He looks at me. "He doesn't fit his background."

"Sebastian is *not* a kid from the streets. Trust me. You can get some who are well read, self-taught like you, but that's rare. You can get some from middle-class backgrounds, good educations, but that's not the story he gave. Did Abbygail come to Rockton wearing a university shirt? Knowing what degrees she wanted? Where to get them?"

"Fuck no."

"He could be faking it. Inventing a future for himself. But that was the one time he lit up. The one subject he engaged on."

"Yeah, I noticed that. Until then, it was like he was reading lines for a role he studied. That last part, though, that was real."

"And I think it's the only part that was."

THIRTY-TWO

According to our plans, the moment the sun breaks over the horizon we'll be in the plane, rolling down the runway, taking April to Dawson. There's a good chance it'll be hours before anyone realizes we aren't just at home, sleeping in while leaving Anders on duty.

The next morning, though, I have trouble getting April moving. My ultra-efficient sister dawdles enough that I start wondering if something's wrong. To be honest, though, "dawdling" isn't the right word. "Fussing" is better. After I pick her up, she insists on stopping by the clinic to check on Kenny, and then she begins fretting.

"April," I say. "We know what to do for him. You practically wrote us a book."

"This isn't right," she says. "You need a full-time doctor."

"Are you volunteering?"

"Of course not. I'm saying that you cannot have a patient in this condition without proper medical care."

I sigh. "We've been over this. The council needs to wait for a doctor to apply for entry. If you think I just haven't fought hard enough, you've never seen me fight. And you've sure as hell never seen Eric fight."

"I know. It's just . . ."

"Do you have any suggestions?"

She shakes her head and opens the door to the exam room, where Kenny is awake.

"You need a doctor," she says to him.

"You volunteering?" he says.

She doesn't snap at him. In fact, I swear her cheeks flush.

"I can't," she says. "I have a job and responsibilities that I cannot ignore."

"I'm kidding, April," he says. "I know you're busy. No one expects you to stay."

She fusses with the bedside tray. "I meant that you need medical care in a place that is equipped to provide it, which this town is not. If they cannot bring you care, then you must go out and get it. While I *am* very busy, I would, under the circumstances, offer to accompany you to Vancouver. I'm sure the town council could arrange transport."

"No, April," he says, his voice low. "We've been through this. If I leave, they won't let me back in."

"You *were* leaving," she says. "Your time is up."

"My minimum time is up," he says. "I realize now that I didn't want to leave."

"So you'll stay, despite the fact that inadequate medical care might cost you your mobility."

"We've been through—"

"That is ridiculous," she says. "You cannot make these decisions while you're on painkillers."

"Which is why I made you stop giving them to me yesterday, and it didn't change my mind."

"Because you were in pain then and therefore still not thinking clearly."

"April?" I cut in. "I understand that you're upset—"

"I am not upset. I'm frustrated and annoyed by the patient's illogical reasoning."

"Kenny," he says. "I have a name."

"I am aware of that," she snaps. "And if *the patient* would act in a mature manner, I would address him by his name, but in this context, his key identifying trait is that he is a patient, one who requires medical and therapeutic care."

"April?" I say again. "We need to go. Either we leave, or you don't."

"I'll be fine," Kenny says.

She turns to snap at him again and then throws up her arms and stomps out.

"Goodbye?" Kenny says after she's gone.

"Sorry," I say.

He smiles and shakes his head. "It's fine. That's her way of saying goodbye. At least she cares what happens to me."

"She does," I say.

"I know. Now get her home before the council finds out she's leaving."

Dalton has the plane ready. He grumbles when we walk in late, and April lights into him, starting up all over again about Kenny. Dalton arches his brows and tries taking her bag, but she wrests it from him, stalks over to the open hatch, and throws it through.

"Huh," Dalton murmurs to me. "Actual emotion. That's a switch."

"Hmm." I raise my voice. "April? Would you like to sit up front? It's a better view."

"I don't want a view. The sooner I'm out of this godforsaken forest, the better."

She starts climbing into the rear seats.

"I'm afraid I can't let you do that," says a voice behind us.

We turn to see Phil.

"Fucking hell," Dalton mutters as he bears down on Phil.

I step between the two men. "Hey, Phil. You're up. Good. I went by your house to talk to you, but it was dark. Not surprising at four in the morning. We're running April to Dawson, and then we're going to do a bit of online—"

"No, you are not."

"We'll be quick," I say. "We just need to look up a few things—"

"You know that's not what I mean, Detective. You are not taking your sister home."

"We've discussed this," I say. "I promised she'd be back in Vancouver for work tomorrow. She's been fully debriefed, just like any departing resident."

"Your sister is a suspect in this crime."

"That is ridiculous," April says, getting out of the plane. "I was in the clinic with witnesses at the time we received word that Casey was bringing Marshal Garcia, wounded. I followed the first responders and arrived on the scene with them."

"*After* them," he corrected. "You arrived shortly after them. Even if you were not the shooter, that doesn't address the allegation that you led Marshal Garcia here. That he was following you."

April starts to sputter.

"The possibility of that is extremely low," I say.

"Low?" April says. "I am not a criminal—"

"*Extremely* low," I repeat. "How Mark Garcia arrived here is something we plan to investigate in Dawson. Eric has a theory."

"As long as there is any chance your sister led him here, she cannot leave."

"If she led him here, why would she *want* to leave?" I say. "If she was somehow, very coincidentally, in danger when I just happened to offer her safe haven, why would she leave now?"

"She is *not* leaving," Phil says. "Until the council agrees to her departure, she must remain in Rockton. That is the price you pay for bringing her in behind their backs. They are not letting her leave the same way. They warned me to watch for this, and when I saw you both heading toward the hangar at daybreak, I knew what you were doing."

"Great," I say. "So you tried to stop us and failed. Tell them whatever story you want. We will fully support it. This is entirely our fault. You did the right thing. We're the ones who disobeyed. Now, we'll be back before sundown—"

Phil pulls a gun from his pocket and points it at Dalton. Dalton's eyes narrow, and he advances on Phil.

"Is that how we're playing things?" Dalton says. "Every time you want us to do something, you're going to pull that fucking gun? Is that how you do it down south, Phil?"

"I—"

"No, it's not. You wouldn't dare. Down south people deserve basic respect. Up here we're just a bunch of savages who need a gun waved in our faces before we'll listen to you."

I'm holding myself still, heart slamming into my ribs, barely able to hear Dalton's words as he walks straight toward that gun.

Please don't do this, Eric. Step back. I know you're making a point, one you need to make, but please, please don't.

The only thing that stops me is seeing Phil's index finger, held far from the trigger. I see that, and I see the gun, and a safety switch flicks on in my head, allowing my thoughts to zoom down another track.

Dalton stops in front of Phil. "There? Does that help? You wouldn't want to miss your target when you shoot me for doing my damn job."

"I—"

"That's what I'm doing, Phil. The council is fucked. You're here, and Val's dead, and the council hasn't gotten its shit together, and it seems in no hurry to do that. When we ask to speak to someone, we get some old lady who doesn't even seem to have the power to make an executive decision. Meanwhile, we have a dead US marshal and a resident with a bullet in his fucking back—a bullet fired by your goddamned predecessor. So what am I doing here? Disobeying orders? No. The damned council hasn't even told me what your position is, so I'm sure as hell not taking orders from you. I'm returning this doctor to the south—as promised—and I'm helping my detective pursue this case. That's my fucking job. So if you want to *kill* me for doing it . . ."

"I'm not going to kill you, Eric."

"You're holding a fucking gun on me!" Dalton booms, loud enough to make Phil jump. My heart stops as I watch Phil's trigger finger. That finger doesn't move, though. If anything, it shifts further back.

"The intention of that weapon is to kill me," Dalton says. "If you pull that trigger, it won't matter if you're shooting my shoulder or shooting *over* my shoulder, you are a dead man."

Phil's mouth opens. Then he follows Dalton's gaze to me, standing with my gun pointed.

"If you fire, she fires," Dalton says. "She's not going to wait until she sees where you aimed."

"Just ask Val," I say.

Dalton winces at that, but it has the desired effect. All the blood drains from Phil's face.

"You do not aim a gun unless you intend to shoot," I say. "I will shoot. You know that."

"Eh, don't worry about it, Phil," Dalton says. "Ignore that loaded gun aimed at your chest, like I'm supposed to ignore the one you're pointing at mine. No big deal, right?"

Phil lowers his weapon. I do the same.

"There," Dalton says. "Now we're back to square one, where I tell you I'm leaving, and you tell me I'm not, and this time, I'll ask if the council has spoken on the matter."

"No, but they consider Casey's sister a suspect. You're putting me in a very difficult position here, Eric."

"Yeah, get used to it. All the positions up here are difficult. All the choices are tough. We don't wave guns around to get our way. If you ever see me doing that, feel free to take my badge. If you want, I can clock you."

"Clock me?"

"Hit you. Jaw's best. It'll leave a mark, and we'll tell everyone that's what I did when you tried to stop me. Not your fault. I'm just an asshole."

"I am not letting you *hit* me."

Dalton snorts. "No, but you were willing to shoot me. You got a strange sense of priorities there, Phil. Fine. Play it your way. If you can stop me without resorting to gunfire, you're free to do so."

"I'll stay."

The voice comes from behind me. I turn to see April, the source of this argument, forgotten by everyone. She steps forward.

"I understand your predicament," she says. "Casey and Eric promised I could leave, and they are attempting to make good on that promise. However, if they do so, they risk both disobeying this council and placing you in an even more precarious situation, Phil. Casey did attempt to warn me about the circumstances here. I thought she was exaggerating. I see now that she wasn't, and furthermore, that no one could have foreseen this collision of events—my arrival coinciding with the arrival and murder of this US marshal. The timing of those events makes me a suspect, and if I were at home in this situation, I'd be told I cannot leave town until the matter is resolved. The same applies here."

"You have commitments," I say. "You're needed in Vancouver."

"Which makes this inconvenient, but emergencies happen. What I will ask, Phil, is that you allow Casey to go to Dawson to conduct her research and, at that time, she can make the appropriate calls, with excuses that will permit me another week here. I know I'm not guilty of any crime, and I'm sure a week is all you'll need to determine that." She looks at Phil. "Is that acceptable?"

"I need to check with the council."

"Fuck the council," Dalton says. "You know they'll waffle, say they can't guarantee anything. She's asking for a promise, Phil. From you. She's staying here, for what you and I both know is no damned good reason. She's putting her professional reputation on the line to save your ass. We all know you're screwed here. The sad truth is that Casey and I can't afford to give a damn. April is throwing you a life jacket, but you're going to need to swim a bit to grab it. You want to swim? Or just keep paddling and hope you stay afloat?"

Phil's jaw twitches, but after a moment, he says, "One week. I will not update the council on this matter, and they will likely forget April is here. She may leave on the weekend."

"Great," I say. "Now, hand over the gun."

"What?"

"This is the second time you've pulled it," I say. "You're a cop's worst nightmare. The dude who carries his handgun to the grocery store and pulls it on the guy who cuts him off in line."

"That is—"

"True," Dalton says. "One hundred percent true. You've got the gun, so you yank it out, with no idea what that means. You're going to get yourself shot. Give it to Casey. We'll lock it up."

Phil slips the gun under his jacket. "No."

"Is that in your *waistband*?" I say. "Please tell me you are not carrying a loaded gun in your waistband."

"The gun is mine, Detective, to do with as I like."

"And you like shooting your balls off?" Dalton looks at me. "It would be wrong to make a crack about him not having any to shoot, wouldn't it?"

"Totally wrong. Phil, I'm giving you one last chance to hand over the gun. It is against town rules for anyone other than law enforcement to possess a firearm. In light of what happened with Val, I would strongly suggest this is not a rule you want to break."

"The gun is for my personal protection, Detective, and as you've pointed out, I have no official role in this town. Therefore, I will continue to carry it."

"That makes no fucking sense," Dalton says. "Unless you're arguing that you aren't a member of this town at all, in which case . . ." He points. "The forest is that way. Hope you've got a knife to go with that gun, or you'll be ripping dinner apart with your teeth."

"Forget it," I say. "We've got more important things to do. We'll take this up with the council. You're dismissed, Phil. April? We need to discuss who I call and what I say. I've got a notebook in my bag. Just let me grab that."

I walk to the plane while Phil turns to leave. As we pass, I grab his wrist and throw him down so fast April yelps.

I pin Phil on the ground, take the gun from his waistband, and then hold it up for Dalton. "You wondered what a three-eighty looks like?"

"Fuck."

"Yes, when we were counting handguns in town, we forgot about this one."

Once Phil gets his wind back, he launches a litany of threats that I ignore, backing away from him with the gun in hand.

"I tried asking for it nicely," I say.

"That is personal property."

"Nope," Dalton says. "It's evidence in a crime, and you refused to surrender it."

"Crime? What are you talking—?"

"Do you keep this weapon secured?" I ask.

Phil gets to his feet, brushing himself off. "Of course I do. I am a responsible gun owner."

"Good. So you knew its whereabouts at all times. Do you keep it loaded?"

"A gun is hardly useful if it's empty, Detective."

"Fully loaded? When's the last time you fired it?"

"At the range, a few weeks ago."

"Mmm, no, I don't think so."

Phil looks from me to Dalton. Then he straightens. "Is that how you handle law enforcement in this town? I fail to turn over my gun, so you're going to accuse me of firing it at you?"

"I have reason to believe this gun was used in a crime," I say. "I knew if I said that, you'd never hand it over." I lift the gun. "A three-eighty. The same caliber as the bullet that killed Mark Garcia."

Phil blusters and then straightens again. "That only means a similar gun was used. I'm sure one of you has such a weapon."

"A three-eighty?" I say. "This is the kind of handgun they sell guys like you. Inferior firepower, but cheap and easy to handle. An amateur's self-defense weapon. I'll do the ballistics, of course, but if you want to lay bets . . ."

I open the chamber and lift it to show two rounds missing. "Didn't you say it was fully loaded?"

"I have not fired that gun in weeks."

"Two rounds were fired at Marshal Garcia. Two rounds are missing from this gun. It's a shame you kept it secured, too. Otherwise, we'd think someone borrowed it without your knowledge."

"I keep it in my bag. Someone could very easily—"

"Now the story changes," I say.

"Phil?" Dalton says. "You are under arrest for the murder—"

"What?" Phil squeaks. Then he clears his throat and speaks a few octaves lower. "Do you think I'm an idiot, Eric? I minored in law. I know that you cannot arrest me for murder based on rounds missing from my gun."

"Fuck." Dalton looks at me. "Have I been doing this wrong all along?"

"You have," I say. "Sorry. You need to speak to the crown attorney's office first and see whether we have enough to charge him."

"Crown what?" Dalton says.

"Ah, right," I say. "Sorry, Phil. The council hasn't sent us prosecutors. Or attorneys. Or a judge. As soon as we get back from Dawson, we'll talk to the council and see how they want to proceed. I'm glad we caught the killer, though. Now we just need to figure out who the marshal came for."

THIRTY-THREE

Dalton leads Phil away. Once they're gone, April says, "Phil shot the marshal?"

"Nah," I say. "Well, it's possible, but I doubt it."

"So you're locking him up because he's a jerk?"

"Pretty much."

"That seems wrong," she says. "But also, oddly fair. Pulling a gun on Eric was unnecessary and dangerous. Phil should have turned it over as an act of good faith. He also shouldn't have lied about keeping it secured."

"Yep. We'll let him go as soon as we're back. Honestly, though, the reason we're putting him into the cell isn't to teach him a lesson. It's to keep him from running to the council and giving them his version of events. Now, if you want to leave, there's no gun-toting stockbroker blocking the way."

She shakes her head. "I have considered my commitments in Vancouver and realized that none of them vitally requires my presence. The most pressing is the surgery I was consulting on tomorrow, but I'd already given my recommendations, and the surgeon doesn't need me to hold her hand. I should see Kenny further into his recovery. The swelling is finally receding. Once it does, I can properly assess his condition."

"All right. Phil gave his word that you'll be allowed to leave on the weekend. At worst, we toss him in the cell again until you're gone. At least now he doesn't have a gun."

If asked to choose between Whitehorse and Dawson City, I'd say it's like choosing between tequila and chocolate chip cookies. I love both, and they serve very different purposes. If I take that comparison literally, Dawson is the tequila. It's the fun sister. The town where you can watch a dance-hall revue and play the slots and drink a cocktail with a dried toe in it.

The streets of Dawson are paved with nothing. They're dirt, with wooden sidewalks, and the first time I came, I thought that was for the weather—because concrete and asphalt might buckle over the permafrost. A perfectly sensible answer. The answer, though, is tourism. Dawson City made its reputation in the Klondike Gold Rush, and apparently people expect that six-hour drive from Whitehorse to launch them back in time.

Yet Dawson also serves as a supply town. It's the second-biggest city in the Yukon, clocking in at a whopping fourteen hundred souls. This time of year, it's bursting with tourists but also miners, of the professional and amateur variety. Last month, I met a miner who looked like he walked straight out of the Klondike, with a grizzled long beard and fewer teeth than fingers—he was also missing a few of the latter. On the trip before that, I met a geology professor from California who'd been bitten by the gold bug as a child and returned every summer, finding just enough to justify her trip.

We arrive at the airport, which is fifteen kilometers outside town. It is the smallest airport I've ever seen. There's no baggage carousel—they push your luggage through a trapdoor into the tiny terminal. We land, and Dalton checks in and gets our car. Dalton hasn't arrived with a flight plan. Most of the air traffic is bush planes like ours trucking people in and out of the wilderness. Dalton radios with plenty of notice, and when he does that, if it's a controller he knows, he can have the car summoned and waiting when we arrive.

There are no taxis in Dawson. No car rentals. No buses. There's a "guy," whom the council apparently pays well enough to come at a moment's notice, bringing a vehicle and then finding his own way home.

After checking in, Dalton chats with one of the ground crew, an older man who's known Dalton for years. Dalton's asking if anyone took an inordinate amount of interest in either our last departure or our last arrival.

The Yukon isn't a place where you ask too many questions, especially up here, where destinations are closely guarded secrets, often lying close to good mining or trapping or hunting. Dalton is unfailingly polite and friendly enough to the staff. He's well groomed. Well spoken. He follows airport protocol and never causes trouble. He tips just well enough to be appreciated, and not so well that anyone suspects he's sitting on a gold mine. His story is that he's an independent contractor with a place in the woods, and he runs supplies to companies that appreciate discretion.

Still, as smooth as Dalton's relationship with the airport is, this is the most likely source of the leak—that Marshal Garcia knew the Rockton supply plane flew in and out of Dawson and made a deal with someone to let him know when it arrived. That would explain his sudden flight from Calgary to the Yukon, tags still on his outdoor gear. He got the call. He came. He followed us into the wilderness.

As Dalton talks to his contact, I wait off to the side, but I can hear the conversation. Dalton is concerned. His clients pay him very well for privacy and discretion, and it seems he was followed on his last flight. He managed to evade his pursuer before his client realized what happened, but his professional reputation is at stake. Did his contact hear or see anything that might suggest anyone noted Dalton's last arrival or departure? Maybe something as seemingly innocent as another pilot asking to be notified when Dalton arrived because he wanted to speak to him? The contact doesn't have anything, but he promises to ask around, and Dalton passes him a couple of twenties for his help.

Our car arrives then. We drive halfway to Dawson. Then Dalton takes a rough road, pulls off, and walks into the forest. This is his stash where he keeps a pay-by-use cell phone and a laptop, wrapped up and insulated against the elements.

Dalton used to use the phone primarily to contact his adoptive parents. When he had questions about a resident, he'd set Gene Dalton on the case. He doesn't do that anymore. Part of that is because he has me, and I can do the research myself. Also, the council revealed that they're aware he's in contact with his parents, and while he hopes that just means they're monitoring the Daltons—and not that his father is informing on him—he'll err on the side of paranoia. We now have multiple SIM cards for the phone. One he uses to call his parents and anyone else he doesn't mind the council tracking. The other one is for me to make research inquiries.

On the drive to Dawson, I send two texts for my sister. The only person April deems "phone-call-worthy" is the surgeon she's consulting with tomorrow. Even then, I just get the woman's voice mail. April has told me to impersonate her, and I do. I keep the call short and businesslike. I inform her that I was away for the weekend, and I have encountered travel issues with my return, which will prevent me from attending the surgery. Everything the surgeon needs, however, should be in the files I sent last week. If she needs to discuss anything, please email me, but my vacation is also an internet sabbatical. That means I have limited access to my email and none to my cell phone, which is why I'm calling from this number.

I text a similar message to April's research assistant and a colleague. That's it. Before my sister came to Rockton, she'd placed one call, presumably a personal one—she'd made the business notifications by email and text. Yet when I asked if I should notify anyone else, she said no. This was, as she said, sufficient, thank you. In other words, her private life shall remain private.

We reach Dawson. It's midmorning, and the town is bustling as tourist season ramps up. That only means it's tough to get decent parking, and lodgings will be full. Even at its peak, the town is never crowded. Just busy. That's still enough for Dalton, and after the third tourist steps out in front of our car, I suggest he drop me at a café while he runs errands outside the town center.

Dawson may be touristy, but this isn't Orlando, with endless chain restaurants and cheap T-shirt stores. There isn't a chain restaurant in Dawson, not even the ubiquitous Tim Hortons. Tourists who come here are a very different sort, eager to experience the Yukon wilderness. Those tourists expect that when they come out of that wilderness, one thing they can find is a nice café, with locally roasted coffee, homemade baked goods, comfortable seating, and most importantly, free Wi-Fi. There are a few of those off the main street. At this time of year, they're all crowded. Dalton drops me at one and happily escapes.

I claim a table outdoors and settle in with my cappuccino and a cookie—okay, two cookies. I have come prepared for an efficient work session. Coffee shops might be good about letting patrons camp out with a laptop, but at this time of year, they're going to notice if I'm here for five hours, and with the amount of research I need to do, I could be, if I didn't come with a ready list of questions and search terms.

The first question is the most pressing. *Please, Google, tell me what you know about Marshal Mark Garcia, from Washington State.*

I don't like the answer.

No, let's not mince words. I fucking hate the answer.

I type his name and occupation into an image search, and within seconds I'm looking at the man I watched die two days ago. Of course, the search engine gives me some unrelated results. A guy named Marshall Garcia. A guy named Mark Marshall, who works for Garcia's Gastropub. But when the page fills with thumbnail images, at least six are pictures of the man who came to our town.

I click on the oldest version of his face. I'm holding my breath as I do. I'm hoping that the word "marshal" is included for some unrelated reason. Maybe it's his middle name. Or he works for the USMS in a clerical position. Or he used to be a marshal but quit two years ago for a private security job. The last is my most fervent hope. It's also the most likely. People give up on law enforcement all the time. Crap pay. Crap hours. Danger, disrespect, and derision. The constant temptation of corruption. The high rates of alcoholism, divorce, suicide . . . It's not surprising that at some point, many realize being a cop isn't all it's cracked up to be. Private police work suddenly looks very tempting. Garcia could have been a marshal once and switched to private investigating or bounty work or even murder-for-hire.

He didn't. It takes only five minutes of typing to confirm, beyond any doubt, that we are dealing with an active employee of the US Marshals Service.

There is a moment, on realizing that, when I am tempted to do something I have never done in my career. Never considered doing. Never could have *imagined* myself considering.

I consider framing a suspect.

Phil, to be precise.

I have known detectives who've done it. Maybe they're desperate to close a case. Maybe they know suspect X is guilty of many things that won't stick, so they arrest him for one that might. It's extremely rare, but it does happen. The reasoning is that we aren't throwing someone in jail for a crime they didn't commit. Okay, yes, we are— they'll be in jail pending an initial hearing and longer if they can't make bail—but the cops who do this ignore that technicality. The point, to them, is that it's up to the prosecutor to make a case, and if the person is innocent, then they have nothing to worry about. Forget the lives you destroy, the prosecution jobs you endanger, the taxpayer money you waste—at least you cleared a case.

I actually consider doing the same. Not clearing a case but shifting the responsibility. If I can make Phil seem like a viable suspect, that puts this mess on the council. He's their guy. They left him here. Give them Phil, make them handle the fallout, and then quietly find the real killer on my own.

If I did that, though, I'd be throwing Phil to the wolves. No, he'd have a better chance of survival if I threw him to *actual* wolves. At best, he'll lose his job. At worst . . . Well, I know what "worst" is, and therefore I don't do more than briefly consider the possibility. I will, however, investigate Phil as a serious suspect, more than I planned to.

The realization that Garcia was a real marshal is also enough to have me ready to slap my laptop shut and walk away. Screw finding the killer. Does it actually matter now? The USMS is our real concern now. I should stop working and go find Dalton and tell him what I've found.

Except I don't know *where* to find Dalton. I'm safely ensconced at this busy coffee shop, and he's out doing whatever, so he has the cell phone. I can't contact him. I can't track him. I must continue my work, which is really what I ought to be doing anyway.

I have arranged the remainder of my list in order of answering ease. When it comes to researching suspects, it's not really about priority. The issue is the likelihood that I'll fall down the research rabbit hole, that I'll find my answers and then chase them for more information, satisfying mere curiosity after I get what I came for. So the suspects who interest me the most go to the bottom of the list. Start with the ones where I'm just double-checking data.

Paul comes first. Dalton has already said he found his case online, and so do I, when I use the real name Dalton gave me. It went exactly as Paul said—during a protest, he beat an FBI agent. Witnesses said he mistook the agent for a rival protester, and there was an altercation, and the outcome was that beating, which led to a hospital stay for non-life-threatening injuries. A federal warrant has been out on him since the incident, which took place four years ago. I skim one article. It's accompanied by a photograph taken during the protest and, yep, it looks like Paul.

I attempt to research Petra next. While I might be more curious about her than anyone on my list, I have little expectation of finding answers. Dalton's given me the name she applied under, and he's had no reason to research her story, so he's never tested it. I do now, and as expected, it seems to be fake. I have a list of keywords to search using her first or last name. I know she was a comic-book artist. I know she's been married. I know she had a child who died young.

Correction—these are things Petra has told me about herself. That doesn't make them true.

Those keywords lead to nothing useful, and I don't have time to dig deeper.

On to Roy. I put in the name from his application, but it's a laughably common one. Roy McDonald. Again, I have my list of keywords. Two lists. The first is specific to his story. The second is a list of things we may know about him—the city where Dalton picked him up, his approximate age, and so on.

I start with the most obvious. Is there a Roy McDonald who worked as an investment manager and was accused of cheating his clients? I'm mildly surprised when I don't get a hit. I keep digging, using my keywords, and then . . .

"Damn . . ." I whisper, because I know Roy McDonald. Not by name. Not even by face. But his story? *That* I know.

It'd been in the news, and it caught my attention because it pissed me off. Roy McDonald was a university prof. Economics, which explained part of his "investment guy" false story.

Three years ago, McDonald caught shit from his university for being a racist asshole. Surprise, surprise. He made some highly questionable comments about race and economic status, and he'd been reprimanded for it. Like too many people in that situation, convinced of the righteousness of their beliefs, he doubled down. He'd started expounding on his right to free speech and how kids these days are sensitive snowflakes, and he's just exposing them to the harsh reality of real life.

None of that would have caught my attention. There are racists and assholes in every walk of life, and having a doctorate degree doesn't cure you of ignorance. What pissed me off was that McDonald then signed up for one of those online services where strangers donate funds to cover medical bills. In Roy's case, he'd been asking supporters to donate to his "cause." That "cause" being free speech. Toss some money his way to show your support for his crusade. And if racism wasn't enough for you, well, he had a few things to say about women, too, in an "economic sense." Every time his fifteen seconds threatened to expire, he found a new cause, and his coffers swelled.

I'd been too wrapped up in a case to catch the end result. Turns out that Roy got greedy, and he screwed up, investing his newfound capital in some very questionable ventures and ending up charged with fraud. So that part of his story was true. He was indeed on the run for money problems. The story just wasn't nearly as mundane as the one he'd given.

For all that, there's nothing here that suggests Roy could have been Garcia's target. Whoever Garcia came for, it's a violent criminal. He warned us, and now I suspect he was telling the truth.

Which resident might have done something like that? The guy at the bottom of my list.

I have Sebastian's supposed real name. It brings back nothing, which is what I'd expect if his story was true. His crimes were too minor to be news, plus he'd been a minor himself. But I know his story is bullshit. Every detective cell in my body screamed it during that interview, and every answer he gave only reinforced my gut instinct. He is not a kid from the streets who grew up jacking cars and selling dope, a high school dropout living in group homes and juvenile facilities. Ten minutes of conversation would have been enough to tell me Sebastian wasn't that guy. Dalton only bought the council's story because Abbygail was his sole experience with that sort of background, and Dalton isn't one to draw generalizations.

So I start throwing in other terms. Most people in Rockton use their real first name, and like Petra's, Sebastian's is just unusual enough that I'm hopeful. I know his age. His papers say he's from Winnipeg, but I hear no accent in his voice, which suggests he's from my region: southern Ontario. His universities of choice are southern Ontario, too.

I still don't find anything. I start tossing out search terms, and one brings back a twenty-year-old named Sebastian, who goes by Bastian. The picture isn't our guy, but my gaze snags on the name, and there's a click, deep in my memory.

Holy shit.

THIRTY-FOUR

I type feverishly, so fast that I keep making typos as my fingers tangle. All I need is four words. Toronto. Bastion. Murder. I might not even require the fourth, but I add it anyway because it's the one that defines this case.

The boy's name was Bastion. His parents may not have realized that was short for Sebastian and mistakenly gave him the diminutive, but in this case, I suspect they were just being creative. "Creative" best summed up Bastion's parents. His mother was a filmmaker, his father an artist. Neither had been particularly successful, but they came from money, and having a fulfilling career was more important than success. Also more important than talent. They'd lived in a historically designated house in one of Toronto's wealthiest neighborhoods. They threw lavish parties. They jetted around the world. Their parenting style had accommodated that lifestyle, their only child raised by nannies and tutors. Bastion had attended private school briefly when he was eight. Then his parents took him out because the class schedule interfered with their own.

Bastion was eleven when he ran to a neighbor's house and banged on the door. The neighbors didn't open it. Instead, they called the police. They'd never seen Bastion before, and all they knew was that a child was banging on their door and screaming at 2 A.M. I'm not sure what they thought. That some street urchin from a Dickens novel had come to rob them in the night?

The police came. They let Bastion take them back to his house and upstairs where his parents lay in their bed, dead. Poisoned. Glasses sat on the nightstands, ice not yet fully melted in their cyanide-laced Scotch. Beside one glass lay a suicide note. They'd had enough. They'd failed in their art. They'd frittered away their lives. They could no longer bear to look at themselves in the mirror, knowing they were talentless failures who'd lived lives of unearned luxury, while people died of the cold and the heat, sleeping in cardboard boxes on the streets. Ashamed of their choices, they'd decided to end it, leaving ninety percent of their fortune to the city's homeless, the other ten to their son, only enough to support him to adulthood.

An astounding moment of clarity in two lives of indolence, a touch of nobility to a tragic end. And it was a lie. A complete and utter lie.

Bastion's parents had been murdered. And their killer? The boy himself.

What struck me most about the case was not the idea of a child murdering his parents, as unthinkable as that might be. What sent even more chills up my spine was the breathtaking maturity of it. An eleven-year-old boy poisoning his parents' nightcaps and then leaving that note, revealing a preternatural awareness of their shortcomings. As a child, I had grumbled about my parents, but it wasn't until I was older that I could step back and analyze them as people, criticize and critique their life choices and my upbringing. A child accepts her situation because it's all she knows. Yet Bastion, at the age of eleven, looked at his parents and judged them and executed them.

When the police accused him, he could have cried. He could have feigned shock. It probably would have worked. Instead, he confessed with an equally chilling equanimity.

You got me. I did my best, but you win.

I don't know if he said that, of course. But it was always the sense I got. Like a career criminal who prides herself on her skills so much that when she's caught, she accepts defeat without fighting.

I screwed up. I accept the punishment.

Or like me, waiting for someone to link me to Blaine's death, telling myself that when they do, I won't fight it. Hoping I won't fight it. That I have the guts to say "You got me."

I do know something Bastion *did* say. It's in the article, reminding me what I'd heard before, over beers with a detective who'd nominally worked the case.

When asked why he killed his parents, the boy said, "I wanted to go to school. I wanted to play hockey. I wanted to have a skateboard and go to the park. I wanted to be a regular kid."

He murdered his parents to get that "normal" life. In a perverse sense, this seemed to bother cops more than the murder.

Wanted to go to school? Play hockey? Ride a fucking skateboard?

Spoiled little brat didn't know what he had, how good his life was. Born with the proverbial silver spoon, and he spat it out.

Yet this I understand. When you have money, people think that solves all your problems and you have no cause for complaint. While it does grant you enormous privilege and opens doors, that doesn't mean it's a perfect life. Not if you're an eleven-year-old boy, being whisked around the world, when all you want is an afternoon in a park and neighbors who know who the hell you are.

That does not justify what Bastion did. Does not even make it comprehensible. At eleven years old, he murdered both his parents in cold blood, and the only crime they were guilty of was self-absorption. If you make that an executable crime, we'd have a massacre of Fortune 500 parents. What happened here was the collision of problematic parenting with an even more problematic child. A boy with a broken psyche. A fledgling sociopath.

Bastion's official diagnosis was borderline personality disorder. Bastion wanted something his parents would not give him, something he deemed essential for his life, and so he got rid of them. Problem solved.

A week ago I met a girl who murdered her grandmother and two other settlers because they wouldn't give her what she wanted. To her, it was a simple and obvious solution. Now, in our town, do we have a young man who has committed an equally horrifying and unthinkable crime?

I can't pull up a photograph and see whether our Sebastian is really Bastion Fowler. He was eleven. I only know his name being in law enforcement.

Bastion was tried as a juvenile and sentenced to a psychiatric facility until his eighteenth birthday. That came a year ago, which would make him two years younger than Sebastian. Ours could easily be nineteen, though.

When he was released, reporters had tried tracking him down. At eighteen, he was fair game. Technically, given that he was tried as a minor, his name was excluded from public records. But he was the only child of a high-profile couple who died in a high-profile murder . . . committed by their son. The papers knew Bastion's name.

Reporters found out when he was being released from prison. I find three photos of him supposedly getting out. I say "supposedly" because it's three photos of three different young men, as if decoys had been used to throw off reporters. Two are very clearly not the young man I know. But the third . . . It's the worst one, taken from too far away, a blurred shot of a guy in a hoodie hightailing it to a car. He's slightly built and average height, like Sebastian. Hair hangs over part of his face. Light brown hair. I see that, and I remember the young man who sat across from me last night, hair hanging in his face.

It's you. In my gut, I know. In my gut, this makes sense.

I read more. According to the articles, Bastion Fowler wasn't the charming, manipulative sort of sociopath. He didn't have that magnetic personality. Instead, he was polite. Calm. Deferential, even. Like the young man I'd spoken to last night.

Unnaturally calm. Unnaturally mature. Highly intelligent. Highly creative.

A boy who intellectually understood the difference between right and wrong. He'd tried to cover his crime, after all. He had also accepted his punishment.

I tried. I failed. You got me.

I'm digging for more when a voice at my shoulder says, "May I join you?," and it's a testament to how deep I am in my research that I look up with an automatic smile, presuming it's Dalton. It is not

Dalton. It's a guy about forty, holding a coffee and a muffin. He has a too-white smile and blond-tipped hair, spiked in a style that would have better suited him twenty years ago . . . when it was in vogue. When I smile, he puffs up in a way that makes me internally smack myself upside the head.

"Uh . . ." I begin. "My—"

"Sorry," he says. "You're hard at work, and I don't mean to disturb you. I just hoped to use the Wi-Fi to check in with my kids and . . ."

He jerks his chin around the patio. Every table is filled.

"My husband will be joining me," I say, "but you can certainly use that seat until he does."

He sits, and I type in more search terms. I don't even get my results before he says, "My ex is home with the kids. I promised I'd send them photos."

I nod and keep my gaze on my screen, hoping his haste to clarify his marital status means nothing. I pull up an article on Bastion's release.

"So you're here with your husband?" he says.

I glance up just enough to see his gaze fixed on my empty ring finger. "Yes. We were out panning this morning. I took my band off before it fell in, and someone thought they struck gold." I smile, but it's a tight one that should warn him off. Instead, he inches his chair toward mine.

"What kind of laptop is that?" he asks.

"No idea," I lie. "It's my husband's."

"Looks state of the art. He's a tech geek, I take it?"

I can't help laughing at that. "No."

"So where are you from?" he asks. "I was talking to a couple just this morning from Tokyo, and our guide said tourism from Japan is booming."

I fix him with a steady, deadpan look. Then I return to my article. It's on the kind of junk-news site that posts pieces by wannabe journalists. Under a dateline nine months old, the writer claimed to have found Bastion's apartment building, which she'd been staking out in hopes of spotting him. Not sure what she hoped to "spot" when no photos of him were available online. Did she think she'd see his crimes writ on his—

"Surgeon or musician?" the man asks.

I look over at him.

"With those fingers, you must be a surgeon or a musician." He smiles as he leans closer. "Although, with that face, I'd say model. You must have done some, right? Former model turned cardiac surgeon?"

I stare at him. He's grinning like he's just paid me the biggest compliment ever, and surely I'll rise to the bait, blushing and stammering, my ego bolstered.

I'm tempted to say I'm a cop, but he might like that. Somehow, I seem to attract the guys who do.

"I'm a travel writer," I say. "And I'm on a deadline. I'm sure your kids are waiting for those pictures."

Kiss-offs don't come much clearer than that.

"Travel writer?" He inches his chair closer still. "Got any hot local tips?"

"The coffee shop down the road is less crowded."

He only laughs. When he opens his mouth again, I snap my laptop shut and stand.

"And if you'll excuse me, I should probably move to that other shop," I say. "My husband's late, and he may have gone to the wrong one."

I check my watch as I put my laptop away. It's been two hours. Dalton should be here any second. I'll find a place nearby to hang out and watch for the truck.

The encounter has annoyed me more than I'd like to admit. On the force, when I dared complain about being hit on, my male coworkers would either tell me I should be flattered or scold me for "misinterpreting," as if I were so conceited that I presumed any guy who spoke to me was flirting. At first, it pissed me off, and I'd try to explain that I knew the difference between conversation and flirtation and harassment. But *that* conversation rarely goes well. So I've learned to deal with it, as every woman does, and it rarely bothers me. Today it does because it drove me from my seat and from my work. So I'm fuming, walking fast, trying to regain my focus.

I stride along one sidewalk and start crossing the road. When I check for traffic, I spot the guy I just escaped, hands in his pockets as he gazes about, his face turned the other way.

Is he following me?

Again, this is always a dilemma. Just because he's left the coffee shop does not mean he's coming after me. However, he's also discarded his unfinished coffee and muffin, which suggests that he didn't just happen to be done and depart at the same time. Still, if I jump to the conclusion I'm being followed, a little voice tells me I'm overreacting.

Don't be silly. He just finished up quickly and decided to leave.

And if I listen to that voice, I hear others—all the voices of all the women I met as a cop in special victims, the ones who admitted they'd had a "bad feeling," and they ignored it because they didn't want to seem paranoid.

That little voice in our heads does this weird thing, conflating self-preservation with self-importance. We express concern over walking around alone at night, and we imagine people scoffing, telling us we aren't "all that." As a cop, I know assault isn't about physical attractiveness. Yet that voice still screams, admonishing us for our egotism.

I'd said I was going to a coffee shop down the road. I can't pretend to do that, because there isn't one. There is a Greek restaurant, and I pop into it and buy a can of pop, which I tuck into my bag. I'm about to ask if there's a washroom—and hopefully a back exit near it—when the front door opens and my pursuer walks in. Seeing me, he pulls up short.

"Hey, small world. I was looking for that other coffee shop you mentioned. I was going to ask in here."

"I think it's closed down," I say, "but I'm sure someone here can help you."

I brush past and out the door. I'm about to walk around the side of the small building. Then I stop. I don't want to ditch this guy just yet. There's still that whispering voice of doubt claiming it's a misunderstanding. More important, though, is the louder one that suggests it's odd for a casual admirer to be so ardent in his pursuit, especially when he's gotten no encouragement in return.

He did admire my laptop. Am I looking at a very different kind of predator here? One who sees a petite woman alone with an expensive piece of tech?

I have no idea, but the cop in me wants to solve this mystery. So I hit the sidewalk, heading the other way at a leisurely pace. The restaurant door creaks open and bangs shut behind me. Footsteps clomp on the wooden sidewalk. I make a left at the corner and then cross diagonally at the next intersection. On one corner is the inn where Dalton and I stay when we make a supply run.

I walk inside. As soon as I duck into the main room, one of the staff appears. His smile of recognition hitches, and he opens his mouth, probably to tell me, with regret, that they're full, but I reassure him that I'm not here for a room.

"I have a favor to ask," I say. "And it's a little strange."

I tell him that a middle-aged guy has been following me, and I ask if I can slip out the rear. He's fine with that and promises that if anyone comes in asking about me, he'll say that he's not at liberty to discuss his guests.

I head out the back and, sure enough, when I peek around the corner, I see my pursuer in the parking lot. I'm wondering what he's doing when I notice the cell phone glued to his ear.

He turns, leaning casually against an SUV, his back to me. I zip to the other side of that vehicle. When I stop, he's laughing.

"Oh, yeah, she was having nothing to do with me. As soon as she realized I was following her she retreated to her hotel. Typical stuck-up bitch. Figures I'm trying to get in her pants and marches off, nose in the air, like I've got some nerve, thinking I stand a chance with her." He snorts. "Anyway, you got eyes on the pilot?"

Pilot?

He's talking about Dalton.

"I'll come help with that," the guy says.

A moment of silence.

"No, I'm coming," he says, firmer. "This bitch isn't going anywhere. Probably figures I'm mooning around the front door, hoping to catch a glimpse of her. Tell me where you are—"

The person on the other end cuts him off.

"Hey," the guy says, the word coming hard and fast. "Don't pull this shit on me. We had a deal, and I'm sticking close until this is sorted. It's my money on the line, too."

A pause.

"No, actually, I *don't* trust you. This whole thing is starting to sound fishy, and I want my damn money. Tell me where you are, or I march up to this bitch's room and tell her what's going on."

I cross my fingers that the person on the other end calls his bluff. But the threat works, and the guy heads for the street, phone still to his ear.

I follow. That isn't easy. Even on a "busy" day in Dawson, once you're off the main street, the sidewalks empty. Ahead, a trio of ravens pick at roadkill, adding to the Wild West ambience. The guy slows to watch them, and I hopscotch along from one point of cover to the next. When he picks up speed again, I let him get a good head start. It's not as if I'm going to lose sight of him. He makes a left onto Hanson, heading for the back of town. Yes, only a few roads away from the main drag is the back of town, with forest beyond. Go in the other direction, and once you pass Front Street, you're in the Yukon River.

I keep my distance. The guy is passing Berton House, heading toward the Jack London Museum and the Robert Service Cabin. He doesn't seem the literary tourist type, and he swings left on Eighth Avenue, the last road in town. He heads straight for a pickup.

I kick it up a notch. He's going to climb into that truck and drive away, leaving me standing on the street, gaping after him. I look around. For what? An Uber? This guy is about to drive off to parts unknown, where he will meet up with his partner, who has "eyes" on Dalton.

Shit.

THIRTY-FIVE

I spot an older sedan to my left. Last night, I quizzed Sebastian on his car-theft techniques. He'd failed the test. I could pass it. An informant once spent an hour teaching me—we were on a very dull stakeout together. Jacking an old car like this one is easy, especially when the windows have been left down. Hell, the keys are probably under the mat.

I don't do more than idly consider the fact that I *could* steal it. I wouldn't. Anything I do out here puts Rockton in danger. I have another idea. It's not a *good* idea, but hey, it'd been a few days since I threw that bear cub. High time for another crazy plan.

I edge along the wooded property while the man does indeed walk straight for that pickup. As he climbs in, I duck behind a bush. The moment the door claps shut, I run, hunched over, toward the back end.

The tailgate is not open. That would make this far too easy. He puts the truck into drive, the carburetor thunking. As soon as the vehicle lurches forward, I pitch a rock over the cab. Then I leap onto the rear bumper. My timing is perfect. The rock hits the hood just as the truck dips under my weight. He slams on the brakes, and I dive into the truck bed.

Okay, I don't dive. That would make far too much noise. It's more of a slide. Then I hold my breath.

My hope is that he'll look out the front windshield, realize he hasn't hit anything, and drive off. Instead the door clanks open. His footsteps thankfully head around to the front. I wriggle forward and plaster myself against the front of the truck bed.

Please do not come around the back. Please do not look in the back.

There's a pause as he tries to see what he might have hit. A grunt. Then the door clanks again as he opens it. He gets in and shuts it.

I exhale.

The truck makes a U-turn and heads back toward town. I stay where I am, up at the front of the bed, so he won't spot me if he looks in the rearview mirror. We reach Front, which is also the Klondike Highway, leading in and out of town. When we pause at a four-way stop, a tractor-trailer pulls up behind us. The driver can see me. I wave and grin and do an exaggerated "finger to the lips." The guy only smiles and shakes his head.

I might complain about being underestimated, but let's be honest—I get a ton of mileage out of it. This trucker sees me in the pickup bed, and he does not for one second think the driver is in danger of having his truck jacked on a lonely road.

We leave town. I peek up periodically to get my bearings. I've been to Dawson a half dozen times since I arrived in Rockton, and I know the surrounding land well enough. We're heading south. We pass the road leading to the Midnight Dome—one of our favorite spots—and take the next left.

We're rolling over rough road for a couple of minutes. When it smooths out, a sudden "Bingo!" startles me. Then I realize it's the guy talking on the phone with his window down.

"I see him right up ahead. His tire just blew. Very conveniently." The guy's braying laugh drifts back to me. "Okay, I'll take this. I'll pull up—"

A pause.

"Hell, no, I'm right here. I don't even see you. I'm—"

Pause.

"Fine. Fuck you, but fine." The pickup swings a sharp right onto an adjoining road. "There. I'll park right here, and you'd damn well better come pick me up or . . ."

I don't hear the rest. The moment the pickup stops, I'm vaulting over the tailgate. I'm sure he'll see me but he's too wrapped up in his phone call.

I run into the forest. Before we turned that last corner, the guy said he could see their target at the side of the road, fixing a flat tire. Their target is Dalton. I'm sure of that. The guy's partner must have tampered with Dalton's tires while he'd been out of the truck, in the expectation that one would blow on these empty roads, stranding Dalton.

I make it to that intersection. When I look out, I expect to see Dalton's truck just ahead. I'll zip to him, and we'll work out a plan.

Instead the truck is a dot at least a kilometer away. I'm going to need to hoof it there before—

Tires rumble along the dirt road. I look right to see an SUV. It pulls up across from my fake admirer's pickup. A woman leans from the driver's seat and calls something to the guy, who's already getting out. He jogs to the passenger side.

I need to warn Dalton, but I can't even cross the road right now, not without them spotting me. Before I can make a decision, the SUV is moving again. As soon as it's through the intersection, I cross to Dalton's side, but I'm still a kilometer away.

I run. I don't care how much noise I make. The two in the SUV won't hear me over the rumble of their tires. If Dalton does, all the better. But that's overly optimistic, given the distance and the fact that I'm not an Olympic sprinter. The SUV reaches Dalton before I'm even halfway.

I slow. Now is not the time to startle him. The SUV crosses the road and stops in front of Dalton's truck. I jog, straining to hear the conversation.

"Lost a tire, huh?" the woman calls. Her door clicks as she gets out.

"Yeah," Dalton says. "Must have run over something."

"My husband's a mechanic. Let me give him a shout." A pause. "Damn. No phone signal. Typical. Been up here two years, and I'm still not used to that. Let me give you lift to town."

"Thanks, but I have a spare."

"I see that," she says as she walks toward him. "The question is whether you know how to change it. And, if you don't mind me saying so, it doesn't seem as if you do."

"I'll figure it out."

She snorts. "Men. It's not a black mark on your masculinity if you can't fix a flat tire."

Dalton says something I don't catch, his voice muffled, as if he's under the vehicle.

The woman laughs. "All right. I won't give you a hard time. But at least let me drive you into cell range, and you can call someone yourself."

There's silence as I creep closer. I pass the SUV, and I glance at it, but I can't see through the tinted glass. I do have a sight line to Dalton's truck. The flat is on this side, and the woman stands by the passenger door. Dalton is indeed bent on one knee. He's rising slowly, gaze on the woman, and I'm close enough to see his expression. It looks calm, blank even, but there's a slight squint that I know well. He's realized this woman is pushing the Good Samaritan routine too hard, and he's wondering what the hell she's up to.

I've given Dalton shit for being overly protective, but I can be the same. Yes, he lacks experience when it comes to the real world, but that's no reason to presume he's going to blithely stumble into this trap. He's cautious by nature. Very, very cautious, and also very aware of his lack of experience out here.

It's true that he'll be struggling to fix a truck tire, but he'll figure it out, being our main mechanic for the plane and ATV. If he can't, he'd rather walk an hour to get cell service than hop into a stranger's SUV in the middle of nowhere. Now that he's suspicious, his guard rises as he gets to his feet.

"I appreciate the offer," he says. "But I'm fine, and I'm sure you have other things to do."

"Not really," she says with a chuckle. "And I do hate leaving any-one stranded on this road. Stop being stubborn. We all need a helping hand now and then. If you feel guilty, you can buy me a coffee."

Dalton answers, but I don't catch it. Instead, I've caught something else—a flicker of movement behind the truck. I don't even have time to wonder what I'm seeing before the woman's partner swings around the rear bumper. Dalton wheels, but too late. A fist slams into Dalton's jaw.

Dalton reels, and I'm running, crashing through the trees. No one even hears me. The guy has grabbed Dalton by the collar and yanked him upright. Dalton stiffens, and I know something's being pressed into his back. I skid to a halt. I don't think I breathe until I see the knife in the man's hand, and I exhale.

Yes, a knife is dangerous, but it's not a gun.

I still stay where I am, breathing hard, watching and resisting the urge to break through the last few meters of forest between us. Startle them, and that blade will slam into Dalton's back.

"My wallet is in the truck," Dalton says, his voice calm. "It's in the console. There's five hundred bucks in it."

"We're looking for a bigger payoff than that," the man says. "We want the money we were promised."

From my angle, I see the woman's mouth set. She doesn't appreci-ate her partner jumping in. Before she can speak, Dalton's face screws up and he says, "Promised? From me? You've got the wrong guy if you think—"

"You're the pilot of that Super Cub that comes in from the bush every couple of months," the man says. "Don't pretend you're not. We—"

The woman cuts him off. "Last Thursday, my partner here flew our client out after you. That client hasn't been heard from since."

"And he owes us money," the man adds.

The woman's jaw flexes, and she shoots her partner a look, telling him to shut up.

"What the hell does that have to do with me?" Dalton says.

"You tell us," the man says.

"You do realize I have no fucking idea what you're talking about, right?" Dalton says.

Dalton keeps talking, but all I see is the man's arm draw back, knife clenched. Then it slams toward Dalton's shoulder.

"Eric!" I shout.

The knife hits, but Dalton is already in motion, spinning away from the blade. Blood drops fly as I run.

Dalton's fist hits the man's arm. The knife goes flying. Dalton hits him again, this time in the jaw. The man sails off his feet. Then the woman is on Dalton. She grabs the back of his shirt, battering at him. He turns, and she falls back, and he hits her. She comes at him again, and he punches. She's a good six inches shorter than him, and the blow strikes the side of her head. She flies into the back of the truck, her head cracking against it. Then she slides to the ground.

The man has recovered. He runs for the knife, but I'm already there. I put my foot on it. He looks like he's ready to tackle me, but Dalton is barreling toward him, and the man changes his mind. He veers to the side and runs. Dalton starts after him, but he turns too fast and slips on the dirt. By the time he finds his footing, the guy has too much of a head start.

I grab the knife and run to the unconscious woman to get her keys. "He's got a pickup around the corner. That's where he's going. I need her keys . . ." Her pockets are empty. "Damn it. Where—?"

Dalton slaps keys into my hand. I don't take time to wonder how he got them. I'm on my feet and running for her SUV. Then he calls, "They aren't for that. They're for this."

He points to the truck's tailgate. Inside, I see a dirt bike.

"Where did that—?" I begin.

"You can still ride, right?"

I don't answer. I race over and open the tailgate.

THIRTY-SIX

It's been years since I rode a dirt bike, but it's the same type as I remember, and motor memory guides me. Make sure the bike is in neutral. Hold the front brake and clutch. Kick-start the bike. Stay upright. That last part is really important, especially at the speeds I travel.

The guy hasn't reached the corner yet. He hears the whine of the dirt bike, and when he glances over his shoulder, the look he gives is one I will treasure for days to come. It's an unadulterated *What the hell?* followed by a wide-eyed *Oh, shit!*

He runs faster, as if that will help. I zoom up behind him, and he glances back, and that earlier look is magnified tenfold. He dives to the side. I veer past him.

I resist the urge to look back at his expression as I continue around the corner. I'm sure he hesitates, wondering if he's made a mistake, and the woman on the bike was just some other random chick zipping past on a jaunt.

He'll know better, of course. Especially when Dalton finishes securing his partner and comes jogging after him. But it still takes him a few minutes to cautiously approach the corner and peer around it.

I sit on the dirt bike beside his pickup tailgate.

"Feel free to run into the forest," I shout. "I'd appreciate the challenge."

The guy looks over his shoulder. By now, Dalton will be on his way. The guy glances from me to him and back. Then he bolts for the woods.

I hit the throttle, and the bike jumps to life. It's a small one. A 125 cc. More for a kid than an adult, but yes, I am kinda kid-size, so it's perfect for me. It's also perfect for this sparse forest. I catch up with the guy easily. Then I play with him for a while. I can't help it. There's no way he can escape, but it's fun to see him try.

I ride up on his heels. Then I whip around and cut him off. Finally, I spot Dalton in the forest, his arms crossed, shaking his head. So I hit the guy. Not too hard, naturally. I wouldn't want to hurt myself.

I bump him and then shove him as I pass. I stop the bike, hop off, and give chase on foot. When I catch up, he tries to hit me. I grab his wrist, throw him down, and pin his arm behind his back.

Then I lean over him. "Not a surgeon. Not a musician. Not a fashion model."

He writhes under my grip, halfhearted at first, as if figuring he can get free easily. When that fails, he puts some actual effort into it, until I twist his arm up far enough to make him hiss in pain.

"Last guy who did that got his wrist broken," I say. "You could ask him about it. But he's dead."

He stops struggling and looks back to see if I'm joking.

Dalton catches up. "Let me do that. You have questions for him."

Dalton isn't nearly as good at literal arm-twisting, but people presume he's the type who *will* break their arm, so they don't test him. I motion to the blood on his arm, where the knife cut him, but he twists it to show it's nothing more than a scratch. I nod and hunker down in front of our captive.

"Let's back up and smooth out your story," I say. "On Wednesday, my partner piloted his plane into Dawson. The next day, you flew your client out, following my partner, yes?"

"I—"

"Just nod."

The guy grumbles but nods.

"Someone notified you that he'd flown in, yes?"

He hesitates. Then nods, abruptly, angrily.

I don't ask for the client's name. I will, but when you're interview-ing a suspect who is hostile yet cooperating, the "hostile" part will outlast the cooperation. At some point, he's going to get pissy and shut up. So I prioritize my questions.

"Someone told you that the plane had flown in. And then you con-tacted this client?"

He nods, shoulders relaxing, as if relieved I haven't asked him for a name.

"This client wanted to know when that plane arrived, and then he wanted to be flown out after it. Yes?"

He nods.

"Pick up the story from there. Client arrives. Client says, 'Follow that plane.' . . ."

"I didn't set it up. That was Lyd—my partner. I'm just the pilot. She's the one who got the call and notified the client. He busted ass up here. Then after you guys left, we followed. Only I'd warned Lyd—my partner . . ."

"Let's just call her Lynn," I say. I'm sure it's Lydia, but I'll let the guy retain the illusion he's protected her.

"Right. Lynn. I warned her that I can't exactly tail you. That'd be as obvious as following a car down an empty highway. I had to stay well back, so I only got a rough idea of where you landed. I thought I'd be able to get closer, picking up satellite signals, but my receiver went all wonky. The guy said that was close enough. I set her down a few miles out, and he took off. I was supposed to come get him when he called, by Saturday at the latest. He never did."

"And what exactly does that have to do with us?" I say. "This guy was covertly following a private bush taxi, so you go after the pilot of the *taxi*?"

"Our client owes us money."

"I got that. But if he's *covertly* following us, obviously we knew nothing about it."

"It's a lot of money." He scowls. "Lyd—Lynn cut a shitty deal. Twenty-five percent up front. Seventy-five on pickup."

So this guy got someone at the airport to let him know if our plane returned, which it had today. Then he bullied Lydia into coming after us to see what happened to their client. It was obvious from the encounter at Dalton's truck that she knew this was a stupid idea.

"Our client paid a lot to come after you," our captive says. "That means something's going on. Something worth you guys paying me the rest of my money to keep my mouth shut."

"What do you think we're doing? Running a meth lab in the wilderness?"

"I don't know but—"

"Think," I say. "Stop and think really, really hard. It's the Yukon. No one is running an off-the-grid drug lab in the forest. No one is keeping a warehouse of guns out there."

"Mining," he says. "You have a rich find—"

"Do we look like miners to you? Could it possibly be something even more secret and completely legal? Like a matter of national security?" I lower my face to his. "Do you know the penalty for treason?"

"W-what? No. Even if it is government work, following you guys isn't treason."

"Bringing a foreign operative to a government facility is."

"*What?*" His voice rises.

"Oh, did an American secret agent fail to disclose his status to you? What a surprise. Did he look like a miner? Like a drug lord? Gunrunner? Or, now that you think about it, did he look more like a cop? Or a soldier? Something about the way he talked. The way he carried himself. The way he dressed."

The man pales. Then he shakes his head vehemently. "He never said anything about being a . . ."

When he trails off, Dalton says, "Yeah, spies don't go around introducing themselves. My partner here is pissed, but you can relax. The situation was handled. We sent him on his way."

"He had a second pilot for the flight out," I say. "If you want to file a formal complaint to the Canadian government, you just need to tell them what you did. I'm sure they'll have something to say about that."

"I–I had no idea there was a government facil—"

"We didn't say that," I say.

"Nope, we did not say that," Dalton says. "But if we hear that completely *untrue* rumor being whispered around Dawson, we'll know who to talk to."

The guy actually buys our story. Now, I love my country, but it's not exactly known for its high-end military programs. Turns out, though, that our guy is quite the patriot, and he goes on at length about how thrilled he is to hear that Canada is taking our national security so seriously because, you know, we normally just rely on the States to protect us. As far as he is concerned, this is a step in the right direction—well, it would be *if* there was a facility up here, nudge, nudge, wink, wink. But if there is, then he is so very sorry for anything he might have done to endanger it, and he will definitely do his patriotic duty by keeping his mouth shut.

His attitude toward us does a one-eighty, too. We're no longer a couple of low-life criminals stiffing him on a job. We're . . . I have no idea what we are now, in his mind, but whatever it is, it's terribly cool. He praises me for my skills—my tracking and my throw-down and my dirt bike riding and, "Wait, did you hitch a ride in my truck bed? That is *awesome*." He even compliments Dalton on his boots, which are . . . regular boots. *And the fact that you two did all this without pulling a gun? That is so fucking awesome. Go, Canada!*

His attitude well and truly adjusted, he's happy to talk. His airport contact is a guy who does part-time groundskeeping, and please don't give him any grief, because he knew nothing about the scheme. Our captive told the groundskeeper that he'd noticed Dalton flying in and out, and he'd love to pitch his own bush-plane taxiing services, so if his buddy would let him know when Dalton came in again, he'd really appreciate that.

The client approached them through Lydia. Our guy doesn't want to say what Lydia does for a living. Whatever business she's in, it's not one where you ask potential clients a lot of questions. Mark Garcia said he wanted to follow a plane that regularly flew in and out of Dawson. The next time it arrived, he needed to be called immediately, and he needed a pilot waiting when he arrived in Dawson, so he could follow the plane on its exit trip. For that, he promised ten grand. For a name, he'd given Mark Marshall. Cute.

So, Garcia worked in Washington State. He got the call Wednesday when we arrived in Dawson, heading to Vancouver for April. We did the quickest turnaround possible getting back to Dawson, but that's not exactly speedy, given the infrequency of flights. He'd have had time to drive overnight Wednesday to Calgary, fly to Whitehorse, drive up to Dawson, and be waiting for us when we picked up the plane late Thursday.

Next we have a tire to change. Our captive does that for us. Very happily does it, and when Dalton gives him a hundred bucks, he's stammering and blushing, like we've just paid him for a very different kind of service.

"No, really, I shouldn't," he says. "We slashed it. Hell, if you guys want me to cover a new tire, I'll do that, too."

Dalton sticks the money into the guy's shirt pocket. "It was a misunderstanding. I understand. You're out a helluva lot of money. That asshole stiffed you."

"Americans," I say, rolling my eyes.

The guy snickers. "They're always giving us the shaft, huh?" He goes off on a brief diatribe, and we let him, nodding where appropriate.

"Would you talk to Lynn for us, please?" I say. "Tell her we're sorry you two got mixed up in this, but please impress on her the importance of silence, for reasons of national security."

"If it *was* a matter of national security," Dalton says. "Hypothetically speaking."

Once the guy and his partner are gone, Dalton exhales, "Well, that was interesting."

"That's one way of putting it. Crisis averted, though. We lucked out. He might not keep his mouth shut after a few beers, but it's not the worst thing if people think there's a government facility out there."

"It's a good cover story."

"It is. And we now know how they found us, and it's not our

security lapse. It's a flaw in the system. If someone knows about Rockton and knows we fly in and out of Dawson, they can easily find a pilot to trail us."

"Yeah, which means we shouldn't be using Dawson. I've argued that before. There are a few places I could put the plane down, stash a four-by-four nearby, and avoid this bullshit runaround."

"Flying into a municipal airport has never seemed wise."

"No kidding. But this is how the council has always done it, so this is how I had to do it. At least now I have a valid reason to say 'fuck tradition.' Any chance you can extend my winning streak and tell me your research revealed that Mark Garcia isn't actually a US marshal?"

"No, he is. I confirmed that."

"Fuck."

"But I don't think he was here on marshal business."

"What?"

I lift the dirt bike onto the tailgate. I'm kind of hoping Dalton will appreciate the impressive show of physical strength, but he just prods me with "Go on. . . ."

"So you promised to tell me the story of this thing." I nod at the bike.

"Sure, after you tell me what the hell you meant. Now talk or I take away your toy."

"It's mine?"

"Do I look like I'll fit on that thing?"

I start to grin. Then I sober, look at the bike, and say, "You don't need to bribe me, Eric."

He opens his mouth to protest.

"I said I'd love a dog, and then I get one. I love chocolate chips, and I get them. I say a dirt bike would be good for town, and now I get that. While the twelve-year-old in me is giddy, the adult worries." I turn to face him. "It's like a guy I dated in high school—the one who got me started on dirt bikes, actually. When I drifted, realizing the relationship wasn't working, I suddenly got a necklace. And then a bracelet. And then a ring."

"Moron. Anyone who knows you wouldn't buy jewelry. Dogs and bikes work much better." He catches my expression and leans in, arms around my shoulders.

"Are you drifting from this relationship?" he says.

"What? No. Absolutely not."

"Then this isn't the same thing."

"But—"

"But yeah, I worry you'll leave. Rockton can be shit, and these days it's shittier than ever, and you have no reason to stay. You aren't actually hiding from anything. But me worrying is just me worrying. Gotta give my brain something to do, 'cause God knows, I don't have enough to think about. I buy you stuff because it makes you happy. I bought you Storm because a dog is a good idea, for tracking and protection. I bought you this because a dirt bike is a good idea, too. We discussed that. I was getting supplies and chasing leads when I saw this at the end of a driveway with a For Sale sign on it. I had cash in my pocket, and the price was right, so you've got a dirt bike."

"Thank you."

"You are very welcome. Now, tell me about your marshal theory, or I'm taking the bike back."

THIRTY-SEVEN

We're in the truck, heading for the airport. With everything that's happened, Dalton wants to get the hell out of Dodge. Or Dawson. Don't tempt fate. Don't give our patriotic captive time to reconsider and intercept us at the airport.

On the way, I explain about Garcia.

"He's clearly a marshal. Spokane office, Washington. I found photos that are undeniably him. I located a reference as recent as last year in a newspaper."

"Okay . . ."

"So this marshal is in the Yukon, alone, pursuing a fugitive, with no apparent assistance from Canadian law enforcement. That's weird."

"We knew that."

"Right. But from the moment I learned he was really a marshal, I've been trying to reconcile his behavior with his position, and the only answer I could come up with was that the council lied, and he's not a marshal. I failed to see the obvious other explanation."

"Which is?"

"I'm a homicide cop."

"Just figured that out, did you? Good timing, considering I'm relying on you to investigate a homicide."

"Ha ha. I wasn't done. I'm a homicide cop. I have the credentials. Look me up online, and you can verify that. But I'm not here as a member of Canadian law enforcement. Just because he's a marshal doesn't mean he was here on official marshal business."

"I thought you said it was different for federal cops. They're kept on a tighter leash."

"They are, which is why it took me longer to consider this. We know that as of a year ago, Garcia was a marshal. Is he still one? Could he be on sabbatical? Medical leave? With the story that guy just told, there's no way this is official marshal business. Ten grand to fly him out and back? Arranging it through a shady local? Hell, no. It was personal. More than that, there's money in it. Serious money."

"Enough to drop ten grand on a round-trip ticket to Rockton."

"Yep."

"Bounty work, then. Not the kind Brent did either, bringing in people who've jumped bail."

"It could be, but it'd need to be a helluva big bail. A bondsman gets ten to fifteen percent. On a million-dollar bail, that's a hundred grand easy, enough to hire someone like Garcia if his client skipped out. More likely, though, it's not legal bond work. I don't think a marshal would be allowed to do that. It could cost him his job, and if you're risking that, you might as well go all the way as a private bounty hunter or hit man."

"So his target wasn't necessarily someone who committed a federal crime."

"Yep."

"We don't even know if we're looking for someone who *committed* a crime. Just a resident that someone wanted brought back—or killed."

"Yep."

I tell Dalton about Sebastian as we're walking to the plane. He says nothing. Not a word. He just grunts and then conducts his checks on the plane. Only when he finishes does he turn to me.

"His parents."

"Yes," I say.

"When he was eleven."

"Yes."

"Premeditated murder."

I nod, and he runs a hand through his short hair.

"I don't understand," he says.

"I don't think anyone can understand. Except maybe Sebastian."

Dalton exhales and leans against the plane. "If this is what happens down south, that's one more reason to stay up here."

"Except that we send all those people up here to you."

"Yeah, stop that. Just fucking stop." He shakes his head. "And I can't even say that. We grow our own here. That's what Harper is, isn't she? Like Sebastian."

"In her way."

"How many people are like that?"

"Very, very few. That's the thing. I can joke that we send all our killers to Rockton, but you're going to get more than your share, considering its purpose."

"I know."

"And while life in the forest isn't going to turn a kid like Harper into a killer, there aren't any safeguards in place out there. No one to recognize what she's becoming and help her before it was too late."

"So Sebastian solves his problems with murder. What's the chance Garcia came for him?"

"About equal to the chance he came for anyone else. Also, we have no way of knowing that the killer was actually Garcia's target. They just thought they were."

"Fuck." He sighs, deeply. "So did we accomplish anything here?"

"We found out how Garcia tracked us. We seem to have plugged the leak. I confirmed Paul's story. Roy's was bullshit—which I'll explain later—but his crime wasn't violent; he's just an asshole, as we already knew. I answered our questions about Sebastian. And I am certain that whatever Garcia was doing here, we won't have a troop of marshals parachuting down on Rockton, looking for their lost man."

"So that's a win?"

"I also got a dirt bike."

He smiles. "Okay, it's a win. We made progress, then, even if we aren't much closer to finding a killer."

"We'll get there."

No one comes out to meet us at the hangar. Anders knows that we can't afford for him to leave Rockton right now, and Kenny obviously can't come running to help as he used to. We could have gotten someone else to watch for the plane and help unload supplies, but we can handle it. We didn't buy much anyway—this was an unscheduled run, so it was just taking advantage of the extra space. Treats and luxuries. Yes, bribes. *It's been a shitty two weeks. Here, have some M&M's and new books and strawberry-scented shower gel.* When the council promised us extra luxuries for the *inconvenience* of taking Oliver Brady, Dalton had muttered about bread and circuses. He understood, though, that up here, those little extras go a long way toward easing discontent.

We load everything into the ATV. Then Dalton takes that while I follow on the dirt bike. When we get near town, I hop off it. Yes, that twelve-year-old in me would love to rip through Rockton on my new toy, but the thirty-two-year-old knows that would be as welcome as the cousin at Easter who rips around on his new BMX when you got a pair of fuzzy socks. So I will quietly walk the bike to the shed and tuck it away until a better time.

The shed is locked tight. The ATVs and snowmobiles—and now bike—represent the best chance of getting out of Rockton for anyone who's changed their mind about putting in their full two years. I undo the double locks on the heavy metal door and it slides open with a whoosh.

Inside, it's pitch-black. It might be bright sunshine out here, but the angle of the doors is wrong for this time of day, and no light filters beyond the opening. I reach for my pack, to get my light . . .

I came from the city. I'm not wearing my pack.

No matter. There's a lantern just inside the door, for this very situation. Eric Dalton is the quintessential Boy Scout, prepared for everything. I reach inside the door and . . . no lantern.

It's awesome that our boss thinks of everything. It really is. The problem is that he's surrounded by people who aren't nearly as conscientious. Someone has needed the lantern to put away a vehicle and left it farther in the shed. I could gripe about that, but it very well might have been me.

I wheel the bike inside. This being a secure building, there are no windows, so once I pass that rectangle of dim light at the entrance, I'm running on memory. The snowmobiles are tucked at the very back until winter. Dalton has the side-by-side ATV. The two smaller ones should be on my left— Ow, make that my *right*. So the spot on my left should be clear and— Ow, it's not.

Having now stubbed my left toe and banged my right shin, I'm considering dropping the bike here. But that's like running into the house and dumping my shoes at the door, and while I was *that* kid, I try not to be these days.

Prop the bike up and then feel around for a place . . .

A figure passes the doorway.

"Will?" I call.

No answer.

"Is someone there?" I say.

I take a slow step, hand dropping to where my gun should be, except, of course, I don't have it. I take a deep breath and consider pulling my knife, but I'm better without it. Another step. Then a figure fills the doorway, and I stop short.

"It's me," a male voice says.

I don't recognize the voice, and the shape is just that: a human figure. It doesn't actually "fill" the doorway. It's average size. Slight build.

The head is slick and round, as if bald, and it comes to an odd point at the back. Then a hand rises and pushes back what was a hood, and light hair flops forward.

"Bastion," I say.

THIRTY-EIGHT

Sebastian goes still. Completely still, and I want to see his face—I desperately want to see his expression—but the light is at his back.

His head drops forward, and his hand rises to shove his hair back as his shoulders slump.

"Shit," he says, as if I've just caught him trying to take an ATV for a joyride.

"Step back," I say. "Hands up."

"I—" He pauses. "Right. Okay."

He lifts his hands over his head and backs out of the doorway. I follow. His gaze goes to my hands.

"Yes," I say, "I do not have my gun. However, if you think that makes me defenseless—"

"I'm not going to—"

"Yep, you're not. Whatever you had in mind by sneaking up, it's not happening."

"I—"

He looks at me, but it's not quite at me. The hair's fallen again, and he's peering through it, as if hiding behind it.

He *is* in hiding, and he must figure the hair helps disguise him. But even if his picture *was* out there, he wouldn't need to hide behind hair to go unrecognized. He is cursed—or, in this case, blessed—with a very average white-boy face. No scars. No marks or freckles. No striking features.

Sebastian puts his hands on his head and lowers himself to the ground, sitting cross-legged. I tense, and then I realize what he's doing. Taking a nonaggressive position. Like Dalton making offenders assume a downward dog. From there, Sebastian can't leap up and attack me without signaling his intentions.

"I came out here to talk to you," he says. "I saw the plane land. I've been watching. I was going to ask if I could help carry stuff to town, but really, I just wanted to see how you reacted. Whether you looked me up while you were in Dawson City. Whether you found out who I am."

"You have your answer."

He nods. "I do."

His voice is calm, resigned almost.

"What are you going to do about that?" I ask.

His gaze rises to mine. "I think the question is what *you're* going to do."

"I'm looking for someone who killed a man to solve a problem. I believe you know a little something about that."

He flinches. It's not a hard, dramatic flinch, just the barest tightening of his face. Then he nods. "I do, and I understand that you're going to think I did this. I didn't. But convincing you of that isn't my biggest problem right now."

He's right. Whatever he's done, he still hasn't zoomed to the top of my suspect list. This particular crime doesn't fit him. I'm still open to the possibility, though, so I say, "Convince me."

He clears his throat, as if preparing for a rehearsed speech. "Okay, well, if he really is a marshal, that has nothing to do with me. You know my crime. I've served my full sentence. Whether justice has been done is another matter, but the court system says I'm free. Also my crimes were committed in Canada. However, there's the possibility he's not a marshal. I'm sure you investigated that while in Dawson City. Even if he is, that doesn't mean he was *here* as a marshal."

He states this as if it should be obvious. I hope my surprise—and chagrin—doesn't show.

He continues. "If he's not here for a fugitive, he'd be here to collect someone for another reason. Are there people who think I shouldn't be out walking around? Of course. That's why I'm in Rockton. But if the justice system is done with me, then the only reason to come after me is to either expose me or execute a higher punishment. Plenty of people wanted to expose me. Again, that's why I'm here. But they're not going to pay a bounty hunter to drag me back. And the only people I hurt . . ." His gaze shunts to the side. "They're dead. Nobody . . . No one else gave a damn, except about the money, and there was barely enough of that left to buy my way up here. Anyone who had any claim to it knows it's gone, and no one else really had a claim."

He meets my gaze again. "That's my defense against being this guy's target. I know he didn't come for me, so I had no reason to kill him. Even if you don't believe that, shooting him makes no sense. I've been in jail since I was eleven. I got out less than a year ago, and there's no way in hell anyone would let me take marksmanship lessons or join a gun club. I don't exactly pass security checks." His lips quirk in a not-quite smile that doesn't reach his eyes.

"Our gun laws don't mean it's impossible to get access to them. You spent years in juvenile facilities. Enough to make contacts. Enough to pose as a drug-dealing, car-thieving street kid."

He gives a bitter laugh. "Yeah, and I pulled that off so well. I thought it'd be easy. You're right—for seven years, I lived with kids like that. When I was told to come up with a story for the sheriff here, I figured I could fake that well enough, as long as I kept my head down. And how long did it take you to see through it? Two minutes? I could tell I'd blown my cover, which is why I came out here to see if you'd found me online."

I say nothing.

He continues. "Yes, I lived with those guys, but as you could tell by my lame story, we weren't exactly BFFs. Those were kids who sold dope or turned tricks to survive. I was a rich brat who murdered his parents because they wouldn't let him go to school. I scared them, and not in a good, respectful way. Even if I wanted a gun, none of them would sell me one, not at any price. So I can't shoot. I barely know which end the bullets come out of. I know you're going to need to keep me in mind as a suspect, and I'm okay with that. I'm not your killer. My bigger concern is that I am *a* killer, and you know it. What are we going to do about that?"

"What should I do?"

That direct look again, almost chillingly mature. "Send me back 'down south' as you say. If I were you, in charge of keeping people safe, I wouldn't want me here. But I'm me, and I know what I'm capable of, and I also know what I'm likely to do, and those are two very different things."

"Are they?"

"I'm not eleven years old anymore, Detective Butler. I could say that I didn't know what I was doing at that age, but that would be a lie. I can hope I'm not the same person who did those things but . . ." He holds my gaze. "I've spent seven years working on not being that person, on overcoming what is missing in here." He taps his head. "Learning strategies to deal with my condition. I have had help— amazing help—and I'd like to think that your council checked with my therapists before they approved my application, and that they would never let me come up here if they thought I was dangerous."

"Do you worry that you're dangerous?"

It takes him a long time to answer that. "Do I worry that I'll flip out and knife some guy who cuts me off in the coffee line? Absolutely not. Do I worry that if someone knifed *me* in the coffee line, I'd retaliate with worse? Yes. I murdered my parents. I have not denied it since those first attempts to cover up my crime. I can never undo what I did. I can never promise that, under the right—or wrong— circumstances, I wouldn't do it again. I know you don't understand that. You can't."

Again, I hope I don't react. I hope I am as stone-faced as I try to be. If I'm not, he doesn't seem to notice.

"You're here to escape that," I say. "But no one exposed you. You weren't hiding."

He lets out a laugh far too bitter for a nineteen-year-old. "I was hiding from the moment they released me. We had to use decoys to get me out. And then I was just . . ." He shrugs. "On my own. I won't whine about that. As far as most people are concerned, I should still be behind bars, and I don't disagree. I'm glad I'm not, obviously, but . . ."

"Freedom isn't quite what you expected?"

That harsh laugh, almost choking on it now. "God, I was an idiot. They kept me isolated in there—from what went on with my case. I figured by now, no one cared, and I'd be a real boy, like fucking Pinocchio." He looks up sharply. "Sorry. I don't mean to swear." A long pause, and then a hint of that laugh again. "The kid who murdered his parents, apologizing for cursing. Fucking hell."

He goes quiet, as if collecting himself, and I don't interrupt. When he's ready, he says, "I thought once I was out, I could go to school. Yes, I'm still that kid. The boy who wanted to go to school the way other kids wanted to go to Disney World. I have my high school diploma. I graduated with a ninety-eight percent average. Clearly, I would get my dream. I'd go to Western for my undergrad, and then off to law school at Queen's. The boy-murderer who became a public prosecutor. A good news story. A story no one, as it turns out, wants to hear. They want the story of the monster, unleashed again on the world and—"

He bites his lip hard enough that blood wells. He looks up at me. "Sorry. That's whining again. I don't want to be like that. I try very, very hard not to. No excuses. No feeling sorry for myself."

There's a blur of movement behind him, and my head jerks up as Dalton steps from behind a tree. He has his gun, but it's only half raised as he assesses the situation.

"We're fine," I say.

A look passes through Sebastian's eyes, a flash of hope, as if I'm saying this to him. Then he hears Dalton's footstep and twists, hands still on his head.

"Got concerned when you didn't make it to town," Dalton says.

"Sebastian wanted to speak to us," I say. "He startled me. So . . ." I wave at his posture. "We're talking."

Dalton stays behind Sebastian, off to the side. He's become adept at hiding his feelings about residents. He has to be. I struggled with that, at first, knowing some of their backstories. I still do. Right now, though, with Sebastian, Dalton is the one who's struggling, and he's staying out of sight there until he can hide it.

"Sebastian knows what we found out," I say. "He figured we'd go looking. That's why he's here. To plead his case for why he should be allowed to stay."

Sebastian nods. Dalton and I exchange a look. It's not up to us, of course. He will stay. The council let him come, knowing his backstory, and they aren't going to allow us to kick him out. But if Sebastian thinks Dalton has that power, it makes things easier for us.

"We've gone through the whole 'I'm not a threat' routine," I say, with a roll of my eyes.

I actually feel a little bad about that eye roll, seeing Sebastian flush, but this too is something I need to hide. I think about what it would be like, to do a terrible thing at such a young age, to realize there's a crossed wire in your brain and that no amount of rehabilitation will undo what you've done. I *know* what it's like to do a terrible thing, without the excuse of youth or mental illness.

If Sebastian had done this during a psychotic break, like from un-treated schizophrenia, I would have complete sympathy for him. I have met suspects who've done that, and I have witnessed their hor-ror on realizing it later. It is as if they'd been trapped in their own bodies, demon possessed; and now they are forever trapped with the consequences and the memories.

Alternatively, I have zero sympathy for someone who murders while high or drunk. You chose to imbibe, and the outcome is on you, the same as shooting Blaine is on me, whatever my emotional state.

So where does Sebastian fall? He knew what he was doing. He was not experiencing a mental break. This *is* his mental state. I realize that it's a mental illness, but he is still culpable. I need to think more about it. Research it.

There is also the very real possibility that, duh, Sebastian is lying through his teeth. He's a sociopath. He shows what I want to see. He knows the role to play. Perhaps it should seem that obviously I wouldn't believe him. Yet nothing I read in those articles led me to think he was *that* type of sociopath. Otherwise, why would he have been so quick to plead guilty when caught?

I know better than to believe his seemingly genuine displays of re-morse and frustration. I need for him to understand that if this is a front, it's not fooling me. So I must roll my eyes when I tell Dalton that Sebastian has been insisting he's not a threat.

"Yeah, that's a shocker," Dalton says. "Usually, when we find some-one here who committed a crime, they can't wait to tell us how they're going to do it again."

"Sarcasm warranted," Sebastian says. "But you may do anything—anything—to protect people from me. Put any restrictions you want on me."

"How about making you take a roommate?" Dalton says. "To watch over you."

"That's not why I refused one, sir. It's the opposite. I . . ." He takes a deep breath. "At the age of eleven, I decided that the only way to escape my parents was to kill them. Not because they were abusive. I had everything . . . except what I wanted. I was a spoiled, rich brat who murdered his parents because they showed him the world when all he wanted was regular school and friends and sports. That's what *you* see. What I see? That exact same kid—I'm making no excuses for him. But in my head at the time, it made sense. To that kid, it was a reasonable solution to his problem. Up here"—he taps his fore-head—"I can never get rid of that kid. No medication helps me grow a conscience. I needed years of therapy to be able to put myself in someone else's shoes and say 'How would I feel if that happened to me?' You do that naturally. I cannot. I never will. It takes a conscious and—to be bluntly honest—exhausting effort. If you're in front of me in the morning coffee line, and there's one muffin left, I immediately think of all the ways I could get that muffin. Not kill you, of course, but only because it's unnecessary and excessive. Before I trick you into leaving the line, I must stop and remind myself that you have as much right to that muffin as me. I can be trusted never to hurt you for that last muffin. I cannot, at this point, be trusted not to hurt a roommate who really, really pisses me off."

"So you might smother a roommate who snores too much?"

"I don't know if you're being sarcastic, sir, but the answer is 'I really hope not.'" He looks from Dalton to me. "I will take any room, if it means I'm alone. I don't care if it's a tent or a storage closet. Think of me as an alcoholic who doesn't want to live next door to the bar. I know that sucks for you guys—one more person needing extra supervision—but I will help in any way I can. Speaking of alcohol, I'll be nineteen in two months, but even when I'm legally allowed to drink, I'll abstain. I took the chopping job because I wanted to pull my weight, but if you're concerned about me with a hatchet, put me on sanitation. I have avoided being a 'joiner' because, frankly, I was terrified of giving myself away. Now that you know what I am, I would love to join in community stuff . . . unless you'd rather I didn't. I know Ms. Radcliffe was a psychiatrist, so please feel free to give her my full background—my therapy file, too, if you can—and I will see her however often you'd like. Therapy has helped. I'd actually *like* to continue, if that's possible."

"Isabel was a counseling psychologist," I say. "She has no experience with your issue. We do have someone who does. A psychiatrist who's an expert in . . . well, killers, actually. Sociopathy and psychopathy, in particular."

Sebastian's brows shoot up. "Seriously? Does that mean . . . are there . . . others?" He shakes his head. "Sorry, I shouldn't ask that, and I guess it's a bit ironic, a killer worrying there might be other killers around."

"Our expert is here because his work brought him into danger," I say. "Not because we have need of his services."

"Sure, I'll talk to him, then. I'd love that, actually. A new shrink means new ideas. New techniques. If he's okay with helping me, then tell him everything. Please."

"He's already guessed at your problem."

His brows rise higher. "Really?" He sounds almost excited. "That's a good sign. May I ask who it is? Devon in the bakery gives off a therapist vibe."

"Mathias."

He blinks. "The . . . scary butcher?"

"Is that a problem?"

"Uh . . ." He gives a shaky laugh. "Besides the fact that he's at the top of my who-else-might-be-a-killer list? Are you, uh, sure he's what he says he is?"

"We are."

"Okay, well, then therapy with scary-butcher dude it is. I'll do whatever it takes to stay."

"Why?" Dalton asks.

Sebastian looks at him, and Dalton says, "Why is it so important to stay here? No one found you down south. Sure, they were looking, but you'd avoided it, and now you pay to come up here, willing to live under whatever rules we impose, and do the worst jobs we have. Why?"

"When my parents took me out of school—it interfered with their travels—I begged to be allowed to go back. I said I'd do anything. Send me to a military school and leave me there year-round. I just wanted to be a normal kid. Now that I'm free, I thought I could finally have that. Be a normal kid. Go to university. Get a job. I can't. Not after what I did. I know I can't hide up here forever, but I paid almost everything I had for these couple of years. A chance to go someplace where no one knows who I am, where I can be just another face in a crowd. Where I can finally experience 'normal.' I'll have to go back. I'll have to admit who I am and face that and deal with whatever comes from it. I know that. People dream of all the exotic places they could go if they had the money. I had it. I went all those places with my parents, and none of them gave me the one thing

I want. This does. It's my vacation to normal, and I know if I do anything to screw it up, I'm gone. That's the biggest leverage you have over me. Threaten to send me back. It doesn't matter what wiring is missing in my brain—I understand that, because it's about me. Use that, and I guarantee, you'll never have a moment's trouble."

A shout sounds from town. Then a roar, like a wild beast. Someone screams. And we run.

THIRTY-NINE

We leave Sebastian, but he follows right behind us at a run. He catches up and says, "That sounds like Mindy."

I glance over.

"Mindy," he says. "One of the, uh . . . I mean, she works in the kitchens."

"I know who she is," I say.

"She's just wondering how you know what her screaming sounds like," Dalton says.

Sebastian's face goes bright red. "Not that. I—"

Dalton waves him to silence. The screaming has stopped, and now there's just a general commotion in town. Running footsteps. Calls of "What's going on?" And a man's voice, his words indistinct as he shouts. That voice, though, is enough.

"It's Roy," I say as we run.

Dalton lets out a string of curses. We can see buildings ahead and the blur of people running.

"Go around," Dalton says. "He's near Will's place."

He keeps running straight. I slow. Sebastian slows with me, and I'm tempted to tell him to go, but there's no time. I take the path circling town.

"Stay back!" Roy shouts. His words are garbled. They aren't slurred, as if he's been drinking, but more like he's talking with something in his mouth.

"Stay the hell back!" he shouts. "Anyone—" I don't catch the next few words. "—break this bitch's neck—" More garble. "—thinks she can disrespect me? Turn down my good money?"

"That would be her right."

Isabel's voice rings out. "It is the right of every man and woman in this town to turn down any invitation to sex. That includes those who choose to profit from such interactions. You have just earned yourself a lifetime ban from the Roc. If you do not release Mindy in the next three seconds, that ban will extend to the Lion and to all alcohol . . ."

Isabel trails off. As I jog, I see her through the trees. She's been walking toward the house beside Will's, the sparse crowd parting for her. Now she's slowed and gone quiet, staring at something I can't see.

I pick up speed, and then I spot Roy on the front porch. He has Mindy strong-armed over the railing, bent forward, and when I see that, I wish to hell I had my gun. But that sexually threatening pose isn't what stopped Isabel. It's Roy himself. He's naked. Completely naked, his potbelly jiggling as he bellows at Isabel. He's put something in his hair, and it stands up at all angles. He's shaved swaths from his beard, and blood drips from the mowed patches.

Roy has Mindy bent over the railing, and as much as that position enrages me, he isn't attempting to do what it looks like. Mindy is fully dressed, and he's standing at her side, his hand forcing her neck against the railing. That's still enough for me to run faster. And it's enough for Isabel to resume striding toward them. It is also enough to have Dalton coming at a run, yelling, "Get your fucking hands off her!"

"Holy shit," Sebastian whispers behind me.

I keep advancing through the forest. When I'm alongside the building, I motion for Sebastian to stay where he is. While I can no longer see what's happening, I can hear it. Dalton is snarling at Roy. Anders has come from somewhere, and he's calmly but firmly ordering Roy to release Mindy, with Isabel echoing it. Roy keeps shouting, his words making no sense.

Once I'm at the rear porch, I hop onto the railing and then I climb to the bedroom balcony. The setup is the same as at our house, and I've used this route before to startle Dalton. I balance on the balcony railing, climb onto the roof, crouch, and cross partway. Then I'm on my belly, slinking forward.

When I near the edge, I see them below. Dalton is climbing onto the porch. He's right there, and Roy doesn't even seem to care. Roy's shouting something while holding Mindy down with one hand, his other dropped down in front—and I'm pretty sure I know what he's doing with it.

"Let her go or—" Dalton begins.

Mindy kicks. Roy has changed position, partly behind her, and when she kicks, the foot goes straight between his legs. He lets out a screech, but he doesn't fall back, doesn't let go, doesn't even stop what he's doing. She kicks again, harder, and then wrenches from his grip and falls on him, kicking and pummeling. Dalton grabs Roy by the hair and yanks him aside. Roy attacks Dalton, and I drop onto the porch.

My assistance is not required. Roy is swinging his arms, flailing like a child as he smacks at Dalton, who simply grabs him by the arm and throws him down. Roy keeps fighting, and Dalton motions to me to take his arm. We switch places, and I twist Roy's arm behind his back as Anders pins his kicking legs and Dalton crouches in front of Roy, telling him to stop fighting, that he's only making it worse.

Roy doesn't care. He's practically vibrating beneath me, and it reminds me of a time when I'd thrown down a suspect who was high as a kite. Some "under the influence" suspects make no effort to fight, just rant and yell. Others fight with preternatural strength. But this suspect had just flailed under me, a ball of adrenaline that he didn't know how to use. Roy is securely pinned, but he keeps flopping like a fish on the bank. When he ignores Dalton's orders to stop, I twist his arm. He doesn't care. I push it up until sweat beads on his broad face, and he pants in pain, but the sensation doesn't seem to register beyond that. I have to raise my voice to be heard over the sounds Roy makes—snarls and howls and grunts, as if we're pinning a wild animal.

"He's not responding," I say to Dalton. "We're going to need—"

"Excuse me," a voice says, cutting through the clamor. "*Excuse* me."

April strides up the porch steps, syringe in hand.

"This will stop—" she begins.

"Thanks," I say, taking it from her. I jab it into Roy's upper arm. He doesn't seem to feel it. He keeps flopping and flailing until he drops with one last gasp, his eyes bulging like that fish breathing its last. Then his head hits the porch with a thunk.

I go to Mindy as Dalton and Anders handle Roy. The house here is empty, being used for storage, and I shuttle her inside, away from the crowd. She walks, stiff-legged. As the front door closes behind us, the rear one opens, Isabel coming through.

"He grabbed me," Mindy says, as if still struggling to understand what just happened. "I was walking home after my shift, and he grabbed me right in the middle of the road. I didn't have time to fight. I know *how* to fight, but I didn't get a chance. He came up behind me, grabbed me by the hair, and dragged me onto the porch." Her eyes fill with tears of sudden rage. "That bastard. That son of a *bitch*. I told him no. Three times I told him, and I was polite about it, and I was discreet about it, and then he . . . he . . ."

"He's gone," Isabel says. "Not just from the Roc. He is gone."

I shoot her a glare and then say to Mindy, "We'll tell the council we want him removed from Rockton. I cannot promise that they'll allow that, but we will insist. If they don't listen, we'll impose so many sanctions on him that he'll beg us to leave."

I check her injuries—scalp abrasions and contusions—and as I do, I am reminded of how quickly an attack can happen. It doesn't need to be in a dark alley, facing four thugs. Grab someone midday, and by the time anyone can react, the situation has escalated to a point where interference becomes dangerous, and all the onlookers can do is shout for real help.

With Roy being taken to the clinic, I don't suggest Mindy go there. April can make a house call while Mindy rests at Isabel's.

As Isabel takes Mindy out the back, I open the front door to find Anders and Dalton loading Roy onto a stretcher. April examines him.

"He appears to be under the influence of an intoxicant or drug," she says.

"Huh." Dalton looks down at Roy, naked, hair on end, beard half shaven. "You think?"

Anders suppresses a snicker.

"I'll go search his rooms," I say. "See what he took."

Dalton nods. "I'll meet you there. After I lug this idiot to the clinic. We may drop him a few times. He's kinda heavy."

"Drop him on his head, and we might knock some sense into him," Anders says.

"That is not possible," April says. "A head injury would only exacerbate his condition and make it difficult to tell the effects of the intoxicants from those of the fall."

I shake my head and take off.

I'm walking to the station for my crime-scene kit when Sebastian catches up.

"I'm not tagging along," he says before I can speak. "I just didn't want it to seem like I was taking advantage of the distraction by walking away. Am I free to go?"

"No," I say as I keep walking. "You're free to go to *Mathias*. Tell him you're working for him now."

"I, uh, don't think he'll like that."

"Too bad. You can apprentice under him, run errands for him, look after his damned dog. Whatever he wants. You're working for him, and you're under his care, and he is responsible for you."

"He's *really* not going to like that."

"He'll survive," I say. "Hopefully, so will you. Now go find him and give him the good news."

I grab my kit from the station and then continue on to Roy's place. As soon as I pull open his apartment door, I smell . . . bacon? I follow the scent into the kitchen. On the counter is a jar of grease. While we don't raise pigs here, Mathias cures other meats into a baconlike product, heavy on the smoke and spices. Roy has been collecting leftover grease in a jar. For cooking, I guess. It's on the counter now—not just the jar, but the smears and clumps of grease, and as I get a better whiff, I realize that's what he put in his hair.

His razor is also in the kitchen, smeared with more of the grease, as if he used it to lubricate the blade. I'm no expert in male grooming, but I think that explains the cuts. There are scissors and hair clippings, too, as if he trimmed his beard first. It's a weird blend of logic and madness—that he knew enough to cut it shorter before shaving, but when he *did* shave, he used no mirror, no water, just . . . bacon fat.

I take a sample of the grease, in case there's something in it that caused his state. Considering that he started cutting his beard in here, though, I'm guessing he was already in that state before the lid came off that grease jar.

Other than the shaving mess, his kitchen is spotless. I open the icebox under the floor. It's full, everything neatly packaged and labeled. I empty it, find nothing suspicious, and repack it for now—I'll come back if I don't find anything.

On to the bathroom. There's something in the sink, specks of a dried material that looks plantlike. I open the medicine cabinet. Tylenol. Benadryl. I open both and find only what the labels proclaim. All Roy's toiletries are as neatly arranged as his food. Nothing out of the ordinary. Then, on the top shelf, I notice the edge of a baggie. I tug it down to find dried mushrooms. They match the color and consistency of the specks in the sink.

I lift the bag and consider the contents. Then I use tweezers to put a few sink specks into a vial. I label both and tuck them into my kit. I search the rest of the bathroom but find nothing.

Back to the main room. On my way to track the bacon smell, I'd passed Roy's clothing. I return now and consider the story it tells. It's in a heap, like someone might leave before getting into bed, letting his clothing fall as he sheds it. That heap sits in the middle of the floor.

I look around and see nothing—

No, that's wrong. The living room is otherwise so tidy that anything out of place stands out. On the coffee table sit a book of word searches, a pen, and a wineglass. I'd seen the bottle in the kitchen. While liquor is strictly regulated, we allow demi—or half-size—bottles of wine to be taken home, and that's what I'd found in the kitchen—an empty bottle in the recycling bin. I return to the kitchen and check it. Drops of red wine linger in the bottom, and when I lift it to the light, I see dampness along one side, where the contents were recently poured out. I tuck the bottle into a paper bag.

Back to the living room. The wineglass has been drained to the dregs. I pour those last drops into a vial and take the glass. I'm lifting the puzzle book when Dalton comes in. He raises his hands to show that he's already wearing gloves, like me.

"Do I need to watch where I step?" he asks, looking around.

"Only in the kitchen, though I haven't checked the bedroom."

"You want me to do that?"

I shake my head. "I'll be done soon, and I'd rather just keep going."

"You want me to take notes?"

I smile. "Sure, though I know you're offering only as a roundabout way of asking me what I've found so far. But since you offered, you are now my secretary. First, while watching your step, go into the kitchen and tell me what you see?"

He steps through the door. "Shit."

"Incorrect."

"Yeah, yeah. I'm glad it's not shit, considering this is the stuff he put into his hair."

That sparks a memory, but it flutters past too fast to grab, and he continues, noting what I did and making notes as I dictate. I send him into the bathroom next. He barely gets through the doorway before saying, "What's the stuff in the sink?"

"I believe it's mushrooms."

"What?" He leans out.

"For your notes: Detective Butler noticed specks of an unknown substance in the sink. She collected samples. She then found a bag of dried mushrooms in the medicine cabinet, which may be the source of the substance."

"Dried mushrooms?"

"Continuing . . . She also notes that Roy has never taken any interest in the forest and seems unlikely to be a forager. He may have purchased the mushrooms. If so, and if they are a hallucinogen—or he believes them to be—it would seem safer to have stored them with his food. His icebox and cupboards suggest he prefers cooking to purchasing ready-made food, and if the mushrooms had been stored in there, they would have appeared to be part of his larder."

"Yeah, but—"

"Which does not rule out the possibility that he simply never thought of that. You are writing this down, right?"

He does as he walks into the living room.

I continue, "A second potential source of the intoxicant is a glass of wine found by the sofa. The glass was finished, the bottle in the recycling and still damp. This suggests he drank it just before his episode. Also, while he may have drained the entire demi in one sitting, it's more likely it was left, opened, in his kitchen, where it would be susceptible to tampering."

Dalton writes.

I continue, "There is also a word-search puzzle, which he seemed to be doing while drinking his wine. He was halfway through a puzzle and then . . ." I turn the book around. The pages are ripped, shredded by a very heavily wielded pen, used to scrawl obscenities across the page.

"Tough puzzle, huh?" Dalton says.

"Evidently."

I bag the book and head into the bedroom. Dalton follows and stays in the doorway. After I look around, I open drawers.

This time, it's Dalton who dictates for me, with "Detective Butler notes that the suspect's clothing is neatly folded, as she might expect from the condition of his apartment. This confirms the overall impression of a tidy housekeeper, which is at odds with the clothing discarded in the living room. It would appear, then, that whatever intoxication he suffered caused the shedding of his clothing, rather than followed it."

"See," I say. "You don't need a detective."

"Nah, I'm just a quick study. You already figured he stripped because he was out of his mind. This is just adding evidence to that conclusion."

"True."

I riffle through Roy's drawers. When I open the bottom one, it gives a clunk, as if something heavy is inside, yet I see only clothing. I dig down and find . . .

"Porn." I lift out magazines. "God, I haven't seen these since I was a kid."

"You read those when you were a kid?"

"I saw them at friends' houses. As for whether I read them, I plead the fifth, though I'll point out that I was young and curious, and the letters and articles were very . . . illuminating. These days, though, people get their porn online, which isn't an option here." I tuck the magazines back. "So residents can bring skin mags with them?"

"They can. We also have a collection."

I look over at him. "What? Wait. I have gone through the entire library and never seen—"

"It's not at the library. Isabel has them. It was her idea. Magazines and erotic novels. She curates the collection to keep out stuff that's 'degrading or problematic,' as she puts it. Pretty sure I don't want to know what *that* is."

"Good call." I lean back on my heels. "Good call on the collection, too. It provides another outlet for sexual urges. Looks like Roy has been taking full advantage of . . ."

I trail off as my gaze snags on something else in the drawer. I pull out a black rectangle. It looks like a fancy necklace box. I open it to find a Swiss watch.

"A watch in a box?" Dalton says.

"A very expensive watch in a box. This baby would cost more than my first car. Hell, it probably cost more than my last car. Looks like someone missed the memo about leaving your valuables behind." I take the watch out.

"Nice enough but . . ."

"Not Roy's style?"

"Can you imagine him wearing it?" I ask.

"It's a woman's, isn't it?"

It's not. It's just a more delicate style than most men's, a sleek gold watch . . .

"I've seen this before," I say.

"Up here?"

Yes. On someone who had just arrived. I'd noticed the watch and laughed to myself, thinking he definitely hadn't fully understood where he was going. Not surprisingly, the next time I saw him, the watch was gone. He'd returned this watch to the bottom of his luggage, where it would remain until he could escape to a more civilized world.

"Can you guard the scene?" I say. "I need to speak to someone."

FORTY

I find my target in his house. When I rap on the door, he cracks it open and narrows his eyes.

"If you are coming to return me to that jail cell, I'd strongly suggest you speak to the council first," Phil says. "In fact, they are quite eager to discuss my initial incarceration."

Anders had let Phil out of the jail cell after we left, and we've been avoiding him ever since. Now, though, I need to talk to him.

"May I come in?" I ask.

He says nothing. Just keeps giving me that narrow-eyed stare, the door staying almost closed.

I lift the watch. "Is this yours?"

The door opens as he reaches for the watch. I withdraw it.

"May I come in, Phil?"

Phil pushes the door and turns, leaving me to follow him inside. I note his luggage, still by the door.

"How long has that been there?" I ask.

He looks from me to the bag.

"Has it been in that same spot since you arrived?" I ask.

"Yes, and before you ask, that is also where I stored my firearm. I misspoke when you asked whether it was secured. I had it in that bag, and the door was locked, so I considered it secure."

I lift the watch box. "This was also in there?"

"Yes, it seems our killer is a thief as well."

"Perhaps."

His brows shoot up. "Perhaps? It doesn't take a detective to deduce that, Casey."

"No, which is the problem. You aren't a detective, so the answer seems obvious to you. As a detective, I know that this watch is only a link that must be investigated. A defense attorney could point out a dozen alternate ways this watch could have gotten into his client's house."

"Which is why we don't have defense attorneys. Logically, it must be the same culprit, and that is all the council requires to take the suspect off your hands. I'm presuming it's Roy? I heard the commotion, which would have led to the searching of his apartment. I spoke to the council earlier today, and they provided a very short list of suspects. Roy was at the top. Therefore, if I am correct, I believe we can close this case. He stole my gun and watch and then killed Marshal Garcia before returning my gun. Guilt and anxiety drove him to that bizarre outburst this afternoon. I will alert the council—"

"No, you will not. I'm still investigating."

"That is a waste of time."

"Is it? Your gun was used, Phil. You told me it was secured. You still had it in your possession, and it seems to be the murder weapon. Would you have wanted me going to the council with that? Telling them I've solved the case *then*?"

He says nothing.

"Yes," I say. "If you don't want me jumping to conclusions when *you're* the suspect, then you can't expect me to do it when someone else is."

"I was never a viable suspect, Casey. You and Eric were playing games with me."

"No, I believe Eric and I were simply participating in the game you began when you waved a gun at us. As for you not being a viable suspect, had you ever met Val?"

"Yes, but—"

"Would you have considered her a *viable suspect*?"

He opens his mouth. Shuts it.

"Yep," I say. "Lesson one of life in Rockton: no one is who they seem to be. You can't look at anyone and be sure they aren't capable of murder. And you can't look at anyone and be sure they are. So, let's talk about your suitcase."

Jen intercepts me when I leave Phil's house. I wave for her to follow as I return to Roy's. Dalton is still there, and I don't want him stuck on guard duty much longer, not when I only have a few more things to check.

"It's about Roy," Jen says as she catches up.

"So I heard. I know you've said he's caused trouble before, and I'd like to talk to you about that."

She shakes her head. "If you're looking for evidence that he's your killer, I don't have it. I'd have said something if I did. What I was talking about was the kind of bullshit you saw with his lynch mob. He's a loudmouth and a bully, and he gets others riled up, but if he'd actually pulled Brady from his cell, he wouldn't have known what to do with him. He'd have just hoped someone else took over. He's a talker, not a doer."

"You might want to tell Mindy that."

Jen's voice drops, uncharacteristically subdued. "Yeah, that was . . . Fuck him. Just fuck him. No one deserves that crap, but Mindy especially. She's a helluva lot nicer about turning assholes down than I am. She's polite but firm, and she doesn't take any bullshit. What Roy did . . . I'd go see Mindy, but Isabel's hovering, and you know how well I get along with that bitch."

I give Jen a look.

She rolls her eyes. "Oh, come on. To Isabel, 'bitch' is a compliment. But back to Mindy. What Roy did was fucking bullshit, and if you don't kick him out, then put him in a locked room with me and Mindy, and we'll settle this. But . . ."

She lowers her voice again. "It could have been worse. I hate saying that, because God knows, every woman has heard that crap. He grabbed your ass? Be thankful that's all he did. I don't mean it like that. I mean that what I saw was typical Roy. Well, it's what I'd expect from Roy if he snorted coke and lost his damn mind. He hurt her, and he humiliated her, and there's no denying that, but . . ."

"It was intended as a show of force and public humiliation. The act of a bully coward who wouldn't actually carry out his threats."

"Exactly."

We climb to Roy's apartment. I tell Dalton that I've got this—I'm almost done, and Jen can take notes. He heads to the clinic to wait for Roy to wake.

As I look around the apartment, Jen says, "The stuff I was going to tell you is just more of that. Bullying. But it ties into what I wanted to speak to you about specifically. You can't leave Roy in the clinic with Kenny."

I stop looking through a drawer and glance over at her.

"It's not fair to Kenny," she says.

"Having Roy in the clinic will be a problem for Kenny?"

She plunks onto the bed. I wave for her to stand and retreat to the doorway. She grumbles but does it. Then she says, "You can't leave them together overnight. You know how I mentioned Roy's a bully? Kenny is his favorite chew toy."

"Kenny?"

"I know, right? It's like kicking a kitten."

I'm crouched, looking under the bed, and I twist toward her. "True. However, there is one person who never fails to snipe at Kenny, snark at him, insult him . . ."

"It's not the same."

"Not the same when you do it?"

She waves that off. "Kenny gives as good as he gets with me. It's sibling sniping. And, for the record, that's exactly what it is like with me and Kenny—*not* romantic bickering." She shivers. "He isn't my type, and I'm not his, thank God. I might needle him, but Roy stabs him in the back, every chance he gets. He hates Kenny because everyone else *likes* Kenny. That's the kind of person Roy is. Kenny's head of the militia—which Roy wasn't allowed to join. Kenny turns down freebies from Isabel's girls, when Roy can't even pay for it. You like Kenny. Eric and Will like him. Isabel does. Even Mathias tolerates him. All the cool kids like Kenny, and none of them like Roy."

"He's jealous."

"Green-eyed with it. I can guarantee you that when Roy looks at Kenny, he doesn't see the town carpenter who can bench-press double his weight. He sees the kid Kenny was—the nerd who grew up to be a high school math teacher. With Kenny, Roy smells a bully's victim, and he treats him like shit. I don't want him sleeping next to Kenny, who can't get out of bed to defend himself. Even if Roy wouldn't do anything, it's the threat that counts. Kenny doesn't deserve that."

This certainly isn't what I expected. While Jen may say her needling Kenny isn't serious, I'm not sure he—or anyone else—would feel the same way. She's the last person I'd expect to champion a victim over a bully.

A few months ago Mathias said that a lifetime of bullying had turned Jen into one. His theory is that she'd been the victim of it herself as a child. I suspect Kenny has, too. The difference is in how it affected them. Kenny is the bullied kid who never stops hoping it'll just all go away. The boy who grows into a man who still wants to "hang with the cool kids" but has learned the difference between the assholes in the smoking pit and the leaders of the student council.

Kenny came to Rockton determined to reinvent himself, and there's something sad in the fact that he thought he had to—that maybe he believed everyone in his life who blamed him for the bullying. Whatever his motivation, though, he has worked his ass off for the town and become a valued and, yes, popular member of it.

Jen, on the other hand, is the bullied kid who says "fuck you" to the world. She fortifies her wall and defends herself and always hits first—with or without provocation—because that's her way of protecting herself. It doesn't make it right, and I don't care how much I might sympathize with the girl she'd been, I won't put up with her bullshit, because deep inside, there's a girl who *is* a bully, who enjoys seeing me flinch at a well-aimed barb.

Hearing Jen defend Kenny does surprise me, and as I search Roy's bedroom, I also search my brain for Jen's ulterior motive. I find none, and as I finish, I say, "You're right," and she seems to visibly relax.

"Don't tell Kenny I mentioned it either," she says. Her face hardens into a look I know well. "If you do, I'll deny it. I'll tell him you're full of shit."

"Yes, please threaten me, Jen, because that's the only way I listen to you."

"That's not a threat. It's a warning."

I sigh and walk past her into the living room.

"I mean that," she says. "Kenny wouldn't want you knowing Roy's being an asshole to him."

I turn to her. "I realize that, and there's no reason I need to explain anything. Roy flew into a psychotic rage this afternoon. No one will question why I'm separating them, okay?"

Footsteps sound on the porch. Dalton peeks in. "Roy's awake. Still groggy, which might be the best time to question him."

"It is. Give me two minutes, and I'm there."

FORTY-ONE

I question Roy about Mark Garcia. In his confused state, he struggles to even remember who I'm talking about, and then he only recalls that he's "that American law guy who died." I ask about Phil, and it takes even more work to remind him who that is. When I show him the watch, he dismisses it as "some frou-frou girlie bling" and rouses himself just enough to sneer at people who waste their money on "that shit" when a fake Rolex is just as good. I show him the gun, and his eyes light up at that. He wants to hold it. Then he rants about Dalton not letting him into the militia, which turns into a rant about his mother not letting him hunt as a kid. This goes on for a while, the upshot being that Roy really likes guns . . . and has never actually handled one, though he's sure he'd be good at it if that asshole sheriff would give him a chance.

As the questioning continues, the sedative wears off, and Roy remembers what he did. That's when I expect him to go into full-on rant mode, blaming Mindy and everyone else and downplaying his actions. Instead, he freaks out—to the point where April needs to mildly sedate him again. After that she retreats to the front porch, where we've wheeled Kenny while we interview Roy.

"No," Roy slurs as Anders lowers him to the bed. "Someone . . . That wasn't . . ." He swallows and then pats his chin, feeling the half-missing beard and wincing as he touches the cuts. "Nightmare. I had . . . I had . . ."

"You had a nightmare," I say.

He nods, his gaze fixed and blank. "I had to . . . I don't . . ." Another swallow. "I remember that part in the nightmare. I needed to shave my beard, because that's why Mindy said no to me."

"Your beard?" Anders says.

Roy runs his hands over his face, wincing again as he touches the cuts. "It made sense in the nightmare, okay? I had to shave my beard and style my hair, and then she'd say yes."

Anders lifts his brows.

Roy keeps going. "I didn't have hair gel, so I used grease. I was shaving my beard, and then I forgot why I was doing that, and I got mad. Really, really mad. I knew she'd never say yes, and I was sick of everyone treating me like shit. I deserve better, and I was going to show everyone who I was. Show that bit—that woman—that she can't treat me like that."

"Uh-huh," I say. "Actually, if 'treating you like that' is refusing to have sex with you, she absolutely can."

His jaw sets. "She's a who—"

I cut him off. "She's a sex worker. Not a sex robot. You don't put your money in and get a blow job."

Anders chuckles, and Roy glares at him. "Sure, *you* think it's funny. You've probably never had a woman say no to you, even if you are . . ." He trails off and has the grace to look abashed.

"A cop?" Anders says. "That's what you were going to say. I get sex even though I'm a cop. Totally true. Women are good about overlooking that. Doesn't mean they never say no. Doesn't mean I never say no. You're digging yourself in deeper here. You realize that, right?"

"You and this detective don't know what it's like because you both hit the genetic jackpot."

"Yep," Anders says. "Totally did. We were both born to parents with brains, and they passed those on to us."

I start to cut off Roy's retort, but I don't need to. He's sedated enough that when he can't think of a quick comeback, he just sits there, his mouth open.

"We'll discuss what you did to Mindy later," I say. "So you shaved and greased your hair to impress her. Then you undressed . . ."

"To impress her?" Anders says, and he chokes on a laugh that has me scowling and motioning that I'll kick him out if he goes there.

"Let's skip that part," I say, and Roy looks relieved. "Back up. You got off work at four, according to your time sheet. You came home and did what?"

"Relaxed."

"Be more specific. If you have any hope of getting out of serious trouble here, Roy, you need to take me through every step."

"I came home. I poured a glass of wine. And, yeah, I like wine better than beer, okay?" He shoots a glare at Anders, who hadn't reacted.

"You poured wine," I say. "I saw the empty bottle. So you drank the whole—"

"No, it was already opened. There was about half left. I poured it, and I drank it in the living room while I worked on a puzzle. I had dinner plans, so I was relaxing with my puzzle and wine—"

His head spins my way. "The wine. It was in the wine, wasn't it? Someone wanted to embarrass me and dosed my wine."

"Any idea who'd do that?" Anders says. "Or should we just question the entire town?"

I give him a look. Then I say to Roy, "Yes, it's possible that someone added your mushrooms to the wine."

His face screws up. "My what?"

I show him the baggie, and I'm treated to Roy's views on drugs, which boil down to *Yeah, I've snorted coke for chicks, but I don't smoke that hippie-dippie marijuana shit, and I sure as hell don't smoke magic mushrooms.* Then he peers at the bag and says, "You sure those are the smoking ones? They look like the kind I put in my risotto." Then he again glares at Anders—who has, again, said and done nothing—and says, "Yeah, I make risotto. I make a mean quiche, too. You got a problem with that?"

"I believe the only person who has a problem with that—or the wine—is you," Anders says. "Also, you don't smoke mushrooms."

Roy sniffs. "You'd know, wouldn't you? You're like that asshole out there." He hooks his thumb toward the porch where Kenny is. "You think if you spend enough time in the gym, no one will notice you're a little soft. A little 'sensitive.'"

"Yep, I am very sensitive," Anders says. "And now I'll go smoke mushrooms and pump iron until I feel better." He gets to his feet. "You done with this gem, Case?"

"I am."

"Then come on, Macho Man. Let's get you back home. You're going to have the pleasure of my company tonight. The clinic is too small for you and Kenny, so you're getting my home care."

Roy looks down at his hospital gown. "I need my clothes."

"Nah, you don't. You can even leave the gown behind. It's a warm night, and you won't be showing off anything *anyone* hasn't seen."

I help April bring Kenny back in.

"You can't keep him here," she says as we reposition the bed.

Kenny clears his throat. "I have a name."

"Which you know, and I know, and Casey knows, and since there is no one else here, everyone knows who I mean."

"Yes," Kenny says, his voice slow, patient. "But when you talk about someone who is present, you should use their name. Otherwise, it seems like I'm an object, like you're saying, 'You can't keep that pile of trash here.'"

April actually flushes. "I didn't say that."

"I'm kidding. And I wouldn't call you on it with anyone but Casey around."

She frowns. "Why not?"

"Because it would be rude. Now, I understand that you need your workspace, April, so yes, I am in your way and need to be relocated."

"I didn't mean that. I meant that you won't want to be here long-term."

"Ah, then *say* that."

"Am I supposed to analyze everything I say for how it could be interpreted?"

"Yes. Kind of. At least pause to consider it."

She throws up her hands and walks into the next room. When the door shuts, I murmur, "I'm sorry. She's difficult. I know that."

"She's not difficult on purpose. It's just difficult for *her*. Everyone just accepts that it's her way and writes her off as difficult or rude or thoughtless."

Now it's my face heating. I nod. "You're right. I never considered that it wasn't a choice. That she might honestly not know how she sounds."

"I know. So we could ignore it . . . or we could try to teach her, which feels patronizing, but I've talked to her, and she's fine with that. She doesn't *want* to be difficult. Or rude. Or thoughtless."

"Thank you. You're good with her."

He shrugs. "My brother had autism. A much more serious case. He . . ." Kenny tugs at his sheet, fussing with it. "He's been gone a long time. We were close. When he was little, my family worked with him, getting him as far as we could. I'm no expert, but I can guide April a little. I'm almost certain she is on the spectrum. I see little hints of my brother's behavior patterns. She's far from his situation, though. She's also an adult, and that's important to remember, too. She's a very successful, independent, brilliant adult. She'll accept guidance, but she shouldn't be treated like she has a debilitating condition. Not like . . ." He taps his legs.

I sit on the edge of the bed. "April says the swelling's going down, and your sensation has improved."

"It's not as bad as I feared. It's not as good as I hoped, either."

"We still don't know—"

"It's okay, Casey. You don't need to sugarcoat it for me. If I was going to recover one hundred percent, I'd be farther along by now. I'm going to have problems. The question isn't whether I'll ever run as fast as I did before. It's whether I'll walk with or without braces. My goal is getting back on my feet, one way or another. Otherwise, the council won't let me stay."

I open my mouth.

He cuts me off with a look. "No sugarcoating, remember? Rockton can't handle a wheelchair-bound resident. I need to be mobile, even if I need braces and crutches. I'm ready to do the work. Just cross your fingers for me."

"They're already crossed."

FORTY-TWO

I'm still working at ten, when Dalton brings our poor, neglected dog to the station and points out her poor, neglected state and guilts me into accompanying them on a long forest walk. He's right, of course. While Roy's episode added a laundry list of new "things to investigate," none of it is urgent.

Until I figure out what happened to Roy, I have no idea whether it's connected to the case. It's probably not. He's a bullying asshole, and he's been getting worse, and it's entirely possible that someone had enough and doped him in hopes he'd go on a banishment-worthy rampage. If that's the end result, I am okay with it. Okay with the *result,* not the way it was done. Mindy suffered in that outburst. Whoever drugged Roy will answer for that.

I have nothing that needs my immediate attention, and my sleep gauge is close to empty, so I agree to that walk with Dalton and Storm. Then I agree to a beer on our back porch while Dalton plays with the dog. After that, I agree to let him play with *me* upstairs. Okay, "agree" might imply I actually consider refusing. I do not. By midnight, I am soundly and happily asleep.

I wake to the odd sensation of something encircling my wrist. I crack open my eyes to bright sunlight, and I have a momentary flash of alarm, thinking I've overslept, before remembering that up here, at this time of year, it's full sunlight by six. I yawn and reach for Dalton. Whatever encircles my wrist tightens, and I find my other hand following the first as if pulled along. No, not "as if"—it *is* being pulled along. My wrists are tied together.

There's not a single second where I wonder whether Dalton's having some fun. I hesitate to call his sexual style vanilla, because that implies boring, and it's definitely not. It's just that kink isn't really part of his vocabulary. He grew up with minimal exposure to mass media—including porn—and by the time he was eighteen, he had older women eager to initiate him into the world of sex. Many women, very eager. Even if he did develop a sudden interest in bondage play, there's no way in hell he'd instigate it while I was asleep, unable to refuse. Those women taught him well.

So when that strap tightens, my heart hammers, but I keep my face relaxed, eyes shut. My hands fall onto the bed, as if I'd reached out in sleep. Then I listen. The room stays silent.

I crack open one eye. I'm lying on the right side of the bed, facing the left. Dalton's spot is empty. On the nightstand, there's a thermos, and a plate with a muffin and berries. The clock lies facedown. A note is tucked under the plate.

Dalton's gone. He's turned off the alarm and left me breakfast. The note will say he's taken Storm in to work while I sleep.

I'm ready to open my eyes when fabric rustles behind me. A floorboard gives underfoot, not a creak, just a whisper of movement.

My hands are tied in front of me. Plastic cuffs. I know that without even looking. They're the ones we keep by the boxload in the station, and we have no reason to secure them.

My gun is under the mattress. Close at hand without lying in plain sight. *Not* close enough to grab. There's a knife in the nightstand drawer. A penknife, for utility rather than defense. It could cut these cuffs off. I peek at the drawer. Three feet away. I need to throw myself across the bed, roll up onto my feet, get the drawer open, find the knife . . .

It'd be an excellent plan if I were alone, with my attacker waiting downstairs.

I am not alone.

Another board gives underfoot. The sound comes from the foot of the bed. My captor is walking around it. Moving slowly. Trusting I am asleep but knowing, from my movement a few minutes ago, that I'll wake soon.

I turn my face in to the pillow with a groan, as if shifting in sleep. I hear breathing now. Slow breathing.

I ease one leg back and brace my foot. My knees are bent, my shoulders twisted, my bound hands against the mattress. The covers lie over my legs, and I consider tossing to get free of them, but I know that's too much movement. The sheet feels loose. I hope it is.

I have my eyes almost shut, and that means I can see only a shape circling the bed. I desperately want to open them a little more, but I don't dare. I wait until the figure moves up alongside the bed. Then I spring. I push off with my legs, an awkward leap and roll on a direct trajectory with that figure. It is only as I hit that I see who it is. My shoulder strikes, knocking her back. I kick as hard as I can and then swing both hands—

"Casey, don't."

She lifts a gun, pointed at me. Pointed not at my head, but at my shoulder, and when I see that, rage fills me. It's the same thing I've done, the same thing I *did* with Phil, to show that it's no idle threat. She does that, and I want her to point it at my head instead.

Don't do what I would do. You are nothing like me.

"Casey? Just sit down, okay? I'm here to talk. That's it. Talk."

I stare at her, and rage blinds me until I see only the gun floating in front of me.

"This is not how you talk to me," I say, my teeth gritted.

Petra eases back, gun lowering a fraction. "It's not how I *want* to talk to you, Casey, but apparently, it's the only way I can."

"Like hell. I may not be happy to chat these days, Petra, but that does not give you any right to—"

"I did what I had to."

"Break into my house? Tie me up while I'm asleep? Hold me at gunpoint? If you try to tell me that I'm overreacting, and you're still my friend, you had better be prepared to shoot me or I swear I will kick your fucking teeth in."

She blanches at that.

I step toward her. "You want to talk to me? Take off these cuffs. Put down that gun. If you do that, I might give you five minutes."

"That's the problem, isn't it?" she says. "If I'm not holding you at gunpoint, you'll decide when and if you listen to me, and when and if you stop listening to me. You're pissed. I get that. I don't blame you. But this . . ." She waggles the gun. "This is the language you and I both understand. It's the only language, under the circumstances, you'll respect. But this isn't the conversation where I try to convince you I'm on your side and hope you'll see I am. This is one where I— we—are in a shitload of trouble, and I need you to listen to me."

"Put down the gun."

"I'll untie your hands, but I am not—"

"If you untie me, and things go south, we'll grapple for the gun. Neither of us wants that. So I will accept the cuffs if you put that gun down. Pull the chair over. Set the gun on the dresser. Out of your reach. Out of mine. Then you have fifteen minutes of my time, and afterward, if I don't think whatever you had to say was this important, you'll be charged with every offense you've just committed. We'll see if your friends in the council can get you out of that."

She puts the gun on the dresser and tugs over the chair. I sit on the edge of the bed.

"I'm the one who doped Roy," she says.

"I know."

She looks at me sharply.

I continue. "All right, I didn't know for certain. There wasn't any evidence. But you were at the top of my suspect list. The council asked you to do it, didn't they? Dose something in his house. Plant the mushrooms. Plant the watch. Hope that he freaks out, and I find the watch and decide he did it and close the case. Phil already tried to get me to do that, as soon as I asked him about the watch. Your setup was clumsy as hell. I'd have expected better."

"Watch?"

"Phil's watch. Which you planted at Roy's."

She shakes her head. "That wasn't me. Seems like I'm not the only one who thinks Roy makes a good suspect. As for Phil, he's drawing his own conclusions. He wasn't part of this. The council is barely speaking to him. They don't trust him. They probably fed him the same story I got, that they had proof Roy was the killer, and they'd made a mistake sending him here. I can guarantee Phil wasn't part of this. He failed with Brady. They've cut him loose. He's our new Val. They just haven't told him that yet."

"So the council—"

"It's not—" She stops herself. "It's people *from* the council. It is not the entire council. That's where you've made your mistake, Casey. Where we both did. It's like the blind men with the elephant, feeling around and drawing conclusions based on one part. Except, with the elephant, they didn't realize they were dealing with the same beast. You and I thought we were dealing with the same beast. And we aren't."

"Uh-huh."

She leans forward. "You see a corrupt council, acting in its own best interests. I see good people who need to make hard decisions to protect the *town's* best interests. But it's not one elephant we're assessing. It's a council comprised of different people, with different agendas. I just got a glimpse of yours, and that's why I'm here."

"Okay."

"I have a primary contact with the council. You spoke to her."

"Émilie."

"Yes. She's the reason I'm in Rockton. She's dealing with health issues, though, so I've been in contact with two others who occasionally give me orders. My order yesterday was to dope Roy. I was told he was the killer."

"Based on what? I know his real crimes, and they aren't violent."

"The council has been investigating, and they discovered he's wanted on a federal warrant."

I start to say he's not but stop myself and let her finish.

She continues, "They directed me to a cache, where I'd find a substance to place him in an altered mental state."

"Which it did. It also could have gotten Mindy raped or killed. Maybe both."

Petra's cheek twitches. "I know, and that was not what I was told it would do. It was to suppress his central nervous system. Lower his defenses. Like involuntary intoxication. Place him in a state where he'd be far more likely to confess."

"In vino veritas?"

"Yes. An easy way to place him in a state of increased suggestibility, while keeping him alert enough to be questioned."

"That sounds like something out of a spy movie. You actually believed them?"

"I've used similar substances before. Not in Rockton but— Anyway, yes, I believed them, and while it was not supposed to make him violent, no one can predict the way a person will react. I was supposed to monitor him and then lead him into a situation where he'd be questioned."

"Except you weren't monitoring him."

"I was. Then I was called to help in the general store, unloading the supplies Eric brought, and I made the mistake of deciding I could leave my post for a few minutes. Roy usually doesn't drink until after dinner, and if I refused to help with the unloading, that would be suspicious. What happened to Mindy is on me. An inexcusable error in judgment. I was also furious with the council, for their error in judgment. That's all I thought it was. In their zeal to stop a killer, they miscalculated his reaction to the drugs. Then I overheard Eric and Will talking about Roy."

"Convenient. Also uncharacteristically indiscreet of them."

She nods. "All right, I'll rephrase that. I was eavesdropping on a private conversation between Eric and Will. Eric said you'd done some digging on Roy, and there was no possibility of a federal warrant. You believed he was being set up and that the doping was tied to that."

"Which is when you realized Roy wasn't the *only* one being set up."

"The council didn't want me to take the fall. They wouldn't."

I snort.

She shakes her head. "Trust me. I have leverage like you wouldn't believe."

"Oh, I'm sure you believe you do."

She starts to answer and then stops with another shake of her head. "That's not important. The point is that I was only set up in the sense that I was given orders under false pretenses. That's why I'm here. Something is going on with the council."

I laugh. I can't help it. I laugh, and when I can finally stop, I say, "Something has been going on with the council for a very, very long time."

"I'm only just seeing that. You can laugh at my naiveté. But you haven't exactly shared your suspicions with me, and until now, I've only seen the council making hard choices, like with Oliver Brady. I'm accustomed to that."

"From the council."

"No, from . . . before. My past life. The council, too, but I lived in a world where people made these hard choices, Casey, and I have always believed they were for the greater good. With Oliver Brady, it was. With other situations I've resolved here, it was."

"Other situations?"

"Minor ones that have not interfered with any of your cases. I still believe in the council as a whole. I have just come to realize that they may not *be* whole. There are elements with an agenda that conflicts with Rockton's purpose."

"You have no idea. You honestly have no idea."

"You're right. I don't. Yet you don't see the side of the elephant *I'm* on. You need to understand that there are good people who can help you. That's a conversation for another time. Right now, I believe you're right. Someone in the council—likely multiple *someones*—wants this case to go away. They may be protecting the killer. They may just want to kill two birds with one stone—close this case and get rid of a problematic resident. That's not evil, but it's sloppy, and it endangers everyone here, forcing them to unknowingly live with a killer."

I want to laugh at so much of what she says. At the earnestness with which she says it. She's like the sheepdog in a cartoon, suddenly realizing one of her flock is a wolf wearing a sheepskin . . . and the scene pans to show half the sheep with wolf tails hanging out the back.

I *don't* laugh, because she *is* earnest. She really is worried that we'll leave a killer—*one* killer—in Rockton. She really is blindsided by the revelation that a council member isn't acting in Rockton's best interests. She's shocked that she's been tricked into framing Roy . . . and I'm sitting here thinking *That's it? A council member lied to you and misled you? Around here, we call that Tuesday.*

While her genuine shock makes me laugh, it also gives me hope. Of course I need to consider the possibility she's lying. Still, if there is a chance her shock is sincere, then I have an opportunity here. One to flip an adversary to an ally and, yep, I've screwed that up before—hello, Val!—but I've also succeeded, and I cannot afford to reject the possibility. Rockton needs all the help it can get.

"I want to see this cache," I say. I lift my hands. "You're going to undo these, and I'm going to take my gun. You'll leave yours here."

Her mouth opens in protest.

I cut her off. "You want me to trust you again? Start by trusting me."

She nods and pulls out a penknife to cut the wrist strap.

FORTY-THREE

I stop at the station first. Petra is with me. Dalton isn't there. I know he isn't. I caught his voice on the wind, like Storm picking up a favorite scent. I avoided him and detoured to the station, in hopes of catching someone there. I do. It's Sam, doing militia paperwork in Kenny's absence. I tell him that Petra and I are going for a walk to chat, and please let Dalton know if he comes by. Dalton will buy the excuse . . . as long as he doesn't see my expression while giving it.

I do consider asking if Sam knows whether Dalton has Storm or he's left her with a sitter. I'd love to take her on this trip. Whatever Petra might do to me, I trust her around my dog. She was Storm's first sitter, and when Jen lashed out at the dog a week ago, it was Petra who went after her. I think back to that now, to the rage on Petra's face, so uncharacteristic it startled me. A hint at deeper wells. I'd known that. I just hadn't pursued it, assuming it was something in her past, no concern to me except as a friend who might want to help her get past it.

I laugh at that.

"So that story about your kid was a lie," I say as we head into the forest.

She tenses and looks over quickly.

"You remember the one," I say. "Not really a story so much as a scrap, tossed my way so I'll feel like you're sharing something personal. You'd joked about Storm being a sign that Dalton wanted kids. Then you said that we should sort that out because you'd been married and you wanted a baby when your husband didn't. You had one, and it destroyed your marriage. When I asked about your child, you suggested he—or she—had died. A poignant backstory scrap that I now realize was complete bullshit."

"No," she says, her voice hardening. "It was not."

"You also suggested, less than an hour ago, that you have the kind of job experience that seems a little inconsistent with motherhood. And when I tried to find hints of you online as a comic-book artist, I came up blank. Was anything you told me the truth?"

"All of it was."

I look at her. "Like hell. You—"

"Let's start with this." She pushes aside a branch. "According to my intake record, I'm thirty-five. That may also be what I told you. I'm forty-two. I'm just blessed—or cursed—with the kind of face that can pass for younger. I think you know what that's like. So I've had time to do more than you might imagine."

She pauses and assesses a fork before swinging left. "In books and movies, people always say 'I'm special ops.' So let's go with that. I was, as they call it, special ops. I won't go into more detail. I can't, as you might imagine. It gave me a unique skill set. In my early thirties, I decided to get out. I quit, as amicably as one quits that sort of work, and I focused on my art. Yes, I was a comic-book artist, but without my real name and very, very deep digging, you wouldn't find me. It's the kind of career where you don't make a name for yourself unless you're at the top of your game, and I definitely was not. I made more of my income inking than drawing."

"Inking?"

"Someone higher up the food chain did the art, and I filled in the colors. Bet you never even knew that was a job, huh? It is, and it paid decently, mostly because artists want to draw, not color between someone else's lines. That's where I met Mike, as we'll call him. We started as friends, and that's really what we always were. Really good friends with really good benefits. But he wanted a baby. Him, not me. I didn't figure I was mommy material with my background. I wanted to give him a baby, though, so I got pregnant, and we got married—in that order."

She stops. Looks around, as if wondering how she got here. Then, with a shake of her head, she backtracks and finds a broken tree and turns right, heading off the path.

"The marriage ended," she says. "Quickly. Yet while I wasn't cut out to be a wife, I was a damned fine parent. My daughter was . . ." Her voice catches. "People talk about miracle babies, and she was—not for any trouble with her birth, but because she changed my life. Although Mike and I split, we co-parented and remained friends."

She finds the spot and stops there, gesturing at it while still talking. "It might sound as if I left my former life behind and effortlessly moved on. I didn't. Anders has said he saw things, as a soldier, that he didn't agree with. So did I. It gets in your head. I drank to get it out. I remember you asked once if Anders and I ever hooked up. We haven't. I wouldn't, because I'm afraid I'd be one of those lovers who says yes to a hookup while hoping for a relationship. I'd be even more afraid of *getting* a relationship. I see too much of my past in him and his drinking, and it scares the shit out of me. Like him, I never graduated to full-blown alcoholic. Just the consumer of a troubling amount of alcohol. I didn't drink when I was pregnant or breastfeeding, though. I went cold turkey then. After Mike and I split, I never drank when our daughter was over. Then came the day . . ."

She hunkers onto a fallen log, lacing her hands. "It was late afternoon. I'd drunk three glasses of wine while I worked. It was Mike's week with Polly. I got a call from him. He was tied up at work in an emergency meeting and the day care needed her picked up ASAP. Could I do it?"

Her shoulders hunch. "I could have said no. I could have admitted I'd been drinking. I could have called a cab. But one thing about drinking is that it blows your judgment to hell. Three glasses in four hours meant I wasn't even legally intoxicated. I'd be careful. I'd drive slow. On the way back, there was this truck in front of us, with a load the driver hadn't secured. It hit a bump and pipes flew off, and I saw them coming and I . . . I reacted too slowly. It might have still been fine except . . ." Her voice goes to a whisper. "Polly wanted the top down. I had a convertible, and she loved riding with the top down and . . ."

Her arms squeeze her legs, her gaze on the ground. "I have seen things in my job, Casey. What I saw that day . . ." Her voice drops to the faintest whisper. "I never see the rest anymore. All I ever see is her. All that matters is her. It is the only truly unforgivable thing I have ever done."

She pauses for a moment and then continues. "Mike lost his daughter, and he lost his mind. I don't blame him—I did, too. But he had a target for his grief and rage. Me. He just . . . He could not cope, and everything that I turned inward, he turned on me. All the blame. All the hate. He became a man I'd never seen before. He told people—family, friends—that I'd never wanted a child. That's true, but he twisted it to sound as if I might have somehow done this on purpose."

She takes deep breaths, eyes closed, and in her face, I see the woman I saw that time in the cave, when she found Abbygail's arm. I remember her scream, and that look, and I remember thinking there must be trauma in her past. Now I know there was. And I don't even want to imagine what she saw that day with her daughter.

She continues. "I couldn't go to Polly's funeral. I didn't dare—after what he was saying, it would be like spitting on her grave. He told everyone about my drinking. Made it sound so much worse. I tested well below the legal limit after the accident, but he told them I was a chronic alcoholic and he pretended I'd hidden it from him. Even that wasn't enough. He went to my very conservative, very religious grandparents and told them about my girlfriends. Told them I was bisexual. Which, yes, I am, but there was no reason for me to tell them. So when I needed my family most . . ."

She takes more deep breaths. "He was in so much pain. I know that, and I forgive him. At the time, though, it felt like I'd been hit by a truck, and Mike just kept backing up and running over me. I snapped. I wanted to be gone. To not exist. It felt like the only answer. I decided to kill myself. The question was how to do it. I needed a foolproof plan. The only thing that could make my situation worse would be to fail, to be found alive and have people to think that it'd been a weak and desperate cry for help. Like Paul—swallow a few pills, knowing it's not enough to kill you."

She pauses. "That's not fair. I don't know Paul's situation, and I shouldn't judge it. I wanted to kill myself, and I delayed while I perfected the method. During that delay, my grandmother swooped in and snatched me away."

"The one Mike talked to?"

She shakes her head. "That's my dad's family. This is Mom's. My gran and gramps—Dad's parents—were stereotypical grandparents. They lived in the country, and I'd spend a month there every summer, learning to garden and bake cookies. Nan was different. Our summer vacations were a week in Paris or New York. I was in awe of her, and no matter how warm and kind she was, I always felt a distance between us. She was the sort of woman I wanted to be, and that's intimidating. When Polly died, she was overseas. She flew back, assessed the situation, and had me kidnapped."

"Kidnapped?"

A soft laugh. "Yep. She knew me, better than I ever imagined, and she knew exactly how to handle the situation. Like a tactical maneuver. Scoop me up, take me to a mountain retreat—a *secure* mountain retreat—and give me a month of support and tough love. Like a detox center for a life that's gone toxic."

"Your grandmother did that?"

"Well, she didn't kidnap me herself. She was eighty-two. But she stayed with me at that mountain retreat, giving me that love and support. She knew me, and she knew what I needed." Her voice falls again as she looks around. "She always knew what I needed, even when I wasn't sure myself."

"She got you here, I'm guessing."

"She *brought* me here."

"Émilie."

Her chin jerks up. Then her lips curve in a small smile. "You're quick."

"I'm a detective."

She chuckles under her breath. "True. I was never good at that part. Show me a target and tell me what to do, and I can figure out how to proceed. Just don't ask me to *pick* a target. Don't ask me to decide guilt or innocence. I used to tell myself that makes it easier. I am the weapon. Nothing more. That works until you realize you're not made of metal. You have a brain, and you can't help using it. You wonder. You question. Then it seems it'd be better to be in your shoes, where you evaluate and decide. Except then it's a choice, like with Val. You chose to shoot her. I acted on orders. Brady and Val were both guilty. My conscience is clean—I did as I was told. Yours is troubled—you made a choice."

"Is this your way of not answering the question about Émilie?"

Petra laughs again. "You weren't asking, Casey. You were stating a fact. Showing off a little, but I'll give you that. You earned it. Yes, Émilie is my grandmother. She told me about Rockton. Told me *more* about it, I should say. I'd always known it existed—it's family history. She asked if I wanted to come to Rockton and resume my old life. To be her agent on the ground. It was my decision. My choice. There are no illusions between us. I've killed before. I will do it again, for the right reason. I feel no guilt over Brady. She understands that. If I'm a hard-assed bitch, I come by it honestly. The hardness, that is. The toughness. The clean, clear-cut decision making, where the greater good stands above pointless moral navel gazing. Brady was a murderer and a threat. I took him out. My only regret is that you saw me, and it ruined the best friendship I've had in a very long time."

She looks up at me. "Émilie is the best of Rockton. She is its heart and its brain. But her health is failing, and others are taking advantage. That's why I'm coming to you with this. For Rockton. It's what she'd want."

I nod. It's all I can do. I need time to process all this. When silence falls, she shakes it off and rises from the log. Then she crouches and tugs a handful of moss from a knot in the fallen tree. She sticks her hand into the hole and pulls out a gun. When I go for mine, she lifts her free hand.

"It isn't loaded," she says. "I'm just taking it out to show you that this is the cache. It's one of several we've used since I got here. There's an extra gun and ammo. There was a vial, with the drugs. The mushrooms were here, too, for me to plant so you'd think that's what Roy took. The council has these caches, and when they need me to use something from them, I get my orders. Presumably, if I take something like ammo, they'll refill it, though last week was the first time I discharged my weapon."

"You've had it, though. In Rockton."

She nods. "In a safe place, in case I ever needed to use it in an emergency."

"And the vial you removed?"

"Discarded immediately afterward. My orders were to destroy it. I followed my orders. That's what I was taught, and it's what I've done here, because I've had no reason not to, until now."

"Is there more of that drug in there?"

"That's what I'm here to find out." She reaches into the hollow tree, up to her shoulder. She removes a rucksack and ammo, a field knife, a rifle and scope. She points at the rifle. "Never used. I'm hoping Val confessed to being your sniper."

"She did."

But the council knew this was here. That Petra had access to a rifle. Yet they brushed off my concern. When I ask Petra if anyone contacted her to see if she might have done it, she says no. So they knew it could have been her, trying to take down Brady, and they didn't care.

"That's it," she says when she's finished emptying the cache. She starts going through the rucksack. "I've emptied this before, and I didn't see a vial."

As she checks the rucksack, I catch movement out of the corner of my eye. It's fast, and that has me moving equally fast, spinning, gun coming from my holster.

Petra snaps up onto her feet, her gaze following mine. When she sees nothing, she doesn't ask what I spotted, she just keeps looking.

The forest has gone still.

Petra looks at me. I'm still gazing about, seeing her only in the corner of my eye. She drops and reaches for the gun. I do look then. She's on one knee, still scanning the trees, her hand reaching blindly to where she'd laid the weapon.

Another flash of movement. This one's to my left, and I was sure the other came from my right. I lower my hand and extend out two fingers. Telling Petra I spotted two potential threats. Ammo rattles. Petra's gun clicks as she opens it.

A figure runs at me from the right, on the other side of the fallen log. I spin, my gun pointed. The man keeps running. One look at mud-spiked hair and a mud-smeared face and a makeshift knife, and I know it's a hostile.

FORTY-FOUR

"What the hell?" Petra whispers.

I fire a warning shot over the man's head. He doesn't even slow.

"Stop!" I say.

He doesn't care. I know he won't, but I have to say it. I have to hope it'll make a difference. Thick bush slows his headlong charge. I leap onto the fallen log, and when he's close enough, I kick. My foot connects with his gut. He staggers back. I manage to keep my balance as pain stabs through my bad leg.

I glance over my shoulder to make sure Petra's watching for that second person I'd spotted. She is. She has her gun loaded, and she's braced, waiting.

My hostile charges again. I kick again, hard enough that I know my foot is doing some damage. He only howls and comes back for a third kick. That one puts him down.

I leap on him before he can bounce up, which I know he will, no matter how badly he's hurt. I knock the knife from his hand.

The man beneath me bucks. I flip and pin him, but he doesn't care. Just like . . .

Just like Roy.

I inhale sharply, and it's not just because this man's actions remind me of Roy. He reminds me of Roy. When he'd charged, I'd had a split-second flash of memory, too quick for me to pursue under the circumstances. The spiked hair, obviously, looks like Roy's. But it was more than that. It was his face, his expression, blind rage. Now the man reacts as Roy did, writhing and howling, and twisting his arm has no effect. It's like when I hit him in the stomach. He doesn't care. There's no handy sedative here. I don't have my cuffs, either.

I can hit him on the head, but that's as likely to do brain damage as it is to knock him out. I'm wrestling with him, and Petra's there, shouting for him to stop, pressing her gun right to his head.

"Goddamn you, stop!" she says. "What the hell is he on? He . . ."

She trails off, and she meets my gaze, and I know she's thinking exactly what I just did.

What is he on?

What indeed.

"Shoot him."

At first, I think that's Petra talking. It's a woman's voice. The words make no sense, though, considering she's the one holding the gun. I think maybe it's a question. Then I look up to see her gaze fixed to the side as a woman steps through the trees.

It's Maryanne. She holds a knife, and Petra's gun swings her way.

"No!" I say. "She's okay."

Maryanne picks up and pockets the man's knife. She comes closer, and she's shaking, her own blade trembling in her grip.

"Shoot him," she whispers.

I shake my head. "We're going to try to help him."

Even as I say the words, I think, *We are?* Is that even possible? Is it wise? But what is the alternative? He isn't going to let us walk away. That's what Maryanne means. We can't scare him off. We can't injure him and hope he slinks away to nurse his wounds. The guy beneath me is like a killing-machine movie cyborg. He'll just keep coming. He *isn't* a cyborg, though. He's a person, and we cannot keep killing hostiles every time they attack us.

"We need to—" I begin, and then the man bites me.

This is my fault. Caught up in my thoughts, I give him the opportunity to bite, and when he does, I jump, more in surprise than pain.

The moment my weight shifts, he's ready, and he fights like the cornered beast he is.

He bites and twists and kicks and hits. I try to pin him. Petra tries to pin him. Then Maryanne is on him. Blood flies before I even realize what she's doing. She howls and stabs, her face a mask of rage even as tears stream down her face.

"No!" she shouts. "No, no, no!"

Petra and I haul her off him. The hostile crawls away, and I try to go after him, but the moment I relax my grip, Maryanne fights harder. Petra can subdue her, but I don't trust her not to hurt Maryanne in the process.

The hostile scrambles to his feet, a hand to his side where Maryanne stabbed him, blood running from the shot to his shoulder. Whatever bloodlust consumed him, the survival instinct overpowers it, and he staggers into the forest. Maryanne doesn't calm down until he's gone.

I sit on my haunches and look up at her. "Maryanne, we—"

"Warned you," she says. "You didn't listen."

"You warned me about him? I know, you said to shoot—"

"Not him. All." She looks around. "They're watching now. Always watching."

She means the hostiles are watching us. That's what she meant with that skull she gave me for Dalton. A warning. Rockton has gone decades rarely interacting with the hostiles, and then we slaughtered a hunting party of them. Killed them because they attacked us, and we tried to avoid even that—it's Val who finished off the injured—but to them, it was a slaughter. They won't hide in the forest anymore. They're watching. They're waiting. They're attacking. I look at the blood soaking the ground. And now we've attacked back.

"Come to Rockton," I say. "Eric's there. He wants to help—"

She shakes her head.

"Maryanne, please."

She lifts her hand with the missing partial fingers and touches her ruined ear and then her filed front teeth. Tears fill her eyes.

"Not like this," she says.

I'm not going back like this. That's what she means. That is the horror of her situation. Something has happened to her since we last met. Dalton made a connection, and she'd been ready for it. She wasn't the madwoman who attacked him years ago. She'd already changed, calmed. When he made that connection, it reminded her of who she'd been and something sparked. She began rising from that pit. Her mind rising, but her body . . . Her body had already changed, and no epiphany could regrow her ear and fingers and teeth. She now had the mental wherewithal to realize that, which made it all the worse.

"It doesn't matter," I say. "We have a doctor. We can help. You can—"

"No," she says, those tears spilling.

She turns and runs in the opposite direction the hostile went. Petra looks at me, poised to sprint after her, and my muscles tense, ready to do the same. I take a deep breath and shake my head.

"It can't be like that," I say.

She nods. Then she keeps looking in the direction Maryanne went.

"That was a . . ." Petra begins.

"Hostile, yes."

She's still staring. "I thought . . ."

"Thought we were lying? Exaggerating? Trying to scare people with tales of bogeymen in the forest?" I hear my voice, harsh, and I shake my head. "Never mind. I'm just tired and frustrated."

She looks over then, meeting my gaze. "I get it now, Casey. I really do."

She pauses and then says, "He was acting like Roy."

"I know."

"What Roy did to himself—the hair, the beard—it's like a stage-one version of this."

"Yes."

"Then whatever I gave Roy . . ." She looks at me. "What are you thinking?"

I don't answer. She knows exactly what I'm thinking, and I'm not putting it into words so she can tell me I'm wrong, tell me there are other explanations. I know there are. I don't need to have that conversation with anyone except Dalton.

"We need to get back to Rockton," I say.

Once I'm back, I go straight to Dalton and tell him everything. I barely finish before Dalton gets called off on an unrelated problem. Before I get ten steps away, Mathias approaches with Raoul in his arms.

"I hope you weren't bringing him for more canine socialization," I say in French. "Eric has Storm, and he's busy. We both are."

"So am I, apparently. Someone has given them to me without asking whether I wanted to undertake it."

"Sebastian. Yes. You're welcome."

His mouth opens.

"Skip the protests, Mathias. You like projects. You wanted this one. You're going to pretend you're doing me a favor, so I'll feel indebted. But I did *you* a favor."

"A favor?"

"I gave you a pet sociopath. Almost as good as a pet wolf, right?" I motion for him to join me as I walk back to the station. "Sebastian says he's reformed. He says he wants to stay reformed, and he wants help with that. I'm not making any judgment calls. Your job is to help him and watch over him. That's why he's your apprentice."

"I do not need—"

"Too bad. He's your apprentice. Your shop apprentice. Not your sociopath apprentice."

I get a reproachful look for that. I continue. "Whatever your own condition, you've learned to rechannel it. I'm not asking you to do that with Sebastian. He isn't you. Just figure out if he's serious about coping with his condition. If he isn't, we can't have him here. If he is, that's a project for you." I glance over. "Did he tell you what he did?"

"Yes. It is a fascinating case study, to be so young and do such a thing. Even more fascinating if he, at his current young age, sees his problem and wishes to overcome it. The issue with sociopathy is that one usually cannot understand that what one is doing is wrong. He seems to. Fascinating."

"You're welcome."

Next I head for Phil's place. Of course he's at home. He answers the door with a notebook in his hand and a look that warns me I'm interrupting something. On the notepad, I see numbers and equations, and there is a moment where I don't see Phil there at all. I see Val, and I feel . . .

Regret. I will admit that. I will always feel regret for what I did, but I feel anger, too, outrage even, that emotion I'm far less likely to admit to than the regret. Regretting murder is natural, expected, whatever the circumstances. The anger, though, rises from hurt. I am hurt that Val betrayed me. I am humiliated by the fact that I worked so hard to bring her into the community, and she turned on me and mocked me for it.

I won't reach out like that with Phil. Right or wrong, I must lick my wounds in hurt silence, and let him do what he will do, and if that's hiding in his home like Val, so be it.

"I need to talk to you," I say. "About the gun and your watch."

His mouth tightens. "I believe we've been through this—"

"No, we actually haven't. I know you had the gun in your luggage, but we have never discussed who had access to it. Now, I'm sorry to interrupt whatever you're doing . . ."

"Budgets," he says. "I'm working on the town budget. It's clear that despite Valerie's level of mathematical expertise, she had no head for accounting. The books are a mess, along with the town's finances. I've already discovered over a thousand dollars a month that can be trimmed from expenses."

I stiffen. "If you are suggesting that we overspend, let me remind you that people are trapped here. Yes, we could cut back on coffee or baked goods or books, but those things are important to residents."

"I agree, which is why I'm trimming in other areas, so that you will have more money for those luxuries."

"Oh." I glance over my shoulder as residents pass, looking over in curiosity. "Can I come in, Phil? It'll only take a few minutes."

He waves me inside. I confirm that both the gun and the watch were inside his luggage. I also confirm that he hadn't seen the watch between the shooting and the time we returned it.

I should have checked on this earlier, ascertained exactly where he'd kept the watch and when he'd last seen it. After Roy's episode, it seemed obvious that whoever drugged him also planted the watch, especially if they were trying to frame him, which Petra was.

Yet Petra didn't plant the watch, and I believe her, because it was a clumsy move, and she is not clumsy. She would take one look at Roy and know he wouldn't covet Phil's expensive but delicate watch. Roy was an asshole, but he wasn't an idiot. Hiding that watch for two years wouldn't be worth the few hundred bucks he could fence it for when he left.

No, it was clumsily done, meaning that Petra wasn't the only one framing Roy.

"Detective?" Phil says, as I stand there, brain whirring, making connections. "You have something?"

I ask more questions about access to his house. He keeps it locked, unlike most residents, meaning whoever got the gun either broke in or had entry. Those who've had entry, though, have barely gotten past the door, meaning whoever did this likely broke in. That person knew what they were looking for, though. Knew Phil had a gun. And the person I have in mind is on the short list of those who definitely knew, having witnessed the aftermath of the first time Phil pulled that damned gun on us.

"You have a suspect?" Phil asks as I'm preparing to leave.

"I have a theory."

He frowns, clearly vexed with my answer, and despite my wandering thoughts, I almost have to smile at his vexation. Phil has that kind of male-model face where every expression looks like something in a stock-photo collection. Type in "vexed man" or "annoyed man" or "man concentrating" and you get someone like Phil, his perfect jawline and perfect mouth set in whatever perfect expression you require.

I notice this, and I'm reminded of my thoughts about Sebastian, and how he could hide because there's nothing extraordinary about his appearance. Phil might have a very pretty face, but it's as cookie-cutter, in its way, as that stock-photo-perfect visage. And as I think this, I'm not really thinking of Phil or Sebastian at all. I'm remembering Roy with his beard half shaved, and then Petra, talking in the forest.

Then I'm thinking of another face, as blandly average as Sebastian's. I'm thinking of a photograph.

I'm thinking of a mistake I've made.

The mistake of looking at a photograph and saying, "Sure that looks like so-and-so," because it did look *like* him. But it wasn't.

FORTY-FIVE

As I'm walking to the station, Diana crosses the road ahead, moving fast, and finger waves. I remember something I overheard at the clinic—something potentially useful. I consider for a moment. Then I jog to catch up.

"You're in a hurry," I say. "Eager to play nurse for Roy and Paul? I heard that's your job today."

She rolls her eyes. "Believe me, I'm only rushing because I'm late and I don't need your sister giving me crap. April is as delightful as always. I've offered to look after Kenny, while she checks on Paul and Roy, but no . . . she gets the *nice* guy."

"Roy's an asshole," I say. "Take backup when you visit him."

"Oh, I do." She pulls a knife from her pocket.

"Uh, yeah," I say. "You do know that, statistically speaking, you're more likely to get stabbed with that than stab your attacker."

Another roll of her eyes, as if I'm kidding. I'm not, but with Roy, if he did try anything, one flash of that blade should stop him.

"Paul's fine, though, isn't he?" I say. "I know he's interested in you. Has he bothered you lately?"

"No more than usual. It isn't harassment, just pestering. He's interested, and I'm not."

"I know guys here make up stories to impress women, since there's no way to do a background check. If you ever have trouble, I can't tell you why someone's here, but I can suggest when they're full of shit. Has Paul said anything like that?"

It's an awkward shot in the dark. But she says, "Nothing specific. He just hints that he's one of the white-collar criminals. A man with money."

"Really?"

"Oh, yeah. He made it clear that I might want to get in on that, an investment toward my future. As if I couldn't possibly be here for the same reason because I'm a woman."

I look around, making sure we're alone. "Have you told anyone that you met Garcia when he arrived? That he took you captive?"

"No. Geez, Casey. How many times do I need to say it? I didn't tell anyone. You asked me not to, and I wouldn't have anyway. No one needed to know that."

"Good," I say. "Then I think it's time to change that."

Diana and I are in line at the bakery. It's just past one, still early for afternoon coffee, but with the longer days, everything shifts, and by now there's a queue, as I hoped.

"I need to know what he told you," I say, keeping my voice artificially low, a harsh stage whisper that everyone nearby can hear.

"I told you, Case, Garcia never said anything."

"Bullshit, you were alone with him for fifteen minutes. He talked to you. I know he did."

"He told me to shut up and behave or he'd shoot me. If you call that a conversation then yes, we talked."

"He was a US marshal. He wasn't going to shoot you. When I got back with Eric, you were talking about who he came for. He gave you a hint. I know he did."

"He didn't—"

"He said to ask you. Those were his last words. I wanted to know who he came here for, and he said to ask my friend, the one he held hostage, the one with the pink hair." I cast a pointed look at her fading pink tips. "Don't tell me he meant someone else."

"That was his final screw-you. With his dying breath, he tells you to speak to me . . . except he never told me anything. Ha ha. Joke's on you. He was an asshole. Trust me. I'm the one who had to sit with him for fifteen minutes as he held a gun to my head."

I look around, as if making sure no one has heard us. Everyone glances away quickly, feigning sudden interest in their fingernails or the menu board or the lovely June sun overhead. My gaze crosses Paul, two people behind us. He's with Anders, whom I asked to drop in on Paul . . . and suggest they grab a coffee.

Anders smiles and shoots me a subtle thumbs-up. Diana and I step to the front of the line and place our order.

After that, I catch up with Dalton and then tell him my theory at the station. I'd rather have done that before I set my plan in motion, but it hasn't proceeded far enough that I can't stop if he points out some critical flaw in my reasoning.

"Paul?" he says, when I tell him who I suspect. "Yeah, he does have a federal warrant, but we're reasonably sure Garcia wasn't here on official business."

"I screwed up."

Dalton sits on the edge of the desk. "Okay . . ."

"I mistakenly ID'd our Paul as the guy in that online photo. Just yesterday, I was thinking that Sebastian didn't need to worry about being recognized because he has a very average white-boy face. So does Paul."

Dalton's brows rise. "Average white-boy face?"

"They look like a million other Caucasian guys their age. No distinguishing features, just a very normal face, pleasant enough but nothing that stands out, nothing you'd notice or remember."

"That doesn't sound . . . flattering. Dare I ask if I have . . . ?"

"No." I lean over and kiss his cheek. "Now, if your fragile ego can allow me to continue."

"My ego is not—"

"Totally can be. And this is *not* the time for it. So Paul has a very average face. Very ordinary. He also has a beard, which he didn't have in the photo. I'm guessing he had that beard when he arrived?"

Dalton thinks. "Maybe? Yeah, I have no idea."

"Because he isn't memorable, right? But I bet he did. It hides half his face, so when I looked at the photo online, it seemed to be him. Brown hair. Brown eyes. Same facial shape. It *looked* like Paul, and I didn't study the photo closely, because I expected it to be Paul. I can't say for absolute certain that it wasn't, but I'm no longer sure it was."

"Okay."

"Then there's the suicide attempt. Petra made a comment about that, in another context, how it wasn't serious, just a cry for help. She's right. He took enough to pass out, knowing we'd come looking for him because of his shift. Given how easily he recovered, he didn't take enough to kill himself. I figured he just didn't know what a fatal dose might be. But he had more pills there, scattered on the bed, as if he dropped them when he passed out. If you're serious about killing yourself, you take them all at once, before the sedative kicks in. Still, that only means he wasn't serious. It happens."

"Okay."

"Then I ask Diana about Paul hitting on her, whether he's hinted why he's here. Turns out he's bragged to her about having money, enough to suggest he's one of our white-collar criminals. Still, yes, he could be puffing himself up, trying to get her attention."

He's quiet for a moment. "None of it says 'I killed Agent Garcia,' but yeah, he makes a helluva good suspect."

"Also, Paul had time and opportunity to shoot Garcia. After the first time Phil pulled his gun on us with Wallace, Paul was the one who escorted Phil home. He knew Phil had the gun, and he probably saw where he kept it. I can confirm that with Phil, but I don't want to toss the council a suspect. Paul has been in Phil's house since, running errands. He could easily have taken it when he found out Garcia was here. Then he offered to man the radio. He *did* offer—Will confirmed that. Paul offered to take the radio and to watch Roy."

Dalton breathes, "Fuck. Yeah. So he gets the call. He leaves Roy's cell door unlocked, setting up an alternate suspect. He runs and tells others to help find Will . . ."

"While he sneaks into the forest and cuts us off. And there's one more thing. Yesterday, Jen didn't want Roy in the clinic with Kenny alone overnight while Kenny was incapacitated. Where did Paul end up after his suicide attempt?"

"In the clinic with Garcia. Well, with Garcia's body, but he didn't know the guy was dead."

"So he attempts suicide and expects to recover in the clinic, alone overnight with a dying man. Easy enough to finish him off. We'd wonder, of course, but hey, it's Paul. The poor guy tried to take his own life, and if Marshal Garcia succumbed to his injuries while Paul was in the next room, that's just really unfortunate timing."

"Okay, so bring Paul—"

The door opens. My sister walks in.

"I need to talk to you," she says.

"Can it wait? We're in the middle of—"

"No, it cannot wait. I wish to apply for residence."

I look at Dalton, but his expression says he also thinks he's misheard.

"You . . ." I begin.

"Your town requires a doctor. I am offering my services for a six-month term. I expect room and board and whatever credit stipend you pay. I also require a private residence. The one beside the clinic would be ideal for its location. I know Nicole is currently living there, but Kenny says that was temporary, pending the arrival of a new doctor."

"Did Kenny talk you into this?"

"I am perfectly capable of making my own decisions, Casey."

"Right, but you have a career—"

"I will take a sabbatical. I have discussed . . ." She trails off, and her gaze shifts, still hard, just not quite meeting mine. "I have raised the possibility recently, so that I might pursue my own interests, as one does on sabbatical. Financially, I do not need to work ever again. I have invested wisely, and I am free to do as I please. You require a doctor. While I am not a general practitioner, I am a trained medical physician, one who, unlike Dr. Atelier, has practiced. Also, unlike him, I am willing to do the work."

She steps toward us. "I don't know who you had as a doctor before me, but they overlooked many opportunities in equipping and stocking your clinic. I realize you are under restrictions here, with the remote location and the limited electrical supply; however, I see that as a challenge, one I would enjoy."

Her eyes shine brighter than I've ever seen them, her face flushed with what I can only call excitement. When she starts to admit that she'd enjoy the work, she stops short, and I see her mentally withdrawing from that word, looking for a way around it. She straightens her shoulders. "You need a doctor. I am willing and able to fulfill that position."

April wants to stay. I have done the impossible. I've shown her something that actually piqued her interest.

I douse the childish thrill rising in me. Tread carefully here. Do not let my own excitement blind me to the fact that this is completely out of character.

"The weather is lovely now," I say, "but when winter comes—"

"It's the north," she says. "I *have* ventured outside Vancouver, Casey, and I do not forget Ontario winters."

"Okay, I just—"

"It's cold and it's dark," she says. "I understand that. I'm not saying I look forward to taking up winter sports. I will leave that to you. For me, a long and dark winter means time to read and focus on my personal projects. I will also require books. I realize that your supply runs are limited, but an ebook reader requires relatively little charge, and I'm sure you could upload books onto it when you are in Dawson. Books of my choosing, primarily work related, but . . ." She clears her throat. "I may also find time for fiction, which I realize is frivolous . . ."

"It's entertainment," I say. "And a much-needed mental vacation. We have absolutely no problem with that. I think we can supply an ebook reader. . . ."

I look at Dalton, who gives a helpless shrug, and I realize he's not even sure what that is.

"We'll work it out," I say.

"Good," she says. "I understand what life is like up here, and I have spoken to Kenny at length about it."

"Kenny . . ." I say.

"Yes, he's one of the reasons I will be staying." She hurries on, "To help his rehabilitation, of course."

I sneak a look at Dalton. Am I imagining that color in my sister's cheeks? Because if I'm not . . .

Does April have a crush on *Kenny*?

I'm not even sure what to do with that. I do know what to do with this situation, though. What I must do, as much as I'd love to leap at the opportunity. Because it is an opportunity, not only to get a doctor but to fulfill that little-girl dream, where my sister actually wants to be near me. It doesn't matter if she hasn't said a word about wanting *that*; this is closer than I've ever been to having April in my world.

"Eric?" I say. "May I . . . ?" I motion to April.

He nods and pushes off the desk. "I'll be out back."

When he's gone, I turn to my sister. "We need a doctor. You know that. I would love to have you. But this is . . . not what I expected. So I need to ask: is there something you aren't telling me?"

The twitch in her posture tells me there is, and my hopes plummet. Still, I push on. "If there's a reason you want to be here, something you have to escape for a while, then we can talk about that. But we need to know. You saw what we just dealt with, having a federal marshal show up. We cannot be blindsided."

"You need a doctor, Casey, and I am offering to be that. I don't believe I require a reason."

"Actually, yes, you do. I'm sorry, April. While I don't know you nearly as well as I'd like, I still know Rockton is not your idea of paradise. It wasn't mine. I came here for Diana, and yes, I love it now, but there are very, very few people who'd hear about a place like this and say 'sign me up.' You aren't one of those. You want to stay for a reason."

She glowers at me, and I'm ready for her argument. One that will make me feel like a bratty child for questioning my sister's motives. I stand firm, and she meets my gaze, and there is a silence that seems to stretch forever.

Then she says, "I need a break."

"Okay."

She wants to leave it at that. When she can tell I'm not going to let her, she marches across the room.

She stands in front of the fireplace with her back to me. More silence. I don't break it. I can't.

"I love my work," she says.

"I know."

"It is not easy work. I appreciate a challenge. I have, in the past few years . . ." She takes a deep breath. "I pushed myself harder than I should have. After you left . . ."

She spins on her heel. "You *left,* Casey. With a ten-second phone call, you left."

"I told you I was going. It wouldn't have been a ten-second call if you hadn't made it clear I was interrupting—"

"I was distracted. I wasn't paying attention. I thought you were . . ." She flutters her hands. "Being you. *Diana has a crisis. Poor Diana. Must run and save Diana.* Forget your family. Forget your sister. Diana needs you."

I step toward her, but she backs up, stiffening. I lower my voice. "You never needed me, April. If you had, I'd have been there—"

"You weren't there."

"Since Mom and Dad died, you have made it very clear you wanted nothing to do with me."

"I still knew you were there, if I ever needed you. And then you weren't. First, Mom and Dad, and then you . . ." She sucks in a breath. "I pushed myself too hard at work. I had an episode. I needed a rest."

A breakdown. That's what she's telling me, in her way. She had a breakdown while I was gone. I remember me quipping that Mom and Dad said a surgeon needed steady hands. It might not have been the reminder of our parents that made her flinch, but the memory of a time when her hands had *not* been steady, made shaky from anxiety.

"April, I'm sorry—"

"No need. I am fine. I have questioned . . ." She stops, her voice quaking. "Regarding my work, I have questioned what I am doing and where I am going. I need a break. I know that. I hated stopping during my episode, and yet when you offered me the chance to come here—the excuse to take a few days off—I jumped at it. When you first suggested I might not be able to leave quickly, I panicked. And then I was relieved. I need a break. This will do."

I nod slowly. "All right. That makes sense. We'll speak to the council, but I suspect it'll be an easy yes. We can take you home to make arrangements. You'll need to speak to friends and colleagues, set them at ease, particularly whomever you called before you came up here—"

"No one." She blurts the words. Her cheeks color, and she averts her gaze. "I feigned placing a call. There is no one . . ."

When she trails off, my heart breaks a little.

"Colleagues then," I say quickly. "You need to let them know you'll be gone."

She nods.

"We'll sort this with the council," I say. "And then we'll take you home to straighten out everything else. First, though, I have a killer to trap."

FORTY-SIX

We put Isabel in charge of talking to Phil about April. I know my sister is eager to get an answer, and this is really not the time for me to handle it. I have a suspect to test, and a plan for doing that. This plan involves Diana again. She knew that, and she's been waiting. While Dalton goes to give Isabel her task, I set out to speak to Diana.

I'm talking to her behind the general store when she spots Paul.

"Perfect timing," she says, and she starts to leave.

"Hold up," I say. "Eric's not back yet, and Paul isn't going anywhere. . . ."

Too late. She's already jogging toward Paul, and if I chase her, he'll suspect a setup. Damn Diana.

I shake my head and glance around for Dalton. Then I turn my attention to Diana, as she walks briskly across the road from Paul. He spots her, slows, and crosses to speak to her.

Bait taken.

I walk from behind the store and peer about, as if looking for someone. Diana grabs Paul's arm and whispers something. He glances in my direction, and then quickly looks away. Diana shuttles him off, their backs to me.

Now, the plan is for her to take him into the woods to talk. I'll follow at a—

"You!" a voice says.

I turn to see Roy bearing down on me.

"I want to talk to you, Detective."

"Not now. I'm—"

"I don't give a shit what you're doing. I am a citizen of this town, and you can take two minutes to listen to me."

I glance toward Diana, to warn her I've been waylaid.

"Do me the goddamn courtesy of looking when I'm talking to you," Roy booms.

"Give me one hour. Come by the station at—"

"You're kicking me out. I just heard it from that pretty boy who took Val's place. He told me to pack my things. This is bullshit."

I cast a surreptitious glance in Diana's direction. There is no way she *can't* hear Roy, yet she hasn't stopped. Hasn't slowed.

Is it my imagination or is she walking even faster?

She sneaks a look back, too fast for me to catch it.

She knows I've been waylaid . . . and she's not stopping.

Roy's going on about his right to stay in this town, and how even Mindy says she doesn't have a problem with him.

"Wait," I say. "You talked to Mindy? You were ordered to stay away from her."

Diana is gone. She was there a moment ago, but when I glance back, she's not.

Damn it, Diana. And damn me, too, as the fool who keeps trusting you.

She knew I was delayed, and she went ahead and took off with Paul.

I turn to Roy. "I know nothing about what Phil told you. I haven't spoken to him all day. Your residency is entirely up to the council. We only enforce their decisions."

"Bull*shit*. You and your boyfriend run this town. A couple of children, barely old enough to wipe your own asses. Overeducated millennials, so concerned with protecting everyone's rights that you never actually accomplish anything."

"Millennials?" Jen says as she walks over. "I resent that. Casey and Eric might be, but I'm Gen X. Whole different set of stereotypes."

"Jen, can you take him?" I ask.

She grabs Roy by the arm. "Come on, big fellow. Let's get you home. Maybe, if you're good, we can cut off the rest of that beard. Though, I gotta say, it's kind of working for you."

Roy doesn't go quietly, of course, but Jen has this under control.

I jog to where I last saw Diana. There's no sign of her. Or Paul.

It takes me far too long to find Diana and Paul. Long enough that they're already deep in conversation, which is how I locate them, picking up the whisper of their words.

"You have about five minutes until Casey shows up," Diana is saying. "She's been hounding me to find out what that marshal said. I saw her just back there. Roy stopped her, and that'll slow her down, but she's going to catch up any second, and when she does, you and I are done with this conversation. The offer closes."

"I told you, I have no idea what you're talking about."

"Mmm-hmm, which is why you were so quick to intercept me to ask what the marshal said? Idle curiosity? You're wasting my time, Paul. You're on Casey's short list of suspects. You were on mine, too, after what the marshal told me. Now I know you're the one he came for. I see it in your face. You've got a day or two before Casey figures it out. You've only got five minutes—three now—to convince me to feed her false information."

"What did he say?"

"That this fugitive is a white, middle-aged male. Very average. Someone we'd never suspect. Probably close to us, part of the town, maybe even on the town council or militia."

"That describes a *lot*—"

"New York City."

Paul pauses and then says, "What?"

"Nice place. Ever lived there? No, actually, I don't think you have."

"I don't know what—"

"Ever joined a protest, Paul? No, I didn't think you had, despite the story that got you in here."

He opens his mouth, but Diana keeps going.

"Those are the hints the marshal gave me," Diana says. "He said his target might have mentioned he was from New York, might have said he'd been defending a girl in a protest march in Washington, got himself in some trouble. It's not true, apparently. It's just the cover story his target was telling. He hoped I could identify his target for him. I couldn't . . . at the time, anyway."

A hand clamps around my mouth. I twist to see . . .

Roy? Seriously?

I fight halfheartedly at first. I'm not alarmed, just pissed off, wondering what the hell happened to Jen. Then Roy slams his fist into my gut so fast and so hard that I double over, gasping in shock and pain. His hand goes over my mouth again, and he hauls me away as I struggle to catch my breath.

When I finally come to my senses, I lash out with fists and feet. He hits me in the side of the head. The world dips into blackness, and I stagger. He grabs the back of my jacket and hauls me upright.

"I paid," he snarls as he keeps dragging me. "I paid a fortune to get here, and I am not leaving. You drugged me. I know you did. You wanted me gone, and you put those mushrooms in my wine to give the council a reason to kick me out."

He's caught me off guard—how the hell did I let this asshole catch me off guard?—and I'm still reeling from that blow. I need to focus. My gun's in its holster, right under my jacket. I'm fine. I just have to get back to Diana and Paul before this all goes to hell.

Goddamn it, Diana. I cannot trust you, and I'm a fool for thinking I can.

I let myself go limp. Until now I've been scuttling along as he drags me. When I let my knees give way, he staggers backward. I close my eyes, as if I passed out.

He curses and drops me. I play dead . . . or unconscious, at least, lying on the ground like a rag doll. He grabs me by the jacket. Then he stops, and I don't have to open my eyes to know what's stopped him. My holster. He sees it. And he sees it's empty.

I swing into the back of his knee. His leg folds, and I give him a shove. He punches at me. I kick him. Then as he's falling, I slam my fist into his stomach. That's petty and unprofessional, and I don't give a damn. With my gun in my left hand, I plow my right fist into his stomach. He doubles over, and I put him down, flat on his back. Then I point the gun at him.

When he starts to rise, I say, "It's only you and me out here, Roy. Give me an excuse. Please."

He pauses and then lies down.

"Hands over your head," I say.

I see movement to my left as Dalton jogs over. I hand him the cuff strap. "Can you take over here? I have no idea what happened to Jen, who was supposed to be guarding his ass."

"He locked her in the bathroom," Dalton says.

I stare at him.

He shrugs. "She went in to get a razor and help him shave. He jammed the doorknob. She escaped out the window and found me. She's fine. Just pissed off." He looks around. "Where's Diana?"

"Don't ask. Just . . ." I look at Roy.

"You go. I'll cuff him and catch up."

FORTY-SEVEN

As I'm jogging back to where I left Diana and Paul, I hear a shout. A scuffle. A yelp.

Goddamn it, Diana!

I race over to find Diana on the ground, pinned there by . . .

"Jen?" I say.

Jen looks up from securing Diana, who is spitting curses. "She was cutting a deal with Paul. I was out looking for Roy, and I heard them. Paul's your killer. Diana here was blackmailing him."

"As I was supposed to," Diana snaps. "That was Casey's plan. Which you just *fucked* up."

"I—" Jen begins.

"She tried to go after Paul," Diana says. "He bolted. She decided I was a fine substitute and let your actual killer go."

"Which way?" I say.

Diana rises, giving Jen a shove and a glare as she does. Then she takes off, waving me to follow.

I quickly tell Jen to take over with Roy and send Dalton this way. Then I race after Diana. By the time I reach her, she's veered onto a path for easier running, and we can hear Paul crashing ahead.

"You saw Roy stop me," I say as I cut in front of her on the path. "You should have waited."

"I knew you'd catch up, and it gave more weight to my story. Anyway, Paul went for it. He gave me this song and dance about how he hadn't wanted to hurt anyone, but Garcia betrayed him, and he isn't really a bad guy."

"Just misunderstood?"

Diana snorts. "Pretty much. I pretended I bought it, didn't blame him et cetera, et cetera. He agreed to pay me to keep my mouth shut. I was haggling on the price, waiting for you to jump in, when Jen showed up. Where were you?"

"Roy, again."

"Seriously? Can't you just shoot him? Or Jen? I would *pay* you to shoot both of them."

I'm not angry at Jen. We both underestimated Roy's threat and wrote him off as a blustering bully. He is, yet that doesn't mean he can't still be dangerous. As for misunderstanding the situation with Diana and Paul, I can't blame Jen for that, either. I just wish she'd chased Paul and left Diana to us.

This is the problem with setting a trap. It's not a controlled environment, as it would be if I just brought Paul in for questioning. I'd known an arrest wouldn't work, though. I'd been operating on a theory with no solid evidence. So I had to trick Paul into incriminating himself, which meant trusting Diana to stay on script and trusting Rockton to go about its business without any fresh crisis erupting until I finished. Which is, yes, kind of like asking the earth to stop revolving for a few minutes.

It's gone quiet up ahead. I stop and put my fingers to my lips. Diana nods. I take out my gun and pivot, searching the surrounding trees for any sign of movement.

Voices drift from somewhere ahead. A laugh. A good-natured "Hey!" More laughter.

A work party. I check my watch. It's almost five, exactly when any work parties would be heading in.

That's why Paul has gone quiet. He's waiting for them to pass. I pinpoint where I last heard him and begin creeping forward while motioning Diana to stay back. She lets me get ten paces ahead and then follows. Good enough. Probably best if she doesn't stay in one place, the perfect target should Paul decide—

A cry from up ahead. A shout. A woman—Nicole—saying, "Let him go, or I'll put a bullet—"

Paul cuts in. "You set that rifle down, or I'll slit this kid's throat."

I break into a run. I round a corner, and I see them on the very path I'd been taking. It's a chopping party, three guys and Nicole, as their militia guard. She's still arguing with Paul, but she's lowered her rifle.

Paul has a hostage.

Sebastian.

He's holding the kid backed into his chest, one arm around him, the other with a knife at his throat.

Paul's trying to get Nicole to put the rifle down, and she's trying to get him to let Sebastian go. I wave for Diana to stay where she is, as I slip through the forest. I come out behind Paul. Nicole sees me. I motion for her to set the rifle on the ground. She does, her gaze locked on Paul.

"Casey!" Paul shouts. "I know you're out there. I heard you."

I glance around and spot another figure by Diana. It's Dalton. He's leaning in as she explains the situation to him.

I turn back to Paul. I can't shoot him from here. Not without hitting Sebastian, too. I could threaten, but I won't with that knife at the young man's throat. Even sneaking up and grabbing Paul is too risky. He could startle and cut Sebastian without meaning to. I have the advantage of surprise . . . and no way to use it.

"Casey!"

I holster my gun and pull my jacket closed. Then I clear my throat and say, "Right here."

Paul wheels, taking Sebastian with him. The young man winces as the knife nicks him. Nicole goes for her rifle on the ground, but Paul expects that, and his head whips around with "Anyone moves, and I kill him. I swear it."

"I'm moving," I say, my voice loud enough for Dalton to overhear.

"I'm going to pass on your left side and walk over to stand with the others, okay?"

"Hands in the air."

I nod, lift them, and walk to Nicole and the other two residents. They're unarmed. We leave the hatchets hidden at the chopping site—along with the wood—until week's end when they haul it back with the ATV and trailer.

"I know you killed Marshal Garcia," I say. "You admitted it to Diana, and Jen overheard. You know there's no way out of this. Just let Sebastian go—"

"Why? If you know I'm guilty, this kid is the only leverage I have."

Sebastian swallows, and when he speaks, his voice quavers. "If I ever did anything to you, sir, I'm sorry. It was an accident. A mistake. I'd never—"

"Shut up," Paul says, and Nicole tenses, outrage fairly pulsing from her. Paul continues. "I didn't even know your name until now, kid. You just happened to be in the wrong place at the wrong time, so you're going to help me get out of this. Just be a good boy and pray that Casey here gives a shit about you."

"Paul, let him go and—"

"If he dies, it's on you, Casey. Just like that dumb-ass security guard who got me into this mess."

I don't ask what he means. I know he's going to tell me. He's itching to tell me.

"I used to take hostages all the time," he says. "It's the one thing people pay attention to when you're robbing a bank. Grab some kid or old lady, and suddenly, everyone pays attention. They do what you ask, and no one gets hurt. Not until some doughnut-munching lard-ass security guard decides to be a hero. Then what can I do? If I don't shoot the hostage, no one's ever going to take me seriously again. I try not to kill the old lady. I shoot her in the shoulder. That's what they always show in the movies. That's even what ol' Deputy Will taught us. You could cost someone the use of their arm, but it's a damn sight better than killing them. The problem is when you aim for the shoulder, and they move. Suddenly, I'm not just a bank robber; I'm a killer. That's when they pay attention. That's when you get a federal warrant on your head."

"Agent Garcia found you," I say. "And you bribed him to let you go."

His head whips my way.

"He wouldn't come here alone on a warrant," I say. "He caught up with you once before. You made a deal with him. But something happened—maybe you stiffed him on his payment when you came up here—and so he followed."

"I didn't stiff anyone. I paid Garcia in full, and he's the one who *got* me up here. He knew about this place. I paid him to let me go, and I paid him for a contact with Rockton. Then . . . who the hell knows. Maybe he got greedy and followed. He wanted more."

"Or he had a change of heart," I say. "He regretted what he'd done and came up here to make you face justice."

Paul laughs so hard the knife wavers, and Sebastian shoots me a look, the frightened-kid facade slipping to show the unnervingly mature adult beneath, the one who isn't terribly concerned about his situation but asks me to please refrain from anything that will get him killed. The look vanishes in a blink, and he starts breathing hard, eyes fluttering.

"L-look," Sebastian stammers. "I—"

"Shut the fuck up," Paul says. Then he turns back to me, and in him I also see another person, a stranger now. I have to remind myself that this is the same man I've known since I arrived, the eager and helpful militia guy I couldn't quite rely on, but only because he was prone to screwing up, never because I doubted his loyalty.

No, that isn't true. I think back to those screwups. To times when Paul disobeyed an order—like when he failed to help me during Roy's lynch mob—and I should have wondered whether it was truly a failure of nerve or a deeper problem. A lack of commitment to his job. A lack of loyalty to Dalton. We'd known not to put Paul in charge of anything critical, and I think we'd all just been hoping problems were "Paul screwing up . . . again" rather than anything serious.

Garcia told me his target would have insinuated himself deep in the community, and that's what Paul had done. He just hadn't been able to fake full commitment to the task.

"Let's negotiate," I say.

"You're in no position to do that," Paul says. "You act like you can give orders, but you're just Eric's girl. You're hot, and you're into him, and he's taking full advantage of that. As he should."

I resist the urge to glance behind Paul, where I know Dalton is in the trees, rolling his eyes.

"Maybe," I say, "or maybe I'm the one taking advantage. You can tell yourself I don't have power here, but you know I do. As long as I share Eric's bed, I have power—over him. I *am* in a position to negotiate, and you'll get a better deal with me than you would with Eric."

He doesn't come back with a rejoinder, which means he sees my point.

"We're going to trade hostages," I say.

Paul snorts. "Yeah, no. This skinny kid can barely heave a hatchet. I've watched you fight."

"Which is why I'm not offering to be your hostage." I gesture, and his gaze moves to Nicole.

"No," I say and point his attention downward. "I'll trade you Sebastian for that rifle. You take the gun and the knife, and you go. You run fast, and you run far. You might even get away."

"I saw how well that worked for Oliver Brady. No, here's my version of the deal. I keep this kid, and you give me the keys for the plane. Been a while since I've piloted, but I can manage it. I'll let the kid go in Dawson. I know that's the nearest town—I'll find it and leave this kid there. I might even leave him alive, if he behaves—"

Sebastian starts to hyperventilate. "Oh God, no. Please don't let him take me." Tears spring to his eyes as his voice quavers. "I-I'm sorry. I just can't do that. I'll puke, or I'll have a panic attack, and he'll kill me. Give him someone else. Please."

"For Christ's sake," Paul mutters. "Grow a damn backbone, kid, and—"

Sebastian's fist shoots up. It smacks straight into the curve of Paul's arm and knocks it away, the blade falling from his throat. I'm ready. The moment Sebastian started sniveling, I saw a setup. I leap. I'm already flying along the path, and Dalton is doing the same from the other side. Sebastian already has Paul by the arm, twisting, and before either of us reaches them, Paul thuds to the ground, with Sebastian over him, knife at his throat.

"Don't move," Sebastian says.

There's no anger in his voice. None in his face either. That's where my gaze goes—to Sebastian's face—because I must see his reaction. I must look into his eyes. I do, and I don't see rage. I don't see excitement either. The expression on Sebastian's face is the same one he might give a kid who accidentally bumped him in the school hallway, mild annoyance, the understanding that these things happen, and it'd just better not happen again.

When Paul tries to stand, Sebastian's hand never wavers. He lets Paul rise right into the blade, the tip piercing his skin.

Sebastian says nothing. Does nothing. He just watches Paul with that same dead-eyed look.

"We have this, Sebastian," I say. "Go on back to town with the others."

The young man doesn't hesitate. He nods and gets off Paul. After handing Dalton the knife, he joins the others. They start slowly back to town, glancing at us as they go.

We wait until they're gone. Then Dalton says, "Paul? You're under arrest for the murder of Mark Garcia. Get up and put your hands on your head . . ."

FORTY-EIGHT

Paul may have laughed at the idea that Garcia came back to arrest him. I believe that, though. I have no idea how he'd turn Paul over without losing his job, but I can't imagine he came all the way up here to ask for more money. He cut a deal with a killer, and he regretted it. He tried to make that right. I know he did.

As for how *we'll* make things right . . .

The council can do nothing about Mark Garcia. We discuss ideas—put his body in the woods closer to Dawson City, to at least give his family closure. Anything we do, though, would only make the situation worse. Garcia must vanish.

It turns out he was on leave from the marshals for a disciplinary action, and so no one knew he'd come up here. He has an ex-wife and two kids he hasn't seen in years. According to his will, everything goes to those kids, including the investments he's been holding, the ones that confirm his payout from Paul. His family won't get his body back—or any answers—but at least they'll have the money when he's declared legally dead. It'll have to do.

We now know how Garcia got here. He knew about Rockton, and he facilitated Paul's arrival through a third party. He figured out that we flew through Dawson, and he arranged the rest from there. There's no leak we need to plug—this only highlights concerns Dalton has been raising for years, like using the local airport. After this the council agrees to his demands on that.

Paul will be shipped out when we fly April home to collect her things. Someone from the council will meet us in Whitehorse and take him from there. He'll be given a new identity and access to his remaining funds. Yes, that seems like rewarding him for murder, but the council needs leverage to buy his silence about Rockton. If he says anything, they'll make sure he pays for what he did. Until then, he's free. It's not fair, but it's what's best for Rockton.

Roy's also being kicked out, and in his case, they're returning some of his payment. *Slowly* returning it, and if he talks, he loses that. Even Artie is being kicked out, for attempting to "murder" Garcia's corpse. Rockton is about to get a whole lot less chaotic. We hope.

Sebastian, Petra, the hostile . . . that all still needs to play out. Sebastian handled himself perfectly with Paul, and so I have no immediate concerns. Petra's backstory helps me understand her role here, and I have no immediate concerns there either. Both go on a watch list.

That leaves my sister. The council jumped at her offer to stay. They'd already vetted her—they started background checks as soon as they knew she was in Rockton. I was right about her breakdown. She spent a month at a fancy retreat for "stress-related health issues," but she resumed her job after that, with a reduced schedule, and the council isn't concerned about her mental state. She must stay for at least six months, as she offered. That's their only stipulation.

I find April in the clinic, reorganizing a cupboard.

"You're in," I say.

She doesn't even turn. "I will require a labeler. We can purchase one in Vancouver."

I lean against the door frame. "I had to fight for you," I lie. "It wasn't easy, but I've convinced them to let you stay. You have to agree to a minimum of six months though."

"I already have."

"You'll also get the house next door. Nicole is moving."

She moves a beaker. "I'll need additional batteries and tape for the labeler. Several refills of tape."

I shake my head. "I love you, April."

She turns, looking alarmed. "What?"

"Put the beaker down. You'll get your labeler, and whatever else you need. Make a list, and we'll leave as soon as we can. Tonight, though, we're going to celebrate."

"Celebrate what?"

"I solved the case. Caught the killer. Yay for me."

She looks at me as if I'm suggesting we celebrate me brushing my teeth every day this week. "That's your job, isn't it?"

I sigh. "Yes, April, it is. But we'll still celebrate. My success and the long-overdue arrival of a new doctor."

"A doctor who needs to clean and organize and—"

"Not tonight," I say, getting between her and the cupboard.

"But Kenny—"

"Hey, Kenny!" I call into the next room. "Can I steal my sister for a drink?"

"Only if you bring me one," he calls back.

"He really shouldn't have alcohol."

"A beer will be fine," I say. "And you can have tea. Long Island Iced Tea."

"I don't actually care for iced—"

"You'll like this one," I say as Kenny's chuckle wafts out from the other room.

"I will go if it is Isabel's establishment. I would not object to socializing with Isabel. She is a very competent businesswoman."

"That she is, and sure, we'll go to the Roc. She keeps saying I should start drinking there, so other women feel comfortable. We'll just have to make it very, very clear to the patrons that you are not there for work."

"Yes, I would prefer not to be accosted with minor medical concerns in my social time."

"Not that kind of work," I say. "Isabel's place is a brothel."

April stares at me. Then she frowns. "I will never understand your sense of humor, Casey."

"Oh, I think you're about to." I shoo her toward the door and call a good-night to Kenny as we leave.